BY JALEIGH JOHNSON

DUNGEONS & DRAGONS
The Fallbacks: Dealing with Dragons
The Fallbacks: Bound for Ruin
Honor Among Thieves: The Road to Neverwinter
The Howling Delve
Mistshore
Unbroken Chain
Unbroken Chain: The Darker Road
Spider and Stone

MARVEL
Triptych: A Marvel: Xavier's Institute Novel
School of X: A Marvel: Xavier's Institute Anthology

WORLD OF SOLACE
The Mark of the Dragonfly
The Secrets of Solace
The Quest to the Uncharted Lands

STANDALONE NOVELS
The Door to the Lost
Assassin's Creed: The Golden City

DUNGEONS & DRAGONS

THE FALLBACKS
DEALING WITH DRAGONS

DUNGEONS & DRAGONS

THE FALLBACKS
DEALING WITH DRAGONS

JALEIGH JOHNSON

Random House Worlds

NEW YORK

Random House Worlds
An imprint of Random House
A division of Penguin Random House LLC
1745 Broadway, New York, NY 10019
randomhousebooks.com
penguinrandomhouse.com

TM & copyright © 2025 by Wizards of the Coast LLC

Penguin Random House values and supports copyright. Copyright fuels creativity, encourages diverse voices, promotes free speech, and creates a vibrant culture. Thank you for buying an authorized edition of this book and for complying with copyright laws by not reproducing, scanning, or distributing any part of it in any form without permission. You are supporting writers and allowing Penguin Random House to continue to publish books for every reader. Please note that no part of this book may be used or reproduced in any manner for the purpose of training artificial intelligence technologies or systems.

RANDOM HOUSE is a registered trademark, and RANDOM HOUSE WORLDS and colophon are trademarks of Penguin Random House LLC.

Wizards of the Coast, Dungeons & Dragons, D&D, their respective logos, Forgotten Realms, and the dragon ampersand are registered trademarks of Wizards of the Coast LLC in the U.S.A. and other countries. © 2025 Wizards of the Coast LLC. All rights reserved. Licensed by Hasbro.

LIBRARY OF CONGRESS CATALOGING-IN-PUBLICATION DATA
Names: Johnson, Jaleigh, author.
Title: The Fallbacks : dealing with dragons / Jaleigh Johnson.
Other titles: Dealing with dragons | Dungeons & dragons
Description: First edition. | New York : Random House Worlds, 2025.
Series: Dungeons & dragons
Identifiers: LCCN 2025000816 (print) | LCCN 2025000817 (ebook) | ISBN 9780593599570 (hardcover) | ISBN 9780593599587 (ebook)
Subjects: LCGFT: Action and adventure fiction. | Fantasy fiction. | Novels.
Classification: LCC PS3610.O35438 F35 2025 (print) | LCC PS3610.O35438 (ebook) | DDC 813/.6—dc23/eng/20250129
LC record available at https://lccn.loc.gov/2025000816
LC ebook record available at https://lccn.loc.gov/2025000817

Printed in the United States of America on acid-free paper

2 4 6 8 9 7 5 3 1

First Edition

BOOK TEAM: Production editor: Jocelyn Kiker • Managing editor: Susan Seeman • Production manager: Erin Korenko • Copy editor: Laura Dragonette • Proofreaders: Debbie Anderson, Emily Cutler, Julia Henderson

Book design by Alexis Flynn

The authorized representative in the EU for product safety and compliance is Penguin Random House Ireland, Morrison Chambers, 32 Nassau Street, Dublin D02 YH68, Ireland. https://eu-contact.penguin.ie

To Tim, for always bringing me the light. I love you.

DUNGEONS & DRAGONS

THE FALLBACKS
DEALING WITH DRAGONS

CHAPTER 1

"How many oozes, skeletons, mephits, and zombies can one gods-forsaken dungeon possibly churn out?" Tess shouted as she aimed her hand crossbow at an undead bugbear's ribs. The bolt put it down, so she jumped over the creature's body to find the next foe. "Is anyone keeping track? It has to be at least twenty so far, right? Solid twenty?" At this rate, she was never getting the smell of mephit blood out of her clothes. She'd have to burn them.

"Don't forget the little critters made out of sticks," Baldric added. The burly dwarf snugged his helm into place and followed Uggie into a cluster of zombies, his mace wreathed in flames that lit up his brown skin and gray-streaked black beard. "Uggie's eaten at least five of those."

The otyugh confirmed this by flapping her tentacles, shuddering, and coughing up a hairball of sticks and tree sap that had once been one of the critters in question.

"They're twig blights," Cazrin called helpfully from across the chamber. She held her staff aloft, the stone at its tip flashing with deep purple light as she prepared to cast a spell. "One of the stranger creatures to infest the Sunless Citadel. I've read that they can root in soil to gather nutrients, then pull themselves out of the ground to hunt live prey for—"

"That's twenty-fiiiiive," Lark sang out, cutting the wizard off as he accompanied himself on his lute. He aimed the magic flowing through the instrument at the skeleton skittering toward him with a sickle clutched in its hands. "Twenty-five skeletons scorched and chopped, twenty-five mephits ready for the pot. Hey there, ho there, what's one more? Hey there, ho there. What's. One. More." His rings flashed, and his voice boomed deep and sinister on the last line, his lips pulled into a malicious grin.

The skeleton quivered, broke off its charge, and scurried out of the chamber.

"Ha! That's right, it's one *less* now, isn't it!" Lark shouted after it. The tiefling glanced around, always looking for his audience. "You see what I did there, right?"

"Don't want... to alarm... anyone," Anson interjected as a zombie shoved him against a lip of stone surrounding a large vertical shaft in the center of the chamber. Using his shield, he blocked a blow from the creature's club and drove forward, impaling the crude wooden weapon with the jagged end of his broken sword. With a deft twist, he wrenched the club out of the thing's grip, following up with a shield bash to its ribs that spun it away from him and knocked it to the ground. He grunted as a *trio* of zombies immediately took the creature's place and shoved him to his knees, using their combined weight to drive him back. Now the crumbling stones were all that separated him from an unknowable drop down the wide shaft. "But I think... this wall is... coming loose."

"What?" Tess pivoted, aborting the dagger throw she'd been aiming at the dust mephit hovering near the ceiling on the opposite side of the chamber. "Lark!" she called out. "Peel those zombies off Anson before they dump him down that shaft!"

Soft violet light shone from the gap in the floor behind Anson. It and the smoky torches on the walls offered just enough wavering light for Tess to see Lark dodge around an ooze's corpse and move nimbly across the room to back up Anson.

The domed chamber had been wide enough to allow the party to spread out, but that also meant there was plenty of room for the swarms of monsters that had flooded the chamber soon after their arrival. Tess hadn't noticed until now that, as the battle dragged on, her party members had gotten cut off from one another.

Not good.

Tess could no longer see Baldric or Uggie among the monsters they were fighting, but she could hear Uggie's yips and growls and the cleric's chants. A golden axe suddenly materialized in midair above the fray, chopping straight down at the nearest undead bugbear.

Cazrin was a bit closer, standing just a few paces to Tess's left. That changed when she finished the spell she'd been casting and vanished. In her wake there came a thunderous *boom*, and the zombie who'd been crowding her into a corner lurched back, dropping heavily to the floor. The wizard reappeared across the room, out of reach of the monsters for now.

Suddenly, a cloud of thick, choking brown dust descended around Tess. Cazrin, Anson, and the rest of the fight disappeared from view as high-pitched, cackling laughter filled the air.

It was the mephit—a small creature that reminded Tess of an imp with its beady, malevolent eyes and exaggeratedly angular features. Tess coughed and cursed herself for getting distracted so the creature could get in another attack. Now she was blinded to what was going on in the rest of the chamber.

Crouching, Tess covered her mouth and nose with her sleeve and began inching forward, her dagger ready to throw once she found her way out of the cloud.

There was movement to her left—a huff of breath and the hiss of a blade parting the air. It was just enough warning for Tess to dive and roll, dodging a sword slash that would have clipped her in the neck.

She didn't get far. Her shoulder slammed into a pair of muscled legs, stopping her progress. There came a muffled growl and the stench of rot that was definitely not from one of her party members. Ignoring the throbbing pain in her shoulder, Tess brought her dagger around and buried it in the meat of an undead goblin's calf. A shriek of pain followed, but Tess was already up, getting to her knees to knock the creature out of her way and deeper into the choking dust cloud.

Tess kept moving, darting forward until she finally burst out of the blinding dust. Her eyes were watering, and her lungs felt like they were full of sand, but she had a clear view to aim her dagger at the single zombie left pinning Anson. The other two that had been harrying him were on the ground, stiff-limbed with magical paralysis.

Lark had taken care of business, Tess thought with satisfaction. One good hit to the remaining zombie would take it down.

Tess raised her dagger, but Anson caught her eye just as the blade spun from her hand. "Don't!" he shouted. "We're going—"

With a loud scrape and groan, the stone lip behind Anson gave way just as Tess's dagger dug in between the zombie's shoulder blades. The creature slumped, and it and Anson plunged backward into the shaft and disappeared.

"Anson!" Tess activated the teleportation power on the other dagger in her hand, letting the magic carry her to its twin. The dust-filled chamber faded in a flash of brilliant white light.

When Tess blinked back into existence, her hand encircled the dagger hilt protruding from the zombie's back, and she was falling through the air. The sudden plunge stole her breath and threatened to empty the contents of her stomach, but she held on to both the dagger and the zombie.

She locked eyes with Anson just below her, who was also holding on to the zombie.

"What are you doing?" Anson shouted, wearing a comically incredulous look as the wind whipped his straight dark hair around his face. The fighter reached for her, grabbing her collar to try to pull her in, as if intending to shield her fall with his body. Tess had the vague impression of thick, slithery vines like pale snakes running up and down the walls of the shaft around them. She reached for the vines, trying to snag one to slow their fall, anything—

They hit the ground first.

Tess landed half on the zombie and half on a carpet of vines and fungi. White-hot pain shot up and down her flank. The breath had been blasted out of her lungs. Anson lay next to her, groaning in pain but still gripping her collar. Blood flowed down one side of his face.

"Baldric!" Tess screeched, and the shout pulsed straight down her throat and into her lungs. Ah. She'd probably broken some ribs in the fall. Good to know.

"We're coming, Tess!"

That was Cazrin's voice. The rest of the party would be close behind, as soon as they dispatched the remaining monsters. Tess's vision blurred, and she had the strong urge to close her eyes for just a minute to rest.

Gritting her teeth, she forced herself to stay awake. A good thing too, because suddenly, a speck of brown swam into view from halfway up the well shaft. It was flying straight toward her, closing fast.

The dust mephit. The damn thing still wasn't dead. Its papery wings fluttered madly when it caught sight of Tess and Anson lying helpless at the bottom of the shaft. Cackling, it sucked in a breath, ready to expel another cloud of blinding dust at them.

Tess reached beneath her armpit and felt around until she found the hilt of her dagger, which was still sticking out of the dead zombie's back. She yanked the blade free and threw it at the mephit, skewering it through its tiny head and left wing. Its gravelly cackle cut off in a choking sound. The creature exploded in a puff of brown dust that dispersed harmlessly in midair before drifting down the shaft. Tess's dagger fell back to the ground, sticking into a mushroom cap between her and Anson.

Tess reached over and grabbed the dagger, flicking the mushroom off. She rolled away from the zombie and, wincing in pain, pushed herself to a sitting position.

The chamber around her was large, like the one above, but instead of being plain stone, this room overflowed with strange, luminescent fungus. It ran up the walls and even across the ceiling, giving off a steady violet light that was hard on her eyes. The rich scents of earth and natural decay filled the air, like a spring garden after the rain.

The grove, Tess thought, clutching her ribs as she inched her way over to check on Anson. If Mel's directions were right—and she had no reason to think they weren't—the shaft had led them to the lowest level of the Sunless Citadel, where the famed Gulthias Tree and its mythical fruit were waiting for them.

Assuming, of course, that it was still the summer solstice. They'd hurried their journey here to coincide with the turning of the seasons so that they could claim the tree's enchanted fruit, a perfect red apple that was said to appear on the tree only during the solstice. If harvested, it would grant healing and health to whomever consumed it.

It wasn't the main or even the most important reason they'd come here, but Tess would love to eat even a bite of healing fruit right now, and Anson, by the look of him, needed the whole apple, core and all.

Tess checked the rise and fall of Anson's chest. He was semiconscious, but she didn't like the look of the bleeding wound at his temple. She reached into her pouch, grabbing the first healing potion she could find. Popping the cork, she tipped it carefully down the fighter's throat in a thin trickle, encouraging him to drink.

Anson's throat bobbed. He coughed, his shoulders convulsing, but he swallowed the liquid. As the magic took effect, the bleeding slowed and stopped, though there was still a nasty gash and a tapestry of bruises left behind. The fighter took a deep breath as his eyes fluttered fully open.

"You all right?" Tess asked with a wan smile. She couldn't have managed a laugh, not with the pain in her ribs. "It's not safe to nap here, you know."

"Don't underestimate me—I can take a nap anywhere." Anson groaned as he looked around the fungus-riddled chamber. "Did I at least break your fall?" he asked, reaching up to wipe a streak of blood off his cheek.

"You broke that one's fall," Tess said, indicating the dead zombie. "Not that it mattered."

Anson nodded, though he still looked dazed. With an effort, he focused on her and scowled. "Why did you teleport after me? I warned you not to."

"Party leader, remember?" Tess said, pointing a thumb at herself. "When a party member is in trouble, that's where I go." She paused.

"Although, I thought I could use the vines to stop our fall, but that didn't happen."

"Tess!"

Tess looked up just in time to see a glowing beam of light fall on her and Anson, and Baldric's murmuring voice drifted down the shaft to them. Tess recognized the light of the cleric's healing lantern, and then his magic flowed over her like a soothing wave. The burning in her lungs cooled, and she drew her first pain-free breath since tumbling down the shaft.

The rest of the Fallbacks came into view one by one, drifting slowly down the shaft to the ground courtesy of Cazrin's magic. Baldric came first, keeping the beam of the lantern steady on her and Anson to bolster his healing magic. Lark was next, still holding his lute and posing in the air like a dancer in the middle of a complicated leap. Anson barked out a laugh at the sight of the tiefling's red tail sweeping back and forth behind him.

Cazrin and Uggie came last. The wizard held her staff in both hands, the purple stone glowing a similar shade to the fungus in the chamber. It lit her dark eyes as she drifted to the floor, her overskirt swirling around her. Uggie flopped down next to her, the otyugh's tentacles whipping around curiously as she inspected the fungus and vines, probably hoping they were edible.

"Are you both all right?" Baldric asked as he made his way over to them, stepping carefully among the vines. He knelt next to Anson and inspected the head wound. "Didn't break anything important, I see," he said with a grunt.

"Not this time," Anson said, chuckling, but it quickly turned into a wince.

Baldric touched the side of Anson's face with his fingertips. "Hold still," he said gently.

Golden light gathered in the cleric's palm and spread outward over the wound. The bruises slowly faded and disappeared. The unicorn symbol of Mielikki glowed briefly on Baldric's cloth of holy symbols tied at his waist.

"The Lady of the Forest has been awfully good to you this trip, Baldric," Lark drawled as he kicked aside some mushrooms to take a seat on the floor near Tess. He cast a hopeful glance at the cleric. "Does she have any favor left for a humble bard who hasn't seen the sun in ages?"

"We've been down here for a day at most, Lark," Tess said dryly. "I don't think you're in any danger of withering away for lack of nourishment."

"Scoot closer to the lantern, and you'll feel better," Baldric advised him. "Mielikki's favor only goes so far, especially since we haven't managed to find her servant yet." The cleric looked over at Cazrin, who was exploring the chamber while he conducted his healing. "See anything, Caz?"

"There are a couple of doors leading out of this room," Cazrin called back to the group. "No harmful magic in the area, but— Uggie, you're going to make yourself sick eating those vines. Come over here, come on." The wizard held out a gloved hand, and Uggie obediently trotted over and allowed Cazrin to scratch beneath her chin. A curtain of vines clung to the corner of the otyugh's mouth.

"What about above us?" Tess asked, pointing to the shaft as Baldric turned the full focus of his healing magic on her. "Is the area clear, or are we going to have company down here?"

"We cleared it without issue," Lark said, flicking an imaginary bit of lint off his white coat. The tiefling frowned. "None of them were carrying an impressive amount of coin or other items, though."

"We'll find something," Tess promised him. "We have to be getting close to the Gulthias Tree. Hopefully, that's where we'll find Keevi too."

The tortle cleric was a servant of Mielikki. They were also a former student of Tess's mentor, Mel, the halfling rogue who'd taught Tess everything she knew. Keevi had disappeared while on a mission to the Sunless Citadel on behalf of the Harpers, a secretive organization dedicated to protecting the innocent and checking abuses of power throughout Faerûn. Mel had asked Tess and the Fallbacks to investigate and rescue the cleric if necessary. Judging by the number of monsters infesting the place, it was definitely going to be necessary.

But that was still only part of their mission.

Tess glanced at Baldric as he finished his healing. There was a deep crease between the dwarf's brows as he surveyed the fungus-covered chamber. Tess thought she could guess what he was thinking.

"Mel told me this place used to be a stronghold for the Cult of the Dragon," she reminded him. "There's bound to be knowledge here that can help us."

"Yet, I haven't seen any sign of anything remotely draconic in this place," Baldric pointed out, gesturing around the chamber. "Just a lot of fungus and monster hovels."

Tess didn't blame him for doubting. And he was right. They'd seen nothing here so far to indicate cult activity. As she got to her feet and began to examine the chamber they found themselves in, she couldn't help but worry that Mel might have missed the mark by sending them here.

The Fallbacks had set themselves up in Baldur's Gate, focusing their efforts on helping Baldric find more information about the mysterious, burning-eyed entity that haunted him, interfering with his sleeping and waking hours and disrupting his bargains with the gods that granted him his powers.

Frustrated by the entity's continued presence in his life, Baldric had settled on a new strategy for dealing with it—go on the offensive. Rather than try to hide from the entity, the cleric had actually begun seeking it out in visions over the past several months, asking it questions about its identity and intentions, trying to get it to betray its true nature.

At first, Tess had been doubtful the strategy would pay off. But she'd forgotten how determined Baldric could be when he set his mind to a task. It had been a risk, goading the entity this way, but one night, after the entity had visited Baldric in his dreams, he'd had a breakthrough. He'd woken with echoes of a language that was strange yet familiar ringing in his ears. He'd repeated some of it to Cazrin, and she'd identified it as an ancient form of Draconic.

Cazrin had then taken that information and begun feverishly researching powerful draconic entities and organizations on the Sword Coast. Tess had brought the findings to Mel, who had also come to stay in Baldur's Gate for the summer. Mel had in turn set them on this course to find her missing Harper student and investigate the Sunless Citadel.

Now here they were, in the depths of the grove. Tess pulled her magical cat's mask down over her face to reveal any waiting traps as she went to examine the doors that led out of the chamber. She owed it to Baldric to do all she could to find a lead here he could use. He hadn't said as much, but she could tell the continued presence of the entity was weighing heavily on him. She didn't know what the thing was whispering to him in the depths of sleep or in his negotiations with the gods, but she knew it was nothing good. And the telltale streaks of white in his hair and beard were a constant reminder of what the entity could do to Baldric if they didn't take steps to stop it.

CHAPTER 2

As the party made their way down yet another fungus-choked corridor, Baldric wondered how the poets and storytellers of the world had managed to make *adventuring* seem like such a glorious calling. A glamorous way to see Faerûn! Make a name for yourself! Become a legend in your own lifetime!

The reality, he'd discovered, was somewhat different.

Yet, Baldric had to admit it was a life that suited him well. He thrived on walking the thin line between power and peril, disaster and triumph. It thrilled him, and he wasn't about to apologize for that feeling. He supposed it was only natural, then, that he'd surrounded himself with people who had similar notions and ways of behaving.

He hadn't been a bit surprised, for example, to see Anson plunge down that shaft clutching a zombie corpse, or for Tess to follow right down after him, her own safety be damned. They were walking disasters, all of them.

Part of Baldric's job was to keep everyone alive and functioning. He mostly thrived on that too, though he might grumble about it at times. All in all, he had no complaints about the unusual turn his life had taken with this group over the past several months.

Except for that single thorn in his side. The metaphorical devil in the dark, whispering to him from the shadows every time he closed his eyes.

The entity was getting stronger.

He hadn't wanted to admit it at first, and he wasn't about to discuss it with the rest of the Fallbacks—that would make it real and certain—but Baldric knew he was operating on borrowed time. The entity had sworn it would claim him, and he wasn't about to wait around to find out what that meant. He needed answers about what he was dealing with, and if Tess and her mentor were wrong about this place, he would be back to puttering aimlessly around Baldur's Gate while Cazrin researched powerful dragons and their machinations in the world.

That just wouldn't do. He was hungry for action, for solutions, even if they led to further disaster.

Lost in thought, Baldric gradually became aware of a hefty weight thumping intermittently against his right leg.

Bump. Bump.

Bump.

He glanced down to see Uggie trotting along beside him, her three stubby legs just barely allowing her to keep pace with his shorter stride. Her eyestalk was fixed intently on him, and a glistening bit of drool slicked from the corner of her mouth.

"What's wrong?" Baldric asked, and was immediately bombarded with a stream of mental images and telepathic speech that buzzed through his brain so fast it was hard to separate them into coherency.

Beard. Want bacon. Baldric person. BACON. Baldric person sad? So hungry. Vines not good. Starving. Feed now or I DIE!

"All right, all right," Baldric said, putting a hand on Uggie's head to calm her. The flood of mental imagery slowed and finally stopped, leaving behind a dull ache in his skull. He reached into his pack and pulled out a pale wedge of cheese and a knife. He carved off a couple chunks and dropped them into the otyugh's waiting mouth. "I don't have any bacon, sorry. Tess, when was the last time you fed Uggie?" Baldric called up to the front of the line.

That was another thing that had changed. He never thought he'd live to see the day he was concerned about an otyugh getting proper nutrition, especially since her diet consisted mainly of the sort of refuse other creatures left behind to rot.

Tess glanced back at them, the eyes of her cat's mask shimmering in the glow of the lights Cazrin had summoned to hover above their heads. "She's been eating nonstop since we got in here," the rogue said. "You have to try to ignore the mental nudges. If you feed her every time she thinks at you hard enough, she won't ever stop."

"Wonderful." Baldric sighed and put away the hunk of cheese. "Nope," he said when Uggie whined and headbutted his knee again, smearing drool all over his pant leg. "Party leader says you've had enough. Complain to her if you don't like it."

"Is it just me, or is her mental voice getting a lot stronger and louder than it used to be?" Lark asked, falling into step beside Baldric as the corridor widened. "She slept next to me in camp last night, and I dreamed about a soup made of stirge wings and rat tails. In the dream, I actually *craved* it." The bard shuddered. "Revolting."

"She's growing up," Cazrin said, turning to pat Uggie on the head. There was a distinct note of pride in the wizard's voice. "Getting more powerful, just like the rest of us, aren't you, Uggie?"

WANT BACON!

Baldric rubbed his temples and sighed again.

"Look alive, Fallbacks," Tess called out, but she kept her voice low. "We've got another chamber up ahead." She hesitated and then added, "Baldric, you may want to come up front."

A prickle teased Baldric's scalp at the restrained excitement in Tess's voice. Quickly, he worked his way to the front of the group, automatically checking on Anson as he went past to make sure the man wasn't still suffering from the effects of his fall. He shot Tess a glance too as he joined her, but she wasn't favoring her ribs anymore and appeared to be breathing without pain.

Then he glanced into the chamber, and a shiver went through him.

The room was full of crumbling stone and more fungus, and that same rich, earthy smell permeated everything, but Baldric wasn't paying any attention to that. He was staring at a large object situated on the far side of the room.

On the western wall, a great marble statue rose up before them. It was carved in the shape of a rearing red dragon, massive wings spread behind it in all their unsettling glory. At first glance, in the flickering shadows cast by Cazrin's lights, the scales of the statue seemed to move, as if the dragon were not a statue at all, but a beast caught in the act of drawing a slow, fiery breath. But as Baldric stepped closer, the rest of the party following behind, he realized that the effect was artificial. It was a lifelike representation, but it was still nothing more than a statue.

Until Baldric looked into its eyes.

The statue's eye sockets were empty, yet a bright glow emanated from them, a gaze that pierced him right through the chest. He felt a pull, like a burning tether woven through his ribs, drawing him across the room to stand before it.

"Careful," Cazrin said, hurrying to his side. She pointed her staff at the floor. A rune-carved tile was situated in front of the statue, with symbols on it Baldric didn't recognize. "Don't step there until I find out if it's safe."

Nothing about this place was safe, Baldric thought, unable to drag his gaze away from the statue's eyes.

Burning eyes.

"That's him," Baldric said, his mouth gone dry. "That's the entity."

"Are you sure?" Anson asked, staring up at the statue dubiously. Glancing at the others' faces, Baldric realized none of them was as unsettled by the depiction as he was.

"I'd know those eyes anywhere," he said. He'd seen them so many times. In his sleep, just before waking. When he made his deals with the gods. More and more now. He swallowed. "Trust me, I'm sure."

"Well, this is good," Cazrin said excitedly. "This is wonderful! I mean, not *wonderful*, of course, but information is power. All we have to do now is find out the identity of the dragon depicted in the statue."

"Is that all?" Lark indicated the statue with a sweeping gesture.

"I don't know about you, but that dragon looks formidable. We're not going to have to kill it, are we? Because I don't feel I've reached the 'dragon-slaying' part of my adventuring career. I'm definitely not being paid enough." He shot a look at Tess.

"Actually, you skipped right over that and went straight to lich-slaying," Anson pointed out. "Not many people can say that."

"Not many can say they used two angry purple worms to do it either," Tess said, taking off her mask and wiping the sweat from her forehead. "If it helps Baldric, I think we're more than ready to take on a dragon. Think of what it would do for our reputations!" Her eyes gleamed as she glanced at Lark. "Think of the song you'd get to write. You're going to need a follow-up to 'Lorthrannan's Fall' at some point, right?"

"I don't know." Lark considered. "'Lorthrannan's Fall' is just starting to get some traction in Baldur's Gate," he said. "But you're right. An artist needs to move on to his next great work before the applause dies down."

"Great," Anson said, rubbing his hands together. "So, we're agreed that we're taking down a dragon? Where is it?"

Baldric crossed his arms. "I can see the rest of you have already slain the dragon in your minds, mounted its head in the Wander Inn, and written a romantic ballad about the battle—"

"More of an epic, operatic piece, surely," Lark interjected.

"But we don't know what we're up against yet," Baldric finished patiently. "I'd like to find out." He knelt next to Cazrin, who was examining the tile on the floor. "What do you think?"

"It's written in that same ancient form of Draconic," Cazrin confirmed, "but it doesn't give any hint to the identity of the dragon depicted by the statue." She stood and shone the light from her staff along the chamber walls. More writing came into view, jagged carvings that seemed sinister, almost threatening in appearance. "Oh my," she breathed.

"What?" Baldric crowded closer to the wall. He wished he could translate the symbols for himself. "What does it say?"

"The writing here speaks of the dragon goddess Tiamat," Cazrin explained. "But the words are intended as a warning to any who represent or support her. They're not welcome in these halls."

"A dragon goddess not welcome in a chamber with a giant dragon statue?" Lark cocked an eyebrow. "Bit of a mixed message there, don't you think?"

"Not all dragons ally themselves with Tiamat," Cazrin said. "There are different factions, different beliefs, same as the rest of us."

"Then what faction does Glowing Eyes here represent?" Anson asked, pointing to the rearing dragon. "If he's—"

"Look out!" Tess, who'd been standing nearby, suddenly drew her dagger and hurled it across the room.

Baldric turned just in time to see a shadow detach itself from the wall behind the statue. Tess's dagger sliced through it and clanged against the stone. The monster hissed in pain but kept coming, surging toward them in an inky curtain that enveloped Cazrin.

"Hold on!" Anson drew his sword and swiped at the shadow, but Baldric waved him off.

"Save it!" He gripped his cloth of holy symbols. Anson's sword had a habit of randomly releasing bolts of lightning in a fight, and Baldric didn't want that to happen while they were all clustered together in a group. "I've got this one."

He traced the unicorn's horn worked into the cloth at his belt. "Mielikki," he murmured. "I promise I won't keep asking, but we're getting close. I can feel it. We're going to find your servant. I just need to keep us alive long enough to do it. Be patient a little while longer, please, and help me."

Baldric was pushing it, he knew. He'd been asking a lot of Mielikki as they slogged their way through the depths of the ruined citadel. But this was where he was at his best: heart pounding, arm raised, making his offer and waiting for the magic to flow through him, to see if his words had been enough to sway a deity to do as he wanted.

And when she answered, adding more weight to one side of the scale, increasing the debt he owed, he couldn't help feeling another thrill. He rode it, releasing a bolt of radiant energy that struck the shadow dead-on.

An ear-piercing screech filled the chamber, and the shadow melted under the force and intensity of the light. The spell briefly lit up the room like midday, revealing another exit on the far side of the chamber. Through the door, Baldric caught a glimpse of stone shelves filled with books, iron-banded chests, and some piles of coin on the floor before the light faded and Cazrin slumped forward, gasping as she was expelled from the cloak of darkness.

"Are you all right?" Baldric put a hand to the wizard's shoulder to keep her steady. Tess was there too, and Anson stood protectively on the outskirts of the group with Uggie, his sword at the ready as he scanned the room for any other shadows that might be moving in a way they shouldn't. Lark had his lute in his hands, prepared to play and call forth his magic, but he'd also seen the doorway leading to treasure, and there was an avaricious light in the tiefling's eyes.

"I'm fine," Cazrin said, waving Baldric off. She shuddered. "That was just . . . unpleasant. Cold, like the Ruinous Child, but thankfully not nearly as powerful."

That was a relief. None of them was eager to encounter a power like the sentient, vile tome that had brought the Fallbacks together for their first job—and had almost been their doom.

"We need a rest," Tess decided, as Baldric helped Cazrin to her feet. "This is as good a place as any—"

"Oh, but did I see a library back there in the corner when you cast that spell, Baldric?" Cazrin asked, craning her neck to see around the statue.

Lark chuckled. "I think she's fine," he said. "But I'd be more than happy to scout ahead for you, Cazrin," he added, inching away from the group.

"We're staying together," Tess said firmly. "We'll rest in the next room."

"Behind us!" Anson called out, and swung at a second shadow approaching from the opposite corner of the room.

Tess went to help, but as Baldric moved to join them, he felt again the piercing gaze of the statue boring into his back. It was unsettling, like a physical touch, a burn on his skin. Baldric turned, staring defiantly up at the statue.

"Trying to taunt me, are you?" he muttered. "We'll see about that."

He cast a quick glance over at Tess and Anson. They were already tearing the second shadow apart. Lark and Uggie had moved in to help, but it was clear they wouldn't be needed. Cazrin was still standing next to him, watching him curiously.

"What are you going to do?" the wizard asked.

"We can't spend all day searching a library for a needle in a haystack while these monsters chip away at us," Baldric said. Then he remembered who he was talking to and shot her a guilty look. "Er, but maybe we could come back later—"

"I agree with you," Cazrin said, smiling ruefully. "We need to find Mel's Harper, as well. So, what are you going to do?" she repeated.

"We need a shortcut," Baldric said, threading his cloth of holy symbols through his hands until he found the symbol of a crystal ball filled with embroidered eyes. He'd done something similar when they'd visited the great library at Candlekeep to find information about the Ruinous Child. But this time, he wasn't relying on the whims of fortune. He needed to get to the truth of the matter, to bring to light what was being concealed. That would take a very specific kind of divine aid.

"Time to drag this entity out of the shadows," Baldric said. Touching the symbol for Savras the All-Seeing, he closed his eyes, considering the offer he was going to make. He'd seen nothing here that would tempt the Third Eye to be as generous as Mielikki, but sometimes a good old-fashioned offer of a favor, when placed in the right context, would do the trick.

Magic once again hummed at Baldric's fingertips when he made the connection. As the power flowed through him, for just a moment, he found he could forget about the burning gaze of the statue.

"I want to find the truth," he murmured, making his case to the deity. "No more and no less. In return, I promise to bring to light any secrets I find here for those who might be seeking their own answers. Truth for truth. That's my offer."

It was a good proposal, Baldric thought, and for a moment, he thought he felt a flash of approval in response. Then it was gone, cut off by a voice that whispered in the back of his mind.

Crawling through the dark, it taunted. *Little mouse searching for crumbs.*

"Go away," Baldric snarled. He didn't have time for this. He tried to push the voice aside, but it filled every corner of his thoughts.

Do you really want to know who I am, mouse? The entity sounded amused. *You're a fool if you think it will make any difference. I will have you in my service, one way or another. Perhaps you need a reminder of that.*

Pain burned in Baldric's chest, so quick and sharp that he gasped. The connection to Savras wavered, the god's granted power fading under the force of the entity's presence.

How disappointing. It's almost too easy to get to you now. I thought you'd be more of a challenge.

I'll give you a challenge. Baldric gritted his teeth and held on, fighting the entity for control. He took a breath and forced the voice to the back of his mind, locking it away in a box with his panic and fear. He focused on Savras instead and found the connection he'd made to the deity still intact. The entity wasn't as in control as it wanted him to think.

But it was so much stronger now, he thought. Ever since he'd accepted the entity's help in discovering a way to destroy the Ruinous Child, its pull on him had grown more and more intrusive, allowing the entity to tease and prod, to interfere with his bargaining and his magic.

Someday soon, it might be strong enough to keep him from the gods entirely ...

No, Baldric wouldn't let it get to that point. He was close now. That's why the entity was taunting him, because Baldric was clawing his way to gaining the upper hand.

"Show me," Baldric called out, seizing the connection to Savras and holding on for all he was worth. "Show me what that monster's trying to hide."

No matter what else he struggled with, Baldric hadn't lost his gift for negotiation.

The Third Eye opened within his mind and pointed the way.

CHAPTER 3

"Ashardalon," Cazrin said, reading from the dragon-scaled book that Baldric's spell had led them to in the adjoining library. "Ashardalon the greatwyrm."

She spoke in a hushed tone, as if the name signified something ominous, but it meant nothing to Anson. Then again, he hadn't made a study of famous dragons. He was just happy that Baldric had finally put a name to his enemy, although he'd expected the cleric to be in slightly better spirits than he currently was.

"Keep reading," Baldric said impatiently. "What's his story?"

He was pacing back and forth in front of a row of collapsed bookshelves. The rest of the room wasn't in much better shape, save for the pair of locked treasure chests that Tess was working on opening. Lark had collected all the coin on the floor and now stood sentinel nearby with Uggie. He was never one to miss a treasure reveal.

"And what's a greatwyrm?" Anson asked. "Are they a lot harder to kill?"

"You could say that, yes." Cazrin tapped the book's spine thoughtfully with her fingernail. "My ancestress wrote some accounts about greatwyrms she'd encountered in her travels. Enough that I could teach a class on the difference between them and regular dragons—"

"Could you do me a kindness and stab me through the eye first?" Lark asked, grinning at her.

"Don't worry, I wasn't going to get out my lectern," she assured him.

"Are you helping me with this chest or not?" Tess tugged on the hem of Lark's coat. "You're supposed to be watching for signs of mimics. We had this discussion."

"Fine," Lark said with a dramatic sigh. "Continue, Cazrin," he invited.

"Thank you, Lark," Cazrin said dryly. "To make a long story short, I was going to say that greatwyrms are extremely powerful, ancient dragons."

"Ah," Anson said, glancing at Baldric. He understood now the reason for the cleric's mood.

"So you're saying he's a dragon god, something like Tiamat or Bahamut?" Baldric asked, his voice tight.

"Not quite." Cazrin shook her head. "At least not according to this account." She made a gesture, and one of her lights drifted closer to the text so she could see it better. "Although it does say he was worshipped here long ago by a sect of the Cult of the Dragon. The cult's followers aid powerful dragons because of their belief that one day, those same dragons will become the rulers of everything and everyone. But Ashardalon was also known to be an enemy of Tiamat, a potential usurper plotting to increase his own power and status, seeking always to prolong his life." Her eyes widened. "It says he once suffered a mortal wound to the heart, but in order to cheat death, he replaced the organ with Ammet, a balor."

"I'm probably not going to like the answer, but what's a balor?" Anson asked.

"An extremely powerful demon," Cazrin said. "Merging with it transformed Ashardalon's features into those of a fiend, his eyes glowing with demonic flame."

Anson gave a low whistle. "Well, that's . . . a creative solution." He looked over at Tess, who had paused in her lockpicking to listen to Cazrin's reading.

"Mel said she sent Keevi here to investigate rumors that the cult was trying to reclaim the Sunless Citadel," Tess said. "Maybe Ashardalon is plotting something new and wants his headquarters back. Maybe that's why the monsters are all stirred up in this place."

"And we're thinking that plot might involve Baldric somehow?" Anson asked.

"It could," Tess said, glancing at the cleric.

"If he is planning to use me for something, he's going to be sorely disappointed," Baldric said. "I know what I'm up against now. Ashardalon can't hide in the shadows anymore and try to intimidate me."

Anson nodded in agreement. He preferred a straightforward fight himself. He'd never been one for subterfuge.

That had always been Valen's area of expertise.

Against Anson's will, his thoughts were dragged back to his brother. There'd been no sign of Valen in the weeks after he'd escaped the service of the lich Lorthrannan and gone on the run. Anson had finally gotten word through a mutual friend that Valen had ended up in Baldur's Gate to hide from the Zhentarim. They hadn't taken kindly to his betrayal in Undermountain.

Anson had hoped to link up with Valen in the city, but by now the party had been settled in Baldur's Gate for weeks, and despite his best efforts, he'd found no trace of his brother.

"Anson? You with us?"

Anson blinked at the sound of Tess's voice. He glanced over and saw she'd picked the lock on the treasure chest and was carefully lifting out its contents. She looked at him expectantly. "Yes, I'm here," he said quickly. "You need the bag of holding?"

"For the coin, yes, and any larger items." She gave him a funny look but said nothing more about his distraction. "We'll sort this stuff quickly, and then we need to get moving to find Keevi."

She pulled out a scroll, which she passed to Cazrin. Next came a neatly folded black cloak embroidered with silver thread. Finally, there was a small gold amulet carved with the stylized image of a closed eye. Beneath the items lay a solid three inches of platinum.

Lark beamed.

Cazrin went through the items one by one, murmuring some arcane phrases as she did so. "The scroll contains a spell that can teleport us out of here if we need to make a quick escape," she said, tucking the rolled parchment into one of her many satchels, along with the dragon-scaled tome that contained the account of Ashardalon.

"Keep that one handy," Tess advised, standing up and dusting herself off.

Anson opened the bag of holding and began scooping platinum coins into it. "What's the cloak's story?" he asked as he worked. "Is it magic?"

Cazrin grinned and held up the cloak, shaking out the fabric to get rid of the wrinkles. "It can be used to disguise the wearer," she said. She glanced down at Uggie, who was taking a nap at Lark's feet. "You know, I think I could adapt it for Uggie, so I wouldn't have to cast a spell on her every time we want to take her into taverns or shops."

"But think of how I could use it onstage," Lark countered, running his fingers reverently over the soft fabric. "To be able to change my face mid-song? It would take my performances to new heights."

"Your face is pretty enough as it is, songbird," Baldric said, cracking a smile.

"Well, there's also the amulet," Cazrin said, running her thumb across the lidded eye. "From what I can tell, it hides the wearer from various forms of detection, both magical and mundane, so that could be—"

She was cut off by Lark, who closed the distance between them in a heartbeat and deftly plucked the amulet out of her hands. "You don't say." He held the amulet up to the light of Cazrin's floating globes. His eyes were large, his crimson skin flushed an even deeper red with excitement. "Mind if I hold on to this one?"

"You can't have them all, Lark," Tess said. "Everyone gets an equal share. You know how this works."

"Just this, then," Lark said. He was already putting the amulet's chain over his head, tucking it between the folds of his coat so it was out of sight.

That was strange, Anson thought. Lark was never one to hide a pretty trinket when he could show it off to the world. Maybe it clashed with his outfit somehow.

The bard looked earnestly at Tess. "I'll take less coin in exchange for the amulet," he promised.

Tess raised an eyebrow. "Since when do you turn down coin? Are you feeling all right?"

"I'm fine," Lark said, waving a hand airily. "I just like my privacy, that's all. I only enjoy being watched when I'm onstage. Offstage, I like to be able to keep a low profile. This amulet will let me do that."

"Whatever you say." Tess glanced at the rest of the party. "As long as no one has any objections?"

The rest of the Fallbacks shook their heads. Anson finished collecting the coin, but his thoughts lingered on Valen. He was anxious to get back to Baldur's Gate. Maybe, in his absence, some of his contacts had come through with new information. He wasn't going to give up until he had word that his brother was safe. If they could just have a conversation, Anson was sure they could resolve some things between them, things that had festered for far too long.

"Anson, you coming?"

Anson looked up, surprised to see the rest of the party already gathering near one of the doors on the far side of the room. Tess hung back, watching him in concern. "We're moving on," she said. "You ready?"

"Yes, I'm coming," Anson said, shaking the cobwebs from his thoughts. Valen would have to wait. He needed to focus on the here and now.

An hour later, Anson wrenched yet another briar from his sleeve, swearing softly as the fabric tore. Usually, he liked being surrounded by nature, but after this trek, he'd be grateful to never see another forest again.

Except that this forest was unlike any he'd ever been in, because it was underground.

From the moment they'd come upon the hidden grove, Anson had suspected that this was not a sanctuary or a shrine to nature. The trees here were sickly shadows of the great ash, oak, and duskwood trees that thrived on the surface. The branches of the briars were thin and fragile, the slightest pressure causing them to snap in two. The leaves of the trees were limp and blighted, always seeking the sunlight but having to be content with the ever-present violet light of the fungus that coated the walls and ceiling.

With Tess leading the way, they moved slowly and furtively toward the center of the vast underground chamber, where a stone wall was erected around a huge, intimidating tree.

The Gulthias Tree.

From what Anson could see of it rising behind the wall, it was the opposite of the kind of tree you'd want to lie beneath on a warm summer's day. The Gulthias Tree was a mass of blackened, twisted limbs pointing like spear tips toward the cavern ceiling. The branches had a charred appearance, as if the tree had been burned in a great conflagration. Though there was no breeze in the underground cavern, the branches swayed, creaking and groaning ominously.

The overwhelming feeling Anson got when he looked at the monstrosity was *hunger*.

"Looks like no one's watered that thing in decades," Lark observed quietly as the party gathered at the base of the wall. Anson and Baldric took up guard positions, watching for signs of anything hiding among the briars. They'd already had to silently dispatch two twig blights that they'd surprised when they'd first entered the chamber.

"This isn't the kind of tree that thrives on water and sunlight," Cazrin said, her face pinched with worry as Tess prepared to scale the stone wall to scout what was waiting for them on the other side.

"'Thriving' is a generous word," Lark said. "What does it feed on, then?"

Baldric gave him a look. "Take a guess," he suggested. "But make it the worst possible thing, and that's probably what it eats."

"Legends about the tree say that it grew from the stake used to slay a vampire down here," Cazrin said. "Which means it's probably—"

"It's blood, isn't it?" Lark said. "You were going to say blood."

"I was going to say blood," Cazrin admitted.

Anson left them to their discussion and went to join Tess at the base of the wall. "Need a boost?" he asked, cupping his hands and offering her a leg up.

"Thanks." Tess had put her cat's mask back on and was tugging her blond hair into a quick braid. When she'd finished, she adjusted her tool gloves and put her foot on his clasped hands, using one hand on his shoulder to brace herself.

Anson hoisted her up, and Tess's nimble hands did the rest, finding gaps and cracks in the stone to hold on to as she scuttled up the wall as quick as a spider.

He waited, keeping watch while Tess scouted, but after a few minutes, he grew restless. He needed to be up there in case she needed help. And he could still keep an eye on the party and their surroundings from the top of the wall.

Anson didn't have Tess's skill at climbing, but what he lacked in finesse he made up for in strength. He dug his fingers into handholds in the stone and hoisted himself up with a grunt. A moment later, he reached the top of the wall, pulling himself up beside Tess, who was looking out over a wide clearing.

Up close, the Gulthias Tree was even stranger and more unsettling. The closest branches were only a few feet away, and Anson swore he saw them shift ever so slightly in his direction, as if the tree were turning its attention to them. It was ridiculous, he knew, but he couldn't help feeling unnerved in the thing's presence. The smell of rot and decay filled his nostrils, causing him to hold back a sneeze.

"What are you doing?" Tess whispered as he settled beside her. "The plan was that I scout and the rest of you keep watch, remember?"

"I can watch from up here and help you at the same time," Anson argued. He pointed down into the clearing, where a hunched figure had been tied to the base of the tree. "Is that our Harper?" he asked. "They're not looking so good."

"Yes, I think that's Keevi, unless there's another tortle cleric imprisoned down here that we don't know about," Tess said, squinting to get a better look. "How have they got them tied to that tree? It looks like . . ."

She trailed off, and Anson shuddered as he realized that the tortle wasn't actually tied up at all. It appeared Keevi was slowly being *absorbed* into the tree itself. The tortle's scarred bottle-green-and-brown shell was already half-covered by the blackened bark of the Gulthias Tree, holding the cleric in place. Keevi sagged in the grip of the twisted trunk, their eyes closed, unresponsive to anything happening around them.

"Do you think they're still alive?" Anson asked, feeling a spike of worry.

"If they were dead, I don't think the tree would be bothering to absorb them," Tess reasoned. "And I don't think they'd be so heavily guarded." She pointed to the other side of the grove, where a group of figures milled about, keeping watch and occasionally casting glances at Keevi. There were at least ten twig blights and a group of four guards—an elf, two humans, and a tiefling.

"Something's not right about them," Anson said. He pointed to one of the humans, a burly man in full plate armor who bore the symbol of Torm, god of duty. He shuffled stiffly around the grove, his face an expressionless mask. In the violet light of the fungus, his skin had a rough, textured appearance and looked as if it were cracked in places. "He looks like a paladin, but his face is . . . is that bark?" he asked incredulously.

"I think you're right." Tess grimaced. "It's like they're becoming part of the grove, or something equally unpleasant. All right, here's the plan," she said. "I'm going to send Baldric and Lark over there to get Keevi. The rest of us will take out the guards, but we need to do it fast. Once we get into a battle, the noise is bound to draw in more twig blights and other monsters. The longer we stay here, the more the odds are going to be stacked against us." She scooted back, letting her legs dangle over the edge of the stone wall, prepared to drop back down to join the party.

"Wait," Anson said, tugging on her arm to stop her. He nodded toward the tree's upper branches. A cluster of them had twined together into a protective bundle, like a gnarled nest. In the center, a bright red apple stood out among the branches like a dot of blood on a black field. "Do you see what I'm seeing?"

Tess followed his gaze and gasped. "That's the fruit we're looking for," she said. "I'd bet any amount of coin."

"I'm not sure I want to eat that," Anson said. It was jarring to see that perfect red fruit, healthy and lush, growing out of a tree that reeked of death and decay, in a cavern full of sickly briars. It was as if any bits of light and life were being drawn inward to sustain that single piece of fruit.

And maybe Keevi was being used to sustain it as well.

CHAPTER 4

Baldric watched as Anson and Tess climbed back down the wall and rejoined the party. Uggie immediately went over to Tess and nudged her hip for attention. Tess petted her absently as she motioned for everyone to gather around. She laid out the situation on the other side of the wall and each member of the party's individual parts in the rescue plan.

Baldric was glad to hear that Keevi was still alive, though he admitted that some of his reasons were purely selfish. Now that he knew Ashardalon's identity, he needed to know more about the greatwyrm's cult and his plans for Baldric. He hoped that Keevi might have at least some of those answers.

When Tess had finished going over the plan, she glanced at him. "Do you think you can get Keevi out of that tree?" she asked. "Will Mielikki still be willing to help?"

"I'd say that tree is a corruption of everything she holds dear," Baldric mused. He could work with that. "Leave it to me."

"All right, everyone get ready," Tess said. She nodded at Cazrin. "You're on."

The wizard approached Baldric and Lark, touching them both

on the shoulder and murmuring the words of a spell. Baldric felt a slight tingling warmth where her magic touched him, but he didn't see the spell take effect until he glanced over and watched Lark fade from sight, his body turning to a clear shimmer in the air before vanishing completely.

Baldric looked down at himself and, disconcertingly, saw nothing at all. His head swam for just a second until his mind came to grips with the fact that he hadn't actually left his body. He'd just been turned invisible.

"Remember," Cazrin warned them, "it doesn't take much to break the spell. Attacking someone or even using magic of your own will do it, so tread carefully when you're freeing Keevi."

"Understood. Ready, Lark?" Baldric asked.

There was no reply, but then Baldric felt hot breath ghosting along the back of his neck.

"Ready," Lark said in a low, ominous tone.

Baldric checked the urge to elbow the bard in the ribs. He didn't want to break the magic before he'd even begun to use it. "I'll pay you back for that later," he promised.

He moved as slowly and stealthily as he could along the wall until he found a gap in the stone. He slipped through, trusting Lark to follow. They couldn't see each other, but the Gulthias Tree was their target. Lark's job was to get the fruit; Baldric's was to get the cleric.

The bark-skinned guards were patrolling in a wide perimeter around the tree, staring at their surroundings with vacant-eyed looks, just as Tess had described. It was clear that some sort of magic was affecting them, but was it the tree, Baldric wondered, or was there someone else controlling this grove whom they hadn't seen yet?

Baldric kept close to the wall as he moved through the grove, stepping over thick underbrush as quietly as he could, dodging more briars, and keeping a watch for the twig blights that infested the underground cavern. Tess was much better suited to this sort of work, but freeing Keevi from the tree was likely going to take strong magic. And even with Cazrin's spell concealing him, he felt like he was being watched. The Gulthias Tree's presence loomed over everything, heavy with malice and the pervading stench of decay.

The smell intensified the closer he got to the tree. As he passed beneath its branches, the air felt noticeably cooler, and the shadows cast in the violet light created spiky, unsettling patterns on the cavern floor.

Baldric cautiously approached Keevi. Tess hadn't been exaggerating about the tree seeming to absorb the cleric. Keevi's thick, weathered shell was already half-covered by the charred bark. The rest of it bore a patchwork of scars: blade slashes, arrow nicks, even a jagged crack that looked like it had been hacked there by an axe.

But through the old wounds there also grew a layer of fine, feathery moss that softened the worst of the damage. Upon this, button-sized wildflowers and forests of white toadstools had sprouted. The whole of it was like a tiny garden that the tortle carried on their back, a tapestry of old pains covered by new joys.

All of which was being eaten by the desiccated heart of the tree.

Stepping close, Baldric examined the seam where the tortle's shell ended and the tree's bark began. After a moment of watching, he began to see the slow creep of the bark across the shell. Going by that, it wouldn't be long before the tortle was completely absorbed by the tree.

He moved in close to the tortle's ear. Keevi's eyes were closed, but the cleric still breathed in a deep, steady rhythm. That was a hopeful sign.

"If you can hear me, Keevi," Baldric murmured, "your rescue party has arrived—sent by Mel, your mentor—but it's important that you don't let on that we're here. Can you give me a sign—quietly—if you're still with us?"

There was an almost imperceptible hitch in the cleric's breathing. The tortle's membranous eyelids twitched and slowly lifted.

"Who are you?" they whispered. Their voice was low and wheezing. Lines of pain creased around the tortle's eyes as they searched the clearing, taking note of the guards. Baldric wasn't sure how long Keevi had been left here sealed to the tree, but it was obvious they'd grown quite weak.

Above them, the lowest branches of the tree dipped and swayed, and Baldric caught a whiff of Lark's cologne. The bard had made it into the tree. The guards were bound to notice once he plucked that fruit, but if they timed it right, Tess and the others' distraction would divert them away for a few precious moments.

"Let's just say the two of us are in the same line of work," Baldric whispered to Keevi. He reached across the tortle's thick, rounded shoulders and touched the holy symbol of Mielikki that hung from their neck. "Mind if I borrow this for a minute?" he asked. "Just in case I need the extra incentive."

"Extra . . . incentive?" The cleric's leathery face creased in confusion as their eyes opened a bit more.

"I'll explain later," Baldric said, as a high-pitched whistle—Tess's signal—echoed in the chamber. "For now, brace yourself. Things are about to get exciting."

The bark-skinned guards and twig blights turned toward the sound. One by one, they headed in the direction of the wall, away from the tree.

Baldric tightened his grip on Keevi's holy symbol and began what he hoped would be the last bargain he'd have to make with Mielikki today.

"Help us one more time," he murmured. "Help your servant. They don't deserve the fate that's waiting for them inside that tree. It's a corruption of everything you stand for. Help us strike a blow against this blighted grove, because that's what it is."

As Baldric spoke, he could hear the low murmur of Keevi's voice joining his. The tortle was speaking too quietly for him to make out the words of the prayer, but it must have been compelling, because the seam between Keevi's shell and the cursed tree began to glow. Slowly, the light brightened, searing into the gap, finding every crevice and weakness it could. The radiant power tore into the tree, and Keevi grunted in pain.

Baldric reached for the tortle's shell, careful to avoid that searing light, and began to pull.

The invisibility spell melted away as he wrenched the tortle's shell free of the cloying bark. He heard a shout—the burly paladin had glanced back and seen them. He raised another cry, but just then, Cazrin, Anson, Uggie, and Tess jumped down from the wall, landing in the midst of the guards.

Cazrin held out her hands, and a burning curtain of flame fanned out from her fingertips. The twig blights screamed and recoiled, and several of the nearby briar trees caught fire.

Tess threw her dagger and caught the tiefling guard in the shoulder, while Anson charged the man in plate mail. Lightning crackled along the broken blade in his hand as he feinted to the left, drawing the guard's eye to the magic sizzling along the blade. He checked the move at the last second and came straight in, hooking the jagged edge of his blade on the hilt of the man's sword and thrusting it aside to get under his guard.

Baldric couldn't spare any more attention for the fight unfolding. The twig blights were screeching an alarm, drawing more of the creatures over the walls to attack.

"We're about to be surrounded," Keevi said as Baldric guided the tortle away from the tree. The cleric's leathery, trunk-like legs shook, but their gaze rested on Baldric's cloth and the unicorn symbol of Mielikki that was prominently displayed there. "I'll do what I can to fight," Keevi went on, "for a fellow servant of the Lady of the Forest."

Baldric cleared his throat. "Well, you see, I'm not exactly . . ." He trailed off as a group of twig blights leaped from the wall and charged in their direction. "You know what, it'll have to wait." He positioned himself in front of the tortle, thinking fast. "If you have the strength to heal yourself, now would be a good time."

While Keevi prayed to Mielikki, Baldric quickly assessed the twig blights. By themselves, the creatures weren't terribly intimidating. They were small, spindly things, like shrubs or stick sculptures made to faintly resemble a human. But as they gathered into an ever-larger swarm, Baldric imagined dozens of those spindly arms reaching for him, claws plucking at his eyes, and he shuddered.

Fortunately, the thing about creatures made of twigs was that it was a safe bet they wouldn't take kindly to fire.

"Time for something extreme," Baldric decided, adjusting his cloth of holy symbols until he found the emblem of Talos. He hadn't had reason to call on the Stormlord for some time, but he thought this situation would be appropriate, even if Mielikki's servant might not approve.

"Aha! Got you!" called a voice from above him, and Baldric looked up to see Lark crouched among the shadowy boughs of the tree, the ripe, juicy fruit of the Gulthias Tree clutched in his crimson hand. "You should see the view from up here, Baldric!" Lark's teeth flashed in a smile. "It's the only way to watch a battle unfold!"

"How about you stop watching and cast some spells or take some shots with Last Resort from up there?" Baldric shouted back. "And stop distracting me!"

"Your wish is my command!" Lark sang out, spreading his arms wide. "I will bolster you and our companions from this unorthodox stage!" The bard teetered as he leaned too far forward, grabbing one of the branches for support.

"Is he with you?" Keevi asked weakly, pointing up at Lark with a large, trembling hand.

"They all are," Baldric said dryly, nodding to the rest of the party as he tried to compose his request in his head. "We're the Fallbacks."

"You're a fallback?" Keevi blinked in confusion. "Who was the first choice, then?"

"No, that's—" Baldric sighed. "That's our party name. It's a long story."

Lark's voice echoed across the grove in song.

*Keep your love
to yourself
It suffocates me!*

*Don't you force-feed me
the fruit
of your poisonous tree!*

For being composed on the spot, it wasn't bad, Baldric reflected, and the power—the magic that drove the words—settled over him, focusing his thoughts and helping him push away the distractions of the battle and the looming specter of the tree.

"Talos," he murmured, "this grove has been hidden underground, safe from the ravages of nature and all its disasters. Isn't it time for it to experience the wrath of wind and fire? Why should it be spared from the devastation that the Stormlord can summon? If you'll help me, I can bring the fire down on this place. What do you say?"

And maybe it was Lark's song inspiring him to a new height of eloquence and persuasion, or maybe it was simply a way for Talos to show up Mielikki, who'd been aiding them so far—Baldric hoped there wouldn't be any hard feelings—but he felt an answer to his request almost immediately.

Heat rose around him, lending the air a sudden heaviness, like a storm about to break in the middle of a hot summer's day. But then the power shifted and built in Baldric instead, gathering inside him like waves of fire. Baldric had just enough presence of mind to thrust his hands skyward, aiming and directing the spell where he needed it to go.

A column of flame streaked down from the chamber ceiling, striking all seven of the approaching twig blights at once. High-pitched screams filled the air but were quickly cut off, and black smoke billowed across the grove.

Near the wall, Anson and the paladin paused in their fight to look at the impressive spell. A flicker of fear crossed the paladin's wooden face, and for a second, Baldric thought the man might be able to shrug off whatever enchantment held him prisoner. But then he blinked, and the instant of clarity was gone. He slashed his blade at Anson, and the fighter just managed to dance back out of the way, ducking and blocking the follow-up strike with a loud clang of steel on steel.

The fire from Baldric's spell had ignited some of the nearby briars, creating a barrier of flame between them and the rest of the enemies in the grove. Using the reprieve, Baldric turned to check on Keevi. There was a line of black running along the tortle's shell where it had been fastened to the tree, but the cleric had been healing themself, and Keevi looked more alert than they had been since Baldric found them.

"Can you run?" he asked, already tugging the tortle's arm to get them moving. "We need to get out of here before more reinforcements arrive."

Keevi allowed themself to be pulled along, but they were staring incredulously at Baldric. Their gaze dropped to his cloth of holy symbols, and Baldric saw the moment Keevi registered the sheer number of different deities represented there.

"What are you?" they asked. "You called on the Lady of the Forest *and* the Stormlord, and they answered! How do you command all those forces?"

Baldric shook his head. "If we live through this, I'll buy you a drink, and you can interrogate me, but right now—"

"Interlopers! How dare you defile the sacred grove!"

Baldric rolled his eyes. "You know, this time I was really hoping we'd get away clean."

The voice had come from the top of the wall, about thirty feet away. Baldric looked over and saw a human man dressed in dark green robes, brandishing a wand of twisted, blackened wood not unlike the branches of the Gulthias Tree. Beside him, at waist height, squatted a giant green-skinned frog, its bulbous eyes staring down at them from the top of the wall. Baldric heard Uggie give a yip and a howl, and the frog turned its glistening body in the direction of the sound.

"We're here to rescue the Harper," Tess called up to the man with the wand. The elf spellcaster she'd been fighting lay unconscious at her feet. "Your servants attacked *us*. We defended ourselves. Let us take Keevi out of here safely, and we won't defile your grove any further."

Baldric glanced up at Lark, who had his crossbow balanced on one knee as he crouched in the tree, aiming it at their new enemy. "Get ready to get down from there," he called out in a low voice, hoping Lark would hear him.

"You stole the fruit of the sacred tree," the man said, pointing his wand at Tess and the others. "Return it, and submit yourselves as supplicants to the grove's will." The man drew himself up, and the briars and dead plants of the grove all seemed to bend toward him at once. "I am Belak the Outcast, caretaker of the grove, and I will make a place for you here."

Tess pursed her lips, pretending to think over that offer. Then, faster than the eye could follow, she hurled her dagger at the hand holding the wand. Belak shrieked as the blade buried itself in the flesh of his arm.

"That's going to be a no from us," Tess said.

She triggered the teleportation magic on her dagger, but she wasn't fast enough to keep the caretaker from activating his wand. As she appeared at the top of the wall, Belak pointed a trembling hand at Anson and Cazrin. Suddenly, the thorny shrubs and sickly underbrush rose and twisted around their legs, holding them in place. They grunted in pain as the briars grew and pierced their clothes and skin, drawing thin trails of blood.

Dodging the giant frog, Tess yanked her dagger free of Belak's arm, eliciting another pained shout. The caretaker swung toward her, hissing the words of a spell. His skin faded to a pale grayish-brown color, becoming roughly textured like that of the other supplicants. Behind her, the frog jumped down from the wall, landing in front of Uggie, who'd been scrabbling and scratching at the base of the wall, managing through sheer luck to avoid the entangling briars.

"Lark, let's go!" Baldric threw a supporting arm awkwardly around Keevi's shell, and when the bard climbed down from the tree, the three of them made their stumbling way across the chamber toward Anson and Cazrin.

Baldric was just trying to decide how best to make another appeal to Talos when Keevi laid a heavy hand on his arm.

"I'll help them," they said. "Can you get us out of here?"

Baldric nodded at Cazrin, who had pointed her staff at the tangling undergrowth but luckily seemed to have thought better of summoning more fire to burn through it. "She's our ticket out of here," he told Keevi. "Get them free if you can, but hurry!" He glanced over at Uggie, who was facing off with the giant frog, the two of them hunched close together.

"Uggie!" Baldric called. "Come on, girl! Get over here!"

CHAPTER 5

Uggie had never felt this way before.
Uggie was a warrior. She'd been on many adventures, had stared death in the face countless times and roared in defiance in order to protect her persons. She had a heart of steel and a stomach to match, and she was smarter than all the rest of her kind. She had to be, in order to care for her persons. Because they were squishy and dainty, and they didn't always make the best decisions.

That was all right. Uggie had their backs, no matter what.

But then the giant olive-green creature with the crooked appendages and webbed feet leaped from the wall. With the grace of a dancer, it landed before her, thumping its rump on the ground and raising a cloud of dust. Its yellowish throat expanded, making a loud *brrruuum* sound.

Was it a challenge? A greeting? Uggie hunkered low, tentacles waving warily, but she found herself off-balance. The creature's huge, wide-set eyes glistened with a fierce intelligence and cunning that matched Uggie's own. Its mouth gaped open, and a thick pink tongue darted out, tasting the air. A sweet, rotting flower scent rose around them, making Uggie's senses tingle with unexpected delight.

As she watched, entranced, the creature hopped forward, examining Uggie as closely as Uggie was examining it. Uggie took a moment to appreciate the dark, raised spots scattered across its back like a spray of freckles. Was the creature's skin really as coarse and leathery as it looked?

The creature expanded its throat again, yellow flesh swelling, and let out another low, rumbling *brrruuum* sound.

Was it . . . asking her name? That must be it. It was caught up in the moment, beguiled, just as Uggie was. But how could this be happening? They were sworn enemies, sitting on opposite sides of a deadly conflict. She shouldn't answer it. She should attack. She needed to protect her persons.

And yet . . .

Uggie. Against all sense, Uggie sent the thought across the insurmountable distance between them. *My name. Uggie. Who you?*

"Kulkek, kill that monster!" shrieked the person on top of the wall, spittle flying from his mouth as he waved his crooked stick at the creature like a child throwing a tantrum.

Kulkek.

Kulkek. That you?

Brrruuum, the creature said. A confirmation.

Kulkek. Uggie thought it was the most beautiful name she'd ever heard.

Now the angry person with the stick was yelling something about making them all pay with their lives, that he would feed them to the tree if his magic didn't strip the flesh from their bones first. Tess person was yelling something too, but Uggie was distracted by her own reflection in Kulkek's beautiful, bulbous eyes. Her heart pounded in her barrel chest. She felt overcome, her stomach churning with happiness, like she'd just eaten a bucket of grass clippings and rotten eggs.

Was this . . . was this what *love* felt like?

Brrruuum, Kulkek intoned, hopping closer but hesitating, as if afraid its presence wouldn't be welcomed.

Uggie blushed from the root of her eyestalk all the way to the ends of her tentacles. She opened her mouth, her tongue lolling out as she turned, showing Kulkek her profile and the impressive web of scars she'd acquired over the years.

Cazrin person ran past them, sweating, stumbling, and trailing a curtain of briars and grass. A blue-white lightning bolt shot from her staff and tore into the yelling person on top of the wall.

"Uggie, we are *leaving*!" Tess person shouted.

Leave? But they'd only just met. Uggie wanted to know all about Kulkek. Did Kulkek like bacon grease and dead birds as much as Uggie did? How high could Kulkek jump with those powerfully muscled legs?

Not fair, Uggie thought to Kulkek. *Need more time.*

Brrruuum. Kulkek hopped toward her, close enough to nuzzle its face against hers. It smelled of algae and moist earth. Uggie breathed it in, committing the smell, and this moment, to memory.

"Uggie!"

That was Baldric person.

She was powerless to ignore that sweet, bearded face as it gazed at her in exasperated fury.

Goodbye, she thought to Kulkek. *Uggie remember you.*

Brrruuum.

And then, before she could change her mind, Uggie was running toward her persons. They were gathered in a group near the scary dead tree, and Cazrin person was reading aloud from a piece of parchment. Maybe she would let Uggie eat it later. Anson person held out his arms for her, and Uggie jumped into them. She craned her eyestalk to look back at Kulkek. The creature flicked its tongue out at her in farewell, catching one of the twig creatures that just happened to be running past and snapping it in half.

Then a swirl of blue light filled the chamber, blinding Uggie. She called out, and thought she heard a faint *brrruuum* in response before everything vanished.

CHAPTER 6

Night had fallen, and the smell of rotting fish filled Tess's nostrils as the party appeared at the edge of a rickety wooden pier. She started to take a step forward and realized almost too late that she was standing right at the edge, and there were no more steps left to take before the plunge into the water. Arms out for balance, she managed to pull herself back, heart fluttering in her chest.

Some of the others weren't so lucky.

"Oh sh—" Lark's voice cut off as he toppled off the end of the pier, grabbing Anson's shoulder and pulling him and Uggie along for the ride. A spray of water went up in their wake.

Cazrin was standing safely a few feet away from Tess, with Baldric and Keevi at her side. They were looking around in confusion at their surroundings. As near as Tess could tell, the teleportation spell had landed them in the heart of the Gray Harbor in Baldur's Gate. The deepwater port was the hub of the Lower City, with the Seatower rising on its western bank, and its numerous cranes and cargo carts like hulking metal beasts silhouetted in the moonlight.

"Sorry about that!" Cazrin said, striding to the edge of the pier. Tess joined her to see Lark and Anson treading water while Uggie doggy-paddled happily between them, drinking as much of the dirty water as possible before Anson stopped her. "I meant to transport us directly to our rooms at the Elfsong Tavern. I don't know what happened!"

"We were in a bit of a rush," Tess said, to reassure her. "Anyone could have made that mistake. I'm just glad you got us out of there. I was getting tired of hearing Belak scream about how painful our deaths were going to be."

"Would someone give me a hand, please?" Lark shouted up to them. He peeled wet ropes of his long dark hair out of his face. "My coat is trying to drown me! I'm never going to get the smell out!"

Cazrin murmured a spell and pointed her staff down at Anson. Purple light flared at the staff's tip, and Anson began to levitate out of the water. Lark grabbed onto his shoulders, and Uggie latched onto Lark's coat with her impressive teeth. Anson teetered and stuttered in midair, their combined weight testing the limits of the spell, but in the end they managed to drift to the edge of the pier, and Tess pulled them onto dry land again.

"Everyone all right?" she asked, checking over each of her party members in turn, then ending with Keevi, who was standing on their own now, though they still looked a bit shaken by their ordeal in the grove. Tess couldn't blame them. Being slowly sacrificed to a cursed tree was not a fate she would wish on anyone.

"I'll live, I suppose." Lark shivered and stripped off his coat, letting it fall to the ground with a wet slap. "Now that we're finally back in a land where the plants don't come to life and try to eat you, that is. Time for a meal?" he asked hopefully.

"I'm in," Baldric and Anson said in unison. Anson was stripping off his boots and dumping water out of them.

Tess turned to Keevi. "How are you doing?" she asked. "We know you've been through a lot, and you're probably anxious to report back to Mel—she's been worried about you—but if you'd like to join us for a drink and some food to recover your strength . . ." She let the thought trail off, as Keevi's attention seemed to be fixed on Baldric, so much so that the dwarf turned away, looking uncomfortable under the cleric's scrutiny.

Finally, Keevi shifted their attention to Tess. "Yes, I think a drink sounds marvelous," they said with a grateful smile that deepened the green seams around their eyes. But then their expression dimmed. "Belak and his followers stripped me of my weapons and belongings, including the coins I had on me. I wish that I could buy you all a drink and a hot meal as thanks for saving my life, but as it is, I'm afraid I can't even afford an ale."

"Don't worry about that," Anson said, putting an arm companionably across the tortle's shell, being careful not to touch the healing wounds. "We collected plenty of loot on our way to that weird garden. I'm sure some of it was yours."

"Not to mention yours truly managed to snag this beauty," Lark said, removing the Gulthias Tree's fruit from his pouch and tossing it in the air before catching it again. "Seems like a lot of trouble for a bit of healing, though. We already have a cleric." He nodded at Baldric.

"Yes, but it's not just a piece of healing fruit," Tess reminded him. "It helps cure poison victims too." She reached down and plucked the fruit from Lark's grasp. "So, the next time we have a carrion crawler incident"—she gave the group a significant look—"we'll be prepared."

"Ahh." Heads nodded throughout the group.

Keevi looked confused. "Carrion crawler incident?" they asked.

"We'll explain on the way," Baldric said.

"Wait." Cazrin gestured to the bag of holding secured to Anson's hip. "Let me see that cloak we picked up in the library. I'm going to use it to disguise Uggie."

Anson obligingly reached into the bag and pulled out the dark cloak, passing it off to Cazrin. Tess gestured to the fighter to keep a lookout while the wizard worked. True, they were back in the city, but it was still Baldur's Gate after dark, and this was the Lower City. Even with the Flaming Fist mercenaries ostensibly keeping order—or harassing people whenever they felt like it—one couldn't be too careful.

"How's it going to work?" Baldric asked, scratching his beard as Cazrin whipped the cloak over Uggie's large form, adjusting the fabric to accommodate her tentacles as best she could. "Uggie's not going to know how to activate the magic, is she?"

BACON, came the familiar mental shout.

"No, probably not," Cazrin allowed. "But back when I was researching the Ruinous Child, I found some variations on spells intended to summon animal or monstrous allies." She lifted the cloak's hood over Uggie's eyestalk. "Using that as a foundation, I've been tinkering with the magical theories surrounding the calling of familiars and other close magical companions, which is a different and fascinating branch of study altogether."

"Caaaaaazzzz." Lark pretended to collapse to the dock in an exhausted puddle. "I want a drink! And food! Sometime before dawn, preferably."

"Right," Cazrin said, her lips twitching. "To cut short what I assure you would otherwise be a fascinating lecture on the subject: I'm using the basis of the magic that summons familiars to create a temporary telepathic connection with Uggie, in order to guide her to activate the magic to disguise herself as a sheepdog."

Baldric snorted in amusement. "And the liches of the world trembled and wailed to see how Cazrin Varaith subverted their legacy."

"I know." Cazrin grinned at him. "Isn't it marvelous?"

"Does that mean the creature will become your familiar?" Keevi asked curiously.

"Let's . . . not go that far," Cazrin said. "No offense, Uggie," she added hastily. "You'd make anyone a wonderful familiar, wouldn't you, girl?"

KULKEK, Uggie barked mentally as Cazrin put her hands on the otyugh's back and began the spell.

"Uggie." Tess rubbed her temples wearily. "Softer, please. What was that last word?"

KULKEK!

"Maybe she took a blow to the head," Lark suggested. "That sounded like gibberish."

"It's that Belak fellow's pet frog," Baldric said. "I heard him shouting at it during the battle." He nodded at Uggie. "I saw the creature and her together. If I didn't know any better, I'd think our girl's got her first case of puppy love. Er, or whatever it's called for an otyugh."

"Really?" Anson said, ringing out his soaking wet shirt. "But Kulkek's a frog. How would that work?"

"The universal song of love," Lark intoned, spreading his arms wide, as if to encompass the entirety of the star-filled sky. "Who are we to question its mysteries or the desires in Uggie's heart?"

"Um, I meant, I'd be just a little bit afraid she might decide to eat Kulkek one day," Anson clarified. "If she got hungry enough."

Tess considered. "Fair point."

Cazrin cast her modified spell, her eyes shut tight in concentration. Tess took a moment to wonder what the wizard might be seeing in the depths of Uggie's mind and resolved to ask her about it later. The wizard's forehead creased, and a shimmer of light passed across the cloak, like liquid gold spilled over a dark surface. Uggie yipped excitedly, spun in a circle, and suddenly, instead of an otyugh in a cloak standing on the docks at night, there was a tall, shaggy sheepdog with gray-and-white fur—and three eyes, and a tentacle poking out of its back.

"Oh dear," Cazrin said, opening her eyes to assess the outcome. "That wasn't quite what I was going for."

"No, no, that's perfection!" Lark spluttered with laughter, his shoulders shaking.

Tess put a consoling hand on Cazrin's shoulder. "We'll work with it," she said. "It's a long walk to the Elfsong."

Keevi stared at the sheepdog-otyugh and shook their head. "Who *are* you people?"

TESS LED THE way down the bumpy, cobblestoned streets toward the Elfsong Tavern—or so she hoped. She'd never had cause to come into the city from the harbor before. But she'd become familiar enough with the tightly packed buildings and narrow, winding streets of the Lower City in the last few months that she was confident she could find her way.

Baldur's Gate was a far cry from Waterdeep, in so many ways. Crouched on the north bank of the River Chionthar, it was a walled city firmly divided between the rich upper crust and the commoners. The Flaming Fist mercenary company held sway in this part of the city, and anyone with a passing familiarity with that organization knew they often led with said fist in keeping order in the roughest section of the city.

Tess used the term "order" loosely, of course.

But so far, they'd managed to keep a low profile and not attract any attention from either the criminal element of the city or its often equally criminal authorities, which was exactly where Tess liked to be as a professional infiltrator.

And they'd done well for themselves over the past several months. Tess didn't consider herself the bragging sort, but she appreciated a job well done, and ever since the Fallbacks had completed—and, more important, survived—their first mission together and rid themselves of the Ruinous Child, things had been proceeding much closer to the plan she'd had when forming the group in the first place.

But though they'd been comfortable in Waterdeep, Tess wasn't about to be content with comfort. Comfort was not in keeping with the adventurer's life, or with building a reputation that would outlast them, a legacy that would echo across Faerûn.

Besides all that, Waterdeep hadn't been able to give them the answers they sought about the entity—Ashardalon—plaguing Baldric. But now, after months of researching, questioning contacts, and following false leads, they'd finally rooted out their enemy's identity. The question that remained was how best to act on that information and plan their next move in this chess game.

Tess had seen Baldric struggling down in the Sunless Citadel. She suspected Ashardalon's presence and influence was intensifying. Baldric hadn't said as much, but she could see the strain in his eyes. They needed to do something soon.

But for tonight, it was time to rest and celebrate their successes. Ashardalon was a formidable enemy, but the greatwyrm could wait one more night.

Tess knew her party. The Fallbacks needed to blow off some steam.

CHAPTER 7

Good enough, Cazrin thought as she severed the mental connection with Uggie—and with it the image of a stew of raw rabbit, mushy vegetables, and mothballs that she wasn't going to be able to scrub from her mind anytime soon. She'd adjusted the spell so that the otyugh looked mostly like a dog. The subtle differences—an extra eyelid here and there beneath her fur—wouldn't show in the low light.

Or so she hoped.

The Elfsong Tavern was alive with activity. Most of the tables were full, but Lark had silver-tongued his way into getting them a spot near the bar. At the back of the room, several patrons had shoved a table in front of a couch against the back wall and were engaged in an enthusiastic game of Baldur's Bones, the dice clattering across the wooden tabletop and bouncing off tankards and glasses amid shouts and curses from the players.

Next to the bar, a young gnome woman was playing a beautiful spruce harp. As she finished a cheerful melody, she bent to take a sip of water and exchange a few words with an eladrin with straight golden hair that she wore at shoulder length on one side of her face and shaved close to her skull on the other. An autumn oak leaf tattoo was situated just above the sharp point of her left ear.

Cazrin's heart did a tiny stutter at seeing her. She'd hoped that Rane would be here to sing tonight, and it looked like she wasn't going to be disappointed. The bard had been booked at the Elfsong for several performances, and Cazrin had been drawn in at once by Rane's voice. Lark had introduced them—he'd known her from the tavern circuit in Waterdeep—and they'd talked for hours that night and the night after. At one point, Cazrin thought they'd been flirting, but she didn't have enough experience at it to be certain. Whatever was happening here, it was as fascinating and confounding as trying to unlock the secrets of some ancient magical tome.

Part of her wanted to go straight over to Rane, but she hesitated, her steps faltering as she tried to think of what she would say. What if they'd exhausted all topics of conversation? Maybe they didn't have as much in common as Cazrin hoped.

What if Rane was tired of talking to her and was only doing it to be polite?

Maybe . . . well, maybe she needed a moment before she went over there. Just to work up to it.

For now she took a seat at the table with the rest of the Fallbacks and tried to relax. It was good to be back. Baldur's Gate wasn't her favorite place the party had visited in their travels, but its rough exterior hid pockets of knowledge and hidden gems of magic for those who cared enough to seek it. It was a wonderful puzzle box and place to learn, if you gave it a chance.

Cazrin was all about taking chances and embracing new beginnings these days. Or, at least, that's what she *hoped* to do. Making plans was one thing, but those first steps weren't easy.

"Falten!" Lark called out to a red-haired human man rushing past, his muscles straining under a full tray of drinks. "Don't forget about us! We're back in town and in a mood to tip generously!"

"I'll remember you said that." The young man smiled and waggled caterpillar eyebrows at Lark as he swept by them.

Eventually, they managed to put in orders for wine and dark beer, and several servings of the night's special: roast chicken with turnips and potatoes and a thick, rich gravy that Falten promised would make them fall at the cook's feet. Cazrin settled in with a glass of Cormyrian blush wine and turned to speak to Keevi, but she found them wholly focused on Baldric.

"It's remarkable," Keevi was saying. They were bent forward, careful to keep their large, curved shell from dragging on the floor behind their stool, to examine Baldric's cloth of holy symbols. The dwarf was holding it up for Keevi's inspection. "How is it that you've sworn yourself to this many deities? I've never seen anything like it before."

Anson was slipping Uggie a handful of peanuts from a bowl on the table. He grinned at the tortle. "How much time do you have, Keevi?"

Baldric shot the fighter a look of exasperation. He turned back to the tortle. "It's not that complicated," he said. Falten came around and thunked a tankard down in front of him, spilling a stream of foam down one side. Baldric immediately seized it and took a drink. He wiped the foam from his beard and gave a satisfied sigh. "I offer an honest bargain to the gods in exchange for the power I need," he went on. "If it's accepted, everyone does their part, the debt is paid, and afterward, we walk away. No expectations or strings attached."

"Strings?" The tortle's leathery brow furrowed, and Cazrin could see they were unsettled. "Is that how you view divine service? As a burden?"

"Not for those who go to it willingly, with eyes wide open," Baldric said. "I'm sure it's quite fulfilling for them." He took another drink. "But it's not my path. I walk my own road, and I choose carefully where I put my loyalty."

Seeing an opening into the conversation, Cazrin leaned forward. "It's not so very different from my path," she said. "I'm always searching for new spells and unique ways of applying magic. I study the research of others who came before me, from all over the world. Why should I restrict myself to studying the work of just *one* wizard, when there are so many perspectives to learn from?"

"I appreciate the spirit of what you're saying." Keevi reached out a tentative hand, looking to Baldric for permission before touching the unicorn symbol of Mielikki on his cloth. "But I don't think it's the same thing. It's not just about being loyal to a certain deity.

There's a bond of trust and caring between a cleric and their god, a promise to use the magic they've been given to serve their faith."

"But the gods already know what Baldric is using his magic for," Tess put in. "I've heard him call for aid when he casts his spells, and he's always up-front about what's at stake and where the magic is going." She looked to Baldric for confirmation.

"It's part of the deal," Baldric said, nodding. "If the gods are upset about what I'm doing, or want to demand more from me, they haven't said so."

Despite the confidence with which he spoke, a shadow passed over Baldric's face. Cazrin thought she was the only one who noticed, as Falten came back just then with their food. There was a clatter of plates and cutlery and drinks being refilled as they all dug into the juicy roast chicken. The gravy was as rich and mouthwatering as promised.

But Cazrin was still watching Baldric. She wondered if he was thinking about Tyr, the one god who had abandoned Baldric when he had been in great need. As a result, Baldric had called out in desperation to any entity who would listen, be they divine or . . . something else. That was how Ashardalon had gotten a foothold in his life.

Anson leaned over, clanking his tankard against Baldric's and sending another wave of foam splashing over the side. "Well, I don't claim to understand what you do, but it's amazing to me," he said. "To have the ear of so many gods, to give them what they want and still come out ahead for yourself—it takes a special kind of skill to make that happen, and Baldric here has it." He gave Keevi a meaningful look. "It's saved us all more than once."

"To Baldric," Lark said, raising his wineglass, his red tail whipping restlessly over the floor. "Our master negotiator!"

"All right, songbird, you don't have to lay it on that thick," Baldric said, shaking his head. "Why don't you go get onstage where you belong? Looks like there's an opening."

Lark glanced over his shoulder and immediately perked up at seeing the makeshift stage empty. He leaped up from his stool, checked to see that he was mostly dry, then grabbed his lute and his wine and wove through the crowd.

Tess watched him go, then turned back to Keevi, her gaze serious. "Mel told us a little bit about your mission to the citadel," she said. "She mentioned that you were looking for signs of renewed interest in the place from the Cult of the Dragon. Did you manage to find any evidence of that?"

Keevi looked surprised, then wary. Cazrin lifted a hand. "We're not asking you to reveal any information that the Harpers want you to keep secret," she assured them. She exchanged a glance with Tess and Baldric, who nodded for her to continue. "We have a particular interest in powerful dragons ourselves. Specifically, a greatwyrm known as Ashardalon." Cazrin watched for Keevi's reaction and noticed that the tortle's hands tightened on their tankard.

Baldric saw the gesture too, and his keen eyes lit briefly. "It might be that we have similar goals here," he remarked casually, but Cazrin recognized that tone. Keevi may not have realized it yet, but it wasn't just the gods that Baldric was adept at negotiating with. "We've got no love for the greatwyrm, and if the Harpers have reason to act against him as well . . ." He let the idea linger and speared a turnip on the end of his knife so he could take a bite.

Keevi glanced between the two of them, their gaze shrewd. "If I did have such information," they said carefully, "I'd of course want to report it to Mel first. I trained with her, and she helped me find a better path when I was struggling, one that ultimately led to my service to Mielikki and the Harpers. This mission was my way of repaying her for all that she's done for me." Their shell creaked as they shifted on their stool. "You all saved my life, and I'm deeply grateful, but I feel I need to be cautious."

Tess nodded. "You want to make sure she can vouch for us." She held up a hand when Keevi started to protest. "It's nothing less than I would expect from one of Mel's students." She grinned. "It's exactly what she would tell me to do in this situation."

Keevi chuckled. "I forgot you said that you were also one of her pupils. We probably have a great deal in common, even if I didn't end up following your path." They licked a bit of gravy off their claws and seemed lost in thought for a moment. "If I did have pertinent information to share," they continued, "are you saying you might be willing to take on a task for the Harpers?"

Now, that was interesting, Cazrin thought. What were the Harpers getting out of all this?

"If there was such a task," Baldric said carefully, "and it meant striking a blow at Ashardalon, I'd say we'd be *very* interested."

"Assuming there was also a fair exchange of coin for this job," Tess added. "You've already seen a sample of what our party can bring to the table, so I don't need to tell you our qualifications."

"No, you don't," Keevi agreed. "As I said, I owe my life to that competence. Very well, then. Tonight, I'm going to rest and repair my shell further, but I'll get word to Mel that I'd like to meet with her tomorrow to give my official report." They nodded to each of them. "Your group should come to that meeting, and we can talk more."

"Sounds like a plan." Tess leaned back in her chair, her hands folded behind her head. She wore a satisfied expression.

Cazrin felt a frisson of excitement. This might be the breakthrough they were looking for. Judging by Tess's reaction and the gleam in Baldric's eyes, they felt it too.

But when Cazrin looked over at Anson, who'd been uncharacteristically silent throughout the conversation, she found his attention had drifted away. He was eating his meal, but his eyes kept straying to the door of the tavern, as if he expected someone to walk in.

No, Cazrin corrected herself. He was fidgeting, as if he wanted to leave.

"Anson," Tess said, nudging the fighter's arm where it rested on the table. "Are you good with the plan?"

"Hmmm?" Anson blinked and looked over at Tess, as if seeing her for the first time. "Oh, um, whatever you want is fine," he said.

Tess frowned at the noncommittal response, but she didn't say anything else.

The conversation moved to lighter topics after that, and as Cazrin finished eating, she found herself scanning the room over the rim of her wineglass, searching for Rane. She tried to act casual, but a swirl of fluttery nerves took over her belly at the thought of talking to her again.

Next to her, Tess cleared her throat quietly and tilted her head toward the couch at the back of the room. "She's over there," Tess said, wiping a bit of chicken grease off her fingers. Sheepdog Uggie was watching her every move, waiting for a piece of food to drop from the table.

Cazrin followed Tess's gesture, and sure enough, Rane was perched on the couch, hands folded around one knee, talking to the tabaxi bartender as he handed her a drink.

"Go," Tess urged her with a chuckle.

"Are you sure?" Cazrin asked, feeling another flash of uncertainty. "I can stay if you need me here."

"It's a celebration," Tess encouraged her, "and the night is young. We all deserve some time to relax."

She was right. Take a chance, Cazrin reminded herself. Before she could change her mind or let her nerves overcome her, she slid her chair back, patted Uggie, and headed across the room. She walked unhurriedly, taking in the sight of Rane's animated face reflected in the dancing firelight.

As if she felt the attention, the eladrin turned and locked gazes with Cazrin just before she reached her. Her eyes widened in surprised pleasure.

"Cazrin! You're back."

Rane held out her hands. Cazrin clasped them and found herself pulled down onto the couch next to the entertainer, who signaled to the bartender to make another one of the drink she'd just ordered. "When did you arrive?"

Rane's voice was soft, barely heard over the din of raucous laughter and conversation in the room, and the sound of Lark tuning his lute in the opposite corner. Hearing that voice, one would never suspect that she was one of the most talented operatic singers that Cazrin had ever heard.

"Just now," Cazrin said, accepting the drink Rane passed to her, though her heart skipped as the bard kept hold of Cazrin's other hand. "How much longer are you in the city?"

"Tonight's my last night performing," Rane said. "I move on to Neverwinter in a couple of days." She squeezed Cazrin's hand. "I'm glad we could meet up again before I leave."

"So am I," Cazrin said, putting on a smile as she sipped her

Rashemi sunrise cocktail. Inwardly, she felt a sharp pang of disappointment that Rane would be leaving soon. She knew it was silly. The Fallbacks wouldn't be staying in Baldur's Gate forever either. But she didn't want whatever this was between them to end just yet, at least not without acknowledging it somehow.

Cazrin tried to think of an opening, a way to bring up what she was feeling, but something held her back. The doubts crept in again, and she found herself withdrawing, her hand going slack in Rane's. An awkward silence fell between them, and they turned their gazes to the stage.

Lark was now warming up the crowd with a foot-stomping number that encouraged audience participation without requiring them to stop drinking or eating. As he belted out the chorus, the tiefling tossed his dark hair over one shoulder, dipped into a courtly bow, and tipped his hat off his head. He laid it at the edge of the stage before returning his hands to his lute.

A casual observer might not notice, but Cazrin had seen Lark perform often enough to know that he'd used the little flourishes to activate the magic of his rings. In response, the light around him brightened, while the rest of the stage seemed to draw back into shadow. A golden glow illuminated his lute strings and sparkled in the air around him. He spun, went to one knee, and pounded the stage like a drum with one hand while continuing to play with the other. The crowd whistled and hooted in appreciation, and he flashed them a brilliant smile.

"Your friend is in particularly fine form tonight," Rane commented, setting down her glass.

Cazrin had to agree. In fact, she couldn't remember the last time she'd seen Lark so at ease while performing. In the past, he'd seemed to enjoy playing to the audience, but at the same time, his attention had always been divided, as if he were keeping one eye on the crowd, one eye on his performance, and the rest of his attention on something she'd never quite been able to identify. It had made him seem removed from the show instead of part of it.

Not tonight. Tonight, he was giving all of himself to the audience and to the music, and the crowd adored him for it.

She shouldn't be surprised, Cazrin thought, as she and Rane joined in for the clapping and foot-stomping finale. In the months since the Fallbacks had been together, they'd all gone through changes, settling more fully into themselves and into their roles in the party.

Cazrin felt like her life had been upended completely, in ways she'd never expected or dared hope for, since the day Tess had walked into that musty old warehouse to recruit her.

She'd finally found people who understood her and her passion for magic. They accepted her and valued her gifts, no questions asked. It had caused a whole new confidence to blossom inside her, like a flame that wouldn't be extinguished. Cazrin couldn't wait to see where the next adventure would take them, and what twists and turns her life would take with it.

So why was she having so much trouble gathering her courage with Rane? Cazrin suppressed a sigh of exasperation with herself. If only the brilliant scholars of Faerûn, who'd written thousands of books on the mysteries of magic, had devoted even a bit of their wisdom to explaining these feelings she was having.

Then again, maybe what she needed was a poet, not a scholar.

Summoning a bit of her newfound confidence, Cazrin shifted away from Rane and quietly murmured the words of a spell, just as Lark was finishing his song. While the applause was still echoing through the room, she sent him a quiet message, her mind connecting to his.

Do you think you could play a slower song, Lark? she asked, trying to catch his eye as she made her request. *Maybe "Mystra's Midnight Walk"? You remember?*

Onstage, Lark was basking in the applause, taking a swig of his wine and wiping the sweat from his forehead. He didn't answer, and for a second, Cazrin worried the spell hadn't worked. Then his lips curved in a sly smile. He looked up, finding her effortlessly in the crowd, and winked.

The applause eventually died down, and Lark began to play the first notes of the slow, romantic ballad. The light around him dimmed, casting shadows over his dusky crimson skin.

"I feel an inspiration, like a voice, a muse, whispering in my mind," he purred. "It's time for a lover's dance. Something passionate. So, find a partner, and make some magic."

He winked at her again.

Cazrin blushed and looked away. She put her empty glass down on the low table in front of the couch. *Now or never,* she thought. She'd fought a *lich.* Overcome a vile, powerful tome.

She stood up.

Held out her hand to Rane.

"Dance with me?" she asked, grateful her voice didn't shake with nerves.

The bard's hazel eyes lit with pleasure, and the gentle bow of her lips curved in an inviting smile. "I'd love to," she said.

Easy as that.

Cazrin felt a heady rush as she led them to the middle of the room, which had been roped off on three sides to mark out a rough dance floor. There wasn't much space among the tables, but fortunately, there was only one other couple on the dance floor: a wiry orc mercenary wearing a skirt that bristled with daggers and a copper dragonborn in an olive-green vest who wore the symbol of Tymora displayed prominently on his barrel chest.

Rane slid into Cazrin's arms, and the two of them began to move to the haunting melody, a song of peace and yearning that Cazrin had always loved.

A year ago, she mused, she never would have thought she'd end up here, on a night like this. If the Fallbacks hadn't rushed headlong into her life, she'd probably still be crawling through that dusty warehouse in Waterdeep, buried under a pile of books. She'd managed to find her own kind of happiness there, but looking back, she could see with a bit more clarity. She had been lonely, like the young girl in Lark's song, who dreamed of a future and a power she couldn't yet comprehend.

Now she was here, surrounded by her friends, fulfilled by her work and study of magic. There were still hard times, and Cazrin wasn't fool enough to believe that facing Ashardalon was going to be easy. It was a dangerous life she'd chosen, but tonight, she felt more at peace than she had in a very long time.

The only sting was that her family couldn't see how far she'd come. She'd long ago given up on the idea of making them proud—she'd made peace with that part of her life too—but she wondered sometimes if they wished her happiness, or if they thought about her at all.

Maybe that was why it was scary to reach out, to make this connection with Rane. Maybe she was still worried about that same rejection happening again, despite everything.

"Are you still with me?" Rane's voice was a warm whisper against the shell of Cazrin's ear. Her hands drifted to the back of her neck, playing with her dark hair as they swayed.

"Mmm," Cazrin said. "If you keep doing that, I'm afraid I might step on your feet."

Rane laughed softly. "I'm not scared." She leaned closer, her eyes serious and kind. "Something you want to talk about?"

"Just thinking about the past," Cazrin admitted. "But I'm also thinking about starting new chapters in my life."

"Sounds right, even if it's not always easy." Rane gently turned them in the dance. "But while we're on the subject of new things . . . I'm happy you asked me to dance tonight. I wasn't sure how you felt about the two of us. I know I'll be leaving soon, but that doesn't mean we won't see each other again." She hesitated, and for the first time, Cazrin thought Rane might be just as nervous, just as unsure as she was. "If that's something you want?"

"I do," Cazrin said. The sound of her heartbeat was loud in her ears. "I just don't—" She stopped and took a breath to gather her thoughts. "This is very new to me," she admitted. "So many things are new in my life right now, and I don't want to do something wrong, to do anything that will mess it up. I don't want to hurt you and . . ." She trailed off as Rane cupped her cheek.

"Hurt is inevitable," the bard said, "but I wouldn't be here if I wasn't strong enough to bear it, and I believe that you are just as strong." She stroked her thumb across Cazrin's cheek. "I wanted to tell you, after I finish my performances in Neverwinter, I'm going south for a bit."

"Warmer weather?" Cazrin guessed, leaning into her touch.

"And a view of the sea," the bard said in an airy voice. "I could live on those two things. But in a month or so, I plan to stop at a village off the Coast Way. It's called Verin's Crossing. You'd love it. There's a little book and tea shop on the square, right across from an outdoor theater. The owner knows me and lets me perform whenever I stop by. We should meet there and spend some time together."

Cazrin had never been to the village Rane described, but she could picture the scene in her head. She'd sit at a tiny table outside the shop, a book in her lap, tea in hand, and wait for Rane to look across the stage and see her. "It sounds wonderful," she said, swallowing. But how could she make a promise to be somewhere in a month when she didn't know where she'd be tomorrow?

"You don't need to decide tonight," Rane said, as if sensing her uncertainty, "or worry about everything that may or may not happen. Tonight, you and I are here together, at the start of something, and that's enough." Rane tilted her head, her eyes gleaming with mischief. "Although I do have one thing to ask you before I leave the city."

"What's that?" Cazrin's chest ached at Rane's sweetness, at the uncomplicated acceptance that she'd offered.

Rane smiled and leaned in, her lips a breath away from Cazrin's, and whispered her request.

Cazrin's face warmed, and she felt she could have danced right up through the ceiling and out among the Tears of Selûne. "Yes, you can," she whispered back, but then she kissed Rane first, right in the middle of the dance floor.

CHAPTER 8

Lark kept a weather eye on Cazrin and her companion on the dance floor, so he got to witness firsthand the kiss that made the wizard gleam and glow every bit as much as Lark did after a good steam at the Hissing Stones bathhouse. He reminded himself to take full credit for it later. His songs always had that effect on people.

Gods, what a time to be alive, Lark thought as the crowd's applause rippled over him. He grabbed a glass of water the bartender had placed on a stool nearby and took a long drink to soothe his parched throat. He felt the weight of the amulet's golden eye resting on his sweat-soaked chest, just below his pendant. It was heavy, like a shield, a glorious barrier against the prying world. For the first time in a long time, he felt he could stand here on this stage, unafraid of eyes watching him from dark corners. When he stepped out the door of the tavern later that night, he would raise his face to the sky and close his eyes, letting the cool night air kiss the flush of his skin.

Instead of looking for a cloaked figure with a dagger to jump out at him from an alley.

Lark put the glass down and shifted his grip on his lute, getting ready for a more upbeat tune, something that would coax a few more folks to dance. It wasn't that he was *always* looking over his shoulder. In fact, ever since he'd joined the Fallbacks, he'd felt more secure. That's what came from travelling with powerful people.

It was just that in Lark's experience, such luxuries never lasted. Take his old band, for instance. There'd been a time Lark had thought that dance would last forever, that he and his friends would travel up and down the Sword Coast scooping up accolades and coin with both hands.

But that had ended too, and Lark had been on his own. Dealing with cloaked figures who seemed to turn up in every city and hamlet he travelled to, without fail. He'd dodged them so far, but he was no closer to finding out who they were or what they wanted with him. What crime could he have possibly committed that would warrant this kind of manhunt?

The not knowing was the most frustrating part.

"If you're not there already, you're going to want to get on your feet for this next one," Lark teased, pointing at his table and the remaining Fallbacks seated there. He was surprised to see there was only Tess, Baldric, and Keevi left. A quick sweep of the room showed Anson slipping out the tavern's front door. The fighter looked like he was trying his best to pass unnoticed, but that was hard to do while dodging a line of gnomes who had just piled into the tavern wearing matching ribbons in their hair and sashes across their chests that proclaimed them to be *The Agile Acrobats of Neverwinter*.

As the fighter disappeared into the night, Lark couldn't help but wonder what he was up to. Had their fearless leader sent him on a midnight errand, or was this personal business? Lark wasn't one to pry, but he loved a bit of juicy gossip, and he made a mental note to ask Baldric about it later. For now he had fresh coin in his pocket, wine warming his belly, and an eager audience to entertain. It truly didn't get any better than that.

Who knew where the night would take him?

Lark spun away and then back toward the crowd, spreading his fingers as if he were throwing out a handful of coin. He sang out a spell, and colored sparks erupted in the air, popping and crackling and sending streamers of gold over the dancers.

That got the crowd's attention. Ale sloshed, shouts and whistles rang out, and more people sprang up from their tables, grabbed a partner, and squeezed onto the dance floor.

Lark let their excitement feed him as his fingers flew over his lute strings. By now he knew the words of "Lorthrannan's Fall" as well as he knew his own name. It was a triumphant anthem about how he and the Fallbacks had descended into the depths of Undermountain and ended up in an earthshaking battle with an evil lich. Lark had begun to conceive the song in his head as he'd been running up the back of a purple worm with a malevolent tome clutched in his hands. He'd had no idea at the time that it would end up being his most popular new piece, or that people would turn a song about the downfall of a lich into a dancing tune, but here they were.

*You cheated death
you burned your bridge
thought yourself so smart*

*But every dog has his day
and every worm eats its way
to your decaying heart*

*The fall, the fall
will take us all
to our own eternity...*

*But Lorthrannan's fall?
You will recall
for its lack of dignity*

Lark hoped that Lorthrannan, wherever he happened to be rotting now, appreciated Lark's attempt to immortalize him in song. It was much more satisfying, in Lark's mind, than trying to preserve mortal flesh far past its expiration. More sanitary, as well.

He finished the song and threw up his hands, sending more sparks into the air amid the applause. People were coming on and off the dance floor at a steady pace now, filing past the stage to drop coins into the hat Lark had placed at his feet. It was hot in the tavern with all the bodies. People were bright-eyed, flushed, and happy, ordering more drinks to cool off. The bartender refilled Lark's water and wineglass and gave him a nod of approval. Lark's music was drawing more customers in the door, and that meant more business for the tavern.

He really had them tonight. His audience was in the mood for a party, and Lark could give that to them. Usually, at this point in the night, even if the crowd was good, he'd surrender the stage before he drew too much notice.

Tonight, he felt invincible.

"Look at all the newcomers." Lark grinned at the crowd as he absently plucked at his lute strings. "You've been an amazing group so far, but I think we can pick things up even more, don't you?"

He sashayed back and forth across the stage as he spoke, and more coins clinked into his hat. Oh, he did love that sound. He had gained an appreciation for a full treasure chest over the past several months, but he was still a busker at heart, and a pile of coins in his hat meant he'd bonded with his audience.

"Let's see where the night takes us," Lark said, waggling his eyebrows amid more cheers and laughter.

He was just about to launch into a new song he'd been experimenting with when a disembodied female voice rang out over him, so sharp and piercing that he fumbled his grip on his lute.

"The night is not yours to claim!"

The lanterns hanging throughout the room all dimmed at once, lengthening the shadows and obscuring some of Lark's view of the crowd.

Gods, not again.

"It's her," whispered a dwarf sitting near the stage.

"She sounds unhappy," said one of the acrobat gnomes, his face pale in the light coming from the fireplace. He pointed at Lark, his eyes wide. "He'd better watch out."

A hush fell over the crowd, and several people skittered off the dance floor and back to their tables, as if they'd been caught doing something wrong.

In his euphoria, Lark had almost forgotten about the Elfsong Tavern's lone quirk. An elven spirit was said to haunt the place, but instead of throwing crockery against the walls or tripping drunk patrons into puddles of their own vomit like any self-respecting poltergeist would, *this* spirit chose to periodically burst into song. Which was not in itself a bad thing, except that the songs the spirit sang were some of the most soul-searing, over-the-top, heartstring-plucking ballads of true love lost to tragedy that Lark had ever heard.

She was a real mood-killer.

"Folks, folks," Lark said, putting on a relaxed air and gesturing over the crowd. "We're all friends here, storytellers and singers. There's no need to worry about competition—"

The disembodied voice rang out again and seemed to take Lark's note about singing as an invitation.

Oh my love, where have you gone?
I fell for your schemes
You took all my dreams
But tell me, will you stay away long?

I carve your name in the sand
Hoping you'll understand
When the tide washes you away
Yet my tongue still betrays
And I can't help but say

Oh my love, where have you gone?

Face raw in the wind
Nails dig in my skin
Tell me, will you stay away long?

The crowd eased into the song, their earlier energy fading. The dwarf sitting next to the stage even gave a sniffle. Lark shot a glance at the Fallbacks' table, but only Baldric and Keevi were left. The two clerics were sitting in silence, listening appreciatively.

Cazrin and Rane had left the dance floor and were sitting on the couch again, their heads bent close together, talking about things only lovers cared to know.

Lark suppressed a sigh. Well, he could either let this happen and surrender the stage to the ghost bard and her song of spurned love …

Or …

Lark waited patiently until the ghost had finished another verse, taking a moment to listen to her voice to get an idea of the direction of the song.

Then he began to accompany her.

She didn't appear to notice at first, but the crowd did. Whispers spread through the room, and people pointed at him, half of them impressed at his audacity and the other half waiting to see if he was about to be attacked by a furious, invisible songstress.

As the elven singer returned to the chorus, Lark smoothly cut in over her.

Oh my love, why didn't you wait?
I came through the war in
Through your door
But you'd already driven
that nail in my coffin

As the tenor of his voice joined to the soprano, the crowd let out a collective gasp. There were more sniffles, glistening gazes locked on the stage as Lark turned the song into a duet and a battle all at once.

And it was a battle he fully intended to win.

The elven ghost's voice cut off abruptly, and there was an angry high-pitched shriek that shattered Lark's wineglass. Lark spun across the stage, smoothly dodging the flying shards.

Things were serious now.

Oh my love, where have you gone?
Oh my love, why didn't you wait?

Another glass shattered at the table closest to the stage, sending a pair of halflings diving for cover. Lark splayed his hand, and the rings on his fingers glowed. The spray of glass shards suddenly shone with a pale radiance, like drops of starlight. Caught between fear and wonder, the audience applauded tentatively.

Oh my love, why didn't you wait?

And the battle raged on, two voices at war, two lovers airing their grievances. Lark reveled in it as they dragged the audience along for the ride. By the time the song battle ended, there wasn't a dry eye in the house—or an intact piece of glassware, come to think of it.

What a time to be alive.

Lark took a bow as the applause went on and on, stopping only when the tabaxi bartender came onstage and hooked a clawed hand around his elbow, towing him off the stage. He only just managed to grab his hat, which was now overflowing with coin.

"I think I have a few more songs in me," Lark protested. He tipped his head at Rane as she moved past him to take the stage in his place. "We could do some more duets—"

"No more duets tonight," the tabaxi declared, and Lark belatedly realized he was being muscled toward the door instead of back to his friends' table. "You started out good, but now the crowd's in tears and I'm all out of wineglasses. Plus, the ghost's furious, and that's going to mean a headache for me for the next month. Out you go!"

"W-wait!" Lark looked around frantically for help from his companions, but they were lost in the crowd. Several of the patrons, in fact, were filing out of the tavern *with* him, complaining to the tabaxi along the way.

"We want another song!" cried the dwarf who had been weeping all through Lark's duet.

"He was just getting started!" argued one of the acrobat gnomes, twisting her sash and stomping her foot angrily.

"It was just getting good!"

"Friends, it's all right!" Lark raised his hands to the crowd, even as the tabaxi was pushing him out the tavern door and slamming it in his face. "A true performer needs no stage, as long as there are ears to hear him!"

He surveyed his remaining loyal audience. He recognized a few of them from his earlier performances. The copper dragonborn and the orc, in addition to the dwarf, who'd come to see him before.

Fans.

He had fans, and they had followed him out the door without

hesitating. Some of them had even carried out their tankards and plates.

Well, Lark wasn't about to disappoint them. They may not have required a stage, but they needed a better venue than standing out in the middle of the street in Baldur's Gate at night.

Lark slid his hand into his pouch, just to make sure his latest acquisition was still safe and sound. When Tess had leaned over to talk to him earlier, he'd taken the opportunity to put some of her recent training to the test. Most of the time he did his best to resist her attempts to mold him into what she considered to be a "proper" adventurer and infiltrator, but in this case, he had to admit that her skills had come in handy.

He held up the small, magical tankard figurine so the crowd could see it. "What do you say, friends? Will you follow me into the darkness as we seek a magical place? A place of story and song, and all the reasonably priced drinks you can imagine?"

Cheers immediately erupted from the crowd.

"Let's go!"

"Hear hear!"

Tankards were thrust into the air, and the dozen or so people pressed in close, ready to follow wherever Lark took them.

He felt a heavy weight bump against his leg and looked down.

Uggie the sheepdog was there, tail whipping back and forth, staring up at Lark joyfully.

"Well, at least one of my party members is ready for a good time," Lark said, reaching down to scratch Uggie behind her false sheepdog ears. "Come on, girl. Let's give them a night to remember."

CHAPTER 9

Tess slipped easily from shadow to shadow as she followed Anson among the tightly packed buildings of the Eastway. He was headed back toward the docks, which was almost as bewildering as the moment back at the tavern when Tess had realized that Anson was no longer at their table, that he was heading for the door without so much as an explanation or a good night.

What business could he have at the docks? And why hadn't he told them where he was going?

It wasn't the first time Anson had acted strangely either. Ever since they'd set themselves up in Baldur's Gate, her friend had been distant, distracted. That was cause enough for worry, but it was even more concerning that he hadn't come to her about it.

They'd known each other for years. They should be able to talk about what was wrong.

Anson turned into a dark, narrow alley that smelled of rotting food. He didn't so much as glance behind him to see if he was being followed. Tess felt a twinge of exasperation at his lack of caution, but then she reminded herself that Anson had always been this way. It was how he'd grown up, living rough on the streets for most of his childhood, his brother always following in his shadow. He'd gotten more than his share of black eyes and broken bones in alleys like this, but instead of that teaching him to avoid danger, he preferred to confront it head-on and bust right through.

Tess kept close to the wall, avoiding puddles and bits of loose gravel that would crunch under her boots and give her presence away. Glancing above her at the ceramic-tiled roofs of the buildings, she made a quick decision. Reaching out, her gloved hands found purchase on the cracked stone, and she pulled herself silently up the wall, bracing herself with her feet. In seconds, she was on the rooftop, moving steadily closer to the harbor while keeping one eye on Anson below her. In this way, she could also scout ahead, making sure there was no one preparing an ambush for a lone man walking the streets late at night.

At the mouth of the alley, Anson glanced in both directions and finally looked over his shoulder. Seeing no one—and not looking up—he made his way across the street and onto the docks. A couple of ships in the harbor looked like they had recently arrived. The captains stood with the dockmaster, directing their crews as they unloaded cargo, shouting orders and curses as they worked.

Tess stayed on the rooftop for the moment, watching Anson pull the dockmaster aside for a private conversation. She saw him take out a small pouch of coin, which the dockmaster took and slipped into his vest. The two of them talked for a few more minutes, though Tess was too far away to hear what was being said. But when Anson turned away a moment later, she could see in the light of the dockside lanterns that he wore an unhappy frown. He turned and continued to stand there for a moment, looking out at the harbor and the crews coming on and off the ships.

Uneasiness rippled over Tess as she watched him. No more sneaking around—for either of them. It was time to confront Anson directly, find out what was going on.

Bracing a hand on the ceramic tile, Tess vaulted off the roof, her cloak billowing out behind her. She dropped noiselessly to the ground, straightened, and walked across the street in Anson's direction. Out of habit and training that had been drilled into her by Mel, she moved without sound. When she was about ten feet away from the dock where he stood, she slowed and let her feet scuff the wooden planks so as not to startle him.

Anson turned, and his eyes widened when he caught sight of her. He ducked his head, and his shoulders hunched defensively, as if he were a boy who'd been caught doing something bad. The reaction only intensified Tess's unease.

"Beautiful night, isn't it?" Anson said when she stopped next to him.

"It's certainly ... something," Tess said, peeling her cloak off and tossing it over her arm. The air was humid and close, and the dock was covered in gull droppings and fish bones. "We missed you at the tavern," she went on, trying to sound casual. "It looked like Lark was just getting warmed up."

"Oh, he was great," Anson said, rubbing the back of his neck self-consciously. "Sorry, I guess I just wasn't in a celebrating mood."

Tess nodded, trying not to read anything into that, even though, up until recently, Anson was often the one leading the way to the nearest tavern after a mission. "Seems like you've been spending a lot of time on your own lately," she said. "I mean, we all need space sometimes, but if there was something wrong, you know you could tell me about it, right?"

Anson hesitated, looking out at the water again. Tess waited, scraping a toe over the rotting wood planks as he gathered his thoughts. She couldn't remember him being this broody before.

"I'm trying to find Valen," Anson said abruptly. He gestured to the dockmaster and the ships' crews. "I keep asking around, placing some bribes to see if anyone's had contact with him. I don't know, I just find myself wondering where he is and what he's doing, whether he escaped from the Zhentarim." His lips thinned. "Or if they hunted him down."

Tess absorbed that. Anson didn't talk about his brother very often. Who could blame him? At the same time the party had found out they were being pursued by a lich during their first job together, Anson had learned that his own brother was in league with the lich via the Zhentarim, the band of smugglers and mercenaries he'd joined up with. Tess knew that even before that, Anson's relationship with his brother had been fraught at best, and hostile on Valen's part at worst.

"From what you've told me about Valen," she ventured, "he seems like the type of person who can look after himself. I'm sure he managed to escape the Zhentarim."

"That's just it," Anson said. "I can speculate, but I don't *know*. Ever since we were kids, I've always been there, trying to look out for him. Even when he would push me away, he needed me at the same time." Anson gazed out over the rippling water of the harbor. "But now he could be anywhere." He swallowed. "He could be dead, and I'm just standing here, doing nothing."

"I'm sure he's not dead," Tess hurried to reassure him, although she had no evidence to support that claim, no more than Anson had reason to think the worst. For all she knew, Valen had run afoul of another shadowy organization and gotten himself into even more trouble. Anyone who threw in his lot with a lich obviously liked to walk the razor's edge. "Your brother isn't a child anymore," Tess reminded Anson. "You can't always be there to keep him out of trouble. You have your own life to live."

He shook his head. "But I get to choose how to live it."

"What does that mean?"

Anson shifted restlessly, walking to the edge of the dock to sit down on a rust-stained barrel. "You told me, that night in Waterdeep, after we'd defeated Lorthrannan, that we'd find Valen." He avoided her gaze as he spoke. "You said that you'd help me get closure, if that's what I wanted. Do you remember that?"

"I—yes." Tess did remember, now that he mentioned it, but in truth, she hadn't thought about that night, or her promise, since. A wave of guilt washed over her. She wasn't one to make promises lightly, but in this case, there'd been extenuating circumstances. "I also made a promise to Baldric, that the Fallbacks would help him be rid of the entity—er, Ashardalon," Tess reminded him. "He needs our help, and I'm sorry, but the needs of the party have to come first."

"*I'm* part of the party too," Anson pressed, finally looking up at her.

Tess fought to keep the exasperation out of her voice. "Yes, and you don't have a greatwyrm trying to take you over or suck the life out of you whenever you pray to the gods. So, yes, I've put Baldric a little higher on our list of priorities. That's my job as party leader."

"We've had plenty of other missions since Waterdeep that didn't involve helping Baldric," Anson said, ticking them off on his fingers. "We've taken time to bolster our reputations up and down the Sword Coast, we've stopped at libraries for Cazrin, and festivals for Lark. We've managed to make time for everyone in the party, one way or another."

It was Tess's turn to look away. "Cazrin was researching things to help Baldric, and Lark *begged* us to go to that bardic festival," she said defensively. "If I didn't give in, we wouldn't have gotten any peace." She hugged herself, even though the night was warm. "And you . . . you just didn't—"

"I didn't push," Anson said quietly. "I didn't poke or bother you about it. I just trusted that you'd keep your promise."

That one was like a knife.

"I will!" Tess insisted. She hadn't been deliberately ignoring him or his needs. Most of the time, Anson never really seemed to need *anything*. He was just there, steadfast and ready to help.

She tried to pull the conversation back on track. "Look, the important thing right now is to keep our focus on dealing with Ashardalon. After that's done, we'll see about Valen, but you have to realize that Baldric needs us."

"You're right," Anson said reluctantly. "I know you're right. It's just hard for me. Valen doesn't have anyone else, and I can't stand the thought that everyone in the world has given up on him, or that he thinks *I've* given up on him. I thought if I could take some time off to find him . . ."

He trailed off, and Tess's stomach twisted into fresh knots. Had Anson actually been considering leaving the party to search for his brother? After all they'd gone through to build it? After Valen had been the one *helping* Lorthrannan hunt them down?

Anger wormed its way through Tess. Without thinking, she said, "Have you ever considered that maybe Valen doesn't want to be found? That maybe *he's* the one who's given up on your relationship, not the other way around?"

Anson flinched. Tess immediately wished she could take back the words, but it was too late. "It doesn't matter," he said, his voice hardening. "I won't stop looking. You don't give up on family."

Sometimes you don't have a choice. But Tess didn't say it. She'd already hurt his feelings, and anything she said now would only make him dig in deeper. Anson was loath to abandon people, and he always tried to see the best in them. It was what Tess admired most about him, and it was also the thing most likely to get him killed in this line of work.

The silence stretched, thick with a tension Tess had never felt between them before. But the fighter eventually stood and began walking back across the dock toward the street.

"We should get back to the tavern," Anson said over his shoulder. "The others will be missing us. Probably not Lark and Cazrin, though. They seemed to be having quite the night." He attempted a smile, though it didn't reach his eyes. That was also so unlike Anson that it set Tess's world off-balance.

"Are you sure you don't want to talk some more?" she pressed, hurrying to catch up to him. Nothing about this felt right. Anson was the person she'd always been able to talk to, no matter what. She'd never felt so closed off from him before. "We could set up the Wander Inn and have some time together, just you and me."

Since arriving in the city, they'd been dividing their time between the Elfsong and the party's own private space, activated by the magical tankard figurine that Tess always carried with her. Staying at a local place had its advantages—connecting with contacts and following up on potential job offers, as well as just soaking up the atmosphere of the city and its people. There was a lot to be said for that.

But there were also times when the party needed security and privacy, and the Wander Inn could be accessed only by a set of magical keys that each of the Fallbacks carried. And Cazrin had put some of her knowledge of the Ruinous Child's security measures to use in some additional protective wards over the last few months. It was a place of their own, a home they could take wherever they went.

Maybe Anson needed that right now, a reminder that *this* was his place. He belonged with the Fallbacks.

Or at least, Tess hoped he still felt that way. She didn't want to think about the alternative.

Without waiting for Anson to reply, she began rummaging through her pouch, searching for the figurine. This was a good plan. They'd have a long talk, relax and laugh, and everything would be all right. This was just a temporary setback.

She dug deeper, but all she felt was the clink of coins. That was strange. Had she put the figurine in a different pouch, or handed it off to Cazrin to put in one of her satchels? No, she would have remembered doing something like that. She always kept the figurine right here, secure at her hip.

"Something wrong?" Anson asked, as Tess's rummaging became more frantic.

"It's nothing," Tess assured him. "It's here somewhere; it's just buried under some coins or—"

She stopped. A memory surfaced, like a lightning bolt hitting her. Hours ago, in the Elfsong, when she'd leaned across the table to talk to Lark, he'd met her halfway, hands on the tabletop, but then he'd slid them forward, moving a plate out of the way. She'd been distracted, and then ...

"That sneaky bard!" Tess burst out. She stomped off the dock, hands on her thick hips in fury, then stomped back to Anson. "He used my own lesson against me!"

"What are you talking about?" Anson asked, brow furrowed. "Who used what lesson? Are you all right? Your face is really red."

"I'm going to kill him," Tess decided, slapping her hand crossbow as she paced in front of Anson. "No, wait, that's not a good idea."

"Killing someone?" Anson crossed his arms. "I agree; let's not do that."

"I'm going to compliment him on what an excellent pickpocketing job he did," Tess continued. "Praise and affirmation—that's what an effective mentor should offer—and *then* I'm going to kill him."

Anson looked nonplussed. "Who are we killing?"

"*Lark.*" Tess groaned. "He took the Wander Inn, and Gods only know what he's doing with it."

CHAPTER 10

The night was young, but Lark was ready to declare it a rip-roaring success. He should have stolen that tankard figurine months ago.

He'd chosen a vacant lot a few streets away from the Elfsong, in one of the seedier areas of the Eastway, to set up the tavern. He hadn't been interested in the aesthetics; he'd just wanted a place with adequate space. Then it had taken him a few tries to remember the command phrase to activate the item's magic. Tess was always the one who'd set up the figurine in the past, and he hadn't known quite what he was doing. But he had an audience of curious onlookers at his back, and Lark always performed better in front of a crowd, so it hadn't taken him long to remember what he was supposed to say—and to find the words inscribed on the bottom of the tankard.

Just as he finished uttering the words "Take us to the Wander Inn," he realized he'd misjudged how uneven the ground was in the spot he'd chosen, so that when it finally appeared in a flash of light and sparkling colors, the full-sized tavern was startlingly lopsided, as if the tankard-shaped building were about to spill its contents all over the ground. But other than that minor flaw, the magic was spectacular, and his companions broke into a round of applause.

Like a parade leader, Lark marched at the head of the crowd, sheepdog Uggie following right behind him. They went up the wooden ramp to the door, ducking beneath the crooked sign overhead that read THE WANDER INN. Inside, it was as if the tavern had seen the guests and prepared accordingly. There were more tables and chairs crowded into the front room, and decks of cards and dice had been laid out on the gleaming bar along with bowls of peanuts and fruit.

"Come in, everyone!" Lark invited, as the crowd lingered outside and in the doorway, peering around curiously to inspect the magical building. "First round's on me!"

That got them moving. As the room gradually filled up, Lark left the door propped open so that more people could find their way in. Then he claimed a spot by the fireplace, tuning his lute while his orc and dragonborn fans appointed themselves bartenders, passing out wine and ale, which the tavern kept up a steady supply of as more people arrived, swelling the crowd size from a dozen to thirty or more. Dice and card games started at the tables, and someone brought in a bunch of baskets of fried fish from a shack down by the docks.

Suddenly, it was as if Lark had opened up his own place. People were leaving coins on the tables, the bartenders were collecting silver for drinks, and Lark's hat was quickly full of coins again.

Lark grasped the amulet hanging around his neck like the world's best good-luck charm.

Gods, he thought, this might turn out to be the best night of his life.

He launched into a round of raucous songs, numbers that had people up and dancing, standing in their chairs, and jumping off tables. The blood roared in Lark's veins every time the crowd broke into cheers and every time they chanted his name, begging for more. Warm air blew into the tavern from the open door, carrying the sounds and smells of the city. It was a glorious night, and Lark threw back his head and howled his joy through his music to anyone who would listen.

About halfway through his second round of songs, the copper

dragonborn came up to him with his scaled arms crossed and a distinctly unhappy downturn to his snout.

"Where's my wife?" he demanded.

"Sorry?" Lark blinked. "How . . . how should I know? Maybe she went outside for some fresh air?" he suggested.

It was distracting when people interrupted him while he was onstage. He shifted away, looking pointedly out at the crowd to signal the conversation was over.

The dragonborn was undeterred. He stepped right into Lark's eyeline, nostrils flaring. "She went in the back," he pressed, "and now she's disappeared."

"Hmmm." Lark wasn't really listening. He put his ear close to his lute to make sure it was still tuned to his liking. It was getting harder to tell in the noisy room. "Maybe she got tired and went home?" Really, why did people expect him to keep track of their spouses? Did he look like someone who should be responsible for someone else's welfare? That was why he didn't own pets.

The dragonborn took a step closer to the stage, and Lark suddenly became aware of how much larger and more robust he was compared to Lark's wiry frame. "She didn't go home," he said. "She's here somewhere." He glanced over his shoulder at the hallway, then looked back at Lark. "This place is strange," he went on. "The rooms . . . they move."

Lark opened his mouth then snapped it shut. "Oh," he said.

All right, so in his newfound sense of freedom and joy, it was possible he'd forgotten the other peculiar feature of the Wander Inn: its tendency to add, change, and move rooms magically on a whim. Well, Cazrin claimed it wasn't a whim. She believed the tavern changed its looks and purpose according to the needs and desires of the Fallbacks. Except that since their party was rarely able to agree on what they needed, and because what they desired tended to change in an eyeblink, sometimes the tavern got mixed up and gave them something they didn't want *at all*.

Like the time Anson had had a particularly vivid dream that the rest of the party was being suffocated by a gelatinous cube that had somehow wedged itself into all of their bedrooms simultaneously. He'd woken up in a cold sweat, and the walls of all of their bedrooms had been covered in sticky slime for the rest of the night. Cazrin had speculated that the tavern had misread Anson's dream as a desire for their bedrooms to be redecorated with slime.

It didn't matter. He could fix this. Lark stood up, jumped down from the stage with a flourish, and called out to the crowd, "Never fear, folks! I'll be back soon. Catch your breath, catch a snack, and tip your servers." Somehow, they'd acquired volunteer servers from among the party guests in the last hour or so. Lark wasn't going to question it. "You've been a wonderful crowd!" He turned to the dragonborn. "I'll find your wife," Lark assured him. "Er, what's her name?"

"Selisa," the dragonborn supplied.

"Selisa, got it." Lark gestured back toward the bar. "In the meantime, I think we have some thirsty patrons over there. Could you help them out?"

The dragonborn sighed and shuffled off, murmuring something about strange magic.

Lark immediately turned and made a beeline for the back hall. The first thing he noticed was that there were five more doors than there should have been, squeezed in close together all along the hallway. Several of them stood open, and when Lark looked inside, he saw that the tavern had been providing the overflow guests with private lounges of sorts, complete with couches and overstuffed chairs, more bottles of wine, and even plates of cheese and meat.

Uggie was sprawled on a couch in one of the rooms, still wearing her disguise. She was lying on her back while the gnome acrobats took turns rubbing her belly.

"Who's a good, snuggly furball?" A gnome with thick brown braids leaned over and fed the otyugh a wedge of cheese. "Your fur is really coarse, though. Like leather. You need a bath, don't you? Don't you, honey?"

"Is that a scar, sweet girl?" said another one in concern. His olive-skinned face creased in confusion. "It looks like ... an *eyelid*?"

"Hush, Brendel," said the one with the braids. "It's not polite to comment on the shape of a lady's scars." She dropped another wedge of crumbly cheese into Uggie's drooling mouth.

It seemed Lark wasn't the only one having the best night ever.

He left the otyugh to her bliss and checked the next room. The door was ajar, and when Lark pushed it open, he saw that it was Anson's bedroom. The fighter was the only person Lark knew who kept training dummies and weapon racks right next to his bed. Lark had sworn the room used to be on the opposite wall, but who knew what the tavern might be thinking.

He was just about to leave and close the door when he noticed a shadow shift against the far wall by the bed. At first glance, he'd taken it for another training dummy, but it was actually a human man. He was tall and lanky like Lark, with silvery-blond hair that he wore long and appealingly shaggy around his shoulders. His back was to Lark, so the bard couldn't make out any further details.

Lark slipped quietly inside the room, drawing on more of Tess's training to soften his footsteps. He would never admit it to her, but her lessons *had* been coming in annoyingly handy lately.

He made his way stealthily across the room, approaching the man from behind. It was possible he'd just gotten lost, like Selisa, and had gone exploring.

Or he could be a thief.

Perhaps a display of pyrotechnics would scare him into confessing, if that was the case.

Lark was just humming a tune under his breath to cast a spell when the man abruptly spun and seized the collar of his coat. Lark felt the tension in the man's arm that heralded an attack, caught the wary flash in an otherwise pleasing pair of ice-blue eyes.

The bard reacted instinctively, opening his mouth to cut the man with magic. But before he could utter any words, the man's eyes narrowed, and he jerked Lark forward, interrupting his spellcasting. Off-balance, Lark abandoned his spell and shoved instead, using the full weight of his body to try to tackle the man to the floor.

At the last moment, the slippery figure twisted, and it was Lark who ended up on his back on the floor next to the bed. But in the scuffle, he'd managed to draw a small knife that he kept on his belt in case of emergency. As the man pinned his shoulders to the floor, he raised the knife and pressed it against the tender flesh of his attacker's throat. At the same time, he felt the point of something sharp digging into his right flank.

For a moment, neither of them moved or spoke. The room was quiet except for the sound of their harsh breathing and the distant laughter from the party in the front room.

It was Lark who broke the silence. "You know," he said conversationally, "in the tales the storytellers spin, the young, handsome couple usually end up sprawled *on* the bed in these sorts of situations."

The man's narrow-eyed gaze softened a fraction. "I suppose it depends on the tale," he said. His voice was a low, gravelly rumble that shivered through Lark. "Is there usually naked steel involved?" he asked, eyes dipping to the knife beneath his jaw.

Lark couldn't help a lazy smile. "So many ways to answer that. But like you said, I suppose it depends on the tale. And my knife isn't the only thing between us."

He glanced down at his flank. What he'd taken for a dagger or a club was actually a wooden practice sword. Anson had several like it in his weapon racks, but this one was much smaller than the others, so small that it was almost like a toy. Lark couldn't remember ever seeing the fighter wield it before. Then again, he rarely paid attention when Anson practiced.

Had the man really come in here to steal a toy sword?

Lark decided he needed to reassess the situation. He put on his most charming smile and eased his grip on the knife. "Why don't I buy you a drink, and we can decide together what sort of story we find ourselves in?"

The man laughed, and oh, what a lovely sound, a private song, just for Lark. He hadn't thought this night could get any better, but apparently, he'd been wrong.

"All right," the man said in amusement. He shifted his weight off of Lark, moving in a slow, nonthreatening way. Lark stood just as carefully, as if the two of them were engaged in a complicated dance. The man placed the practice sword in the nearest weapon rack and followed Lark out the door and back down the hallway.

Lark paused before they reached the common room. "I forgot I was supposed to be looking for someone," he said, glancing back over his shoulder.

The man cocked a blond eyebrow. "Tired of me already?"

"Oh, I'm just getting started," Lark assured the blue-eyed menace. "But I promised— Oh, that might be her!"

An orc came stumbling out of one of the rooms near the back of the hall. Sweat poured down her face, and her eyes were very large.

"Selisa?" Lark asked hopefully.

The orc nodded. She shuffled past Lark and hooked a trembling thumb over her shoulder. "Thought it was the water closet," she murmured, shaking her head. "It . . . wasn't."

She moved past him, and Lark exchanged a glance with his new friend. "I wonder what it actually was?" the man asked.

"Probably best not to know," Lark said.

He led the way back to the common room. The tables were still full, so Lark grabbed a bottle of wine and two glasses and went to sit on the edge of the stage, nodding for the man to sit beside him.

He watched the stranger as he moved. Graceful he was, but so wary. He kept his eyes moving over every corner of the room, checking for threats or figures he couldn't see clearly. It was a technique Lark was all too familiar with.

The stranger was a hunted man. A scruffy, dangerous, hunted man.

So many of Lark's weaknesses all rolled into one.

"All right, then," the man said, leaning back on his elbows on the stage. "What's the story of this place? A magical tavern dropped into the middle of Baldur's Gate."

"Dropped?" Lark gave him a look of mock affront. "This was the result of careful planning and architectural savvy, I'll have you know."

Across the room, the gnome acrobats were rolling Uggie down the distinctly slanted floor.

"Of course it was," the stranger said dryly.

"All right," Lark allowed, "you caught me. It's a temporary magic, something we carry with us wherever we go, so we always have a place to sleep at night."

"Seems like more than just a place to lay your head," the man said, looking around at all the people, the food and drink flowing freely. There was a flash of hunger in his eyes, but when he glanced back at Lark, it was gone. "Who's 'we'?" he asked.

"My associates and me," Lark said. He uncorked the bottle of wine and poured for them both. He handed the man a glass. "Professional adventurers for hire and legends in the making." He grinned and sketched a bow where he sat. "The Fallbacks, at your service."

The man took the wine and sniffed it appreciatively. "Never heard of the Fallbacks," he said, shrugging.

Lark wasn't offended. He was used to this reaction. "You will someday," he promised the stranger. "I'll make sure of it."

"I'll drink to that," the man said, tapping his glass against Lark's. "To being known," he murmured.

"To being known."

The man took a drink, swallowing half the glass, while Lark took just a sip, savoring the rich Waterdavian red, letting it sit on his tongue for a few seconds before swallowing.

"What makes the magic that runs this place?" the man asked, gesturing to the common room with his glass. His gaze shifted to Lark, zeroing in on the amulet around his neck. "Is it that pretty bauble?"

Lark's hand went to the amulet automatically in a protective gesture. "No, this one's entirely for me," he said. "To keep away prying eyes."

"Handy," the man said. He'd shifted closer, and Lark caught the faint scent of sweat and leather. The man's nose was slightly crooked, as if it had been broken sometime in the past. Lark watched his throat bob as he took another drink of wine.

Lark was a suspicious sort by nature. It was necessary for survival, even if it wasn't always fun. He was in the mood for a bit of fun tonight, but not at the expense of being taken for a fool. "If you're interested in a magic lesson," he said, sliding to the edge of the stage, "you should talk to my friend Cazrin. She can lecture about this place for hours and hours."

He started to stand, and the man laid a casual hand on his wrist to stop him. Lark paused, meeting the man's gaze with a raised eyebrow.

"I want to talk to *you*," he said. "What's your name?"

"Lark Silverstring," Lark said, still wary, but his skin tingled where the man touched him. His hands were rough and callused. A worker's hands. Or a brawler's. Yes, this one had been in his share of fights.

The man smiled wolfishly. "A pleasure, Lark. Tell me," he went on, "do you have a room of your own in this magical place?"

Lark laughed. "You're bold," he said. "As a matter of fact, I do have a—"

"Lark, what in the *Hells* is going on here?"

Lark's head snapped around at the sound of Baldric's voice. He and Cazrin stood in the inn's doorway, staring open-mouthed at all the people. The acrobats were standing on one another's shoulders, forming an archway of gnomes in the center of the room through which couples were dancing while another bard played a fiddle in the corner as accompaniment.

"Baldric! Cazrin!" Lark spread his arms wide in welcome. "Come join the party!"

The cleric and the wizard squeezed their way through the crowd. Cazrin had a distressed look on her face.

"Lark, you can't have this many people in the Wander Inn at one time," she scolded him.

"You shouldn't have *any* of them here," Baldric said, though he gazed with interest at one of the card games in progress on the other side of the room. He shook his head, lips twitching. "Tess is going to murder you and dump your body in the Chionthar."

"You don't sound nearly as concerned about that as I would like," Lark said, putting on a look of hurt. "Won't you defend me from her wrath?"

"No, I'm going to get a tankard of ale and watch," Baldric assured him with a grin.

"How are you making sure no one's getting lost in the extradimensional spaces?" Cazrin demanded. "You know how unreliable the tavern's magic can be. Did you warn everyone?"

"Of course," Lark said breezily. "In fact, I was just telling my friend here all about it."

He turned, but the man with the ice-blue eyes was gone. Lark scanned the tables and the dance floor, but there was no sign of him.

"What friend?" Baldric asked.

"He was just here," Lark said, wilting a bit. "You must have scared him off."

"Or he got lost," Cazrin said, her eyes widening. "Lark, we have to get these people to go home."

Come to think of it, there *were* quite a bit more folks here now than when they'd started the party. Lark wasn't sure what the capacity of the place was, but somehow, the tavern had made room for everyone.

"I'm sure it's fine," he said. "They found their way in off the street. I'm sure they'll find their way out again." He picked up the bottle of wine. "Care for a drink? I wondered where the rest of you had ended up after I was unceremoniously tossed out of the Elfsong."

"We saw that," Baldric said. "The ghost quieted down after you and the rowdy bunch left." He grinned. "Never thought you'd be bested by a ghost singer."

"Oh, I'll have a rematch with her before our time in the city is done," Lark promised him. "What did *you* think of my song, Cazrin?"

But the wizard was gone. Lark spotted her across the room, herding people out of the back hallway and ushering them toward the door.

Well, even the best of nights had to come to an end eventually. And he *was* starting to get tired.

"Gods above!"

Oh no . . .

Lark looked over at the door again. There stood Anson and a red-faced Tess, hands on her hips, snaring Lark with an expression that suggested she was going to take her daggers and peel him like an onion.

He squared his shoulders and prepared to face his doom. "Tess, I can explain."

CHAPTER 11

"You stole the tankard figurine so you could throw a *party*?"

Hands on her hips, Tess squared off with Lark, who had retreated behind the bar. Anson and Cazrin had gone searching for some missing revelers in the back, while the rest slowly filed out the front. Baldric sat on a stool nearby, drinking ale and watching in amusement.

Tess stabbed a finger at the mess. Several chairs had been broken during the acrobats' antics. Dirt had been tracked all over the room, and there were puddles of spilled ale and food scraps ground into the floor. "You stole the tankard figurine—we worked for weeks on your pickpocketing technique, and you were terrible, and somehow, tonight of all nights, you got lucky—"

"It wasn't luck!" Lark was indignant. "I'm always listening during our delightful training sessions," he assured her. "The way you demonstrate each gesture, every sleight of hand in gripping detail, meticulously explaining *every single part* of the process—"

Baldric cleared his throat. "You're digging the hole deeper," he muttered into his tankard.

Tess gritted her teeth and counted to ten. When that didn't work, she took a deep, meditative breath.

A copper dragonborn leaned between her and Lark with a glass of water. "Drink?" he asked politely.

"Thank you," Tess said, snatching the glass. She smiled wearily at the impromptu bartender. "You should really go home now," she advised him. "It's getting late."

He nodded, clasping his scaled claws in front of him. "My name's Derlarran," he said. "My wife, Selisa, and I were hoping you were hiring. We're looking to retire from mercenary work, and this place is just wonderful! A little strange at first, maybe, but we'd love to be considered for a position, now or in the future."

"We don't even care that the building's crooked," said Selisa, stacking clean glasses on the shelves behind the bar. She adjusted the portrait of the purple worm hanging on the wall.

Tess took a long drink of water. She tried to picture the couple's reaction when she told them that whenever they weren't inside it, the tavern shrank into a figurine that could fit in the palm of her hand. Could people still be inside when that happened? Would they be trapped? She would have to ask Cazrin about that later.

"I'll keep you in mind," she said, smiling apologetically, "but I'm afraid we're not taking on any new employees at this time." Her tone turned icy as she jerked a thumb at Lark. "I've got my hands full with the ones I already have."

"It was just a bit of harmless fun!" Lark protested. "Isn't that what tonight was supposed to be about?"

"Except it *wasn't* harmless!" Tess snapped when Derlarran and Selisa were out of earshot. "We don't fully understand how the magic of this place works. People could have gotten hurt wandering around on their own." She put her glass down with a loud *thump*. "And even if it was safe, you *stole* from the party and invited a bunch of strangers into our private space. This place is supposed to be for the Fallbacks."

"*I'm* one of the Fallbacks!" Lark shot back. "Shouldn't I get a say in what goes on here too?"

"Of course!" Tess threw up her hands. "But the point is, we discuss things as a party. We don't steal and keep things from each other!"

Tess took another gulp of water and prepared to continue her lecture, but as she put down her glass, she noticed the bard's hunched, defensive posture, so similar to Anson's earlier when they'd argued at the docks. She was still stinging from that conversation, and now she was at odds with another member of her party.

Suddenly, Tess felt very tired. "I just thought we were past things like this," she said. "We've been training together, making so much progress, and then you pull the rug out from under me. It's not a great feeling, Lark."

Lark looked at her, and some of his defensiveness melted away. "I'm *sorry*," he said. This time he actually sounded contrite. "I'll make it up to you. I'll take extra lockpicking classes, or I'll train with that backpack full of bricks again." He winced. "Just don't look at me with that disappointment."

Tess sighed and reached behind the bar, grabbing a mop. She pressed it firmly to Lark's chest. "You're on cleanup duty," she said. "Make it sparkling in here."

"I—really?" Lark asked. "No other punishment?"

"No." She finished her water and set the empty glass on the bar. The dragonborn grabbed it and added it to the others that still needed to be washed. Tess resolved to pay the couple for the night's work. "I'll go help Cazrin and Anson find the stragglers," she said. She hesitated, then added, "We'll try again with the training. We'll keep trying, right?"

Lark met her gaze and slowly nodded. "We will."

Satisfied for now, Tess headed for the back hallway to find Cazrin and Anson. She glanced over her shoulder once. "Spotless!" she called.

Lark immediately began mopping the floor with vigor. "I promise!"

LARK WATCHED TESS disappear down the hallway. He dutifully returned to his cleaning while Uggie inhaled the leftover scraps of food on the floor. Baldric nursed his ale and watched him.

"You could help, you know," Lark said casually, after he'd started on his fourth circuit of the room. How did one get wine stains out of floors anyway? He would have to learn the secret if he ever decided to open a place of his own.

Derlarran and Selisa had finally gone home—leaving the bar in perfect condition, Lark noticed—so it was just him, Baldric, and Uggie left in the common room. The otyugh eventually got full and collapsed into unconsciousness in her bed by the fireplace.

"I think I'm going to sit this one out," Baldric said, leaning one elbow on the bar. "You put Tess in a hard spot, and she went easy on you in the end." He raised his tankard to a pair of elves who had just stumbled out of the back hallway, looking dazed as they made their way to the exit. "Have a good evening, you two."

"I know I messed up," Lark said, grunting as he scrubbed a particularly stubborn stain beneath one of the tables. "I said I'd make it up to her, and I will."

"Good to hear." Baldric took a drink and regarded Lark curiously. "You still seem to be in a good mood tonight, despite everything."

"Why shouldn't I be?" Lark said. "We had a successful mission with lots of loot, and we're getting ever closer to solving your little nightmare. Isn't that reason enough to put me in a good mood?"

"Just making an observation," Baldric said. "I didn't realize you were worried about my problems." He grinned. "I'm touched, songbird."

Lark sank into one of the chairs he'd pulled out so he could clean beneath the table. He watched Baldric in silence for a moment. "I'm not blind, you know," he said casually.

Baldric paused in the act of raising his tankard, one eyebrow quirked. "Never said you were. What's this about?"

"Just that you seem a bit more cheerful tonight too," Lark said. "Those white bits in your beard may lend you distinction, but the hollows under your eyes that you've had for the past few weeks were slightly more concerning." Lark knew what it was like to have your worries gnawing at you in the middle of the night and dogging your steps during the day. "I'm just glad you're getting answers, that's all."

Baldric leaned back, the stool creaking beneath him. "Thanks," he said. "I admit, I was beginning to wonder whether I had a future at all." He shrugged. "Whatever's ahead isn't going to be easy, though."

"But you have a face for your enemy now," Lark said. He knew what that was worth too. He didn't have a face for his enemies, but in place of that, he now had a very big shield. "And you have the rest of us, of course, along for the ride."

Baldric met his gaze, and the two shared a look of silent understanding. That part—having people to watch their backs and help them deal with their problems—was something both of them were still getting used to.

CHAPTER 12

The next morning, Anson rose early and made his way quietly down the hall, past his party members snoring in their bedrooms, and peeked into the common room. He breathed a sigh of relief when he saw it was deserted. The gray light of dawn was just starting to seep in through the windows, giving him enough illumination to see that Lark had been true to Tess's command. The room was spotless. It was as if there had never been a wild party.

Anson slipped out the front door and used his key to relock it. He paused for a moment, running his fingers over the lightning bolt engraved on the key's triangular bow, remembering Tess's words from the night before. She wanted him to be focused, to concentrate on the party's mission to help Baldric.

Fair enough.

But how could he do that effectively when his brother was out there somewhere, maybe in need of Anson's help? He needed to find Valen, and if he had to do it on his own time, then so be it. The Fallbacks were asleep; they didn't need him right now, which meant he was free to search the city in these hours before the day began.

He made his way down the narrow streets, stepping over revelers passed out in alleyways and nodding to workers who'd been up before the sun to get to their jobs. He liked this time of the morning, when the city was quiet, the streets not yet packed and bustling with traffic. When he was a child, growing up in cities like this one, this had been his favorite time, and his favorite season—when he didn't have to worry so much about finding a warm place for himself and his brother to sleep. All he needed was a hidden nook to curl up in, to let the warm summer nights give way to slow, dewy mornings.

Sometimes, on the hottest nights, he would climb to the top of the tallest building he could reach, searching for just a breath of wind. He'd fall asleep with the night breeze cooling his skin. At dawn, he would look out over the city and watch it come awake.

Anson looked up at the building nearest to him: an old, ramshackle warehouse with peeling paint and cracked windows that had probably been rented cheap by some merchant and then been left to rot. He wasn't as skilled a climber as Tess, but he could probably find a way up to the roof if he tried. Maybe the change in perspective would help him see things more clearly, help him make a plan to find Valen.

He had tried bribing his way around the docks to see if Valen's name or one of his aliases had been on the passenger list of any of the incoming ships, but none of the captains he'd spoken to had had anyone on board with that name or description. He'd known it was a long shot. Valen was probably disguised and travelling under a new name since his time with the Zhentarim. His brother was many things, but he wasn't a fool. He knew how to disappear when it was necessary.

Anson stepped up to the wall of the warehouse and tested his weight against the closest windowsill, which was situated about a foot above his head. The wood groaned ominously, but he decided to try his luck anyway. It wasn't as if he'd never fallen down before. Cuts bled and bones broke, but they eventually mended.

He'd learned that lesson early too.

As he reached up and grasped the wooden ledge, he heard a soft sound behind him, the barest scrape of a boot on loose gravel. It was so subtle that he almost missed it, but his senses were on alert after he'd discovered Tess following him the night before.

Whoever was behind him now was not nearly so silent as his friend, but they were good.

Anson kept his back to the figure stalking him, pretending to be oblivious as he flexed his arms, ready to pull himself up the warehouse wall. The figure behind him stepped closer, close enough that Anson could smell the hint of sweat that wafted to him on the breeze. He waited for the figure to take one more step . . .

Anson spun, his hands seizing the front of a cloak and a fistful of shirt. He pulled the figure around to the place where he'd just been standing, pinning him against the warehouse wall with a *thud* so loud, a flock of doves took flight from under the eaves. He registered that the man had a weapon in his hand at the same moment he grabbed the wrist that held it, pressing it against the cool stone of the building.

"Got you," Anson said, looking up into the stranger's face. As he watched, the blond hair shortened, the brighter color disappearing in a swirl of illusory magic, revealing sleeker, darker strands. The blue eyes turned brown and cunning, and the angles of the stranger's face rearranged, becoming sharper, making Anson blink to adjust his vision.

He had been in disguise, as Anson had predicted, but even with the spell, he would have known his brother anywhere.

"Valen." His hands went slack and dropped to his sides.

"Well met, Anson." Valen straightened his shirt and cloak where Anson had rumpled them, leaning casually against the wall. "I see you haven't lost your keen senses."

"I've had a knifepoint pressed into my ribs too many times to let my guard down in dark alleys," Anson replied. "Why were you following me?"

"I was about to ask you the same question." Valen's easygoing demeanor vanished, and there was a hard glint in his eyes that Anson remembered all too well. "I'm out here trying to lie low, and you're asking every merchant and midwife in the city about me, drawing attention that I can't afford. What were you thinking?"

"I—I'm sorry," Anson said, belatedly glancing around to make sure their little scuffle hadn't drawn attention from any passersby. "But I heard you might be in Baldur's Gate, and I wanted to see if you were all right. You know, after..." Now that it came to it, he found he couldn't bring up the lich's name. It churned up too many other questions, and Anson wasn't sure he was ready for the answers.

Why were you working for the Zhentarim?

How did you fall in with a lich?

Why did you set yourself up as my enemy?

"It hasn't been easy, I can tell you that," Valen said, bitterness creeping into his tone. "The position I had with the Zhentarim made me more coin than I've ever seen in my life, and the opportunities to move up in that organization are endless."

"I'll bet," Anson said, crossing his arms. "Slip a dagger in the ribs of the person in front of you, and there you are, moving up the ranks like a champion."

Valen's eyes narrowed. "You're in no position to judge me, brother. We've always done what we had to do to survive. Not everyone can join up with a group of adventurers and have endless coin and magical wonders falling into their laps."

"That's just how the bards tell it," Anson scoffed. "We've had our lean times too."

But not so lean as Valen. Now that he got a good look at his brother, Anson noticed the threadbare cloak, the rips and dried bloodstains on his shirt, hastily covered by a vest that looked like it hadn't been washed in weeks. Those were surface details. The real story lay in the gauntness of his cheeks and the dark shadows beneath his hunted eyes. From the looks of it, Valen had been on the move for some time, sleeping rough and skipping more than a few meals.

"Well?" Valen spread his arms, as if to give Anson a better view for his inspection. "If you're satisfied that I'm not dead in a ditch, I can be on my way."

He started to move past Anson, shifting the weapon he carried from his left hand to his right. Polished wood caught the meager light, and Anson realized what it was Valen was holding.

"How did you—" He snatched the practice sword and held it up. His large hand nearly swallowed the child-sized hilt, but he remembered a time when a sword like this had felt as heavy as the world.

There was a familiar notch halfway up the wooden blade. Anson stared at his brother in disbelief. "You've been in my room."

Valen shrugged, unrepentant. "You've been looking for me; I thought I'd return the favor, see what you'd been up to with your new friends." He stopped just short of sneering the word. "They're an interesting bunch—especially the bard. You'll want to watch that one, though. He's charming, but he's not the trustworthy sort."

"How would you know that?" Anson asked, raising a skeptical eyebrow.

Valen's smile was as sharp as a blade. "Takes one to know one." He held out his hand for the practice sword. "That one's mine, you know. Only fair that I should have it back. I left yours in your room."

Anson hesitated. "The last time we used these swords, you threw yours down and said you wanted nothing more to do with them." He met Valen's eyes. "You said they were worthless."

"Was I wrong?" Seeing that he wasn't going to hand over the sword, Valen pointed to the notch marring the blade. "Anyone who can make a dent like that in a practice sword is ready to move on to the real thing."

That wasn't how Anson remembered it at all.

Valen had stolen the wooden swords from a market stall while Anson haggled with a fruit vendor, trying to trade his last coppers for a bag of bruised apples. He'd been eleven, maybe twelve at the time. The apples had been mushy and brown, but the polished oak swords were a treasure beyond price.

They'd practiced with them every day, and even though he was bigger, Anson always lost to his younger, faster brother, who seemed to move with the grace and speed of a striking snake. A blur of motion and *whack*, Anson's forearm or shoulder would be red and stinging from the slap of the wooden blade.

"Was it because I finally won?" Anson asked. "Is that why you wouldn't spar with me anymore?"

Valen made a noncommittal sound. "You know, I used to get so frustrated with you when we first started learning," he said. "You always lost because you'd just charge straight in, never paid attention to what I was doing with my sword or my feet, nothing. You just ran at me with this big smile on your face, even when you knew you were going to get hit." He shook his head. "You don't still use that technique on your opponents, do you?"

"Sometimes," Anson said, chuckling. But he sobered quickly. "I only used to do that because I was excited to be sparring with you. I knew you would never really hurt me."

"Exactly my point!" Valen did something then that Anson had seen Tess do many times, and he still couldn't explain how. He took a step toward Anson, and suddenly, the practice sword was gone from Anson's hand, and Valen was holding it. "You never doubted that things would turn out all right, or that the world would treat you fairly, even when some dung-stained merchant wheedled two coppers out of you for a bag of rotten apples."

"They were all right—"

"They were rotten, and he cheated a starving *child*!" Color suffused Valen's cheeks. "That's why I hit you as hard as I could, as often as I could, with this sword. So you'd finally learn not to trust everything and everyone that crossed your path. So you'd stop chasing lost causes!"

"Well, you made your point!" Anson could feel himself getting angry, though he tried to push his feelings down. This happened so many times when he spoke to his brother. Why did it have to be so hard? "I took my lumps and my bruises, and I fought back, just like you wanted."

And during their last match, he'd hit Valen's sword so hard that it had notched the blade and sprained Valen's wrist. He'd been fine after a few days, but Anson had felt terrible.

They'd never sparred again, but Anson had kept both swords. He would never have cast them aside.

Valen picked at the notch in the sword with a dirt-encrusted fingernail. "Yet here you are today," he said, exasperated, "looking for me, meddling where you shouldn't."

"We've barely spoken in years," Anson pointed out. "You don't know me as well as you think."

"Don't I?" Valen stepped toward Anson again, using the flat of the wooden blade to unsheathe Anson's actual sword. It came out easily, exposing the jagged, broken-off end before Anson grabbed and re-sheathed it. "You never replaced it," Valen said. "I'm not even remotely surprised."

"It's a good sword," Anson said defensively. "It's just . . . difficult, that's all."

"Find a better sword, one worthy of your skills."

"I don't abandon things when they're difficult, Valen."

His brother was silent at that.

"Why did you join Lorthrannan?" Anson blurted out.

Valen's face shuttered. "Here we were getting along so well," he said, "and you had to go and ruin it."

Anson wouldn't be put off. "A *lich,* brother? Out of all the beings you could have sworn your loyalty to, you chose the one that wanted me and my friends dead?"

"It wasn't about *you,*" Valen snapped. "I'm sorry if this crushes your gentle spirit, but I don't stroll through life constantly considering your feelings or needs. I saw an opportunity with the Zhentarim, and I took it. That's all." A muscle worked in his jaw. "I didn't know who they were actually answering to until it was too late."

Anson nodded, feeling a bit of the weight he'd been carrying these past few months lift from his shoulders. For all his mistakes, his brother hadn't set himself against Anson on purpose. That meant something.

"At least you got away," Anson said. "You can start fresh now. I can help you."

Valen snorted. "If you really want to help me, you'll stop trying to find me," he said. "Or, better yet, if you have a way to help hide me from the Zhentarim—who still want to flay the skin from my bones—that would be most welcome."

"Of course I'll hide you," Anson said, feeling like he was on even footing at last. This was a problem he could tackle head-on. "It's only a matter of time before the Fallbacks will be leaving on another mission. You can come with us. We'll protect you."

He'd love to see the Zhentarim try to take on all of his friends. Anson would personally make sure they never threatened his brother again.

Valen barked out a laugh. "Oh yes, I'm sure that would go over well. 'Friends! Remember the man who sold you out to your worst enemy? Well, here he is! Make a place for him by the fire.'" He shook his head. "Even you can't expect that to be a rosy picture, brother."

Anson wanted to argue. His friends all had secrets, things they'd done in their pasts that they weren't proud of. But then he remembered his conversation with Tess at the docks, the look on her face when she'd said that Valen could take care of himself. It was clear she didn't want him in their lives. His friends might be willing to forgive Valen—eventually—for his actions, but that didn't mean they'd trust him to travel with them.

"I'm not just going to leave you to fend for yourself against the Zhentarim," Anson said stubbornly. "There has to be something I can do to help."

Valen examined the sword in his hands thoughtfully. "There might be something," he said. "That tavern of yours is a cozy spot. Your bard friend said that you carry it around with you, like a portable hideout."

"We do," Anson said carefully. "It becomes a small figurine when we're not using it. Are you saying you want to hide in there?"

Valen shook his head. "I'm saying I want you to give me the figurine. It's the perfect thing to carry with me, a safe place that I can use whenever I need it."

"You want—" Anson opened his mouth then closed it again. "You want me to *give* you the Wander Inn?"

"Why not?" Valen twirled the practice sword again. "You're adventurers, aren't you? You probably come across magical trinkets like that one all the time. Surely, you'll find something to replace it, and your companions will understand, once you explain how worried you are about me, and how much you want to *help*."

Anson shifted uncomfortably. He was fairly certain his companions *wouldn't* understand, no matter how well he phrased it. They'd be furious, in fact. The Wander Inn was one of the very first treasures they'd found together as a group. In the months since, they'd made it their own, a home they could all share. He had no right to give that away.

But Valen's life might depend on it.

He looked up to find his brother watching him. A rueful smile curved one side of Valen's mouth. "It's all right, brother," he said. "Don't tie yourself in knots over this." He spun the practice sword, balancing it on the palm of one hand as he offered it to Anson. "I'm glad you kept this sword all these years. It's a good reminder of better times."

Anson took the sword, and suddenly, it felt as heavy in his hands as it had when he was a child. "Where will you go?" he asked, his throat tight.

"Don't worry about me," Valen said. He pulled on the hood of his cloak and looked up and down the alley. "I'll be fine. Just stop looking for me, eh? It'll make things easier."

He started to move off down the alley, gravitating to the shadows. In a moment, he would vanish, just like Tess did whenever she went ahead of the party to scout. Just like that, he would be gone. And maybe it would be the last time Anson ever saw him.

"Wait," he said, before he could change his mind. "I think I know what to do."

CHAPTER 13

Baldric followed Tess up a narrow flight of creaky wooden steps that corkscrewed through the boardinghouse on Tiven Street. The place was clean but old; it smelled of incense and fried onions from the kitchen downstairs. But the walls were thick, and no voices carried from the individual rooms. Tess's mentor had chosen a good place for clandestine meetings.

He glanced back over his shoulder to check on Keevi. The tortle was having a difficult time navigating the tight stairwell with their large shell, scraping off bits of dirt and wildflowers as they rubbed the walls, but otherwise they seemed fully recovered from their ordeal in the Sunless Citadel.

The stairs ended at a low-ceilinged hall at the top of the building. Tess led the way down the hall and knocked on the last door on the left. But she didn't just rap on the wood. She knocked twice in the center of the door, once near the knob, and two more times near the floor. When she'd finished, she looked back at Keevi with a raised brow. "That still the code?" she asked.

Keevi huffed a quiet laugh. "It is," they confirmed. "You really are her student."

The door opened, and a gray-haired halfling woman peered out at them. "Tessalynde," she said warmly, the skin around her dark eyes crinkling as she smiled at the elf. She glanced around, and her gaze fell on Keevi. A bit of tension went out of her posture when she saw them safe and well, and she beckoned the group inside. "Come in and sit down. We have a lot to discuss."

Mel's rooms were sparse. There were no windows and only a couple of dusty rugs on the floor to dampen their footsteps. It was clear this was a place for business, not comfort. She led them to a small table in the corner with a lit lamp in the center and just enough chairs for all of them to sit.

As he watched Mel clear away the remains of a breakfast tray, Baldric noticed a familiar pattern in the way the halfling moved. At first he couldn't place it, but then when Tess strode over to take one of the chairs, he recognized where he'd seen it before.

Though Mel was much shorter than Tess, her hands smaller and bony, the knuckles prominent when she grasped a ceramic mug, the two were echoes in more ways than one. Mel also wore gloves full of lockpicking tools, and she moved through the room as lightly as possible, footfalls making no sound, just like Tess. It told Baldric more in that moment about how much Tess admired and respected her mentor than he could have ever learned by talking to the elf.

"So," Mel said, when they were all settled. Her voice was soft and rough. "You have a story to tell me."

They did. Tess told it in bits and pieces, starting from their journey into the Sunless Citadel and culminating in their rescue of Keevi. Baldric listened and put in a comment here and there, but he was anxious, waiting to see what information Keevi had to impart about their own investigation.

Finally, the tortle leaned forward, the lamplight casting deep shadows over their papery green skin. "You sent me out to learn whether the Cult of the Dragon had taken a renewed interest in the citadel," they said, addressing Mel. "At first I could find no evidence that they'd occupied the place in some time." The tortle moved their large hands restlessly over the rough wood of the table. "However, I encountered a pair of humans while exploring the upper levels of the citadel, a man and a woman who spoke in Draconic and seemed to be conducting some sort of ritual, though they were not wearing any symbols or vestments."

Baldric leaned forward. Finally, they were getting somewhere. "Could you tell what or who they were appealing to?" he asked.

Keevi swung their sharp gaze to Baldric, and by the look on the tortle's face, he could guess the answer. "Ashardalon," they said. "I wasn't close enough to make out all the words as I was eavesdropping, but I recognized that name, and when you mentioned it later, I knew we were onto something."

"We may be dealing with a new sect, Ashardalon gathering followers and trying to reclaim his old haunts," Mel observed. She nodded to Keevi. "Go on. What happened next?"

"They spoke of the possibility of moving some of their followers into the citadel, if it could be purged of its current inhabitants," Keevi said. "It appeared they were worried about having too many people in their current base of operations. They didn't want to attract undue attention."

"Where are they operating from?" Tess asked. "Somewhere near the citadel?"

Keevi shook their head. "This is where it gets interesting. Apparently, they've managed to carve out a place within the Hosttower of the Arcane, in Luskan."

"The Arcane Brotherhood's stronghold?" Baldric blew out a breath and exchanged a bewildered look with Tess. "They're one of the most powerful organizations of arcane spellcasters in Faerûn. How did a cult manage to weasel its way into that tower without being found out?"

"The Arcane Brotherhood is formidable," Mel observed, "but they also have their own concerns, ones that often affect the wider world. It's possible that a splinter cult like this one could pass beneath their notice."

"They're ruled by *five* archmages," Tess pointed out. "You'd think they could spare at least one of them to pay attention when a greatwyrm sends spies into their home."

Mel clucked her tongue in amusement. "The great folk of this world can't be expected to have their attention on all threats at all times," she said, and gestured to Keevi with a glint in her eye. "That's what we have Harpers for."

Keevi inclined their head in acknowledgment. Baldric glanced at Mel. "What's your part in all this, if you've got Harpers at your beck and call?" he asked. "Most folk can't claim that privilege."

Mel just gave him an enigmatic smile, but Keevi said, "I was happy to do a favor for my teacher. It was my intention to take the information I learned from the cultists and arrange for an investigation into the Hosttower to see how far their influence now runs. However, the cultists discovered that I was observing them and attacked me. They might have killed me, but we were interrupted by an ambush that targeted all of us—a group of twig blights and kobolds broke into the chamber and attacked. That's when I was captured and taken to the caretaker of the grove."

"What happened to the cultists?" Baldric asked. "Were they captured like you?"

Keevi shook their head. "I don't believe so. I never saw them again, so I have to assume they escaped."

Now Baldric understood the cleric's chagrin. "Which means they'll be watching for you," he said.

Keevi nodded. "Unless I thoroughly disguise myself, I've been compromised," they said. "I'll have to bring in other Harpers and inform them of the situation."

Again, Baldric exchanged a look with Tess. He could practically see the wheels spinning in the rogue's head.

"What if we pursued a different plan?" Tess said. She slid her chair back and stood so she could pace the small room, hands on her hips, fingers tapping her belt absently. "Because it seems to me that you need an infiltration party."

Mel's lips twitched. "Oh? And wherever would we find such a group on short notice?"

"Think about it." Tess leaned over the table, putting her hands on the wood. "We already have a score to settle with Ashardalon because of his hold on Baldric."

Mel already knew this, but Keevi glanced at Baldric with open curiosity. Baldric waved a hand. "Long story," he said. "I'll tell it to you some other time." He looked to Tess, snagging her attention. "I appreciate that you want to defend me, but we can't confront the greatwyrm directly. He's too powerful, and I wouldn't even know how to begin."

"We don't have to," Tess assured him. "All we need to do is break his hold on you. So, we go into the tower under some pretense, and we root out the cultists, one by one if we have to."

Baldric nodded slowly, seeing what she was getting at. "You believe by weakening the cultists' power, it'll disrupt the grip Ashardalon has on me?"

He touched his chest reflexively. The night the greatwyrm had drawn out some of his life energy, it had felt so cold, so empty. That feeling still haunted him. The thought of having that hold on him severed—it was a tantalizing notion, he had to admit.

But much like his negotiations with the gods, these sorts of dealings were more complicated than they often appeared.

"How do we know that taking out some cultists will do any real damage?" he asked. He had no experience with these types of organizations. Merchant empires and straightforward dealings—those were his strong suit.

Tess looked to Mel, who shrugged. "You don't," she said. It was blunt, but Baldric appreciated plain speaking. He didn't believe in sugarcoating things. "But if these cultists are targeting the Hosttower, it means that Ashardalon wants a foothold in a place of powerful magic. Destroying that and taking out his followers will strike a blow he can't ignore."

A thorn in the greatwyrm's paw, Baldric mused. He knew the old nursery tale. Sometimes even the mighty could be chastened by something that stings long enough, and remains constant.

He could do that, if that's what it took to free himself. He could be a nasty thorn indeed.

"You're smiling," Keevi said, bringing Baldric out of his reverie. "Does that mean you'd consider working with the Harpers on this?"

"Well, there'd of course be some details to work out first," Baldric said, leaning back in his chair and crossing his arms. He fell effortlessly into the familiar rhythm of the deal. "The Fallbacks are all about working for the betterment of the world and all that . . ."

Tess picked up the thread. "But adventuring is an expensive business," she said, "and we can't afford to do it out of the kindness of our hearts, you understand. Not at the level we operate at, in any case."

Mel snorted quietly, but she was giving her student a look of pride. "They grow up so quickly," she said, pretending to dab at her eyes and sniffle.

Keevi smiled. "Of course, we wouldn't ask you to freelance for us for no compensation," they said. "The Harpers would be in a position to offer you four thousand gold for any intelligence you can bring to us about the cult and their activities." They hesitated, calculating. "We could offer seven thousand for you to root them out, capturing as many of them as you can."

Baldric scratched his beard thoughtfully, careful to keep his expression neutral. Never let the person on the other side of the negotiating table know how much you like their offer, he reminded himself. This mission was important to the Harpers and to Keevi; that much was clear.

"What about any loot or magic items that we recover in the course of the mission?" he asked casually.

Keevi inclined their head. "If by 'recover,' you mean items taken from the cultists themselves, I have no qualms with that. But we cannot condone stealing from the Hosttower or its residents."

"Of course," Tess interjected. "We wouldn't dream of it."

Baldric reminded himself to mention that particular rule to Lark before they entered the tower.

He glanced over at Mel. "And you won't tell us what part you play in all this?" he asked her. "Do you represent the Harpers as well?"

"Me?" Mel affected an innocent air. "Not at all."

"I see," Baldric said. "You don't represent any of those other powerful folk you mentioned earlier, the ones looking out for the interests of the wider world?"

Mel laughed. "I'm simply a teacher," she said, spreading her hands. She winked at Tess. "Though I'd like to think I'm a fairly good one."

"You are," Keevi said quietly, and Tess nodded her assent. The way she looked at Mel—Baldric had to give the woman his respect for that alone.

"Well, then." Tess cleared her throat and brought them back to business. "While your offer is fair—"

Baldric hid a smile behind his hand. Tess was a fine negotiator herself. He enjoyed watching her work.

"—we'll have to talk the mission over with the rest of our party," she finished. "We'll have an answer for you soon."

With those matters settled, Baldric rose from the table and headed for the door. He noticed Tess lingering, casting glances at her mentor. Obviously, there was more she wanted to say to Mel in private.

Baldric gave her a nod. "I'll wait for you downstairs," he said.

Keevi followed him out the door. "Would you be willing to share that story now?" they asked. "The one about Ashardalon?"

Too curious for their own good, Baldric thought with a quiet sigh, but he nodded. "Let's go outside," he said.

When Baldric and Keevi had gone, Tess sat back down at the table, but she was still restless, fidgeting in her seat and scratching at a stain in the wood.

"Out with it, child," Mel said with a chuckle. "You're making me nervous. What's got you so wound up?"

"It's . . ." Tess tried to find the words for all the knotted-up feelings inside her. In the end, she just looked at her mentor helplessly. "Is it always going to feel like this?"

Mel's forehead creased. "Like what, Tessalynde?"

"Like I'm trying to shepherd a pack of monkeys through the streets!" Tess burst out. She raked her hands through her hair in frustration. "The Fallbacks are powerful, talented, and courageous, and just when I think I have a handle on how to lead them, they turn around and try to run straight off a cliff!"

Mel let out a hearty laugh at her vehemence. "Surely, it can't be that bad?"

"It is!" Tess insisted. "We pulled together when we had to and survived our first mission. After that, it felt like we understood each other. We bonded! I was sure everything would fall into place, but now it seems like everything is unraveling."

She ticked the problems off on her fingers. "Baldric still has a powerful evil entity trying to take over his life. Anson's unhappy because he wants to find his brother, the same brother who was working for the *lich* that tried to kill us, but never mind that, Anson's going to make everything all right again." She groaned. "And Lark! Lark has resisted almost every attempt I've made to turn him into a more professional adventurer, except the one time he was paying attention to my lessons and managed to pick my pocket for a powerful magic item, all so he could throw a *party*." She shook her head. "Cazrin and Uggie are the only ones I'm not worried about at the moment, except that'll change as soon as we find the next evil tome or diseased rat carcass."

Mel scrunched up her small nose in disgust. "All right, I'm assuming you mean—"

"That Cazrin will go for the tome and Uggie the rat, yes." Tess chuckled despite herself. "If it were the other way around, I'd be tempted to quit adventuring."

She looked to Mel for sympathy, wisdom, guidance—*anything*. To her dismay, her mentor simply shrugged. "Well, what did you expect?" she asked.

"What did I—" Tess thought Mel must be joking. "It's not like I planned for any of this to happen!"

Mel leaned back in her chair, surveying Tess with amusement. "Didn't you? You knew that all these people had secrets and desires of their own when you recruited them. You knew that Anson never gives up on anyone if he can help it. You knew the bard was going to be trouble. You wrote about it in your letters. I can show you, if you like?" Mel grinned. "And you told me how impressed you were with Baldric's abilities and his prowess in negotiations."

"Yes," Tess said, "that's all true, but—"

"But nothing," Mel said. She reached into a pouch on her belt and pulled out a small black skeleton key, which she held up for Tess to see. "Do you recognize this?"

Tess's fingers closed around the key, and suddenly, it was like she was a child again, running barefoot through the forests outside her village, splashing in streams, her hair tangled with sticks and moss. She remembered crouching beside the bole of a knotty, scarred oak tree, reaching her hand into the crack where she kept all her most secret treasures . . .

"I didn't know you still had this," she said softly, running her fingers over the key. "I was so mad when you took it from me."

"Oh, I remember," Mel said. "I didn't know they taught elven girls how to swear in halfling, but there you were, cursing and shaking those pale fists at me like I'd wronged you and your whole family line, swearing you'd get your vengeance."

Tess groaned. She'd been a bit overdramatic in her younger years. "It was just because I'd been working on that key for ages," she said. "It opened nearly every door to every home and business in the village. I was so proud of my work."

Of course, it was more the mark of a poor village locksmith than her own talent at the time, Tess realized now. But that key had served her well while she'd had it.

"You used that key to break into the general store." Mel began ticking off her own list. "And the mill. The village baker, the blacksmith—"

"I never took anything from any of those places." At Mel's flat look, Tess amended, "I never took anything that I didn't bring back later."

Part of it was that she'd needed things—like the rope to climb down into the ravine to explore the cave she and her friends had found. But she'd also wanted to see if she could get away with it, sneaking into a place where she knew she didn't belong. That secret little thrill had goaded her on, until she'd learned to channel those feelings into more noble pursuits, with Mel's help.

"The point is," Mel said, "I knew exactly what I was getting myself into when I agreed to take you on as a student." She smiled fondly. "You weren't the biggest challenge I'd ever had to face, but you were no slouch."

Tess took a moment to imagine all the students Mel had taken in over the years, the patience the halfling woman must have had to cultivate to make them into whole, functioning individuals, forces for good in the world.

Like Keevi, who'd begun their career as a rogue and was now a servant of Mielikki, uncovering the plans of Ashardalon's cult and working to stop them.

She shook her head in wonder. "How do you do it?" she asked Mel.

"You make a lot of mistakes," Mel said bluntly. "You learn from them, adjust, and then you make a whole bunch more. Eventually, if you're lucky, you stumble your way through to your goal, and it will probably look nothing like you'd expected or planned. That's life, Tessalynde. That's leadership, and that's the path you've chosen." She gave her a keen look. "Assuming that's still what you want?"

"It is," Tess said immediately. She swallowed, gripping the key in her hands. "It's just I never thought I'd feel so alone while doing it."

Mel frowned. "You have an entire party surrounding you," she said. "You just told me how talented and powerful they are. Aren't they capable of taking on some of this burden you're feeling?"

"They are," Tess said hesitantly. That was part of the problem. She relied on Anson. He was the one person she'd never doubted would be there for her, and now . . .

"Cheer up, Tess," Mel said, reaching over to lay a hand on her shoulder. "It's natural to doubt yourself—I'd be worried if you didn't, in fact—but the Fallbacks have followed you this far. There's a reason for that. Trust them, and trust yourself. That's all you can do." She sat back. "Listen to me! I'm getting sentimental in my old age." She pulled a flask from her belt, unscrewed the cap, and took a drink. "That's better. Now, let's talk dragons and cults. That'll be much more fun."

Tess laughed. "Yes, it's going to take more than a skeleton key to get into the Hosttower of the Arcane," she said. "Any advice?"

Mel chewed her lip thoughtfully. "Vellynne Harpell," she said at last. "An old friend of mine. Seek her out if you can, and use my name. It'll help to have an insider you can trust not to be corrupted by the cult." She leveled a warning finger at Tess. "There will be plenty of other wizards in that place corrupted by other forces. Keep your wits about you."

That, Tess thought, she could safely promise her mentor. "I learned from the best," she said.

CHAPTER 14

"Luskan?" Anson said, once Tess and Baldric had finished telling the party about their meeting with Mel and Keevi. "But we only just got back. How soon are we leaving?"

They were gathered in the Wander Inn. It was still lopsided, but the common room had been set to rights again, and the Fallbacks had clustered around the bar to listen to Tess and Baldric describe the party's new mission.

"Assuming I can get us passage on a ship, I was hoping we'd leave tomorrow," Tess said. "That gives us the whole day to wrap up any business anyone has in the city. Is that all right?"

She was looking at Anson, a crease between her pale brows. Anson turned away, his thoughts racing. "It's . . . it's fine," he assured her. "I was just surprised, that's all."

He hadn't thought they'd be leaving so soon. He'd thought he'd have more time to address Valen's problem, maybe find a better solution than the one he'd come up with.

"I, for one, am ready for a change of scenery," Lark commented. He was draped over one of the barstools, propping himself up on his elbows, eyelids drooping as if he was about to fall asleep. Not a surprise, really, considering how long he'd spent cleaning the previous night. "I'm ready to win over a new crowd, and Luskan is a tantalizing place."

"You ever been there?" Anson asked. "It's about a thousand miles up the coast from here, a city perched at the edge of the sea, ruled by pirates, a haven for smugglers, scoundrels, and sometimes desperate folk."

Lark hummed appreciatively in his throat. "Like I said . . . *tantalizing*."

"The rest aside, the Hosttower of the Arcane is said to be a marvel," Cazrin put in, a faraway look in her eyes as she took a seat at the bar next to Anson. Uggie was sprawled at her feet, sleeping. "You know, when I was a child, I used to daydream about running away and applying for membership in the Arcane Brotherhood." She smiled. "In my imaginings, the wizards would accept me immediately, of course, and give me a room at the top of the tallest tower to study magic all day long."

Baldric chuckled. "Sounds like the perfect plan. Caz will move in, take over the place, and we'll have the cultists cleaned out by summer's end." He cocked his head. "Except that the Arcane Brotherhood has a reputation as one of the most ambitious, power-hungry organizations of spellcasters in Faerûn. If they have a code of ethics, it's a loose one at best."

Tess looked thoughtful. "It won't be easy, but I think Cazrin could be our key," she said. "A powerful wizard seeking membership in the Arcane Brotherhood could be a good cover for entry. Let me think on it some more." She surveyed the rest of them, and Anson again felt her gaze lingering on him, making him shift uncomfortably. "Are we all agreed, then? We travel to Luskan, take care of these cultists, and hopefully"—she shot a meaningful look at Baldric—"we're another step closer to getting Ashardalon out of our lives for good."

There were nods of agreement all around—Lark's came out as more of a snore, as he was falling asleep at the bar—and Anson found himself automatically going along, though his thoughts were still on Valen.

Could he get his brother to change his mind about coming with the party? Luskan was a dangerous place, but Anson had to admit it might appeal to Valen for that very reason. A person could disappear there, start over, just as his brother wanted.

But what would happen when they reached the city? Even if the rest of the party agreed to travel with Valen, was he going to infiltrate the Hosttower with them? Make himself a target of Ashardalon and the cultists, all so Anson could keep an eye on his brother and protect him from the Zhentarim? He'd just be trading one danger for another, and no one would be better off.

Anson suppressed a sigh, running his hand over the wooden practice sword he'd tucked into his belt. Valen had told him what he wanted, and though Anson couldn't give him the Wander Inn, he knew what he had to do to help his brother.

When the meeting broke up, Tess left to tell Keevi and Mel that the Fallbacks were taking the job. Baldric and Cazrin drifted back to Cazrin's room. Anson heard them discussing places in Luskan where they might gain more information on greatwyrms and their powers.

Uggie was still passed out on the floor, and Lark was now fully asleep, with his head on the bar.

Steeling himself, Anson went over to the bard and shook his shoulder gently. "Lark," he whispered. "Lark, are you awake?"

Lark snorted, jerked, and opened his eyes, staring up at Anson in bleary annoyance. "No," he muttered. "I was asleep, and it was magical." He gave a back-cracking stretch. "What could you possibly want right now?"

"Um." Faced with Lark's irritation, and with his own misgivings churning in his gut, Anson almost changed his mind. But then he remembered the expression on Valen's face, the desperation.

He needs this more than Lark does, Anson told himself. Besides, the Fallbacks encountered magical trinkets like this one all the time. Sometimes they kept them and sometimes they sold them, but there were always more. He'd find one to replace Lark's amulet.

"If you're not going to say anything, could you at least bring me a pillow and blanket?" Lark said, slouching onto the bar again. "Merciful Gods, so tired . . ."

"I need to borrow your amulet," Anson said in a rush, before he could lose his nerve. "Just for the afternoon."

All traces of exhaustion vanished from the tiefling's expression. His gaze sharpened on Anson, and his hand rose to cover the amulet.

"Why?" he demanded.

His reaction caught Anson off guard. He'd expected Lark to hem and haw and maybe whine a little before handing over the amulet. He hadn't expected this sudden wariness, and Anson knew he was not the best liar in their group.

"I just . . . need it, for a little while." *Good job, Anson. What an eloquent request. He won't be suspicious of that* at all.

Sure enough, Lark's eyes narrowed. "Oh, well, if that's the reason, then *no*," he said. "Go away and let me sleep now." He slumped over the bar, turning his face away from Anson as if to emphasize the end of the conversation.

What would Valen do in this situation? When they were younger, he'd always been the one who could charm a tavern keeper into giving them the dregs of that night's dinner special, or sweet-talk one of the stable boys into letting them sleep in the barn loft. He always knew exactly how to appeal to a person.

What would appeal to Lark in this situation?

Anson cleared his throat. "Um, Lark?"

"What is it now?" The bard turned back to him with a glare, his tail lashing the air like a whip. Anson had to step back to keep from getting smacked. "Did Tess put you up to this? Did she tell you not to let me get any sleep? Is this part of my punishment?"

Anson held up his hands. "It's nothing like that," he assured him. Inspiration struck him then, and he blurted out, "It's about a girl."

A hot flush shot up his neck, but at the same time, Anson knew he'd said the right thing. Lark's annoyed gaze turned speculative, and a sly smile crept across his lips. "Is that so? Do tell, and please make it good."

Oh Gods, he'd really stepped in it now, Anson thought. Well, he might as well push all his chips in. "I met her last night, and, um, we really hit it off, but there's a problem, and I was . . . hoping I could talk to her in secret, help her out before we left the city. But I need the amulet to make sure no one knows what I'm doing."

He was babbling, but so far, Lark seemed to be on board with the story. "What sort of *problem* are we talking about?" he asked. "Jealous former lover? An impossible debt? Assassins stalking her in the night?" Anson could practically see Lark composing a song in his head. "Why do you need to hide?"

"Well . . ." He didn't want to go this route, but it would appeal to Lark's sense of melodrama. "Jealous former lover," he decided. "You see—"

"Don't tell me!" Lark leaned across the bar and seized Anson's forearm. "You saw her across a crowded room, the two of you instantly smitten, unaware that there were other eyes watching. Malevolent eyes that refuse to let your love flourish in peace, so now you need to meet with her in secret to declare yourself!"

"Er . . . yes, that's basically it," Anson said. He should have known Lark would fill in a better story himself if given the opportunity. He was just glad the bard was exhausted from being up all night cleaning. He didn't think he would have gotten away with the lie otherwise. "So, can you help me out? Please?"

Some of the wariness crept back into Lark's expression as he considered the request. His hand was still on the amulet, gripping it reflexively. Finally, the bard let out a dramatic sigh and removed the amulet from around his neck. He held it out to Anson, frowning. "Do what you have to do," he said, "but I want this back today, you understand?"

"I do. Thank you, Lark."

Anson swallowed, feeling a rush of shame as he took the amulet and put it around his own neck. He turned and left the inn before he could change his mind.

I'll make it up to him, he promised himself. He had some coin saved up. He'd give it all to Lark. Or maybe he would get the bard some amazing magic item to enhance his performances. He'd talk to Cazrin for ideas.

Everything was going to be fine.

CHAPTER 15

Anson quickly made his way back toward the alley where he and Valen had met earlier. It had taken longer than he'd expected to get the amulet. He hoped Valen hadn't left, thinking that Anson wasn't coming.

As soon as he stepped into the deeper shadows of the alley, he heard the sounds. Close-quarters fighting. He'd been jumped in dark alleys enough times in his life to recognize the signs. The scrape of boots on gravel, a pained cry that was quickly cut off, and an *oomph* as someone took a blow to the stomach.

Anson drew his broken sword, lightning crackling softly along the blade. He pressed himself to the alley wall and moved as swiftly and quietly as he could toward the sounds.

He saw Valen first. His brother was near a brick wall, bent double while a pair of burly hooded figures—one a dwarf with a short blond beard, and the other a human with a shaved head and a serpent tattooed on the back of his neck—held each of his arms. They had them twisted so far behind his back it looked like they meant to tear them out of their sockets. A third, lanky figure stood off to one side. His face caught the meager sunlight from the end of the alley, revealing elven features and scraggly brown hair left long to the shoulders.

Three targets. A triangular formation. In seconds, Anson had the cramped battlefield mapped out in his mind. He noted the positioning of his targets' feet, where their weight was distributed, how he could set them off-balance. He couldn't see if the burly ones were wearing armor under their cloaks, but it didn't matter. He would find the weak points.

He always did.

Anson slid into a crouch, making himself as small and unobtrusive as it was possible for someone his size to be, intending to come in low on the closest target. But at the last moment, his foot found the remnants of an old crate, half-crushed in a puddle of water. It crunched under his boot, and the man with the tattoo turned and looked him straight in the eyes.

So much for the element of surprise.

He brought his sword up in an arc, scraping the broken end over the brick wall to his left. Sparks flew, and blue-white radiance briefly lit up the alley, revealing Anson's face to his opponent. Energy surged into Anson's limbs, the blood roaring in his ears as he let out a fierce shout.

And, just as he'd hoped, the man's eyes widened, and he took a faltering step back, his grip on Valen's arm loosening a fraction.

That was all the opening Anson needed.

He feinted left, sparks still dancing off his sword, then came in around the man's right flank, slashing as he went by. His blade bit deep into the fabric of the man's cloak and cut through the leather armor beneath. The man cried out and pulled back, letting go of Valen completely.

Anson was still moving. He reached for Valen, seizing his brother's shoulder and yanking him free of the dwarf still holding on to his other arm. He switched places with Valen, spinning his brother away from his captors and positioning himself in between them now.

Valen took advantage of the momentum Anson had given him and drove his fist into the stomach of the scraggly-haired elf. They scuffled, grunting and cursing each other, slamming into the opposite wall of the alley, but Anson had to focus on the opponents in front of him.

They were big but slow, and the human was still reeling from the swipe he'd taken to his flank. His cloak was soaked in blood on that side. It had been a deeper gash than Anson expected.

Planting his feet, Anson went low again and thrust straight at the dwarf's abdomen. The smaller figure tried to dodge but mistimed the speed of Anson's strike. He took the blade in the shoulder, cursing in pain, spittle flying from his mouth. Anson pushed the attack, driving the dwarf into the wall, trying to daze him and knock the wind from his lungs so he wouldn't be able to mount a counterattack.

"Watch your back!" Valen hollered at him, a reprimand that was quickly cut off when the elf wrapped his spindly fingers around his throat and slammed him into the wall.

Anson wished he could. But that was the danger of fighting in dark alleys, of flashing blades and stinking bodies in the dark. The shadows were your best shield, and even they couldn't always protect you when your enemies were right there, pressing in from all sides.

Movement caught the corner of his eye. There was nowhere to dodge, so Anson flattened himself against the wall. He still took the tattooed man's dagger thrust to his thigh, and oh Gods, that was a deep gash. At first he felt nothing but cold wetness soaking his leg. Then the fiery-hot pain swept through him, laced with something else: a numbing, pins-and-needles sensation, and a bitter taste that stung the back of his throat.

Poison.

Sweat broke out on Anson's skin, and a sickening feeling clenched his stomach. He'd half hoped these were common cutthroats or pickpockets, but they weren't. These were Zhent agents, or assassins employed by them, sent to capture Valen. They needed to end this fight quickly, before the poison incapacitated him.

For an instant, Anson turned inward, emptying his mind, hearing nothing but the breath hissing in and out of his lungs. His senses sharpened, an awareness that momentarily pushed back the poison, the pain, and the fear that these men were going to take his brother.

He walled off those feelings inside of him, and in their place came a swell of calm, of strength and surety.

You're never out of the fight until you've breathed your last. You can always find something more if you dig deep enough.

For a long time, Anson hadn't known how to do that. Until he realized that he needed to turn the feeling outward, to fight for someone else. It wasn't enough to stay alive just for himself, not after everything he'd lost. But as long as someone needed him . . .

Anson drove his elbow back into the tattooed man's gut, so hard he felt one of the man's ribs crack. That gave him the space and time to grab the dagger hilt sticking out of his thigh. He barely felt it as he yanked the blade free. An oily black substance dripped from the blade, fed from a small compartment in the hilt. He'd seen a similar mechanism on Tess's blades.

Just as the tattooed man was recovering his breath, Anson stabbed him with the poisoned dagger in the same place he'd just been elbowed. This time the man folded, dropping to his knees and clutching the wall to keep himself upright.

The dwarf was coming at him again, but he might as well have been moving through molasses. Anson could have choreographed his attack. He wasn't a finesse fighter. This one was pure strength, the muscle that subdued and held the target.

Anson brought his broken sword in again, which fizzed with the magic that was both a blessing and a curse. He never knew when it would obey his commands or strike indiscriminately. But seeing the flash of the chain mail the dwarf was wearing under his cloak, Anson didn't care.

He feinted again and then came in hard. He wedged the blade into the dwarf's hip, grazing the chain mail, and this time, blessedly, the magic in the blade responded just as he wished, the lightning bolt brightening the alley like fireworks on a festival night, reflecting in the dwarf's wide eyes right before he screamed.

Anson let go of his sword as the dwarf collapsed, just in case the magic reflected back on him. He didn't think he could take a hit from that right now. His right leg dragged as he moved, and he pivoted so he could see how Valen fared against the elf.

He needn't have worried. Valen had been disarmed by his attackers, probably when they'd ambushed him, but his brother had never needed a blade to defend himself. He was standing behind the elf, hoisting him in a choke hold as he braced himself against the alley wall.

Anson checked one last time to make sure neither of his opponents was getting up again, then shuffled across to help. By the time he reached Valen, the elf had slumped in his grasp, and Valen dropped him to the ground. Then, gasping, Valen bent double, clutching his knees as he got his breath back.

"Are you hurt?" Anson demanded, taking his brother by the arm so he could get a better look.

Valen shrugged him off. "I'm fine," he snapped. "Stop pawing at me and give me a moment."

"We need to move," Anson said, gesturing to the three Zhents. "They're not dead. We'll find a Flaming Fist patrol and tell them where to find them."

"Or we could just finish them off," Valen said pointedly. He reached down, retrieving his daggers from the elf and returning them to their sheaths.

Anson shook his head. "We're not slitting throats in alleys while they're unconscious," he said. "Besides, you're better off if we let the authorities know there are Zhent agents roving the streets. I'll put some coin in their hands, and they'll keep a lookout for others. You'll be safer that way in the long run."

Valen seemed torn, but he finally nodded. Anson was relieved. He didn't want a fight. He just wanted to get out of the stinking alley and back into the sunlight.

Except the poison had other ideas. As Anson tried to get his legs to move, he found the right one numb and dead. He glanced down at himself, at the blood and black ichor-like substance streaming down his leg, and realized the thigh wound might actually get him before the poison did.

"Huh," he said as he found himself sliding to the ground, riding a wave of dizziness. "I probably shouldn't go out into the streets like this. Going to . . . scare small children or something."

"What?" Valen strode over, and as soon as he got a look at Anson, he cursed loud and long. "Why in the fiery depths of the Hells didn't you say you were hurt?"

"I'm f-fine," Anson said. When did he start slurring his words? "Just need a s-second to catch my breath." He leaned his cheek against the brick wall. This probably wasn't the cleanest place to take a nap. Oh well.

A stinging pain whipped across his cheek.

"Stay awake!" Valen barked.

When Anson opened his eyes, his brother was crouching in front of him, arm raised to slap him again. "Heyyyy," Anson complained as he rubbed his cheek. "That hurt. Your nails need a trim."

"They do not—oh, never mind."

Valen rummaged in his vest, probably searching in one of its hidden pockets. Anson used to help his brother sew them into his clothes when they were children. Best places to hide coin stashes.

When Valen drew his hand out, it wasn't a coin he held. It was a small potion bottle. He popped the cork and held it to Anson's lips.

"Drink," he commanded, and without waiting for Anson to comply, he shoved the vial into his mouth, the glass clinking painfully against Anson's teeth.

"Ow." Anson swallowed the contents of the vial, trying not to choke on the thick, syrupy liquid. The potion warmed a path down his throat. His head, which had felt like it was filling with cotton and bees, suddenly cleared, and the sounds of the city outside the alley came rushing back.

"Better?" Valen asked, leaning closer to peer into Anson's eyes. "Your pupils are still big as marbles, but that should fade soon. Damn Zhent poison is strong, but I think you'll be all right."

Anson blinked at his brother. Was it his imagination, or was there actual worry in Valen's expression? He couldn't be sure, so he lifted his hand and palmed one side of Valen's face, pulling him closer.

"What are you doing? Get off!" Valen shoved at Anson's chest. "That poison obviously melted your brain. Let g—" He stopped as his gaze snagged on the amulet hanging around Anson's neck. "What's that?"

"What's—oh," Anson said. He lifted the amulet for Valen's inspection. "I almost forgot. It's for you."

He lifted the amulet from around his neck, struggling as the chain tangled with his shirt. Valen leaned forward to help, taking the magic item from him and cradling it in his hands. "What does it do?" he asked.

"First, I'll tell you what it doesn't do," Anson said, wincing as he adjusted his leg. The wound was closed now, so he tried to clean himself up as best he could. "It's not the key to the Wander Inn, but I think this might be more useful to you."

Valen gave him a skeptical glance. "Oh, really? Do tell."

Anson explained the amulet's purpose, how it would keep Valen from being tracked magically. "You can disguise yourself all you want," he said, "blend in and try to disappear, but if the Zhents have something that they can use to find you with magic, it won't matter." He tapped the amulet in Valen's hands. "This will level the playing field."

Valen nodded slowly, appearing to think it over. He put the amulet on, tucking it inside his vest so it wouldn't be visible. "I think you're right, brother," he said finally. "I think this is even better than having a place to hide." He glanced at Anson. "Are you sure you want to part with it?"

Anson hadn't been sure at all. He'd almost turned around a dozen times and gone back to the inn to return the amulet to Lark. Only when he'd entered the alley and saw the Zhents holding his brother had all of his doubts vanished.

This was the right thing to do. Valen needed him, and this time, at least, Anson was going to be there for him.

"It's yours," he said, patting his brother on the shoulder. He glanced over at the Zhents, but they were still unconscious. "Let's get out of here," he said, wrinkling his nose. "I'm pretty sure I sat in a puddle of urine just now."

Valen sniffed. "I don't think there's any doubt of that."

CHAPTER 16

After they'd informed the authorities about the Zhents, Anson and Valen ended up back at the docks, watching the ships glide in and out over the pewter water. They stood for a moment in silence, but Anson could tell his brother was getting fidgety, wanting to be on the move.

It wasn't just because he was being hunted, Anson thought. Valen had always been like this, ever since they were on their own as children. He wondered what Valen was afraid would happen if he stood in one place for too long.

"Where will you go?" Anson asked. He picked up a rock and skimmed it over the water, watching it take four graceful hops before it disappeared beneath the surface.

"Better that you don't know," Valen said. When Anson scowled at him, he just shrugged. "I can't have you dogging my steps in every city on the Sword Coast. If I'm going to disappear, I'm going to do it right." His expression softened. "Look, don't give me those doleful eyes. I'll find my way back around to visiting you again."

But he avoided Anson's gaze as he spoke, and Anson knew it would probably be a very long time before he saw Valen again. What was it Tess had told him that night in Waterdeep? That he needed closure with his brother? But how was he supposed to accomplish that? The only common ground he'd found with Valen had been when they were fighting for their lives in that filthy alley—because they'd done it so many times before.

"Would it really be so bad," Anson asked quietly, "if you came with us? Became an adventurer? We're a walking pack of bad decisions and dangerous skills. You'd fit in eventually, and we'd protect you. Why won't you consider it?"

Valen sighed. He looked out over the water, eyes half-closed under the bright afternoon sun. "It wouldn't be so bad," he admitted, surprising Anson and causing an ember of hope to flare within him. "Maybe I'd carve out a place for myself—dally with that bard, annoy your lovely leader. It would be fun for a while."

"Yes, exactly, dally with—" Anson furrowed his brow. "Wait, what? And what about Tess?"

"But it wouldn't last," Valen went on smoothly. "Not because your friends wouldn't trust me or even particularly like me. I could deal with all of that."

"Then what is it?" Anson demanded, growing impatient. "Whatever it is, we can—"

"It's you," Valen said, giving Anson a look that was like a swift kick to the gut. "Sooner or later, you'll go back to trying to 'fix' me, make me more like you, and you know I can't stand that. I'm not like you, brother, and I never will be. We live different lives, and I've made peace with that. You're the only one who hasn't."

The words hurt. Anson wanted to deny it, but he saw the truth in what Valen said. He *would* try to make his brother into something different: a man less violent, less desperate and greed-driven, someone who didn't constantly walk that razor's edge that was probably going to get him killed one day.

Even as he acknowledged that truth, Anson skimmed another rock across the water, hard, and bit back the reply he wanted to make.

Would it be so bad to try to be like me? What's wrong with me?

"At least you're honest," he murmured, glancing over at Valen. "Thank you for that."

Valen nodded. He put his hand against his chest where the amulet was hidden. "Thank you for this," he said. "You always have my back, no matter what."

"We're family," Anson said.

The only family they had left.

Anson kept his gaze on the choppy water, the sun's glare making his eyes sting, and felt the moment when Valen slipped away, leaving him alone.

WHEN HE ARRIVED back at the Wander Inn, he expected it to be deserted, everyone having gone about their own personal business for the day in preparation for their departure to Luskan early the next morning. So Anson was surprised when he shut the door to the common room and heard a gasp behind him.

"Anson, what happened to you?"

He turned. Cazrin was sitting at one of the tables, her feet propped on an adjacent chair, a book open in front of her. Tess and Baldric were sitting across from her; it looked like they'd been having a meeting. Lark was sitting beside the fireplace with Uggie, trying to wrestle what looked like the remains of one of his shirts out of the otyugh's mouth.

They were all staring at him.

Anson looked down at himself, belatedly remembering the gash in his thigh. Although the healing potion had closed the wound and blunted the worst effects of the poison, his pants were still ripped and covered in drying blood, and the smells of the alley clung to him. He couldn't remember if he'd taken a blow to the face or not, but a stinging pain in his cheek made him think he must have.

"I'm fine," he assured everyone as he limped over to the table. Cazrin jumped up and pulled out a chair for him. He sank into it with a grateful nod. "Really, you should . . . um . . . see the other guy," he said as they all continued to stare at him, open-mouthed.

"What happened?" Tess demanded. She stood up and came around the table to tower over him.

Anson shrank in his seat. He'd forgotten how intimidating Tess's glares could be when they were aimed in his direction. Why did she look so mad? *He* was the one who'd gotten injured. "I got jumped in an alley," he said, waving it off. "Nothing I couldn't handle."

His gaze strayed involuntarily across the room to Lark, who was staring not at Anson's wounds but at the empty space on his chest where the amulet should have been.

He shrank a little more in his seat.

"Except, um, they did rob me," Anson said, thinking fast. He'd thought he'd have more time to think up a story for how he'd lost the amulet, but this was as plausible an excuse as any. "Took all my coin and swiped the amulet too." He forced himself to meet Lark's gaze. "I'm really sorry. I promise I'll get you something to replace it as soon as I can."

Silence met his tale. Anson shifted uncomfortably in his chair. His leg was still aching, but more disconcerting was the way his party was looking at him. Tess's glare was still firmly fixed in place, Cazrin had her head bent toward her book, avoiding his gaze, and Baldric had gotten up from the table to intercept the bard, who had suddenly jumped up, surrendering his shirt to Uggie, and was striding across the room toward Anson with a murderous look in his eyes.

Anson flinched, but Baldric got to Lark first. "Easy, now," he said, clamping a gentle but firm hand around the tiefling's forearm. "Let's give him a chance to explain."

"Explain?" Anson felt heat rising up his neck, wreathing his face in scarlet flames. "I just did. I got ambushed in an alley, poisoned even, and—"

Tess took a step toward him, bent down, and pulled his coin purse off his belt. She tossed it onto the table. The strings, already loosened during the fight with the Zhentarim, came free and allowed a pile of gold and silver coins to spill across the tabletop with a loud, damning clinking sound.

"Care to try again?" Tess asked, cocking an eyebrow at him.

Anson opened his mouth then closed it again. His flush deepened. He should have known better than to try to lie to all of them at once, especially Tess.

He sat up straight. "I did get attacked in an alley," he insisted. "But I was ... helping Valen. He'd been ambushed by Zhent agents sent to capture him."

"Is he all right?" Cazrin asked, concern furrowing her brow.

Anson nodded. "I got there just in time," he said. He glanced at Tess. "This wasn't the first time I've met with him," he admitted.

"So you found him," Tess said, her voice neutral. "Why didn't you tell us?"

"Actually, *he* found *me*," Anson said. "He came to the Wander Inn last night when Lark threw his party." He looked over at the bard. "He said he met you."

But Lark didn't seem to be in the mood for talking. His cheeks had gone an even darker shade of crimson, and he was trying to free himself from Baldric's steel-armed grip.

"Where is my amulet?" Lark demanded. "Did the Zhents take it? If so, I'll track them down and—"

"The Zhents didn't take anything," Baldric interjected, a note of weariness in his voice. He put his other hand on Lark's shoulder and glanced over at Anson. "Did they?" he asked.

"No," Anson said quietly. "I gave the amulet to Valen so he could hide from the Zhentarim."

Lark jerked his arm out of Baldric's grasp. He started to move, trying to dart around the cleric, but Baldric was an impenetrable wall. "That's what you intended all along," the bard accused, straining against the cleric. "You were never *borrowing* it for anything, were you? You were always intending to steal it!" His voice rose; he was angrier than Anson had ever seen him.

"Look, Lark, I'm really sorry," he said, raising his hands in a placating gesture. "I would never have done it if it wasn't a matter of life and death." A spike of defensiveness went through Anson. Why couldn't they understand? Why was Lark looking at him like he'd done something unforgivable? "He's my brother," Anson said, frustration causing his own voice to rise, "and he was about to be murdered in a filthy alley, alone! What was I supposed to do, just let it happen?"

"You lied to me," Lark spat. "You stood right there, just hours ago, and lied to my face, feeding me a sob story about some noble cause you were on, and I swallowed it whole." He threw up his hands, giving up on trying to get past Baldric. He dropped into a chair at one of the other tables. Uggie slunk over to huddle at the bard's feet.

A slew of mental images assailed Anson's thoughts, mostly images of the party members growing ten feet tall, haloed by darkness, yelling at one another and brandishing their weapons.

"All right, let's all take a breath," Tess said. "You're upsetting Uggie, and I want to sort this out like reasonable, levelheaded people." She pointed at Anson. "You first. You're telling me that Valen found *you*? That he's been here, in the Wander Inn—for what, to spy on us? What's his game?"

"Why does it have to be something nefarious?" Anson shot back, feeling his temper fraying. "He obviously needed help. He came to me and said so."

"Oh Gods!"

They all turned to look at Lark, who'd dropped his head into his hands and was rubbing his face. A peal of helpless laughter escaped him. Anson wondered if he'd finally lost it.

"The attractive snooper," Lark continued, shaking his head. "The man I caught in Anson's room—I thought he was a party guest who'd gotten lost or was looking for some souvenir to pocket." He looked at Anson. "That was your brother, wasn't it?"

Anson nodded. "Probably." He rubbed the back of his head. "He was disguised when I saw him, so there was no way you'd have known who he was."

Tess narrowed her eyes. "So he came here, to our home, in disguise, to sneak around the place. That doesn't sound like some desperate soul in need of help."

"Sounds calculated to me," Baldric agreed. Anson glared at him, but the dwarf just shrugged. "The truth's the truth, whether you want to hear it or not."

"What did he say to you, Lark?" Tess asked, leaning against the table. Cazrin rose from her seat and went behind the bar to make some tea, calling Uggie to her side to calm the otyugh.

The bard huffed a laugh. "Oh, it was a master play," he said. "We talked and flirted, shared a drink. He was the consummate charmer. I'd be impressed if I wasn't so furious." His expression darkened. "But it was the amulet he was really admiring. He saw me wearing it and asked about it."

Anson was confused. "No, that can't be right," he said. "It was the

Wander Inn that Valen was interested in. He wanted to use it as a place to hide."

"He what?" Tess demanded.

Behind the bar, Cazrin fumbled the teacups in their saucers. Baldric's eyebrows rose.

"He's a bold scoundrel, I'll give him that," the dwarf said.

Lark just laughed again, shaking his head. "Ah, Anson, you fell for one of the oldest cons in the land."

"I wasn't being conned," Anson insisted, but he didn't like the way the others were looking at one another, as if they knew something he didn't.

Baldric elaborated. "I think he was aiming for the amulet the whole time, Anson," he said, his tone caught between sympathy and exasperation. "He started out by asking for something he knew you couldn't give him. It made you that much more motivated to get the amulet instead. Valen had a well-thought-out plan in place when he contacted you. He'd already collected information on the entire party so he'd be prepared."

"That's not what happened," Anson said. "You weren't there. Valen needed my help, and if I hadn't taken the amulet, the Zhents would have hunted him down, and he'd probably be dead now."

"We don't fault you wanting to help your brother," Baldric said, "but the way you went about it isn't how we're supposed to do things."

"You should have come to us the minute Valen contacted you," Tess said. "And Lark," she said, pointing a finger at the bard, "you're also responsible for this. This is what happens when you open up our private sanctuary to anyone and everyone in Baldur's Gate."

"True," Lark acknowledged, a muscle ticking in his jaw, as if the admission pained him. "I'll know better next time." He met Anson's gaze. "And I'll know better than to trust someone when they ask me for a favor. Even if they're in my own party."

"Lark, I'm *sorry*," Anson said, his voice pleading. "I'll make it up to you, I promise. I'll cover the cost of the amulet and more. You can use it to buy yourself something nice for your performances."

"It wasn't about some trinket!" Lark snapped, and this time he did dodge around Baldric, reaching Anson in two strides. Anson stood up, half expecting the tiefling to throw a punch, as angry as he looked. But Lark just got right in Anson's face and snapped, "Your brother may be safe from the Zhents now, but what about *me* and the people hunting *me*?"

That stunned Anson and the rest into silence.

Tess found her voice first. "What do you mean, the people hunting you?" she demanded, pushing between Anson and Lark. "What's going on here?"

Lark's expression shuttered, and he cursed under his breath. "It's nothing," he said, his voice still heated. "It doesn't matter now."

"Lark, please tell us what's wrong," Cazrin said. She brought five cups of steaming chamomile to the table and began passing them out, but only Baldric grabbed one and drank. "This isn't the time for you to hedge or make up a story," she continued. "If there's someone after you, we need to know about it."

"Did you rack up some gambling debts while we were in Neverwinter?" Baldric asked. "Because I can tell you how to take care of that."

Lark picked up one of the cups of tea, cradled it in his hands, then turned and hurled it at the fireplace. The porcelain shattered against the stones, scattering gleaming shards all over the floor.

Uggie whined and ran over to hide behind Cazrin.

"No, Baldric," Lark said bitingly as he wiped tea off his fingers. "This isn't about a gambling debt." He speared Cazrin with a glance. "And sometimes I make up stories because I don't know what the truth is." His voice dropped as he spoke, and he sank back down into his chair.

Tess's face was set in a grim frown. "Go on," she said, waiting for Lark to elaborate.

The bard sighed, giving in. "It started a few months before you recruited me," he said. "Before that tacky dockside theater in Waterdeep, even. I hadn't been in the city long before I realized I was being followed." A haunted look flashed across his face. "It was subtle at first, and I wasn't exactly paying attention. I was still with my old band at that point, and our star was rising quickly. Sold-out shows, festivals, private performances for the nobility—all our dreams were coming true."

"When did you know you were in danger?" Tess asked. She wore an unreadable expression.

"Believe it or not, I got ambushed in an alley." Lark shot Anson a sardonic look. "Luckily, there was extra security on hand for our show that night. They chased off the attackers, so I got away with a couple of broken ribs and a fat lip." He reached for another teacup, but he didn't throw this one. He just wrapped his hands around the warm cup, as if he needed something to hold.

"How do you know they weren't just common cutpurses?" Baldric asked. He took the seat beside Lark.

"Because I practically threw my coin purse at them when they jumped me," Lark said. "Even offered them my lute as they were punching me in the gut, so you can see how desperate I was." His lips thinned. "After that night, they just kept coming back. I never saw their faces—they were always cloaked and hooded, sometimes masked—but I came to recognize their builds and the way they moved, even memorized the cadence of their voices in case I ever heard them in the light of day." He shook his head. "But I've never been able to identify them."

"What about your band?" Cazrin asked. "What did they make of all this?"

"Surely, they could have hired some bodyguards," Anson reasoned, "since your group was doing so well."

Lark sniffed. "I suppose they might have. We discussed it, but much like you all, they assumed this was a gambling debt or some other mess I'd gotten myself into. They didn't believe me when I said I honestly had no idea what the hunters wanted. 'How could you not know?' they said, over and over."

As Lark spoke, his shoulders slumped, and he rubbed his eyes, exacerbating the dark circles beneath them.

The story was making Anson feel worse and worse. He'd messed up. He'd assumed the amulet couldn't be that important to Lark, so he'd taken it without a thought. And he couldn't even go back and retrieve the amulet to make things right. The very magic item he'd given to his brother would make it impossible for him to find Valen.

And if his brother had really orchestrated all this from the beginning . . .

No, he wasn't going to think that, no matter what the others said. Valen wouldn't do that to him. He just wouldn't. He'd come to Anson needing his help, and Anson wasn't about to abandon him.

Everyone was looking to Tess now. Anson expected her to immediately come out with a plan, something to fix the situation, but when he looked over at the elf, he found her uncharacteristically silent. In fact, she looked almost as frustrated as Lark did.

"Why didn't you tell us about any of this?" Tess asked finally. "I know in the beginning you had no reason to trust us—"

"That's right," Lark said, cutting her off. "I didn't know any of you, but I respected the fact that all the rest of you had secrets, pasts that I didn't pry into." He pointed to Cazrin. "Family issues." He canted his head in Baldric's direction. "Deity issues." He glared at Anson. "Worse family issues."

When he looked back at Tess, she spread her hands. "Go ahead," she invited. "What am I hiding?"

Lark's mouth worked. "I haven't found out yet, and that's even scarier! The point is, I was handling things just fine on my own, until Anson decided to put his own needs over the party's. Isn't that what you're always saying, Tess?" he asked pointedly. "That the party comes first?"

"Yes, that is what I've said." Tess glanced at Anson as she spoke. He wilted at the disappointment and anger he saw in her eyes. "Well, you got what you wanted, Anson," she said. "Your brother is safe, and I hope he makes the most of his second chance, because we're the ones who paid for that chance, in the end." She turned back to Lark. "As for you, you may not have owed us an explanation at first, but anything that puts the party in jeopardy is something I needed to know about. You left us exposed and unprepared for too long. But more than that, if you'd told us what was going on, we could have helped you. We would have taken care of it."

Tess stood up and headed toward the back hall. Before she left the room, she glanced over her shoulder. "We still have a job to do, Fallbacks. Baldric needs us, so be ready to leave for Luskan first thing in the morning. Whatever else we have to settle and plan for, we'll do it on the ship. But I need everyone focused on the mission. Got it?"

There were echoes of agreement from Cazrin and Baldric.

Lark said nothing.

Anson glanced over at the fireplace to see that, sometime during their argument, the inn's magic had gathered up all the broken teacup shards, and an intact cup was now sitting on the mantel.

"It fixed it," he murmured, but no one heard him.

CHAPTER 17

Do you really think they're strong enough to help you?
   Baldric knew he was dreaming, but he couldn't wake himself. He was frozen in place, listening to the familiar deep, mocking voice that grated like embers stirred in a fire.
   They can't even fix their own lives. How can they help you with something so vast and terrible as my power? You're wrong to put your faith in them. They are children in a world that will eat them alive.
   Unless I get to them first.
   Baldric woke with a gasp, his heart hammering in his chest. The chill air cooled the sweat dripping down the back of his neck, making him shiver.
   Well, he wasn't getting back to sleep after that.
   Baldric stared at his bedroom ceiling, listening to the deafening silence coming from the rest of the inn. There were none of the usual sounds of rustling bedsheets or loud snores from the other rooms. Which told Baldric that everyone else in the party was probably also lying awake, wrestling with their own personal demons.
   His were just a bit more tangible.
   Giving up, Baldric rose from his bed and slipped out of his room,

walking barefoot toward the common room. The stones cooled his hot feet, bringing him a measure of calm. It reminded him of when he was a child, padding through the winding tunnels of his home, looking for one of his mothers when he couldn't sleep at night.

The feeling of the smooth, hard stone also served as a reminder of what was real and what was a dream.

Baldric shook his head to clear the cobwebs. He just needed a few minutes to gather himself and a drink to warm his belly before he went back to sleep.

But when he entered the common room, he found he wasn't going to have his solitude after all. Lark was sitting in front of the fireplace, poking at a small blaze, while Uggie snored in her bed nearby.

At least someone was getting some sleep, Baldric thought as he passed the otyugh and pulled out a chair from one of the tables. "You know it's the middle of summer," he said, nodding at the fire. "It's not that cold at night."

"Believe it or not, *I* didn't light the fire," Lark said, laying the poker on the hearth stones. "It was here when I arrived." His face creased pensively. "Although I do remember dreaming about long winter nights spent in feast halls, listening to music in front of a roaring fire." He glanced at Baldric. "Surely, that's just a coincidence?"

Baldric sagged into his chair and shrugged. "Who's to say what it's capable of? Cazrin says we've probably only scratched the surface of its magic."

"Maybe we should have let Valen take the inn," Lark said, picking up the poker and stabbing viciously at one of the logs. "I don't know if I like the idea of an entity intruding on my dreams." He shot Baldric a look of chagrin. "Sorry."

"I happen to agree with you," Baldric said dryly. "What's that you've got there?" He pointed to a bottle of zzar that Lark had tucked against his side, cork out and forgotten on the floor. "Holding out on me, are you?"

"I assumed I'd be drinking alone." Lark passed the bottle over. "Can't sleep either?"

Baldric took a sip before replying. "Too crowded in my head these days," he said. "What's your excuse?"

"What else—the brothers Iro." Lark took the bottle back and raised it in a mock toast. "To Valen and Anson, liars and con artists after my own heart." He took a swig, his throat bobbing in the firelight. "You know," he said after he'd swallowed and put the empty bottle aside, "I was half-convinced that our dear Anson didn't have a deceitful bone in his body. He made me dredge up some of my lost faith in good and noble souls." He gave a sardonic chuckle. "Well, that's been taken care of."

"Your anger's more than justified," Baldric said quietly.

Lark's lips curled, and his tail lashed back and forth. "I sense a 'but' coming on. This should be good."

He was raw, Baldric thought. More than he'd expected from the usually flexible bard. "Do you remember the night you came out here and found me doing what you're doing now?" he asked. "It wasn't long after we'd met, and you thought I was going to leave the party."

"I'm going to need another bottle for this conversation," Lark muttered. "Yes, I remember," he said, when Baldric just continued to stare at him patiently. "What of it?"

"You were right, that night," Baldric admitted. "I *was* thinking about leaving. I accused you of being afraid, and I wasn't admitting my own fears." He inclined his head. "I'm sorry for that. Now that I know what you've been holding on to, I feel like I understand you a little better."

"Yes, you know all my dark secrets now," Lark said. He stood up, dusting off his pants as he went over to the bar. Baldric couldn't help but notice that the tavern had already provided another bottle of zzar within easy reach, along with a pair of glasses this time. Lark grabbed everything and brought it back over to the table.

"Why didn't you tell us sooner?" Baldric asked. Unlike Tess, there was no censure in his question. Oh, she had a right to her own anger. She was the party leader, and she had two party members stealing and keeping secrets from her. But for him, it was sheer curiosity. "You helped save this party from two purple worms. Did you really not think we'd have your back against some bounty hunters, or whoever they are?"

"The thought crossed my mind," Lark admitted, pouring two glasses and grabbing one, though he didn't immediately drink. He just stared at the liquid sloshing around in the glass. "But you'd be surprised how many different ways people can disappoint you."

Baldric watched him, thinking back to some of the bard's most intense performances, the songs he'd written about relationships ending in disaster or betrayal. "Is that the real reason why you left your old band?" he asked. "Did they want you gone because of the people hunting you?"

Lark avoided his gaze, staring at the fire again. To Baldric, it appeared to be getting smaller, maybe because he'd been worried about the heat in the room. It was a little disconcerting, he had to admit, the idea that the inn was listening that closely to their desires.

"It wasn't their fault," Lark said at last, dredging up the words. "I didn't tell them I was leaving so much as I slipped out in the middle of the night and ended up halfway down the Sword Coast before I dropped them a note." He winced. "I suppose they had a right to be miffed."

Baldric raised an eyebrow. "But why didn't you tell them—" He stopped. "Ah, I see. You were worried about them, weren't you? Afraid that your problems would get one of them hurt, maybe killed, and you didn't want that."

Lark snorted. "Please, I'm not that altruistic. It was just all becoming a bit much, so I left. There's nothing more to it than that."

"If you say so." Baldric picked up the glass of zzar Lark had poured for him and took another drink. Too sweet for his taste, but the warmth was making him pleasantly drowsy. Maybe he would be able to sleep after all. "If you'd confided in them, they might have been more sympathetic than you thought. Maybe that's a good lesson to learn here too."

"This is veering far too close to a father-son lecture, and I'm getting bored." Lark eyed Baldric, his expression suspicious. "Why are you out here consoling me anyway? You've got bigger problems than any of us. Bargaining with gods, trying not to anger them or dig in too deep at any given moment, and now you've found out that an evil dragon so old he might as well be a god is after you. Yet here you sit, playing counselor to me, listening to me drone on and on about ordinary mortal enemies."

"Best way to forget your own problems is to concern yourself with someone else's," Baldric said. "You may not have a greatwyrm after you, but you're being hunted. You don't know why or by whom, and for the longest time, you've felt like you were on your own to deal with it. I understand that feeling all too well."

He still remembered the night Tess had told him that the Fallbacks would help him deal with the entity. So matter-of-fact, as if he weren't a person they barely knew. Baldric hadn't believed that she would keep her word, even if she wanted to.

Yet here they were, leaving for Luskan tomorrow, seeking answers and a way to fight Ashardalon, even knowing how powerful the greatwyrm was.

He finished his drink and carried the glass to the bar. "I'm going back to bed," he declared, but as he walked past Lark, he put a hand on the tiefling's shoulder. "We're not your old band," he said. "We're not a bunch of musicians out on a tour of the coast. We fought a lich together, and we've saved each other's lives. I think that's worth a little bit of trust."

"Trust, eh?" Lark drawled. "What about Anson, then?"

"He messed up, and he'll make amends somehow," Baldric assured him. "He's probably lying awake in bed right now planning his grand apology."

Lark said nothing.

Baldric sighed and left the tiefling in the common room, though he hesitated for a moment outside his bedroom. Was Lark considering running again? He didn't think the tiefling would do it, but then again, what did he really know about Lark? He was still a damn good liar, and the story he'd told Baldric might be just another tale he spun to gain sympathy.

But something told Baldric there was more truth in it than in all the other tales Lark had told. That was progress, and it was enough to make him head back to bed, trusting that Lark would be there in the morning.

TESS SHIFTED ON her bed, listening to Baldric's footsteps heading back toward his bedroom. She recognized the dwarf's heavier tread, the extra pause on the right from the knee that sometimes pained him. Just as she'd recognized Lark's dancer-like steps earlier, and the soft swish-drag of his tail that happened when he was tired.

How was it, Tess wondered, that she could know her party's movements so well and yet be completely in the dark about the most important aspects of their lives?

She'd tried to build trust with this group. She'd tried to have Mel's patience and tenacity, the belief that they could succeed together. And she thought she'd been making progress.

Now she realized it had all been an illusion. Her party members had stolen and lied, kept secrets that affected the whole group.

If Anson would have confided in her, she could have warned him about Valen's manipulations. But would he have listened?

And if Lark had just told them about the people hunting him, they would have taken care of it. They would have made him feel safe. Or at least they would have tried.

And Tess was their leader, so, ultimately, their behavior in the group was her responsibility. Where had she gone wrong with getting them to trust her?

And how could she fix it?

Tess forced her eyes shut, but she couldn't slip into her usual, peaceful trance. She needed to get her party together or they had no hope of taking on Ashardalon's cult, let alone Ashardalon himself.

Well, if she wasn't going to rest, at least she could plan. Tess rose from her bed and went to sit at her desk in the corner, lighting a candle so she could see. She glanced over at the wall that separated her room from Anson's. She briefly considered going next door to talk to him, to see where they went wrong.

No, she would let him sleep. There would be time for that later.

Bacon.

Sleepy.

Scritches.

Bacon.

Tess looked up as the images pushed their way into her thoughts. Uggie was nudging open her door with a tentacle.

"Well, that's one way to distract me," Tess said, chuckling as the otyugh launched herself onto Tess's bed and flopped down onto her pillow. "I don't have any bacon, but you can sleep here if you want, as long as you don't eat the pillowcase again."

She went over and scratched the otyugh beneath the chin. Almost immediately, Uggie fell asleep, drooling down one side of Tess's pillow.

"At least someone's going to be refreshed and in a good mood tomorrow," Tess murmured.

CHAPTER 18

"I like it," Baldric said as the group made their way down the pier to where their ship, the *Red Nautilus*, was docked. "Small, sleek, fast—good choice, Tess."

"Oh yes, it's a beautiful vessel," Cazrin said, coming to stand next to Baldric, Uggie trotting beside her. The otyugh was once again wearing her disguise, which Cazrin had spent some time refining. That was fortunate, because it would be hard to hide her in broad daylight on the deck of the ship.

When no one else spoke, Baldric glanced over his shoulder to see the rest of the group lagging several yards behind. Tess, Anson, and Lark looked like they hadn't rested at all, and though Baldric was still a bit tired, he found himself in good spirits now that they were getting the mission underway. Cazrin too seemed to be her usual good-natured self, after spending the evening with Rane.

"Well," the wizard said, leaning closer to Baldric and dropping her voice as she too surveyed the stragglers, "what do you suppose we should do to cheer them up?"

"*We?*" He slanted her a look. "This isn't really my area of expertise." He was still worn out from talking to Lark last night, and he wasn't sure he'd done any good. "Why don't you take this one?"

"Even I can't possibly do this alone," Cazrin said, heading for the gangplank. "We need to divide and conquer."

Baldric followed her up. "Fine," he said, "how about you take Anson, and I'll take Tess?"

Cazrin cocked her head in consideration. "Why are we splitting it that way? I'm sure I can cheer Tess up."

"Of course you can," Baldric agreed. "But I need you for Anson—family issues," he clarified. "You can relate."

"Fair." Cazrin shifted the satchel of books she was carrying. She'd finally replaced all the ones that had been fire-damaged by the Ruinous Child. "What about Lark? Am I getting him too?"

Baldric watched the bard shuffling down the pier toward them. He hadn't tried to sneak away in the night, but there was a hunch to the bard's shoulders and a wary shadow in his eyes that he hadn't had the night of the party. That was disheartening.

"No, I'll take him," Baldric said. "Lark's an ongoing challenge." His gaze lifted to the horizon. "I'm hoping it'll be better once we're on the open water."

Because if nothing else, it was a glorious day for sailing. The sun cast bright shards of light on the water's surface, and the breeze lessened the ever-present heat. It had been a long time since he'd been aboard a ship, but Baldric felt the familiar, subtle shift in his stance as he stepped onto the deck, and suddenly he couldn't wait to get underway.

On the quarterdeck, a figure in a long, dark coat turned their way. She was a tall, reddish-furred tabaxi, with a wavy scar cutting across her chin and bright yellow eyes that assessed the Fallbacks as they came onto the ship one by one.

"Welcome aboard," she called out, raising one clawed hand in greeting as she strode over to Tess. "You're on time—that's good."

"We're all here and ready to depart when you are," Tess said. To the others, she added, "This is Captain Imber of the *Red Nautilus*. We spoke yesterday. Captain, these are the Fallbacks."

She introduced them all. Baldric noticed Anson and Lark sticking to the back of the group and staying as far away from each other as they could.

Fortunately, Imber didn't seem to notice the tension threading through the party. She gave a nod to everyone. "We're packed in pretty tight for this trip," she said, "so you'll be sharing quarters, but the weather looks fair today, so we should make good time. We'll get underway once the rest of our passengers arrive." Her gaze fell on Uggie the sheepdog, and she pursed her lips in displeasure. "Make sure you clean up after your pet and keep it out from underfoot."

"Absolutely," Cazrin promised, as Uggie ran to the ship's starboard side and put her paws up on the rail. The wind blew into her face, and she let out a crooning yip that didn't sound anything like a dog.

Baldric heard one of the crew members working near Uggie mumble to another, "I could really use a sandwich, couldn't you?"

"Aw, I know what you mean," her partner said. "Big piece of raw chicken on buttered bread. The best."

The woman arched an eyebrow, and the man cleared his throat. "I mean, *roast* chicken, with beans stewed in dirt clods and... wait..." He put his hand to his temple and rubbed. "I think I need to go lie down for a minute."

Baldric shook his head as the man tottered away. He turned to Cazrin. "This is going to be a disaster."

"Uggie's just excited," Cazrin said, trotting over to pull the otyugh away from the rail so she wouldn't fall overboard. She towed the struggling "dog" back over to Baldric. "She can't keep her thoughts to herself right now, but she'll settle down."

Baldric nodded absently, but his attention was drawn to another group of figures striding up the gangplank. A human woman walked in front, with long, straight black hair draping down her back. She wore a full cloak with the hood down, but as the wind tossed the fabric, he could just get a glimpse of fine leather armor and the bulge of a weapon beneath it.

Behind the woman walked three other figures: another human, a blue-skinned tiefling, and a goliath, all similarly cloaked and armed. It reminded Baldric of the people hunting Lark. Could these be some of them? Likely not, but still, now that he knew someone was after the bard, Baldric resolved to keep a closer watch on the group's surroundings, especially in these tight quarters on board the ship.

Anson apparently had the same idea, for he drifted over to Baldric, pretending to look up at the sails as he murmured, "You noticed them too?"

"Mm-hmm," Baldric replied. "Well armed and capable-looking, but then, so are we. Let's just keep an eye on them for now."

The fighter nodded and wandered off, and Baldric stepped out of the way as Captain Imber shouted orders to the crew to make ready to sail. He had a feeling that, one way or another, it was going to be an eventful voyage.

Thankfully, the next few hours passed without incident, and when they reached the mouth of the River Chionthar and struck out into the Sea of Swords, Baldric stood at the rail and turned his face toward the setting sun. The salty air blew through his beard, and overhead a pair of gulls wheeled and squawked. He savored the moment of peace as the *Red Nautilus* quickly put the coast behind them and headed north.

That's when Baldric noticed Cazrin approaching Anson, who stood talking to a couple of the crew at the base of the crow's nest. He'd wondered how soon she would enact her plan to boost party morale. It seemed she wasn't wasting any time.

Only when she'd almost reached him did Baldric notice that the wizard's face was covered in sweat, and she was turning an alarming shade of green. As he watched, she teetered, covered her mouth with one hand, then turned and sprinted to the railing, where she leaned far over the side.

Baldric didn't see her emptying her lunch into the sea—he was distracted by Lark doing the exact same thing on the port side of the ship, although he hadn't managed to reach the railing and had instead painted the deck with the contents of his stomach.

"Really?" Baldric put his hands on his hips, squinting at the sky in the general direction of the gods or whoever else might be listening to his plight. "That's how it's going to be, then?" He shook his head and went to find Tess.

She wasn't hard to spot, her light blond hair whipping around her face as she stood at the bow of the ship, head bent to examine the figurehead attached to the vessel. It was a carved nautilus, its chambers echoing with the hollow sound of the wind. It wasn't the best depiction Baldric had seen, but he appreciated the way the artist had managed to make it seem as if the creature were emerging from the prow, as if the ship itself were transforming, becoming something new.

Tess looked up as Baldric approached. Her cheeks were windburned, and the sun had made her freckles more visible, but she wasn't showing any signs of seasickness. That was some luck.

"Lark and Cazrin are down," Baldric said, hooking a thumb over his shoulder.

Tess looked where he pointed and wrinkled her nose. "I had a feeling Lark wouldn't take to the water, but I didn't expect Cazrin to go down so quickly."

"Tirin!" Captain Imber yelled from the crow's nest down to one of the deckhands, a gangly human boy with straw-colored hair and freckles all over his face. "Get your mop and bucket and clean up that mess! What are you waiting for?"

Tess pulled her hair back and tied it into a quick braid to keep it out of her face. "Can you do anything for them?" she asked Baldric. "We need them functional tonight; I want to have a planning session for when we reach Luskan."

"I'll take care of them," Baldric assured her. He winced at the sound of more retching coming from Lark. Did the bard do *nothing* quietly? "Once their stomachs are empty, I mean."

"Good, thank you." Tess turned back to stare at the open sea, a distracted look on her face.

Baldric briefly considered leaving her be. Outwardly, she seemed fine.

But he knew better.

The Tess he knew would be up in the crow's nest right now, learning about every aspect of the ship and probably assigning Lark to help the crew as part of his training. Instead, here she was, off by herself, with only the figurehead for company.

He cleared his throat to get Tess's attention. "Listen," he said when she turned, "I haven't gotten a chance to say it yet, what with everything going on, but I wanted to thank you."

Tess's pale brows rose in surprise. "For what?" she asked. "I just asked you to take care of our seasick passengers. There's *vomit* involved."

He chuckled. "True, and I'll pay you back for that later. But I meant . . ." He paused, gathering his thoughts. "You're keeping your promise to me. About dealing with the entity—Ashardalon. It means a lot."

"I said we would help." Tess cocked her head. "You didn't believe me?"

Baldric shrugged. "When I was a merchant, people made me promises all the time. But it was mostly talk and bluster. I accepted that as part of the business, but it can still make you a cynic if you're not careful."

Tess's lips twitched. "You, a cynic? Perish the thought."

"Ha," he said. "The point is, I don't tend to expect much of people, even when they're well intentioned, like you are." He dipped his head, not quite meeting her eyes. "I didn't expect anything to come of your promise, even if I wanted to believe in it." He spread his hands. "Yet here we are, and I know things aren't perfect right now—"

"A disaster, you mean," Tess said, her humor fading. "I heard you say it earlier, and you're not wrong."

He shook his head. "It's a disaster we'll come back from, Tess. That's what I'm trying to say. You'll get us there, even if you have to drag everyone kicking and screaming. I have faith in that." He patted her arm. "And in the meantime, I'll do what I can to help you hold the others together. You're not on your own. Isn't that what you told me once?"

Tess blinked, her eyes glistening for a second before she cleared her throat and looked out to sea. "Damn this salty air anyway," she said. "It's terrible on my eyes."

"The worst," Baldric agreed.

They turned away from the horizon, walking past a confused-looking Tirin, who was holding a mop and a bucket of water, looking around for something to clean. Lark was still draped over the side of the ship, but the mess he'd left behind earlier was gone.

"Don't just stand there, boy!" the captain yelled down again. "Clean up that deck!"

"Um, of course, Captain!" Tirin called back. "Right away." He wandered off, stepping around sheepdog Uggie, who was rolling around happily on the deck.

CHAPTER 19

"Everyone comfortable?" Tess asked as the group squeezed into the tiny cabin that she, Cazrin, and Uggie were sharing. Baldric, Anson, and Lark's room next door was just slightly bigger, but it smelled too much like fish for everyone's liking, so they'd chosen to have their meeting here instead.

"Comfortable?" Lark said incredulously. He was squished into the farthest corner of the room. A lantern perched on a side table illuminated his sallow features. Baldric had worked his magic on the bard and Cazrin to get them upright, but neither of them looked good. Cazrin was propped up against Anson on the opposite side of the room, fanning herself with one limp hand.

Baldric was sitting near the only porthole in the room. Faint moonlight shone on a circle of floor next to him, where Uggie was asleep, letting out loud, honking snores at regular intervals.

"Bad choice of words," Tess amended. "I won't keep us here any longer than necessary, but we need to talk plans. I want to arrive in Luskan ready to go straight to the Hosttower, with everyone on the same page." Her gaze lingered on Anson and Lark, but the bard's eyes were half closed, and Anson was helping to fan Cazrin and wouldn't meet her gaze.

Tess suppressed a sigh. But, remembering Baldric's words, she drew herself up and pressed on. "I think if we explore the Hosttower in one big group, it's going to attract too much attention. We need to split into two groups for this."

That prompted groans from everyone. Tess couldn't exactly blame them. It felt like nothing good ever came of them splitting up, though she couldn't fathom why.

"Hear me out," Tess said. She leaned forward on a rickety three-legged stool. "Two groups with two separate missions gets us into different parts of the tower simultaneously. I've already spoken to Cazrin about how we can keep in contact magically to keep everyone informed of our movements and progress."

"Assuming magical communication isn't restricted within the tower," Cazrin pointed out. "That's something I can't guarantee since I'm not familiar with its inner workings."

"You're saying there's a chance we might be cut off from each other from the very beginning?" Anson said. "I don't like that idea."

"I've made allowances for that," Tess said, undeterred. "One of our first jobs in Luskan will be information-gathering about the tower. When we do go in, we won't be flying blind."

"What's the cover story for each of the groups?" Baldric wanted to know.

"Glad you asked." Tess pointed to him. "You, me, and Lark will be making contact with Mel's wizard on the inside, Vellynne Harpell. She's the ace up our sleeve. We let her know about the cult activity, and she'll get us access to search parts of the tower that we may not otherwise be able to see."

Anson scowled. "Again, we're putting faith in something that may not pan out," he said. "What if this Harpell wizard isn't even at the tower when we get there?"

Tess gritted her teeth. What was Anson doing? Was he trying to be difficult just to get under her skin? "I trust Mel's information," she said curtly. "Harpell will be there." She turned to Cazrin. "In the meantime, Cazrin will lead the second group. As we discussed before, she'll be applying for membership in the Arcane Brotherhood, with Anson and Uggie as her bodyguards."

Everyone looked over at Cazrin, whose sweaty face lit with a spark of excitement. "Really?" she said. "I like it."

"I do too." Baldric stroked his beard thoughtfully. "Fresh off her encounter with a powerful, sentient tome, it makes sense she'd be looking for the next step in her studies. It's a good cover."

"Hopefully, I'll be able to request a tour of the place and search that way," Cazrin mused.

"I don't know if we should be letting our dear Cazrin loose in a tower full of magic," Lark said, managing the first hint of humor Tess had seen in him since he'd lost his amulet. "She'll settle in and forget all about us lowly adventurers."

Cazrin chuckled. "Let's not get ahead of ourselves." She sobered. "But I can handle this. I think splitting up is what's needed here." This she aimed at Anson, who lapsed into silence.

"All right, if we're all agreed, then let's get some sleep," Tess said. "We should reach Luskan by nightfall tomorrow."

"As long as we're on land," Lark mumbled, dragging himself to his feet.

Cazrin patted him on the back in commiseration. "Some of us just weren't meant for life on the water," she agreed.

"And some of us don't have the spells to keep up with seasickness," Baldric said dryly, heading out of the room.

Lark went to follow, but Anson caught the bard's arm. "Can I talk to you for a minute?" he asked, his big frame filling up the small doorway. "I owe you an apology, and I'd really like the chance to make amends before we go any further on this mission."

Across the room, Cazrin stilled as she was shaking out a blanket from her travel pack. Tess pretended to arrange some stacks of papers on the small hammock-side table while listening for Lark's response. If the two of them could come to an understanding before they made landfall in Luskan, it would go a long way toward easing her worries about what was to come and whether the group was ready to handle it.

But the bard brushed off Anson's arm and turned away. "Sorry," he said, his tone flippant, "I suddenly feel another bout of vomiting coming on. Wouldn't want you to be in the path of that."

And then he was gone.

Anson hung there awkwardly in the doorway for a moment before he walked away. The wooden ladder leading up to the deck creaked under his weight.

Tess was torn. Her instinct was to go try to comfort Anson. He was making an effort, and she appreciated that. But a part of her was still frustrated with him, and the way he'd questioned her judgment just now, in front of everyone, hadn't cooled her temper any.

Cazrin put her blanket down on her hammock and headed for the door. "I'll talk to him," she said.

Tess gave her a grateful smile. "Thank you," she said. "I just don't . . ." She couldn't find the words.

Cazrin nodded. "I know," she said. "It's never easy, fighting with your best friend. Sometimes you need an outside perspective."

Tess swallowed. "I hope he still is . . . my best friend, I mean." It was painful to admit it, but at the same time, saying the words out loud lifted a weight Tess hadn't realized had grown so heavy.

"Of course he is." Cazrin came over to Tess and seized her hand, giving it a squeeze. "This is *Anson* we're talking about. You know he's not going to give up on your friendship that easily."

Tess wanted to believe that, but her doubts and fears must have shown on her face, because Cazrin went on, "Anson is your rock, the person you lean on when things get tough. And he does his job so well, I think we've all come to see him as indestructible." She smiled sadly. "But no one can be that strong all the time, can they? Everyone breaks, and when family is involved, it can hurt so much."

"I—" Tess stopped, forcing herself to consider Cazrin's words. She was right. Anson was her right hand, the one she turned to when everything went wrong. She'd been so scared of losing that.

But she'd never considered how hard it was to be that person, to take on that burden. Anson had done it over and over, without complaint, even as he grappled with his own pain and his relationship with Valen.

She looked up at Cazrin. "He's been struggling, hasn't he? And I missed it." She shook her head. She felt awful. "How could I have missed it? Like you said, he's my best friend."

Cazrin squeezed her hand again. "You can't be everything for everyone all the time either," she said. "Trust me, Anson's going to come through this all right. I should know—I've been where he is now."

She had, and Tess was reminded again of what a remarkable person Cazrin was. She'd endured her own struggles, and now she saw the people around her as clearly as she saw her own magic.

"Thank you," Tess said. She took in the wizard's pale face, determined to do better at noticing what her party members were going through. "How are you holding up?"

The wizard considered. "I love being on the open ocean, but I wish my hair didn't smell like vomit," she said. "We can never get everything we want, can we?"

Tess chuckled. "A truth for the ages."

CAZRIN FOUND ANSON standing at the rail on the starboard side of the ship, gazing down at the dark water. The pitch and roll of the deck still assailed her insides with the occasional wave of nausea, but Baldric's magic had eased the worst of it. Cazrin lifted her face to the wind, drew a breath of the fresh, cool air, and went to stand next to Anson.

When he turned to look at her, his face was pinched in misery. "I keep messing up," he said. "I don't know how to fix this! Lark won't even talk to me, and Tess is still mad at me."

"I think she was frustrated that you were questioning her plan in front of the others," Cazrin pointed out as gently as she could. "Tess is never going to like that."

"I wasn't trying to question her!" Anson said, scrubbing a hand over his face. "I was just trying to contribute. She says I've been distracted, so I was trying to let her know that I was listening and thinking about the plan and . . ." He looked at Cazrin and groaned. "I stepped in it again, didn't I?"

"It's going to be all right," Cazrin said. She gripped the railing as the deck pitched gently. "You and Tess will talk, and Lark will come around eventually. You'll see."

"You know what the worst part is?" Anson said softly. "I keep thinking, what if Lark was right? What if Valen was just conning me all along, and I broke everyone's trust in me for *nothing*?"

"Oh, Anson." Cazrin took a step closer and put her arm around his broad shoulders. "You made a mistake. Everyone makes mistakes, especially where family is concerned."

"How did you handle it?" Anson asked. "Your family being so different from you? Valen and I—sometimes it feels like we aren't really brothers at all."

"I left," Cazrin said simply. Her family feared magic because her ancestress had misused it, so they'd forbidden Cazrin from studying it. That's when she'd known she had to leave. She still felt the sting and the consequences of that decision, but she couldn't bring herself to regret it, not considering where it had led her since. "I loved my family—I still do—and I wanted so much for them to be proud of me. But I couldn't change myself to be what they wanted me to be and give up the things that I thought were important. I felt like I was betraying them when I left to study magic, but if I had stayed, I would have been betraying myself."

Anson nodded, but he looked pained. "Valen said something like that to me when we were arguing. He told me he was never going to be like me." He looked at Cazrin. "Is that what I've been trying to do all these years? Make him miserable by betraying who he is?" He gripped the railing, shoulders tense. "I wasn't trying to . . . but maybe that was the whole problem. I was trying to do what was best for *me*, not him."

"You were doing it because you love him, and you want him to be safe," Cazrin said. "The choices your brother has made, the life he's chosen to live, it's not an easy or a safe path. I don't blame you for wanting him to choose differently, but we can't control the people we love. All we can do is support them. You helped Valen, gave him a chance to be safe and maybe seek out a better life. That's all you can do."

"You're right," Anson said. His throat bobbed as he swallowed. "It's just so hard to feel helpless, like I can't fix anything."

"Sometimes broken things need to mend on their own," Cazrin said. She leaned into him and was happy to feel some of the tension ease from his shoulders. "And some things need a little help. Keep trying with Lark. He'll come around. You'll see."

He gave her a wavering smile. "Thanks, Cazrin," he said. "It's really great being able to talk to you like this."

"You're welcome." Cazrin laid a hand on her stomach as it clenched and gurgled. She groaned. She'd known trying to eat that apple earlier had been a mistake. She stepped away from Anson, toward the railing, and gave him a look of chagrin. "If you'll excuse me for a moment, I'm afraid it's time to throw up again."

She expected him to scurry away as fast as possible, but he didn't. He stayed and held her hair back.

CHAPTER 20

Uggie did not like this boat. The ground beneath her was constantly moving, up and down, up and down. It made her belly feel funny, and it was upsetting her persons. There was water *everywhere*, but she couldn't get to it to drink it, and there was NOT ENOUGH FOOD!

Above her, Cazrin person swayed back and forth in her cloth bed and mumbled in her sleep, "Not enough food..."

Cazrin person was hungry too.

That settled it. Uggie would get her persons some food. If she didn't, they might starve, and then Uggie would never forgive herself.

Slowly, she crept from beneath the swinging bed, shrugging off the big blanket that Cazrin person insisted Uggie wear, even though it was hot and scratchy and Uggie didn't like it. Once she was free of the clinging monster, Uggie immediately felt better.

Stretching her tentacles, she inched her way over to the door, nudging it open with her eyestalk. Quickly, she scurried out into the dark hallway. She could smell her other persons in the room next to this one, but she didn't try to get into the room. There was no food in there either, and Uggie was on a *mission* for food.

For her persons, of course.

Keeping close to the wall, Uggie made her way down the hall, sniffing the air as she went. She caught the faint whiff of rodent hair before a small rat squeezed its way underneath the door to her right and out into the hall. The creature didn't see Uggie crouching in the shadows and ran straight toward her. Dropping to the floor, Uggie scooped the unfortunate rat into her mouth.

Ah, the taste of it brought back good memories in Uggie, memories of her time stalking the sewers and feasting on the biggest rats she'd ever seen. She wondered if there were more rats hiding in the room where that one had come from. Oh, but her persons didn't like rats. Uggie had tried bringing them some as a treat, and they had not been happy. Still, there was another smell wafting from beneath the door to the rat room. A scent of cured meat, fruit, and nuts.

Uggie could work with that.

She thumped her way across the hall, hooking the end of one tentacle around the door latch and tugging. It swung open, protesting with a loud *creeeeaaaak*. Flinching, Uggie looked left and right to make sure no one had heard before scrambling inside the room. It was full, crammed wall to wall with boxes, barrels, and crates. The most tantalizing of smells wafted to her nose. The nearest crate was nailed shut, but that didn't trouble her.

Uggie had plenty of teeth, and they were sharp.

When she finally stumbled out of the room sometime later, it was still dark, but Uggie's belly was full—she'd even found a few more rats—and she swayed happily as she lumbered down the hall, back toward Tess person and Cazrin person's room.

Uggie stopped dead.

She'd eaten all the food.

She'd eaten all the food, and she'd forgotten to bring some back for her persons!

Panic seized her, but Uggie forced herself to remain calm. She was excellent in a crisis. She could fix this. She would just have to seek out more food. It was still dark. She could search the rest of the boat before anyone saw—

"Who's out there? What's all that noise?"

Uggie froze as a door swung open at the end of the hall. Light spilled onto the floor, threatening to expose her, but Uggie darted away from it and down the hall as fast as she could, heading for the narrow ladder that led up to the top deck.

"What's going on out here?"

The voice was louder this time. Wrapping her tentacles around the wooden ladder, Uggie gave a mighty pull, hoisting herself up, rung by rung. When she was almost at the top of the ladder, she swiveled her eyestalk in the direction the voice had come from, but whoever it was must have been calling out from one of the other rooms, because Uggie didn't see anyone in the darkness.

If she was caught out of bed, the other persons on board might take Uggie back to her room and thwart her important food mission. Uggie couldn't have that.

With a low growl, Uggie redoubled her efforts, pulling herself the rest of the way up the ladder, finally popping out onto the shifting deck of the boat. The air smelled thickly of salt. Overhead, a large white bird circled the ship, outlined by the sliver of moon hanging in the sky.

Uggie sighed. Birds were delicious. There was yet another source of food, so close, yet still so far out of reach.

She sniffed, trying to pick out the scent of food up here, but it was hard. Everything was so salty . . .

Wait.

Uggie's nose twitched as she detected the faint but delicious smell of ham and . . . was that cheese? And . . . *pickles*?

Uggie loved pickles, and so did Tess person.

Quiet as a shadow, she followed the delightful smells across the deck to a short flight of steps. At the top, she could see the outline of a figure standing behind a large wheel. He was about as tall as Baldric person and had the same kind of beard, though it was red and not nearly as long and magnificent as Baldric person's. But it was still managing to catch and store small bits of ham and bread that were falling from a sandwich the figure held in one hand, while he used his other hand to hold the big wheel steady.

Uggie crept stealthily up the steps, slithering along on her belly. If she was quick and careful, she might be able to charge the sandwich wielder and knock him off the boat and into the water. He would drop his sandwich, and Uggie would catch it before it fell into the water after him.

Uggie liked this plan.

She hunkered down low to the deck, scrunching her three little legs to prepare for a surprise charge, when suddenly, a bright golden light spilled across the deck, catching her fully in its glow.

"There it is! Kill the monster! Kill it!"

Uggie spun in time to see two persons coming up the ladder. One of them held up a lantern, shining its light right on her. The other one was holding a big curved bow with a wicked-looking arrow, and it was pointed right at Uggie.

"Shoot it, Sim!"

Uggie braced herself. She wasn't afraid. She'd faced far worse things than these persons. Whipping out her tentacles to make herself as big as possible, she opened her mouth and gave a menacing howl.

The man holding the weapon paled, but he kept his hand steady on his bowstring as he pulled it back, aimed—

And froze in place as a sweet, soft melody drifted across the deck from somewhere in the darkness.

Uggie let her tentacles drop and stared at her attackers. The man with the lantern had also gone completely still, his eyes wide and fearful.

"Let's all take a moment to calm down," said a familiar voice.

Uggie looked across the deck. Out of the darkness stepped Lark person, holding his song box and looking at the two men with an expression he usually wore only when he discovered Uggie had chewed on his hat.

Lark person strode across the deck to Uggie, put a hand on his hip, and stared down at her. "What have you done this time?"

CHAPTER 21

"I can explain," Tess assured Captain Imber. The Fallbacks stood on one side of the deck with what looked like half the crew standing opposite, hands on their weapon hilts as they stared down at Uggie, who was wedged between Lark and Baldric. The latter had a protective hand on one of her tentacles.

She wasn't quite sure *how* she was going to explain—that sometime during the night, their pet otyugh had shed her disguise, slipped out of her and Cazrin's room, and managed to eat through half the ship's food stores, a barrel of rum, and two crates of expensive truffle mushrooms the ship was transporting to a wealthy merchant family in Luskan.

That one was going to cost them.

Was *everyone* in Tess's party determined to wreak havoc on her life?

"I want that creature off my ship," the tabaxi said, the fur on her arms standing up as she regarded Tess, her lip curled in disgust. "It's dangerous cargo that you concealed and brought on board without anyone's knowledge. Throw it overboard, and maybe I won't turn you over to the authorities in Luskan as soon as we hit the docks."

"Now, now, there's no need to be talking like that," said Anson. He tucked his thumbs into his belt, his stance deceptively relaxed as he kept his hand close to the hilt of his blade. "No one's throwing anyone overboard."

"We'll pay for all the damage our companion did to your cargo," Tess said, lifting the weighty coin pouch from her belt for emphasis. Her hand crossbow was within easy reach, but she didn't think it would come to that. "Plus interest for the inconvenience to you and the scare Uggie gave your crew. We didn't conceal her true nature for nefarious reasons. We simply do it so that her presence won't unsettle people. She's perfectly harmless."

Imber made a noise of disbelief. Fortunately, she was eyeing the coin pouch with interest. Tess suspected some of Imber's anger and bluster was an act, aimed at just this kind of extortion. Although Tess doubted the tabaxi had ever extorted anyone over an otyugh before. She should have expected this on a ship that operated out of Luskan, but once again, she'd been distracted by other things, and she'd missed an important detail.

"The cargo your pet destroyed was extremely costly and hard to come by," Imber warned. "And you're going to need to keep that thing belowdecks, locked in one of your rooms, at all times."

"Is that really necessary?" Baldric spoke up. He stood near Tess, wearing an amused expression. He nodded at Uggie. "She's a young one of her kind, and she hasn't harmed you or any of your crew. I'm sure there's a deal to be made here." Tess noticed him standing so that his cloth of holy symbols was clearly visible. "I thought I saw a couple of your crew looking sickly, maybe a little sluggish." The dwarf cocked his head. "I'd be willing to take a look at them if it would help smooth the way here."

Imber's gaze turned speculative. "It's true, we've had a bout of illness run through the ship—some vegetables in our last shipment that had spoiled. It's put us behind schedule."

"We'd be happy to help you with that," Tess said. She held out the pouch of coins. "What do you think? Can we forgive and forget?"

Imber took the pouch, clawed fingers curling around the leather. She weighed it in her hand, met Tess's eyes, then nodded. "We have a deal," she said, adding, "as long as there's nothing else you're hiding."

"Nothing at all," Tess assured her, and held out her hand to shake on it.

Imber clasped her forearm briefly and then turned to the rest of the crew. "All right, the rest of you break it up! Nothing more to see here today. Go about your business, ignore the otyugh, and it'll ignore you."

Gradually, everyone moved off, going back to their respective jobs. Tess breathed a quiet sigh of relief. "Thanks," she said to Baldric, as the rest of the party gathered around. "That was quick thinking."

Baldric snorted. "Well, she wasn't going to be closed up in *our* room, that's for sure. Not after eating all that jerky."

Cazrin leaned down and scratched Uggie beneath her chin. "No more getting into trouble for the rest of the trip," she said. "You've learned your lesson, haven't you?"

"I'll keep an eye on her," Anson promised. He patted Uggie on the head. "No more sneaking off at night either," he said.

"That's funny, coming from the master of slipping away on his own," Lark muttered.

"Let's focus, everyone," Tess said, before tempers could flare. "Back to the mission. We've still got some planning to do and—"

"Hold up a minute," Baldric said. He gave a subtle nod toward the main mast, his gaze lifting to the crow's nest.

Tess glanced up. One of their fellow passengers, the woman with the dark hair and fine leather armor, stood in the crow's nest, looking down at them.

No, Tess realized. She was looking at Baldric. An amused smile curved her lips as she beckoned him to join her.

It was the first time Tess had seen her on the main deck since their voyage began. Something about that smile, and the way the woman looked down on them all, made uneasiness snake up her spine. She'd learned through hard experience not to ignore that feeling.

"Something we should know about, Baldric?" Lark asked, one

eyebrow cocked in curiosity. "Are you making new friends on this trip? Taking new lovers?"

"If I did, it'd be none of your business," Baldric said, "but no, the woman and I are not acquainted."

"It looks like she wants to be," Anson observed.

"She wants something," Tess said, "but I don't know if I trust whatever it is."

"You think it's something to do with Uggie?" Cazrin asked. "Maybe she doesn't like the idea of an otyugh on board the ship either."

"Maybe she noticed my holy symbols and was curious, just like Keevi," Baldric said.

"Or maybe it's a threat," Lark said, giving voice to what Tess had been thinking.

"We can speculate, but there's really only one way to find out," Baldric said. He put on his helm. "I'll go up there and talk to her."

Tess nodded. "Be careful," she said. "The rest of us will be down here acting casual, but we'll be ready to back you up if she's not friendly." She nodded at Lark and Cazrin. "You two find a good place to use your magic in case it's needed. Uggie and I will stay near the crow's nest."

"What about me?" Anson asked, glancing at Tess hopefully.

Tess met his eyes, thought for a second, then said, "Stay near me and back me up?" She didn't mean to phrase it as a question, but she was still feeling unsure of just where she stood with Anson.

His face immediately brightened. "Absolutely."

"All right, let's do it," Tess said, and the group broke up.

It was a small thing, but it was the closest the Fallbacks had come to acting in accord for days. Tess took it as a good sign, but it couldn't quell her uneasiness as Baldric climbed the ladder to join the woman.

THERE WAS AN unexpected chill in the air when Baldric reached the top of the crow's nest. The western sky had darkened, and the smell of rain sat heavily in the salty air. Still, it was a breathtaking view. An anvil cloud stretched across the wide, storm-blue horizon, and whitecaps teased the surface of the sea.

Baldric took a moment to appreciate the view, and to quietly survey the woman standing before him. Up close, he noticed that her eyes were such a deep shade of brown they looked almost black, a sharp contrast to her pale, angular face. He guessed she was in her late thirties. Her hair was the color of fresh ink, and she looked at him the way some of the elder merchant families of his clan did when sizing up their competition.

He'd never liked that look. Hungry.

"You wanted to talk to me?" Baldric asked. "If it's about the otyugh, we're not paying off everyone on the ship, so don't bother."

The woman nodded to the horizon. "I was just watching the oncoming storm and thought you might also admire it. Nothing but the wind to intrude on our solitude."

"What a lovely sentiment," Baldric said dryly. "Is that the only reason?"

The woman regarded him thoughtfully. Then she lifted her hands and pushed back her hood, allowing the wind to whip her dark hair around her shoulders. "I want to know what it is my master sees in you, Baldric Goodhand," she said.

"Your master?" A coldness seized Baldric, but he did his best to affect a bored tone. "Who's that? And who are you? Because if you're going to play games, I'm not—"

"You may call me Antea," the woman interrupted. "It's as good a name as any, even if it isn't my true one." Her smile widened. "And you bluff well, but I can see by the shadows in your eyes that you already know who my master is."

She took a step toward him. Baldric stood his ground. There was little room up here, and no place to go, so he stared her down. "You're a part of the cult, then?" he guessed. "Did you pay the caretaker of the Sunless Citadel to tell you who had breached it, or did you track us some other way?"

Antea gave him a pitying look. "Don't you know by now that you're always being watched?" she asked. "Ashardalon the wise and powerful looks down upon his *favored*"—she said the word like it was something foul as she looked at Baldric—"and follows them wherever they go in the world. But yes, I tracked you from the citadel, because I had to see for myself how my master could have chosen a weak, non-believing, blasphemous creature like you to be his servant."

Baldric's thoughts raced as he tried to sort out the woman's intentions. Had she and her companions been sent to capture him, to bring him to Ashardalon? Cazrin had read that the greatwyrm had made his domain on the Astral Plane, someplace called the Bastion of Broken Souls. He wasn't about to let himself be taken there, unless it was over his cold, dead body.

But the murderous glint in Antea's eyes suggested that she'd much rather see him a corpse than a captive. Ashardalon had dropped many cryptic hints about the plans he had for him, but Baldric had never thought they included his death.

What was going on here?

"Are you satisfied with what you've seen, then?" Baldric asked, palms sweating, itching to reach for his mace. But he needed more information. He needed to know what they were dealing with here. "Was it worth it to follow me all the way out here?"

"Oh, I believe it was," Antea said, glancing at the empty expanse of horizon that just a few minutes ago had seemed so beautiful, and that was now making Baldric realize just how vulnerable he and the Fallbacks were. "I think I've chosen the perfect spot."

Keeping his expression neutral, Baldric made a subtle gesture to Lark and Cazrin below. Seconds later, he felt the magic of a spell take hold and heard an answering signal from Lark that sounded like a seagull's call.

"But I still don't understand why it was you," Antea said, a fury sparking in her eyes. The flap of her cloak fell back, revealing a scimitar strapped to her hip. Runes carved into the blade shone with magical radiance. "I served my master faithfully for many long years," she went on. "I have reclaimed knowledge and ancient magic that were once his. I have put his name on the lips of followers who would now gladly die for his glory."

"Sounds as if you're very committed," Baldric said, leaning back against the railing of the crow's nest, muscles tense in preparation. "The two of you obviously deserve each other."

"Yet he chose *you!*" Antea's pupils dilated, making her eyes go completely black. "I demand to know why. What did you promise him? What did you offer that could possibly eclipse all that I am?"

"I don't serve Ashardalon," Baldric growled, feeling his own anger rise. "I'm not his toy, and whatever plans he has for me, I won't be a part of them."

"On that, we most certainly agree," said Antea, and then she laughed, a loud and unsettling sound that lifted the hairs on the back of Baldric's neck. He heard murmurs drifting up from the deck below. A quick glance showed him the crew had noticed the two of them up here. They were probably wondering what was going on.

That was the one thing Baldric hadn't accounted for. If there was going to be a fight, he liked his chances against Antea and her cultists, but he didn't want to put the rest of the crew in danger.

"Let's settle this on land, then," he said. "There's no need for anyone here to be involved. And you don't want to draw undue attention to your master, I'm sure."

"Oh, don't worry," Antea said. "Ships disappear often out here. They run afoul of all manner of storms and strange creatures. It's truly sad."

And then Baldric saw it.

A speck of color appeared on the cloud-filled horizon behind Antea's shoulder. From this distance, it might have been a gull or a heron, but with a sinking feeling in his gut, Baldric knew that it was not. As the shape drew closer, a flash of lightning showed him a wide span of leathery wings and dusky reddish-brown scales. For a heart-stopping moment, Baldric thought it was Ashardalon himself, come to swallow the ship whole. But though it was big, this creature was not a greatwyrm or a dragon. It had only two scaly legs, and a long tail tipped with a wicked-looking curved stinger big enough to impale a person through the chest.

It was a wyvern, and it was headed right for the ship.

The time for subtlety was over. "Fallbacks!" Baldric shouted.

And drew his mace.

CHAPTER 22

Baldric jammed his mace into Antea's midsection, hoping to catch her unawares, but she danced aside, somehow finding room in the small space to draw her scimitar. Necrotic energy sizzled along the blade as she pivoted back toward him. Baldric just managed to pull his mace up to block the strike. Power vibrated through the weapons, making his arms ache.

"Tyr, if you're feeling kindly toward me at all right now, I could really use your help," he murmured, channeling the force of his request into his mace.

In response, the metal warmed beneath his hands, and streaks of red light shot along the shaft and into the head of the mace, wreathing it in orange flame. Baldric felt a surge of relief and satisfaction as Antea's gaze snared on the fiery weapon. She pulled back and fell into a defensive stance.

With his opponent retreating, Baldric risked a glance below him. By now the crew had seen the approaching wyvern and were scrambling to grab weapons and find cover as the beast bore down on them.

"Stand strong!" Captain Imber shouted. "Protect the ship! Eyes to the sky!"

The Fallbacks had taken up a position near the bow. Anson stood among the crew, but then Baldric saw him swing around and give a warning cry as an arrow nicked his shoulder.

Antea's companions surged up from belowdecks, weapons out and heading straight for his party.

That was all Baldric could take in before Antea came at him again, the necrotic blade whistling through the air. Baldric blocked the strike and pushed toward her with the flaming head of the mace. But Antea was fast, ducking and dodging around him in the tight quarters. Baldric landed a glancing blow to her sword arm as she went, hoping to make her drop her weapon, but she kicked out at him viciously. He couldn't recover fast enough to get out of the way, and the blow caught him in the upper chest.

Air whooshed out of his lungs as the force of the kick drove him back against the crow's nest railing, and Baldric toppled over the side.

But the flying spell that Cazrin had cast on him was ready and waiting to catch him.

Baldric let himself drop below the level of the crow's nest then shot upward, coming back around the other side, behind Antea. This time, hefting his mace, he landed a solid blow across her back. He felt the impact shudder through her armor, blackening her cloak and driving her to her knees.

Then the wyvern arrived.

Baldric turned just in time to see the beast clamp onto the starboard rail with its clawed feet. The weight of it shifted that side of the ship, knocking down three unfortunate sailors. The wyvern let out an ear-piercing shriek, its wings beating in fury. Several more of the crew broke and tried to run, ignoring Captain Imber's shout to stand their ground.

Faster than Baldric's eye could follow, the wyvern whipped its tail around, impaling one of the fleeing sailors through the hip. The man screamed as he was lifted off his feet and tossed casually into the sea.

Baldric shifted his mace to his right hand and flew down toward the wyvern, grasping his cloth of holy symbols with his left. He considered and discarded several requests to different gods, frantically thinking about what might motivate them the most in this battle.

"Umberlee," he said at last, reaching out to the Queen of the Depths. "This upstart cult has invaded your domain, daring to challenge you by preying on the people who pay homage and give you offerings for a safe voyage. Help me protect them now, and I'll send this beast to the bottom of the sea!"

It was a good bargain, just the right mix of passion and appeal to the sea goddess's pride. He knew it the second he thrust out a hand, feeling the spell rise inside him. It was as unsettling as Umberlee herself, like the feeling of being drowned, consumed, but in magic instead of water.

Sometimes the best, most satisfying bargains came about when you could convince the gods you didn't need something from them, that really, you were doing *them* a favor.

A bolt of light exploded from Baldric's hand, streaking toward the wyvern. It struck the creature just beneath its left wing, outlining it in golden radiance. The wyvern roared in pain and tipped sideways under the force of the blow. It pulled back and launched itself off the deck, leaving deep gouges in the wooden railing.

Baldric rose higher in the air, grateful that his flight spell was still in effect. He glanced down and saw Cazrin crouched near the bow, her staff pointed at him as she concentrated. Lark stood over her, shielding her with his body while he played a furious tune on his lute, aiming a spell at two of the cultists—the elf and the human—as they charged toward the pair. The bard finished his spell, and a wave of thunderous magical force rolled across the deck, slamming into the cultists and tossing them overboard. The edge of the spell's wave caught one of the sailors, a woman with a long gray braid and a black sea serpent tattoo encasing her left arm. She tumbled over the rail, but Tess was suddenly there, leaning over to grab her and pull her to safety.

Behind the rogue, Anson was fighting with the goliath, who wielded a large, two-handed axe, making the fighter seem small and his broken blade a toothpick by comparison.

With the wyvern still reeling from his spell, Baldric took the opportunity to fly for the crow's nest again. Antea had gone down under the blow from his mace, but he had no illusions that she was out of the fight.

His suspicions were confirmed when he flew over the crow's nest and found it empty. Antea was gone.

Cursing himself for letting his attention wander, Baldric surveyed the battlefield quickly, searching for the dark-haired woman and the necrotic blade. There was no sign of her on the main deck. It was possible she'd gone below to heal herself from the wounds she'd taken from his mace, but Baldric didn't have time to waste searching. She'd be back in the battle soon enough.

Turning, he flew toward the wyvern again.

Lightning flashed, and thunder rolled in from across the sea as the storm broke around them. The rain came all at once, lashing him in the face and making it difficult to see. Baldric scrubbed his face to clear his vision and then dipped low, coming up under the wyvern. He swung his mace with all his strength, slamming the flaming head into the underside of the wyvern's jaw. The creature shrieked and reared back, its claws raking the air. Baldric dodged, and he thought he'd gotten away clean until he felt the burning pain shoot from his right shoulder to his elbow. He glanced down and saw the wyvern's claws had sliced through his cloak, sleeve, and armor.

Time seemed to slow, everything going soft and gray around him, except for the bright spots of blood welling from the slash wound. The roar of the rain turned to a dull murmur. Even his heartbeat felt sluggish, and a burning pain flooded Baldric's chest.

And then came the voice.

Do you see how easily the claws tear flesh from bone? This is a taste of what the least *among our kind can do.*

"Get out of my head," Baldric snarled. He snatched the frayed edges of his coat sleeve and bound the wound in a quick, dirty bandage, refusing to take the time to heal himself. He had a wyvern to kill.

Adjusting his helm, Baldric flew straight up, weaving in and out of the sails through curtains of rain, drawing the creature away from the deck and the scrambling sailors. Below him, he caught a flash of dark hair. Antea was on the quarterdeck, fighting with Captain Imber. The tabaxi held a silver rapier in her left hand, and she moved with speed and grace, leaping up onto the rail to parry a strike from Antea's sword. But that rapier looked like a toy in comparison to the wicked scimitar and its necrotic energy.

I give my servants many such gifts, the voice cooed in Baldric's mind. *I could give you more. I could give you such power. You would only have to bargain for it once.*

A bargain for his soul, Baldric thought, suppressing a shudder. "Maybe instead of showering me with gifts, you could tell your servants to stop attacking my companions."

You don't need them or their petty concerns, the voice needled him. *In fact, maybe you need to see how fragile they really are.*

"Don't you dare," Baldric said furiously, but the wyvern that was pursuing him had already peeled off and now dove toward the deck. Baldric followed, trying to see around its bulk, to catch a glimpse of its target.

"Lark, look out!" Baldric shouted.

The bard, who'd exchanged his lute for his crossbow and was firing across the deck at Antea, wasn't looking at the sky. At Baldric's shout, he glanced up, saw the approaching doom, and cast the crossbow aside. He dove out of the way, in the only direction that gave him a chance of escape: over the rail and into the water.

The wyvern pursued, its scaled legs outstretched toward the tiefling as he dove beneath the waves.

Baldric reached for his magic, intending to call upon Umberlee again. He tried to think of a bargain, an appeal to entice her a second time, but all he could hear was the amused laughter of that voice filling his mind. He couldn't concentrate. He teetered in midair, momentarily losing his balance.

Then he looked down and saw that Cazrin had taken a blow from the goliath's axe. She dropped to the deck, and Baldric felt the flying spell slipping away from him. His body grew heavy. He was going to fall.

"Gods be damned, I can do it without magic!" Baldric shouted. He used the last of the spell's energy to shoot himself up and over the wyvern. His body dropped, and he landed heavily on the creature's back, right between its leathery wings. The sudden weight caused it to dip and tilt in midair, its claws barely missing Lark's back as the bard thrashed in the water.

"I hope you impale yourself on your own stinger!" Lark yelled, his words carrying the force of magic. "Stab your own eye, rip out your nostrils, and shove it up your leathery—" The rest of the words were cut off as a wave slapped him in the face, but the magic hit the wyvern, making it falter as it tossed its head from side to side.

Baldric hung on to the creature through the dizzying motions, but he couldn't swing his mace and keep his grip on the wet, slippery scales at the same time. And every time he tried to reach for a spell, there was a buzzing in his ears, and that hissing, draconic laughter, breaking his concentration.

Was Ashardalon stripping his connection to the deities?

Panic choked him at the thought, but then he noticed the head of his mace flare with a sudden, brilliant fire. He felt the warmth of it on his face, and the power temporarily cut through the voice whispering in his ear.

Baldric felt a surge of gratitude at the unexpected show of support. Tyr was still with him. He could fight this.

Tightening his grip on his mace, Baldric locked his knees around the wyvern's body, holding himself in place. Just as he raised his weapon, he saw a flash of light out of the corner of his eye.

A dagger buried itself at the base of the wyvern's wing, and a second later, Tess appeared holding its hilt, scrabbling for purchase on the creature's back. She yanked the dagger free and met Baldric's gaze, and they raised their weapons simultaneously, attacking the wyvern in tandem.

"About time you joined the fun!" Baldric shouted to her as the wyvern did a barrel roll in midair, screeching, frantically trying to dislodge the two of them.

"Been a little busy fighting cultists!" Tess shouted back. She ducked and clung as the wyvern plowed straight into the mainsail, ripping through it like parchment.

Baldric's mace nearly slipped from his hands, but he managed to brace the weapon against his hip, then brought it down for another strike. "How many of the cultists are left?" he asked, his voice barely audible over the wyvern's cries.

"They're gone," Tess said grimly. "That woman gathered them all up and teleported away, leaving us the wyvern to play with."

Baldric cursed. He'd hoped to capture Antea so he could interrogate her, but now that chance was lost. "We need to kill this thing before it cripples the ship," he called to Tess.

"Already got a plan for that," Tess said, stabbing the wyvern again to get a firmer grip and keep herself steady.

"I was hoping you would," Baldric said in relief. "What do you need me to—"

The wyvern wheeled and climbed again, stealing Baldric's breath. Higher and higher it went, then it made a hairpin turn that nearly threw him and Tess off. It dove toward the main mast. With its momentum, it would snap the thing in half if it hit it dead-on.

Tess yanked herself up next to Baldric, reaching out to grab the wyvern's wing. "Pull!" she shouted.

Following her lead, Baldric grabbed the wing, leaning far out across the creature's back. He didn't know what Tess had in mind until he caught a glimpse of Anson standing near the port rail, his broken sword clutched in both hands and raised above his head. Lightning danced along the blade, and Anson planted his feet, a grim expression on his face.

"Aim for the sword!" Tess cried, wrenching the wing again.

"*This* is the plan?" Baldric grunted as he pulled on the wing like a set of reins, trying to point the wyvern toward Anson. If they timed it just right, they would rake the creature's belly right over the jagged blade and its lightning magic.

Of course, if they didn't get clear in time, the lightning would hit them too.

Never a dull moment where these damned dragons were concerned, Baldric thought. He leaned forward, picturing Ashardalon's burning gaze until it felt as if the greatwyrm's eyes were actually upon him, settled in the shadows at the back of his mind.

"Here's what I think of your servants," Baldric growled, hoping

Ashardalon would hear him. He yanked on the wyvern's wing, setting all his weight on it. "Turn, beast! See what we've got for you!"

The wyvern shrieked as its wing buckled, and it went into an inadvertent dive, gliding along the ship's deck. Sailors dove out of the way or were knocked prone, and suddenly there was only Anson, setting his feet and thrusting the broken sword into the air. The wyvern saw him and the lightning-struck blade, but it couldn't pull up in time, not with Tess and Baldric both hanging off its wing.

"Let go!" Tess screamed. "Now!"

Baldric didn't have to be told twice. He let the muscles in his legs go loose and fell away from the wyvern just as the lightning surged over its scales, lighting up the entire ship and blinding him for an instant.

He hit the water on his back, the breath blasting from his lungs. The shock of cold water struck his system next, momentarily paralyzing him. That was bad enough, but then his armor, clothing, and mace immediately dragged him beneath the surface. He thrashed, clawing his way back up, but he was weak from the effort of holding on to the wyvern's back. He tried to call out to Umberlee again, readying another bargain, but he could sense her presence fading. She'd aided him once, and now she was done with him.

Maybe the lightning would have been better, Baldric reflected as his chest began to burn. This wasn't one of Tess's better plans . . .

A hand grabbed the back of his coat, pulling him up. Baldric's head broke the surface, and he sucked in a grateful breath. The salt water stung his eyes, and the rain was still coming down in blinding sheets, but he could see clearly enough to spot the wyvern about thirty feet away, its body sinking slowly beneath the waves.

Cheers rose from the deck as the surviving crew gathered at the rail and began fishing their comrades out of the water.

Baldric looked over his shoulder to see who had saved him.

It was Lark, who was holding them both upright as the white-capped waves bobbed them up and down. When he caught Baldric's gaze, a sly grin spread across his face.

"Yes, it's me, your savior," the tiefling said, striking as proud a pose as he could while treading water. "Snatched you from Umberlee's embrace and dragged you back into the light. No need to thank me," he said, when Baldric opened his mouth to reply. "The song I'll get out of this grand aerial combat will be compensation enough, but of course, if you're still inclined to sing my praises, I certainly won't stop you."

"I was going to say you had my thanks," Baldric grumbled good-naturedly, "but now I'm thinking I'd rather I drowned."

CHAPTER 23

Tess stood on the pebbled beach, her spirits sinking as she watched the *Red Nautilus* sail away. Not that she was surprised. When the battle ended and the survivors had gathered on the deck again, Captain Imber had thanked the Fallbacks for their help while at the same time holding them directly responsible for the cultists being on board in the first place. At least they'd been escorted ashore first instead of just being tossed overboard.

In the wake of the storm, the sunset was spectacular, every shred of cloud alight with a fiery orange glow above the turbulent sea. Under other circumstances, the sight would have filled her with a sense of awe, but watching their transportation to Luskan disappear naturally put a damper on things.

There was no use dwelling on regrets. Tess turned and regarded her tired and bedraggled party. Baldric had his healing lantern out and was tending to Cazrin's wounds while Lark, Anson, and Uggie kept a watch to make sure nothing attacked them from the nearby woods.

Cazrin had been the most wounded of all of them, but Baldric had also suffered a nasty slash to the arm. At Tess's insistence, he'd eventually healed the wound, and he tried to downplay it, but every once in a while, Tess noticed him flexing that arm and rubbing it, as if it still pained him.

The cleric had also been quiet as he'd gone about his healing. Tess didn't know what he was thinking, but she could guess. Ashardalon's followers were actively hunting them now, and who knew how many cultists the greatwyrm had at his disposal?

"Are we camping here?" Anson asked, holding up a piece of driftwood he'd found on the beach. "On foot, we're still a few hours from Luskan. We won't make it before dark. I'll start building a fire if we want to stay here."

"I don't care where we sleep, I'm just happy to be back on land," Cazrin said, closing her eyes as she basked in the light of Baldric's magic. "It's nice to be standing on ground that doesn't heave beneath my feet."

"I don't think it's a night for camping." Tess reached into her pouch to fish for the tankard figurine. "We'll find a hiding place in the woods to put up the Wander Inn. We could all use some sleep in our own beds, and I don't think the cultists will risk another attack tonight."

"As long as Anson hasn't taken the figurine," Lark said with a sardonic smile. "Careful he didn't sell it to those cultists." He nudged Baldric, causing the cleric's lantern to bob back and forth.

Anson wilted a little, and Baldric shot Lark a look of irritation. "About time for you to try something new," he muttered. "I'm getting a little tired of hearing the same song from you over and over."

Lark's mouth fell open, but he recovered quickly, pursing his lips in indignation. "Well, excuse me for being angry when someone betrays me and—"

"He made a mistake," Baldric cut in smoothly. "We've all made them—you included—and we're going to make more." He shook his head. "Can't you see we've got bigger problems?"

"Yes, and walking to Luskan seems to be our biggest one at the moment," Lark snapped.

Tess stepped in before Baldric could hit back. "He means that the cultists know about us," she said. "We thought we were going to have the element of surprise, infiltrating the Hosttower, but if they've been following us, they might know about our mission." She found the tankard figurine and held it clasped in her hands. "But that's not what I'm most concerned about right now."

Baldric's eyebrows rose. "It's not?" he asked. The rest of the party, even Cazrin, looked equally surprised.

Tess looked at each of the Fallbacks, gathering her thoughts. Her gaze rested last on Cazrin. "I had a lot to think about while we were on the ship, about everything that's happened in the last few days and months. I realized some things need to be addressed before we go any farther."

She turned to Anson. "I've been taking you for granted," she said, and she saw a flicker of surprise in his gaze. "I promised you closure with Valen, and I didn't try hard enough to keep that promise. I told myself you were fine, because you're always fine, and you're always there to support us, sacrificing your own needs to do it. I'm sorry, Anson," she said, meeting his eyes. "I never should have treated you that way."

Anson's throat bobbed as he swallowed. "Thank you," he said. "But it doesn't make it right, what I did." He glanced at Lark. "I know it was unforgivable, and I know that's what I've been trying to do, get you to forgive me, because of how *I* was feeling. That was wrong." He squared his shoulders. "From now on, whether you forgive me or not, I'm just going to make it my mission to protect you from the people hunting you. If that means getting you a magic item to replace the one I took, I'll do it. I'll go back down and plumb the depths of the Sunless Citadel or Undermountain or anywhere else until I find something that'll help hide you. In the meantime, I'll guard your back. Now that I know to be on the lookout, I promise you, nothing is going to get to you while I'm around." He put his hand on his sword hilt. "You have my word on that."

Tess felt her chest squeeze at the earnestness in Anson's expression. She didn't know if she'd ever heard the fighter make a vow like that before.

Lark seemed just as surprised. He blinked several times and fiddled with his wet coat, as if he needed something to occupy his hands. "Well, that's . . ." His brow furrowed.

"Don't tell us you're at a loss for words," Baldric said, putting a hand over his heart. "Never thought I'd see the day."

Lark scowled. "I'm just taking it in, that's all. I'm not used to such passionate declarations from people who weren't my lovers." He arched a brow, regarding Anson critically. "It's true, you are a formidable bodyguard, and I didn't take that into consideration before. I might . . . *might* consider us even, if you could eventually find the people responsible for my current situation and put an end to them."

Anson smiled and clapped him on the shoulder. "It would be my pleasure."

Tess felt some of the knots that had twisted her up inside these past few days begin to loosen. They still had work to do, but she was happy to see Anson and Lark take a step toward reconciliation.

She turned her attention to the bard. "Anson wasn't the only one who made mistakes, Lark," she said. "You kept a huge secret that could have affected the whole party if the people hunting you had come after us."

Lark snorted in disbelief. "You're *adventurers*. If I thought you couldn't handle an ambush from mysterious forces, I would have had you thrown out of my dressing room the afternoon you tried to recruit me."

"Exactly," Tess said. She sat down on a jagged shelf of rock jutting from the sand. "The day Anson and I came to ask you to join us, you were sizing us up too. Seeing if we were capable of protecting you." Lark opened his mouth to interject, but Tess spoke over him. "Yes, Anson and Valen used you, but you were using us too, surrounding yourself with powerful people and not telling the truth about your intentions. If you'd come clean just a little sooner, Anson never would have taken the amulet from you. You share responsibility for digging yourself into this hole, Lark. I think that's part of the reason you're so angry—you haven't admitted that to yourself."

Lark set his jaw, a mulish expression on his face, but when Tess only regarded him steadily, he gave in and closed his eyes. When he opened them, there was an unexpected vulnerability in his expression.

"Fine, it's true," he said, his words nearly lost in the steady roll of the waves breaking onshore. "I was using you in the beginning." He glanced at Baldric. "And I very nearly left several times when our situation seemed far more dangerous than any unknown persons hunting me. We had a lich after us! Could you blame me?"

"I think we all wanted to run," Anson said.

Tess smiled as the two shared a look of commiseration. Lark shook his head. "But then you all had to go and start being so damned *loyal*," he said, as if he still couldn't believe the turn of events. "I was stuck on that magical trap in Undermountain, on the verge of being bones in a pit, and none of you would abandon me." He glanced up at Anson. "And you stood between me and a monster. I haven't forgotten that."

"Is that why you stayed?" Baldric asked.

"Partly," Lark hedged. "I also stayed because it was *fun*." He looked around the group. "Even when we were running for our lives, I felt more alive than I had in a long time. It's embarrassing, but there were times I actually *forgot* that I was being hunted. And I went so long without telling you my situation, and I'd gotten so comfortable here, I was afraid of what might change if I told you the truth."

"You were afraid we'd be angry, weren't you?" Cazrin guessed. She crossed her arms, staring at Lark in fond exasperation. "Did you really think we'd throw you out of the party, after everything we'd been through with Lorthrannan and the Ruinous Child?"

"Well, when you say it like that, yes, it sounds absurd," Lark said, squeezing water out of his coat. "But you should know by now that I carry more than a bit of the absurd with me wherever I go." He adjusted his rumpled hat, sending another stream of water down the back of his neck. "For what it's worth, I'm sorry for not telling you. I shouldn't have kept the secret for as long as I did, and yes, I realize I'd still have the amulet if I'd come clean." He glanced at Tess. "That part's on me."

Tess nodded, satisfied. She turned to the others. "If anyone else has any deep, dark secrets they'd like to confess while we're here, now is a good time," she offered, spreading her arms wide. "No one will judge you, and we'll leave them all here on this beach for the tide to take away."

"Believe it or not, that was the last of my dark secrets," Lark said.

"You all helped me face my inner demons," Cazrin said. "Even when they took on a physical form."

"You already know about mine too," Baldric put in. "You've met its representatives and everything."

Anson grinned. "It's not often someone's checkered past comes with its own entourage." He shrugged. "I don't have any deep, dark secrets, except"—his brow furrowed in dismay—"I worry that you were right, Lark," he said to the bard. "That my brother doesn't really care about me at all and was just using me."

Lark winced. "That perhaps came out a bit harsher than it should have," he said. "I don't claim to know your brother, but speaking as a person of questionable character myself, I can say that we often act out of fear, and sometimes that causes us to hurt the people we *should* be caring about. When I talked to Valen, he didn't seem completely beyond hope. Arrogant, cocky, and insufferably handsome, but not beyond hope."

Anson smiled faintly. "That definitely describes him—I'm not going to comment on the 'handsome' part." He nodded to the bard. "Thanks, Lark," he said. "That . . . that helps."

"I'm so glad we're starting to talk again," Cazrin said. She'd taken off her boots and was wiggling her toes in the wet sand. "All the tension in the group was killing me!"

"Says the woman who carried a murderous tome up and down the Sword Coast," Lark commented. "Surely, you can handle a little intraparty conflict."

"Before everyone gets too full of happiness and rainbows," Baldric said, "I'd like to bring us back around to our cultist problem. What are we going to do if they're waiting for us in Luskan?"

"We adapt," Tess said simply. When the others turned to stare at her, she added, "We don't know if Antea represents the interests of the entire cult or if she's following her own agenda. I'm actually encouraged to know that things aren't as straightforward as we thought."

"You mean the fact that Antea regards Baldric as a usurper," Cazrin said.

Tess nodded. "I don't think she came here at Ashardalon's order," she said. "I watched her during her conversation with Baldric in the crow's nest. She wasn't trying to recruit him. She was furious, and she was out for blood. That tells me there are cracks in Ashardalon's armor, dissent in the ranks. We can use that to our advantage."

Baldric nodded thoughtfully. "It's possible," he said. He looked at Tess, and there was a cunning spark in his eyes that she liked to see. "Are you thinking that if we weaken Ashardalon's cult, neutralize a high-ranking individual like Antea, it might be enough to break the greatwyrm's hold on me?"

"There's no clearer signal that you'll never serve him," Tess said. "If he thinks that you'll just keep hunting down his followers, chipping away at his power base, it will show him that it's in his best interest to back off."

"Sounds marvelous," Lark said. "And then we celebrate our good fortune by availing ourselves of every delight that Luskan has to offer." He stretched, his mouth gaping in a yawn. "Let's get some sleep and put this plan into motion."

"Lark's right," Tess said. She nodded to a stand of trees in the distance. "Let's find a place to put the Wander Inn, and then we need to get some rest. We'll be in Luskan tomorrow." She met Baldric's gaze. "And we're not leaving until we get what we're after."

CHAPTER 24

Baldric was happy to be back in his own bed in the Wander Inn, not listening to the sounds of Lark's stomach gurgling ominously in the middle of the night aboard the ship. He didn't mind sharing a room out of necessity, but he preferred his solitude at night.

He had that now, and he felt better about the Fallbacks and their ability to handle the mission than he had in days. Tess had worked her magic yet again, helping them to find common ground. He hadn't always believed she could lead a group like theirs, but he didn't have any doubts now.

So why was it, when things seemed to be going well, and the party was united in having his back, that he still felt so unmoored?

He sat up, reaching over to the bedside table where he'd left his cloth of holy symbols. Picking it up, he ran his fingers over the scales of justice that represented Tyr. The god had been with him in the battle against Antea and her cultists. He'd come through in a moment when Baldric had doubted himself and his unique connection to the gods.

Would he come through again if Baldric asked for help? Or

would he be stubbornly silent, as he had so many times before when Baldric had needed him?

There was only one way to find out.

He slid on a robe and fastened the cloth of holy symbols around his waist. Then he retrieved his mace from a rack on the wall and carried it to the center of the room. He sat down on the floor and laid the weapon in front of him. His hands lingered on the head, seeking that same comforting warmth he'd felt in battle. But the mace lay dormant now, as if waiting for him.

He didn't have to do this, Baldric reminded himself. Tyr was one of many gods, and there were several whose favor he could usually count on before the god of justice. Sometimes, the safer bet was the better option.

But this felt different. Tess's notion of weakening the cult was a good one, but if he wanted to take on a dragon with near godlike powers, he was going to need the help of the most powerful deities to do it. Tyr was one of those. Whether he liked it or not, Baldric needed guidance from the god of justice.

Baldric closed his eyes and put his hand on his mace. "I know we've had our differences in the past," he said, speaking aloud to the empty room, "but you were there for me when I fought Antea, so you must hold no love for Ashardalon. If that's so, I'm asking you to help me." He shifted, feeling the chill from the stone floor seeping into his legs. "I know I've gotten myself into a tangle, and the last thing I want is for the others to get hurt trying to get me out of it. If I can free myself, if there's a way, I need you to show me." He hesitated, then plunged all in. "Whatever deal you need me to make, I'll do it."

The silence in the room was heavy in the wake of his speech. Baldric kept his eyes closed, breathing in and out, deep, steady breaths that centered him. He knew Tyr would not be quick to answer, if he answered at all. The god of justice would not be rushed, or cajoled, or charmed the way some deities might be. Tyr was stubborn and implacable, traits that Baldric admired.

And sometimes they infuriated him.

His thoughts drifted back to that long-ago night he'd been jumped in the alley. That's when all the trouble had begun. He'd called to Tyr that night when the figures had surrounded him, weapons bare, and he'd known they didn't intend to just rob him. He'd been desperate and afraid ... and Tyr had refused to answer his cry for help.

A familiar spark of anger kindled in Baldric at the memory. As if in response, the mace beneath his fingertips warmed, and a soft humming sound filled his ears.

He opened his eyes. The weapon glowed with a soft golden light. As he watched, the light grew brighter until it spilled from the weapon and pooled on the stone floor like liquid. Baldric suddenly felt very warm, the chill of the floor banished by the light, which was now moving in a line away from the weapon. It stopped a few feet away and then expanded, spreading into a large circle upon the floor. There was a ripple across the liquid's surface, like a rock had been dropped into its center. When the ripples reached the edge, the golden light dimmed, revealing something inside the circle.

It was a portal.

Baldric had seen a few in his time. On the other side, he could make out a rocky outcrop overlooking a vast mountain range. He didn't recognize the landscape, and as he peered over the edge of the circle, feeling suspended between one place and another, for the first time Baldric wondered if he might be dreaming all of this. Or, if it wasn't a dream, maybe it was the strange, malleable magic of the Wander Inn reacting to his desire for answers and reassurance. Maybe it had created all of this, and it was just an illusion, thin and fragile as parchment.

"I'll try it anyway, and look the fool if I'm wrong," Baldric murmured.

He stood up, automatically reaching for his mace, but he stopped short of picking it up. There was still a line of golden light connecting the weapon to the circle, and with a prickle of awareness, he realized it was a tether keeping the portal open.

He stepped up to the edge, drew another steadying breath, and took the plunge.

There was a second of weightlessness as he stepped through the portal, and darkness cloaked his vision. Again there was the feeling of suspension, as if he were an hourglass just spinning and spinning, forever trapped in a moment of time. But then the feeling passed, his vision cleared, and Baldric was standing on the outcrop, looking out over the mountains.

He should have been cold. Wind howled across the landscape, but somehow it couldn't touch him. He looked down at himself to see that he was still wearing his robe. He had no weapon, but he wasn't afraid.

More signs that this was a dream.

Baldric turned to look behind him. The portal loomed in the air, its golden edges frayed by the wind, but through it, he could clearly see his bedroom in the Wander Inn, and his comfortable bed beckoning to him. Maybe he should just go back, pretend this whole absurd exercise had never happened.

"You're too stubborn to turn back. You always have been."

The voice rumbled from the heart of the mountains, cutting through the wind and making the ground shudder beneath Baldric's feet.

He turned. Thick clouds hung low in the sky, edged in sunset orange, but as Baldric watched, they changed shape, writhing and twisting until a face emerged. It might have been human, but just when Baldric had convinced himself it was, the shape changed, and a dwarven face stared out at him. Then a dragonborn visage. A tiefling. The clouds were constantly moving, shifting to become something else. It hurt his eyes to stare at the images too closely, so Baldric aimed his gaze at the distant mountains instead.

"Am I addressing Tyr?" he called out. "Or have I finally lost my wits entirely, talking to clouds?"

"This is your magic, your mind, your place," the figure answered. "Only you can say."

"I've never been here before," Baldric started to argue, but then something, a memory, teased the back of his mind. True, he'd never seen these mountains before. But when he was a child, living deep beneath the earth, he used to tell his mothers how he'd have dreams at night about soaring through the mountains until he'd seen and explored every inch of them. He hadn't thought about those dreams in a very long time.

He stared off into the distance, letting his gaze go unfocused, remembering that soaring feeling from his childhood, that sense of pure freedom.

How do I get that back, and break the hold that Ashardalon has over me?

How do I protect my friends from his wrath?

What does the greatwyrm want from me?

The questions had been burning him from the inside out, the questions he'd needed answers to for months. Now here he was, standing before a manifestation of a being that might give him the answers he'd long sought.

Baldric's gaze snapped back into focus. But instead of voicing those questions, he felt that spark of anger rising inside him again. "Why did you abandon me that night in the alley?" he demanded. "I almost died, and you weren't there." He was surprised at the venom he heard in his voice—and the hurt. "None of this would have happened if it weren't for you!"

He felt dizzy in the wake of the outburst, as if the admission had been pulled from him by force. He blinked, staring up at the ever-changing figure, belatedly realizing he might have crossed the line.

"Those are words you've held back for a long time," the Aspect of Tyr said, the rumble of the voice like an approaching storm. "They've been poisoning you."

"What of it?" Baldric tasted defiance in his throat. Maybe he was being reckless, but suddenly, he didn't care. He wasn't seeking the Aspect's approval. "Will you smite me for telling you what I feel?"

The clouds roiled, and lightning danced inside them, casting eldritch shadows over the landscape. Baldric held his ground, resisting the urge to retreat.

"You blame the gods for not standing ready at your hand, like a weapon you wield against the world?" The voice held a note of amusement, but there was an edge to it, a warning. "You are smaller than a grain of sand on the shore."

"Maybe so," Baldric said, "but I managed to make my presence known, and I kept the bargains I made. Why wasn't that enough for you that night?"

"Because there was a more important lesson to be learned," the Aspect intoned, and again, Baldric felt the stones shift beneath his feet. He would have accused the Aspect of being dramatic, but he was all too aware of his precarious position on this hilltop. "The path you walk comes with power but also great risk, and a price that must be paid."

"So it *was* a punishment," Baldric said, bristling. "I was the unruly child, and you thought you'd knock me down a peg, make me beg for help."

For just a moment, Baldric saw the dwarven face emerge from the cloud bank again, with a look that was too close to pity for his liking. "No one made you do anything, Baldric Goodhand," the Aspect declared. "You chose the unknown, risked the wrath of mysterious powers rather than face your own death. You made a *choice*, and now you live with the consequences."

A denial rose automatically to Baldric's lips, but it died before he could give it voice. As the wind howled across the hilltop and he stood there, alone, stripped of his weapons and armor, facing this being who may or may not represent the god of justice, Baldric found that he couldn't lie to it, or to himself.

He *had* been afraid that night, but not just of death. He'd been afraid of what that meant. What would his family think of him? That he'd left them and his responsibilities behind only to end up dying alone in a dark, stinking alley? That his life had come to nothing, in the end.

"I wanted it to mean something," Baldric admitted. "My life and my death. I want to make my mark on the world. Are you telling me that your followers don't want the same?" he challenged.

But the Aspect didn't take that bait. "Your life does mean something, though it is not what you intended. It means something to Ashardalon."

"So, you *do* know what the greatwyrm wants." Despite his anger and frustration, Baldric finally felt like he was getting somewhere. "Tell me, damn it! If you won't help me fight him, that's fine, but tell me what I need to know! You can't want Ashardalon's influence to grow in the world. Where's the justice in that?"

"Do not presume to tell me where my concerns should lie." The voice rose in warning. "*You* created the link that gives Ashardalon power. *You* drew the greatwyrm's interest because he sensed your connection to all the deities you've had dealings with. He sensed the potential to exploit this, though the creature may not know how. It wouldn't be the first time Ashardalon sought to exploit something powerful to fuel his ambitions and plans for longevity." The clouds roiled again. "You are one of many schemes Ashardalon employs to gain power. Even in this, you are a small piece in a large, long game."

Well, that was depressing, though he supposed he shouldn't have been surprised. Was that why the Aspect had brought him here? Baldric wondered. Had he been placed on this tiny rock in the middle of a vast mountain range to remind him of his own insignificance?

"Is there nothing I can do, then?" Baldric demanded. Again, he felt that spark of defiance, and he seized on it. He was terrified that otherwise he might succumb to despair. "If Ashardalon wants to feed on some divine connection I have to you and the other deities, does that mean that I . . ." Suddenly, he couldn't speak for the lump in his throat, and a growing sense of doom. "Shouldn't you just abandon me, or kill me, to prevent that from happening?"

There was a lengthy pause, and Baldric wondered if the Aspect was considering his fate, placing his life upon an invisible scale. Or was he simply drawing out the tension to make him squirm? Either way, he loathed the feeling, but he needed to know what was in store for him. He wouldn't run from gods or greatwyrms or anyone else.

"Much depends on what you do next to extricate yourself from this binding," the Aspect said, and the image in the clouds began to break up under the force of the wind. Baldric could feel the presence receding. "More eyes than mine will be watching."

And with that, the clouds broke apart, allowing a glorious sunset to shine through, casting threads of red-gold light across the landscape. The view was breathtaking, but Baldric was too unsettled to properly appreciate it.

So, Ashardalon had sensed Baldric's connection to the other gods and was intrigued by it. It wasn't about Baldric at all, but what he represented in the greatwyrm's bid for power. He was truly a pawn and nothing more.

"Now you finally understand your place."

Baldric's skin prickled.

This was a new voice. A very different voice from the Aspect's, but one that he recognized.

He looked up. The sunset colors that had blazed so beautifully across the mountains had deepened in an instant to blood red. Smoke filled the sky, obscuring the snowcapped peaks. Baldric blinked, and he was no longer standing on the outcrop. Instead, he found himself in the middle of a barren, broken plain. The temperature had risen, making him break out into a sweat. The smoke filled his lungs, choking him.

A pair of glowing eyes materialized out of that billowing smoke, which twisted and reshaped itself in a parody of the clouds he'd just seen. The features that emerged were a frightening meld of dragon and fiend, and they were very, very large. Seeing the face of the greatwyrm, even formed as it was from smoke, sent a cold chill through Baldric's body.

"No one ... invited you ... to this ... meeting," Baldric said, coughing, trying not to show his fear. Flames shot up from the cracks in the ground around him. The heat was like a physical force.

"I am always with you, pet," Ashardalon said in a voice that grated against Baldric. "You can't escape me, and the gods won't save you." The draconic image drifted closer, towering over Baldric. "I'm here to offer you another chance to give yourself to me."

Pain exploded in Baldric's chest, and he dropped to his knees. He thought something had struck him through the heart until he looked down and noticed the red thread of energy emerging from his chest. The tether corkscrewed through the air, reaching upward until it connected to Ashardalon, passing through the greatwyrm's mouth and into the smoke. The eyes flared, and another shock of pain went through him, so intense he wanted to vomit.

"I can make the pain go away," Ashardalon cooed, as Baldric pressed his forehead against the ground, trying to catch his breath. "All you have to do is say you'll serve me. Come, now. It's not hard. You're already on your knees. Just speak the words, and the power will follow, power beyond your imagining."

"To the Hells with you," Baldric snarled, forcing himself up. He raised his head, glaring hatefully at the greatwyrm. "I'll die first!"

"That can be arranged."

CHAPTER 25

The smell of smoke and the sound of Uggie's howl brought Tess out of her meditative trance.

The smoke was faint, drifting beneath her door in tiny wisps. Leaping from the bed, Tess grabbed her weapons and ran toward it. The door burst open before she reached it, and Uggie pelted into her room, claws slipping and skittering on the stone floor. The otyugh was frantic, yipping and biting at the sleeves of Tess's nightshirt.

"I know something's wrong, Uggie," Tess said impatiently. "Show me what it is!"

A familiar image filled her thoughts as the otyugh projected the source of her worry and fear: Baldric.

Or, rather, his beard. But that was the universal symbol for the dwarf in Uggie's mind.

Tess didn't question it. She burst into the hall, yelling for the rest of the Fallbacks.

Anson was already up, dressed and haphazardly armored. Uggie must have gone to him first. Lark and Cazrin stumbled out of their respective rooms, looking half-asleep and confused. But they snapped to attention when Tess pointed to the door to Baldric's bedroom.

Smoke poured in thick black clouds from beneath the door, which was outlined in red.

"Everyone get back!" Anson barked. He drew his sword, positioned himself squarely in front of the door, and kicked.

The door splintered, tore off its hinges, and fell inward, slamming to the floor in two pieces. Tess darted in, daggers out, though it occurred to her belatedly that she might need a bucket brigade. The smoke was thick, making her eyes stream.

"Cazrin!" she called over her shoulder. "Can you do anything about this smoke and—"

She stopped. Across the room, she glimpsed a strange sight. Baldric's mace lay on the floor, glowing with golden light. A thread of that light led from the weapon to a circle of fire burning on the floor in the middle of the room. As Tess approached, looking down, she realized the flames wreathed a portal. A barren, fiery landscape was visible within the circle, and at its heart . . .

"It's Baldric!" Tess shouted as the rest of the Fallbacks emerged from the smoke to join her. "Everyone get ready, we're going in!"

"Where does this go?" Lark demanded. He had his crossbow out and loaded, staring warily at the flames. "It looks like the Hells themselves."

Before Tess could reply, Uggie tore past her, launching her body through the crackling flames and into the portal. Smoke flared from the circle, briefly blinding Tess. When she could see again, she glimpsed Uggie on the other side of the portal, charging across the wasteland toward Baldric.

Anson went next. Sword brandished, he leaped into the portal with a shout.

Lark shrugged out of his white coat, which he'd somehow managed to don over his nightshirt. Then he tucked his tail close to his body and dove through the flames.

That left only Cazrin. Tess met the wizard's eyes across the flame-wreathed portal. Cazrin gave a nod, and the two of them jumped together.

There was a brief sensation of falling, of dizziness, when Tess didn't know what was up or down, before her feet landed on hard stone and she found she'd arrived on the blasted plain.

The heat was intense. Tess sucked in a breath that burned its way down to her lungs. She surveyed the landscape briefly, looking for enemies either on the ground or in the sky, but she saw nothing. Baldric was on his knees about fifty feet away from them, clutching his chest. A draconic form made of smoke and shadow towered over him with burning eyes, curved, fiendish horns, and an aura of such malevolence that Tess had to fight to get her legs to move.

The rest of the party appeared to be having the same trouble. They had their weapons ready, but it was as if some force held them paralyzed. Even Uggie had stopped and was whining and pawing anxiously at the dirt, as if she wanted to charge but couldn't.

Baldric looked over his shoulder then and saw them all. His eyes widened in fear. "What are you doing here?" He pressed one hand to his chest and waved them away frantically with the other. "You have to get out!"

That's when Tess noticed the thread of light that blossomed from Baldric's chest and rose up into the air, a physical tether to the greatwyrm.

Horror overcame Tess. Was Ashardalon *feeding* off of Baldric?

"We're not abandoning you!" Anson shouted. With a growl, he ducked his head and charged, bull-like, toward Baldric. He raised his sword, then brought it down on the red thread.

Lightning flashed from the blade, and the thread flared in response. A spear of crimson light slammed into Anson's chest, throwing him back at least ten feet, tossing him to the ground like a rag doll. Stunned, Anson lay there, coughing and clutching his midsection.

Lark fired the Last Resort at Ashardalon. The crossbow bolt passed harmlessly through the smoke, and a rumble of laughter echoed across the plain.

"You use sticks and toys to challenge me?" The scent of brimstone filled the air as the greatwyrm cracked its jaws and released a gout of flame into the sky. Baldric cringed, as if the release of power pained him.

Why wasn't the greatwyrm attacking? Tess thought. If it was powerful enough to get to Baldric in the Wander Inn, why didn't it take him, or strike at Anson as he lay prone on the ground?

Something didn't feel right. Tess tore her gaze away from Ashardalon, pushing back her fear and focusing on the landscape around them. Flames shot up from thin fissures in the barren ground. But when Tess looked closely at the rocks, she saw their edges were blunted and feathery, and when she leaned down to touch one, her fingers passed through it.

An illusion.

"This isn't real," she murmured. Then, louder, she called to the rest of the party, "This is an illusion!"

Lark gave her an incredulous look. "This burn on my arm feels fairly real to me," he said. "And that *thing* is sucking the life out of our cleric right before our eyes!"

Tess looked at Lark's wound and then over at Baldric, at the pain in the cleric's eyes. "All right," she allowed, "some of it's real, but not all of it. The landscape looks strange, and so does Ashardalon."

"The Wander Inn might be involved," Cazrin said, dodging to avoid another gout of flame shooting up from the ground. "It could be reacting to Baldric's fears, creating an image of the thing that's been foremost in his mind."

"If the tavern's made an enemy, why can't we fight it?" Anson demanded as he hauled himself up. "And how do we save Baldric?"

Tess didn't have any answers for him. And Lark was right. Whether or not this was an illusion, the danger felt very real.

A memory stirred in Tess. She'd felt a similar way during one of Mel's training sessions, when her teacher had cast a spell to blind and deafen Tess then fought her in unarmed combat. Stripped of two powerful senses, Tess had been forced to rely on other instincts to see her through.

She tried to see the current threat through that lens. If they couldn't trust what they were seeing and hearing, what could they trust in this place?

"I've got an idea," Tess said, and sheathed her daggers.

"Your plan is to put your weapons away?" Lark said incredulously. "So far, I'm hating this."

He kept his crossbow raised as Tess focused on Baldric, doing her best to ignore Ashardalon and the fear that tried to hold her in place. Forcing one foot in front of the other, she made her way over to Baldric, until she was crouching by the cleric's side.

"I told you to get out of here," Baldric said through gritted teeth, his hands pressed to his chest. Red light seeped between his fingers like blood. "Don't let it take you too."

Tess shook her head. "If that was really Ashardalon come to fight us," she said, tilting her head in the direction of the greatwyrm, "we'd all be charred to ash right now. But it's only hurting us when we try to free you. Why do you think that is, Baldric?"

"Because it wants *me*," Baldric said. "So just let it take me and you'll be safe!"

"That's what you're really afraid of, isn't it?" Tess said. "You're worried about protecting us from your burdens. You've built it up so much in your mind that it's overwhelming you, panicking you."

"Don't be a fool!" Baldric drew back as Tess reached toward the red stream of energy. "It'll blast you just like it did Anson!"

"No, it won't," Tess said. Oh, she hoped she was right. "Because I'm not trying to fight anything here. I just want to help you."

And with that, she laid her hand flat against Baldric's chest, covering his hands with her own. The red light flickered for a second, but there was no burst of energy, no pain.

Baldric's forehead wrinkled in confusion. "I don't understand," he said. "I feel your hands. I feel . . ."

"Is it disrupting the pain?" Tess asked. "Making it fade in and out?"

"How did you know?"

Tess squeezed his fingers. "Because *this* is real," she said. "The pain's in your mind. Maybe Ashardalon is using the connection to make it seem real, and the tavern's magic is mixed in somehow. I don't know, and I don't care. All I care about is that you see that *we* are real." She nodded to the rest of the Fallbacks. "We're here to bring you back, and we're not going anywhere."

"You don't want any part of this." Baldric freed a hand, gesturing helplessly to Ashardalon. "I got myself into this. There's no reason to drag you down with me."

"Of course there's a reason." Cazrin appeared next to Baldric, staff in hand. The stone gave off a bright purple glow that chased away some of the crimson light. "We said we were going to face our demons together. Don't you remember?" The wizard laid her free hand on Baldric's shoulder. Once again, the dwarf flinched in surprise at the touch. Tess took that as a good sign. Maybe they were getting through.

Anson and Lark came up behind Baldric, laying their hands on his arms. "You know me well enough to know I'm not going anywhere," Anson pointed out with a grin. "So you might as well not even try to talk me into leaving."

Baldric gave a weak laugh. "That's true," he said. He glanced at Lark. "What about you?" he asked. "I know you'll tell me the brutal truth. You think this is all in my head?"

Lark snorted. "Would I be this close to that thing if I thought otherwise?" He pointed up at the glowering figure of the greatwyrm. Tess noticed the smoke beginning to lose its form, the glowing eyes flickering.

Uggie nudged her way around Tess's hip and bumped her head into Baldric's chest, her tentacles slapping against his shoulders.

Baldric made a face. "I definitely felt that," he muttered. He met Tess's gaze and took a deep breath, his chest rising and falling unsteadily. "All right, then, I trust you," he said. "How do I get out of this? Out of my own head?"

"Close your eyes and let go," Tess advised him. "We've got you."

Baldric nodded. He hesitated for a second, then closed his eyes and sagged into their grip.

"Let's get out of here," Tess said, and together, the Fallbacks pulled Baldric to his feet and began leading him back toward the portal. Tess kept her eye on the red thread connecting Baldric to Ashardalon, watching closely for any sign that the greatwyrm—or whatever it was—was hurting the cleric. The strand of energy began to flicker, weakening as they got closer to the portal.

When the party stepped through, the thread snapped.

Ashardalon and the blasted landscape winked out of existence. Tess breathed a sigh of relief as the familiar trappings of Baldric's room appeared around them, and the portal itself shrank to the size of a gold coin and vanished, leaving behind nothing but a blackened circle and Baldric's mace sitting nearby. The weapon was no longer glowing, but Tess thought she could still feel the power radiating off it.

Baldric went over to the mace and picked it up, holding it contemplatively in his hands. "I didn't think this was how the night would go when I tried to commune with Tyr," he admitted. "Thank you for coming after me." He looked at each of them in turn, his gaze settling last on Tess. "How did you know that the vision I was seeing of Ashardalon wasn't real?"

Tess hesitated, but she decided to be honest. "I think some of it *was* real," she admitted. "Mixed in with the Wander Inn's magic. I think Ashardalon's connection is getting stronger by the day. We need to move fast to sever it."

Baldric nodded, as if he wasn't surprised to hear this, but there was a haunted look in his eyes. "You really think we'll find answers at the Hosttower of the Arcane?"

"I do," Tess said, putting all the confidence she could into the words. "We've got your back," she reminded him. "All of us."

As she spoke, Tess automatically found herself glancing over at Anson, who was leaning against the wall by Baldric's bed. He met her eyes and gave a nod. And with that simple gesture, Tess knew the two of them were going to be all right.

They were stronger together, all of them, and Tess needed her party as much as they needed her.

"Get some sleep, everyone," Tess said, gently herding the rest of the party toward the door. "Tomorrow, we're going to invade a tower full of powerful wizards to find some cultists who want to kill us."

Anson laughed. "Wouldn't have it any other way."

CHAPTER 26

Lark's first glimpse of Luskan, the City of Sails, made his fingers itch for a quill and parchment. This was a city made for song. Not the gentle crooning melody of a ballad you sang for your sweetheart; maybe a bawdy tavern rhyme or two, in the right context. No, what the city really called for was poetry that cut. Words breaking like waves against the jagged cliffs. A song that could make you bleed and that didn't care if you lived or died. Baldur's Gate was a city that tried to rob you blind, but it did so with a facade of civility that Lark had no time for. Luskan didn't bother to hide its intentions—or its blades.

Lark was in love at first sight.

The city draped itself belligerently across the span of the River Mirar, erected on twin escarpments of rock, with islands like chipped teeth lying between them. Long before the Fallbacks reached the city gate, they walked in the deep shadow of its thick stone walls and guard towers. Out of the reach of the sun, the air held a sharp northern chill. The summer heat was nothing but a memory.

Lark tucked his coat closer around himself as they entered the city. He trailed at the back of the group to take in the sights, sounds, and, Gods yes, even the smells that drifted out from taverns—meat and potatoes, crusty loaves of bread, and other simple fare that stuck to the bones, along with the tang of ale from freshly tapped kegs.

"Stay close," Tess advised from the front of the group, where she walked with Baldric and Anson, who was minding Uggie in her sheepdog disguise. Cazrin walked just in front of Lark, craning her neck as much as he was to take everything in. "Mind your coin purses and mind your own business as much as you can," she continued. "We're heading straight for the Hosttower of the Arcane."

It was a very Tess thing to say, and ordinarily, Lark might have objected to the single-minded course she'd set. After all, what better way to get a feel for a city than to saunter through its streets, peek into its back alleys, and interact with the people?

They passed a tavern on a wide thoroughfare just as a group filed out, showing off colorful tattoos on their arms and faces that marked them as members of one of the city's five ruling Ships. Baldric had warned them that "Ships" didn't actually refer to sailing ships, but to neighborhoods in the city. Lark wasn't sure to which Ship they belonged, but the way they carried themselves, spreading out across the breadth of the street as if they owned it, a spark of challenge in their eyes to anyone who got too close, told Lark they were highly placed. If you made trouble in Luskan, you'd risk not just a knifing in a dark alley but retribution from the ruling Ships and their allies.

Lark didn't want any more trouble than their group was already carrying, and since he was back to looking over his shoulder again, he took Tess's advice and kept a low profile. Still, he marked every sharp edge and brutal cut the city offered, vowing to record it all later.

Because this was a city he could lose himself in.

There was a time he might have considered putting down roots in a place like this, hard edges and all. It would take a lot of effort to win over the tavern crowds with his songs, but Lark relished the challenge. And he might have romanticized the idea of sailing off on a pirate ship alongside one of the High Captains of Luskan, like Kurth or Suljack. That was before he'd discovered how violently seasick he got, even on a swift ship hugging the coast in calm waters. The fates were uncommonly cruel to his romantic soul, that was certain.

"Oh my," Cazrin breathed, stopping so quickly in front of Lark that, absorbed in his own thoughts, he almost barreled into her.

"Cazrin, dear, if you're going to stare, you should close your mouth," Lark told her. "Otherwise the flies might wander in, and there are a considerable amount near the mouth of these alleys."

"Lark," Cazrin said, tugging on his arm. "Look up."

Lark followed her pointing finger, and his lips curved in a knowing smile. He'd thought Cazrin's eyes had gleamed like stars at seeing the great library of Candlekeep. But the sight of the Hosttower of the Arcane, bastion of archmages and an endless trove of unfathomable magic, had to be its own unique source of wonder for her.

The five-spired tower grew like a great stone tree from Cutlass Island and was connected to the mainland portion of the city via a span of heavily monitored bridges. Lark noted these details in passing, but seeing the tower as a poet might, he considered it the epitome of a wizards' stronghold: forbidding, aloof, grandiose for its sheer audacity; a stone tower on a thin spear of rock, exposed to the elements, protected from those on the ground, but inviting anyone to strike at it from the air. It was a place assured in its magical protections. And though it seemed to be a slender building, Lark was certain that the tower contained far more than it appeared from the outside. Wizards had a habit of making spaces for themselves that sat outside the normal boundaries of the world, much like the Wander Inn for the Fallbacks.

"Are you sure you want to study in a place like that?" Lark asked as Cazrin continued to stare up at the stone edifice, transfixed by its silhouette against the pewter clouds that promised more rain to come. "It's formal and standoffish in a way that you are decidedly not. I mean that as a compliment," he added as Cazrin turned to look at him.

"It's not a place I'd choose to stay," Cazrin clarified. "But the chance to sample the magical knowledge those wizards have amassed?" She shook her head with a wistful sigh. "Yes, I would put up with a great deal to have that chance."

"We have to get there first," Anson interjected, eyeing the heavily fortified and guarded bridge that led to Cutlass Island and the tower. "How are we going to get across the bridge to find this Vellynne Harpell?"

Tess and Baldric exchanged a glance before Tess put her hand briefly on her coin pouch. "The Harpers are helping fund a path to the tower," she explained.

"Bribery?" Lark was vaguely disappointed that there wasn't something more nefarious afoot. "Couldn't the Harpers have come through with a more creative solution?"

"Not if we want to slip in without drawing attention," Baldric said. "Sometimes it's worth being quiet and greasing the right palms to ease the way. This city runs on bribes and shakedowns. We're just fitting in."

"I suppose." It wasn't exactly the stuff of grand songs and heroic tales, but when they crossed the bridge toward the entrance to the imposing tower, with the River Mirar rushing below them and the brittle wind snapping at their cloaks, Lark was quickly back in the poet's mood.

He turned his gaze from the river upward to the tower's peak and experienced a brief instant of vertigo. He put a hand out to the nearby railing to steady himself and rubbed at his temples.

"Don't look at the tower too closely," Cazrin said, leaning near to whisper in Lark's ear.

"Feels like a hundred bees buzzing and bouncing around my skull," Lark muttered. "What's wrong with it?"

"Nothing's wrong with your head," Cazrin assured him.

"I meant—" He stopped when he caught her looking at him in amusement. "I'm starting to rub off on you, aren't I? I'm not sure how I feel about that."

"I'm not sure either," Cazrin admitted, her lips twitching. They'd stopped a short distance from the large doors leading into the tower. "It's the sheer amount of magic cast on and within the tower. It's going to be a bit of a headache if you look too closely."

"Lovely," Lark muttered. "And we're going to spend a considerable amount of time in this place."

"It should pass," Cazrin said. "In the meantime, get ready. You're onstage soon, remember?"

Of course he remembered. He knew the plan backward and forward, courtesy of Tess. He made his way to stand with her and Baldric before the doors, and Cazrin, Anson, and Uggie remained a few feet behind, dividing the party into two separate groups for entry.

After a long few minutes, the door to the tower swung open, revealing a neat but sparse foyer lit by driftglobes hovering near the ceiling. Lark stood up straight, ignoring the ache at his temples, as a towering magical construct stepped into view, filling the doorway with its presence. Instead of flesh and bone, it was composed of silver, steel, and magic. Lightning danced at its joints and glowed from its penetrating eye sockets. Its entire frame was covered in magical carvings, and it carried an axe as big as Lark's body, the edge of the blade alight with purple radiance.

"Do you have an appointment?" the construct asked in a booming, metallic voice.

"I do, in fact," Lark said, recovering from his initial surprise. He put on a charming smile and got straight to the point. Sometimes it was better to be succinct than loquacious. "My business is with Vellynne Harpell. My associates and I come at the behest of Mel, an old friend of hers. Could you show us the way?"

The construct tilted its head in acknowledgment and gestured with its axe over Lark's shoulder to the second group. "What about the rest of you?"

Cazrin stepped up next to Lark. "Cazrin Varaith and bodyguards," she said, indicating Anson and sheepdog Uggie. "I've come to petition for membership in the Arcane Brotherhood."

The construct made a dismissive gesture with its free hand. "I'm sure you've paid a great deal of coin to get this far, but I'm afraid you've come in vain," it said. "We don't accept candidates for membership who walk in off the street. Unless you have a referral, or a sponsor—someone from within the Brotherhood who will speak for you—or a compelling reason why you should be granted an interview."

Cazrin casually reached into one of her satchels and pulled out Keeper, her spellbook and personal journal. "I was part of a group that recovered the Ruinous Child and kept it from the hands of the lich Lorthrannan," she said, laying out the revelation as if they were discussing the weather or the price of milk.

Now was the time for a more exuberant performance, Lark thought. He just hoped it would work on the construct—though he suspected by its manner that there was a person in the tower somewhere watching and speaking through the thing.

He turned to Cazrin, putting on a look of amazement. "Wait a minute," he said, "that was *you*? The wizard who tamed that evil tome? Why, that was all anyone was talking about in Waterdeep when I went through there a few months back. That lich burned down two city blocks trying to reclaim his tome. That must have been quite the powerful artifact."

"It wasn't easy to handle," Cazrin admitted, "but we managed."

As they spoke, Lark shot a glance at the construct out of the corner of his eye. Its glowing gaze was fixed on Cazrin, but Lark couldn't tell if it was interested or not. Well, it wouldn't be fun if it wasn't a challenge, Lark thought as he mentally cracked his knuckles.

"You know, I myself am something of an adventurer, and a teller of tales," Lark said, deliberately turning away from the construct at the door. "I'd love to hear the story of your exploits, and what you learned from the Ruinous Child. It would make for a fascinating account."

"Well," Cazrin said, shooting a quick, apologetic look at the construct, "I do have a fairly detailed summary and notes about my time with the book." She held up her journal and spoke to it. "Keeper, go to the relevant entries on the Ruinous Child, please." She waited while the tome floated up from her hands, its cover flipping open. Pages fluttered as the spellbook searched for the requested section.

"Oh, this is wonderful," Lark said, eyeing Keeper with an avaricious gaze. "You know, I also have a friend who teaches at Blackstaff Academy, and I'm sure they would be more than happy to take a look at—"

"Excuse me," the construct interrupted. "This is a private interview with a petitioner. I will send word for you and your companions to be escorted to Vellynne Harpell. In the meantime—" The construct stepped back, opened the door wide, and gestured for just Cazrin and Anson to enter. "Please follow me."

"Thank you very much," Cazrin said. Anson and Uggie went ahead of her, slipping easily into the bodyguard role, and just before Cazrin followed, she turned and shot a wink at Lark, Tess, and Baldric.

Then she was gone, and the door closed behind her.

Lark turned to Tess and Baldric, giving them the smile of a satisfied cat. "Sometimes this job is too easy," he commented.

Baldric laughed. "Could you look a bit more pleased?" he said. "I don't think you've managed to give yourself enough credit."

"Good job, Lark," Tess said. "Now we see if Mel's contact can help."

"And is worth what we—or, rather, the Harpers—paid to get here," Lark said.

"Just stick to the plan," Tess said, "and keep your eyes open. We're not in Candlekeep now. I have a feeling this place is going to be even more dangerous than we thought."

CHAPTER 27

The construct escorted Cazrin, Anson, and Uggie down a series of hallways lit by more of the driftglobes they'd glimpsed in the foyer. Thick red carpets muffled their footsteps and kept away drafts, but there was still a noticeable chill in the air. Cazrin nodded to a handful of other wizards they passed. They were dressed in some of the most ostentatious robes she had ever seen. She tried not to stare as the embroidery on a tiefling's sleeve wiggled and changed before her eyes, the image of the sun rising over a forest darkening to a star-filled sky above a roiling sea. Other robes were infused with a magical glow that flashed and shifted colors every few seconds, as if each wizard were trying to outdo the others.

Several of the spellcasters were surrounded by the same intimidating construct that was leading them through the tower. The constructs carried armfuls of books or scrolls, marching behind their masters in a precise formation that reminded Cazrin of an army. It was wondrous and unsettling at the same time, and she watched it all with an ache in her chest.

"You all right?" Anson asked her in a low voice.

"Just a little overwhelmed," Cazrin admitted. "We've been to some amazing places on our adventures together, but this is . . ." She bit her lip and lowered her voice so the construct guiding them wouldn't overhear. "When I was a child, sometimes I would pretend I was a member of the Arcane Brotherhood. I'd run around with a carved stick for a wand, chasing my younger siblings and pretending to chant spells." She cringed at the memory of what had come after those play sessions. "As you can imagine, it didn't go over very well with the rest of my family."

She'd been banished to her room, where she would pretend that she had locked herself away in her own magical laboratory, in the topmost room of the Hosttower of the Arcane.

And now here she was.

"Do you wish they could see you here?" Anson asked, then amended, "I mean, do you wish they could see what you wanted them to see, all those years ago?"

Cazrin nodded. It took a moment for her to speak. "That's exactly what I wish," she said. She nudged his arm with her elbow. "But I'm glad you're here too."

"I've got your back," he assured her, and Cazrin felt infinitely better. She clutched her staff, feeling the pulse of its magic, and an answering wave from the space around her.

Everything about the tower spoke to her. It was the magic, carefully contained, yet enveloping the place like a stunning work of art. It spoke to her of spaces. Protected spaces, where powerful magic was kept from prying eyes and eager hands. *Watched* spaces. The entire tower felt as if it were its own presence, tracking her every move. It was the kind of guardedness that expected a certain level of behavior and respect. *Watch your conduct, for there are more eyes than you know upon you.*

Most impressive of all were the hidden spaces—rooms that were bigger, that contained more than the naked eye could at first perceive. Cazrin had been expecting this, but seeing it in practice was another matter entirely.

They passed rooms that from the outside appeared to be little bigger than a closet. She peered into one of these, hoping for just a quick glimpse of its secrets. Her mouth dropped open when the room she observed suddenly morphed into a cavernous space. A single wizard stood in the center, staring up at a map of the Astral Plane projected across the ceiling. Glowing green arrows marked points of interest in the celestial void.

Anson had to physically pull her away from that one.

They passed a room where a menagerie of familiars trained under the sharp eyes of their eladrin keeper—hawks, snakes, snowfoxes, tressyms, and faerie dragons all cavorting together in the same space. In another room, a circle of wizards appeared to be repairing a magical tome, page by page, with hundreds of sheets of parchment floating in the air. The wizards stared up at the pages with identical gazes of hunger, as if they couldn't wait to claim the knowledge for themselves.

Cazrin had never seen a magical tome being *created* before. She stopped just short of begging Anson and their guide to let her stop and watch as disembodied hands stitched the pages of the book together one by one. This whole journey through the tower was the most wonderful, torturous experience of her life.

Her head was spinning by the time their escort stopped before a nondescript wooden door at the end of a narrow hall. The construct opened the door and gestured for them to go inside. Cazrin's breath caught as she found herself in an expansive laboratory. Bookshelves and racks of alchemical supplies lined the walls, the elegant arrangement broken only by the white stone fireplace at the back of the chamber, where a cauldron of liquid that gave off a spicy scent bubbled over a low flame.

Cazrin's eye was drawn to a circle of runes carved into the floor nearby. Scorch marks and clawlike furrows marred the stone inside the circle, and the runes gleamed with blue-white radiance. In the center of the room, there was a massive wooden table that looked like it might once have belonged in a noble family's dining hall, except that it had been scarred by numerous experiments. Acid burns marred the length of one side, and what looked like teeth marks had broken off two corners. The entire surface of the table was stained with powders, paints, inks, and possibly blood, though Cazrin wasn't close enough to inspect it to be sure.

A human woman was standing at one end of the table, staring down at a stack of parchment. She looked to be in her late fifties, with short white hair and a black eye patch covering her right eye. As Cazrin, Anson, and Uggie approached, she removed a quill from a brass holder shaped like a serpent, dipped it in ink, and made a note on the parchment. A tremor went through her hand, and she paused, waiting for it to still before she made another mark and then looked up at them.

"Vellynne, here are the guests you were contacted about," said the construct before stepping out of the room and closing the door behind itself.

Vellynne? But that was the wizard Tess, Baldric, and Lark were supposed to see. Cazrin exchanged a confused look with Anson, who mouthed the woman's name and shrugged, waiting for her to take the lead.

"It's a pleasure to meet you," Cazrin said, swallowing her nervousness as she approached the woman. "I'm Cazrin Varaith." She nodded to Anson. "These are my companions, Anson and Uggie."

Vellynne Harpell regarded her with a look of curiosity. Her left eye was dark brown and piercing, her mouth firm. "My apologies," she said brusquely. "I would have come to greet you myself, but I've been struggling with this tricky bit of translation for days now. A tantalizing puzzle, but even my patience isn't infinite."

"We apologize for disturbing you," Cazrin said. "You see, I've come to petition for membership in—"

"You look like her," Vellynne interrupted. "Your ancestress was known as Merana the Weave Speaker during her time in these halls—they were not precisely *these* halls, of course. Still, you might hear the echoes of her footsteps. Some say great magic can still be felt long after its passing, and it's said she created many of her most powerful spells here."

Cazrin did not feel the echo of great magic in that moment. What she felt was a creeping flush across the back of her neck. She was exposed, peeled raw under the wizard's intense scrutiny. Vellynne had caught her off guard, mentioning her family. She hadn't realized the woman would recognize her name. Was that why they'd been brought straight to her? And where were the others now?

She put her shoulders back, gathering herself, and met Vellynne's gaze squarely. "I've come here to pursue *my* magical education," she said firmly. "I believe I have a great deal to offer the Arcane Brotherhood. In addition to my own skill in magic, I bear knowledge of the Ruinous Child, and I believe my experiences with that ancient tome will be of interest to your organization."

"Undoubtedly," Vellynne said. "When word reached us of the reappearance of that particular tome, it was a subject of much discussion and excitement." She rested her hip against the table and frowned. "Imagine our disappointment when we heard that same valuable tome had been destroyed by the people who had initially recovered it." She clucked her tongue. "The Weave Speaker committed many crimes against magical institutions in her day, leading even the Brotherhood to—publicly—condemn her actions." Vellynne's lips thinned. "But I doubt she would have condoned the wanton destruction of such a valuable source of magic."

An awkward silence fell. Cazrin had hoped that the wizards of the Hosttower wouldn't be aware of that particular part of her story with the Ruinous Child, but obviously, that hope had been in vain.

Anson spoke up. "It's possible the tome wasn't destroyed," he said. "We never actually saw it blow up. We just . . . you know . . . shoved it into the belly of a purple worm . . . which then exploded . . . burying it under a few tons of rock . . . hidden in the depths of Undermountain." He shifted uncomfortably. "It might turn up again. You know, someday."

"In any event," Cazrin said, taking back the reins of the conversation, "I'd be more than happy to discuss my experiences with the tome."

"I will take it under consideration," Vellynne said, coming around the table. Her robes were dark gray and fur-lined, not nearly so extravagant as those Cazrin had seen on their way here. She eyed Cazrin, once again making her feel self-conscious, as if she were being judged on standards she didn't fully understand.

Then Vellynne's gaze fell on Uggie, and she raised both brows. "There's no need to conceal your familiar's appearance," she said, glancing up at Cazrin. "We've seen far stranger things walk through these doors, I can assure you."

Cazrin glanced down at the disguised Uggie. She wasn't terribly surprised the wizard had seen through the illusion. "You're very kind," she said.

"I wouldn't go that far," Vellynne said, tucking her hands into the sleeves of her robe. "Membership in the Arcane Brotherhood, as you can imagine, is not something granted lightly. Your connection to the Weave Speaker makes you a strong choice, it's true, but I am required to test all potential candidates in order to determine their worth."

"Test?" Anson repeated. He shot a quick, concerned look at Cazrin. "What sort of test?"

"An assessment of her magical abilities, of course," Vellynne said, looking at Anson as if he were a speck of dust that had collected in her pristine lecture hall. "The Brotherhood doesn't waste their time pulling in every common wizard off the street."

"Of course not," Cazrin said, doing her best to sound unbothered. "However, we were hoping to get more information about the Brotherhood and your facilities here at the Hosttower. Perhaps in the form of a tour?" Which would allow them to discreetly look for cultists and ask questions about any recent suspicious activities taking place in the tower that might point to Ashardalon. At least, that had been the hope.

Vellynne gave her an icy smile. "As a wizard yourself, and the descendant of the Weave Speaker, you of all people should understand that we do not share our secrets lightly, nor do we open our doors freely. If you pass the initial test, then we may discuss such things. Unless you feel you are not up to the task?"

Cazrin heard the challenge in the older woman's voice. "I'm more than willing to undertake any test you can devise," she said calmly.

"Then we'll start at once." Vellynne clapped her hands together, then made a series of quick, complicated gestures. The room around them darkened, and Cazrin felt a rush of magic sweep her up, making her head swim.

When her vision cleared, they were no longer standing in Vellynne's laboratory. Instead, they'd been transported to an empty room with bare stone walls. Uggie pressed her nose to the dusty floor, sniffing and sneezing and searching for food.

"Hold on," Anson said, frowning as he looked around. "You

could at least give her a little time to get ready. She hasn't studied for this."

"Study for—" Vellynne blinked at him, then she actually chuckled, a soft, papery sound in the quiet room. "Forgive me. An outsider would naturally be confused." She gestured around them. "The test I'm speaking of is not the sort that involves quill and ink, and this room is far more than what it appears."

She was right. Cazrin could sense it now, the raw power radiating from the walls. "You mean that this is a chamber for testing actual magic use," she said, feeling a spike of nervousness. "My power pitted against yours."

"In a manner of speaking, yes," Vellynne confirmed. "At the conclusion of the test—should you survive—I'll assess the results and see if it's worth going any further."

"*Survive?*" Anson was shaking his head. "No, no, no. No one said anything about a test where death could be part of the score. Cazrin, we don't have to do this. We can leave right now."

"Your companion is oddly protective for a hireling," Vellynne remarked. She shrugged a thin shoulder. "The choice is yours, of course. But you will not have another opportunity to present yourself for testing. If you leave now, you leave for good, and the only legacy for your family within the Arcane Brotherhood will reside with your ancestress."

Her voice had the ring of finality. Cazrin could tell from the amused light in her eyes that she expected her to walk away.

Well, that wasn't going to happen.

"As I said, I'm here to pursue my magical studies," Cazrin said, shifting her staff from one hand to the other, trying to ignore her sweaty palms. "And perhaps educate the Brotherhood as well." Ignoring Vellynne's raised brow, she continued, "You may administer your test, and afterward, I'd like to know more about your organization . . . to see if it's worth *my* time." She gestured to Anson and Uggie. "If you could give my companions a place to wait for me—"

"We're staying," Anson cut in. When Cazrin gave him a look, he smiled apologetically. "I'm simply doing the job I was hired for—being your bodyguard." He glanced at Vellynne. "I promise not to interfere with the test in any way."

"You couldn't if you tried," Vellynne said indulgently. She was looking more enthused by the moment. "I'll observe from outside the room, and the test can begin immediately." She gave a nod. "Good luck to you, Cazrin Varaith. May you do the Weave Speaker proud."

As soon as the door closed behind Vellynne, Anson rolled his eyes. "'May you do the Weave Speaker proud,'" he mimicked in a dull, ominous voice. "Bunch of self-important, stuffy old dust balls if you ask me."

"I'm sure she's listening to you right now," Cazrin admonished him, though she couldn't help the chuckle that escaped her.

"Good." Anson bent to take the cloak off of Uggie, breaking the illusion. The otyugh shook herself, tentacles waving in the air, and licked Anson's outstretched hand. "What do you think we have to look forward to in this *test*?" he asked her.

Cazrin had been wondering about that herself. She turned in a slow circle, examining the room first with her eyes, and then she chanted a spell to reveal the presence of magic in the room. She wasn't sure what she expected to find, but as the spell took effect, the room lit up in a painfully bright convergence of colors and layers of magic that had Cazrin immediately dismissing the spell and clutching her head in her hands. It was just too much magic to sort out. It was overwhelming.

"What's wrong?" Anson demanded, coming quickly to her side. "Are they doing something to you? Have they started the test already?"

"It's not that," Cazrin said, rubbing her forehead with two fingers. "It's this room. It's some kind of magical repository. Spells cast on top of spells. Illusions. Magic that triggers under specific conditions. I've never seen anything quite like it before."

As she stared at the walls, they began to tremble, melting before her eyes, like they stood in the middle of a freshly painted canvas that had gotten caught in the rain. A low vibration started beneath her feet.

She grabbed Anson's arm and Uggie's tentacle, towing them to the center of the room, where the vibration was less intense. "I'm not sure what's about to happen," she said, "but best be prepared for anything."

Anson drew his broken sword, and Uggie assumed a protective stance beside them, opening her mouth wide to expose all her jagged teeth, her tentacles waving menacingly in the air.

PROTECT!

And then all the lights in the room went out at once, plunging them into complete darkness.

CHAPTER 28

After Cazrin, Anson, and Uggie had disappeared inside the tower with their guide, Baldric and the rest of the Fallbacks waited impatiently for their own escort to take them to Vellynne Harpell. It was nearly twenty minutes before a halfling in emerald-green robes appeared. Dark brown dreadlocks spilled over her left shoulder, her brow pierced by a silver hoop that winked in the light of a purple Ioun stone drifting in a steady orbit around her head.

"I am Deva Steen," she said, "Professor Harpell's aid. Please follow me."

Tess motioned to the others, and they followed the halfling down a twisting set of hallways and up several flights of stairs in the tower. Baldric prided himself on being able to keep track of where he was, whether he was in a labyrinth of city streets or roaming the caverns beneath a mountain, but trying to chart their progress through the Hosttower quickly gave him a pounding headache behind his eyes.

He glanced over at Tess to see her scowling in a similar state of frustration. Lark was fiddling with his lute and seemed unconcerned, but then, Baldric rarely turned to the bard for advice on survival in the wilderness.

They passed a few other groups of wizards on their journey through the place, but Baldric didn't recognize any of them from the ship, nor did he see any signs of Antea, or any hint of activity that might indicate a connection to Ashardalon. Then again, the place was massive. When he'd first pictured the Hosttower, he'd imagined a group of decrepit wizards gathered in a handful of drafty rooms. He hadn't expected a thriving community in a building that was magically enhanced to within an inch of its life.

"It might take years to search this place," Baldric said under his breath, leaning close so Tess would hear him. "I hope this Harpell wizard can be useful."

"She will be," Tess assured him, as they made yet another turn and started down a wide hallway. It ended in a set of double doors lined with arcane carvings.

"Through here, please," their guide said, gesturing to the door. "You can wait inside. Professor Harpell will join you shortly."

"Thank you," Baldric said, fighting his impatience. When he crossed the threshold, his mouth dropped open.

The room was cavernous. Rows of glass display cases lined the walls, each containing a different monster magically preserved, like an exhibit one might see in a museum. What drew Baldric's gaze was not the displays, but rather what was hanging above them.

Two huge monsters towered over the room, their bodies suspended on thick wires sprouting from the ceiling and the walls. The one on the right had the legs and body of a huge centipede. Its flesh was a deep, glacial blue, with bony ridges sprouting all along its back, and winglike appendages flaring out from its sides and behind its head.

"Remorhaz," Tess said breathlessly. "I've heard of these monsters, but I've never seen one in person, and certainly not so . . ." She trailed off, gesturing to the wires holding the creature in a rearing pose.

"Articulated?" Baldric finished for her. The remorhaz was clearly dead, though well preserved, with only a hint of discoloration near the back end to indicate it had been dead for some time.

Then there was the creature on the left.

"Ah, memories," Lark said, gazing up at the preserved purple worm, which had been posed in a loose corkscrew, with the center portion of its body positioned near the ground.

"Even dead, it's still impressive and threatening," Tess commented.

"One of my finest specimens," said a voice from behind them.

Baldric turned to see an older woman in burgundy robes tied with a yellow sash. She had short, wavy white hair that made her skin seem even paler than it was. A patch covered her right eye, and the stern set to her thin-lipped mouth told Baldric she suffered no fools. A snowy white owl perched on her left shoulder.

"Vellynne Harpell?" Tess asked, stepping toward the woman.

"I am," Vellynne said, inclining her head. "And you must be Tess."

"Mel's student, yes," Tess said, and introduced the others. "Thank you for agreeing to meet with us. We wouldn't have disturbed your"—she shot a glance at the display case—"research unless it was important, for us and for the Arcane Brotherhood as well."

"Is that so?" The wizard arched a skeptical brow as she approached one of the few empty display cases in the room. She opened the glass door and then reached into a satchel at her side. Baldric wrinkled his nose in disgust as Vellynne pulled out a large, preserved rat, the creature's brain partially exposed in a nest of short, wiry fur. Gently, she laid the specimen inside the case. She glanced up at Baldric, a flicker of amusement in her eyes. "Is this sort of research not to your taste?" she asked.

"Not my sort of magic," Baldric admitted, but he gamely walked over to examine the display case, pulling Lark along with him, though the bard muttered a protest under his breath. "What do you do with all these creatures?"

"Some of them I dissect to learn more about their anatomy," Vellynne explained as she arranged the rat—cranium rat, according to the small placard on the display case. "Others are used in experiments to discover how their component parts can be incorporated into potions and poisons, or how the whole can be used in reanimation."

"Why is it called a cranium rat?" Lark asked, looking at the thing in distaste. "Aside from the obvious, of course."

Vellynne glanced at him. "It's actually a fascinating topic," she said. "Mind flayers create them. Do you know what a mind flayer is?"

"I'm familiar with them," Lark said dryly.

"Good." Vellynne pointed to the rat's exposed brain. "They lash the creatures with waves of psionic energy, altering their minds and creating a swarm of creatures capable of merging into a single intelligence, a unified whole that overwhelms their victims with sheer numbers—and teeth."

"How very... efficient." Lark looked as if he was sorry he'd asked the question, but Vellynne seemed like she was just getting started.

"Come," she said. "Let me show you the remorhaz. Most people who find themselves this close to one end up dead. This is a rare opportunity for you all."

Baldric leaned over to Tess and spoke under his breath. "Cazrin would be loving this," he said.

Tess nodded. "Maybe not the cranium rat, but everything else, yes," she agreed. "She'll be sorry she missed it."

Baldric watched Vellynne Harpell walk among the specimens, pointing out features of each to a reluctant Lark. Cazrin might have enjoyed the lecture the woman was giving, but as far as Baldric was concerned, the two wizards were nothing alike. There was a coldness to Vellynne, to all the wizards he'd seen here so far. They carried themselves with an arrogance and superiority that Cazrin had never shown. She may have dreamed of living here in her childhood, but Baldric didn't think she could ever be comfortable here. She was too good for the place. Still, he hoped that wherever Cazrin was, she was experiencing the Hosttower in all the ways she'd longed for.

CHAPTER 29

Cazrin had been lost in the dark before. She wasn't afraid. And she also wasn't alone this time. She could hear Anson's and Uggie's quickened breathing beside her. It would take more than a simple spell like this to unnerve her.

"Hold tight," Cazrin said. "If the darkness is magical, I can dispel it."

She'd just raised her staff when a sudden *whoosh* of hot wind blew straight at her, stealing her breath and driving her back several steps.

Into nothing.

A scream tore from Cazrin's throat as she found herself suddenly falling, the ground ripped from beneath her. Her heart hammered wildly, and she forced herself to concentrate, murmuring the words of a spell that would save her, making her body weightless as a feather. Her staff flared with purple light, and then she was drifting in midair, getting strange, shadowy glimpses of her surroundings that made no sense.

She saw an image of herself floating upside down. A night sky, stars drifting in the background. Water or some other substance flowing below her—and then the light on her staff snuffed out, and she was alone in a dark void again.

"Cazrin, where are you? Are you all right?"

"I'm fine!" Anson's panicked shout came from somewhere above her, but it was so far away. How far had she fallen? What *was* this place?

And then, as quickly as it had descended, the darkness lifted. Cazrin blinked at a sudden brightness, but it wasn't the wash of sunshine or even the subtle, artificial warmth of magical light. It was a painful, gleaming whiteness emanating from the walls around her. There was no color. Cazrin floated downward in a room whose walls seemed to go on forever, with no visible ground or ceiling.

But there were details. Cazrin spun in midair, trying to take it all in. White staircases pushed themselves out of the walls, leading up, down, and sideways, ending in midair, or melting right back into the walls. Sandwiched among them were slivers of mirrored glass, endlessly reflecting her own image and the images of the staircases. It hurt her eyes to look at it all, to stare into the bright white light.

"Gods, that makes my head ache!" Anson shouted. "Is this an illusion?"

"I'm not sure."

Cazrin had sworn Anson was above her, but now his voice seemed to echo from below. She heard Uggie whining nervously, but she couldn't see the otyugh either.

"Some of it likely is an illusion," she went on, "but I don't know how much. We should tread carefully, but . . . isn't it beautiful?"

Though she felt a spike of fear in being separated from Anson and Uggie, at the same time, she couldn't help but be fascinated by her surroundings. The amount of magic it must have taken to create this landscape, the detail . . .

"It's like a painter working on a composition," she said. "Only instead of layers of paint, it's magic, spells meticulously woven together. Maybe a tapestry would be a better comparison. Oh, I don't know if that's right either!" Her fingers automatically went for Keeper. She needed to take notes, figure out how the magical connections worked and—

"Um, Cazrin," Anson called out, sounding anxious. "I hate to interrupt, but isn't this supposed to be some sort of test? Because we need to solve it and get out of here."

"Right!" Cazrin flushed. She had momentarily forgotten why they were here. She slid her journal deliberately back into its satchel. "I need you to keep talking so I can find you." The spell she'd cast to stop her fall wouldn't last forever.

"You can't see me?" Anson called back, sounding even more anxious. "I can see you. You're about a hundred feet below us. We're up here."

Cazrin looked up, eyes straining, but all she could see were the staircases and mirrors, her own image reflected back to her hundreds of times.

"It must be part of the test," Cazrin said. "They want us confused, separated." She looked around. Since there were no visible exits, the object of the test must be to escape.

"I can't hear you," Anson called down, his voice sounding even farther away. "The voices are drowning you out."

"Voices?" Cazrin said sharply. She listened, but there was no sound in the room. The absoluteness of the silence was eerie, in fact. It raised gooseflesh all along her arms. "I don't hear anything, Anson. Are you sure?"

She waited, but there was no response.

"Anson?" Cazrin repeated. "Uggie? Can you hear me? Where are you, girl?"

Still, there was nothing, just the all-encompassing silence.

Anger flared in Cazrin. This test was meant for her. If the wizards of the Arcane Brotherhood hurt Anson or Uggie, they were going to answer for it.

Raising her staff, she chanted the words to a spell that was intended to remove magic in a given area. She put as much power into the casting as she could. Maybe it would burn away only a few layers of this strange, mazelike trap, but she had to start somewhere if she was going to find the way out.

Before Cazrin could finish the spell, movement in the corner of her eye made her turn. One of the staircases jutting from the wall opposite her was moving, swinging out in an arc toward her. Cazrin tried to dodge, but the protruding rail caught her in the shoulder, spinning her in midair. With a gasp of pain, she lost her hold on the burgeoning spell. Images of herself clutching her shoulder surrounded her, making her dizzy and sick to her stomach.

As she tried to regain her equilibrium, the sound of stone grinding on stone filled her ears. She looked up, only to see part of another staircase detach itself from the wall and fall toward her like a massive scythe cutting through the air. She wheeled sideways, narrowly missing being crushed by the moving stairs.

All around her the staircases were changing—some of them growing, some shrinking, others sprouting strange glowing flowers and toadstools. Iron spikes jutted from the rails, and several of the nearby mirrors shattered, raining glass down on her. She cast a quick shield to protect herself from the falling debris, but it wouldn't last long. She needed to get under cover.

"Anson!" she called out again. "Uggie! Can you hear me?"

Amid the chaos, something was niggling at the back of Cazrin's mind. In her periphery, she watched a white lily grow from the wall and be devoured by a large wart-covered toad hanging upside down from a nearby staircase. They were illusions—even if the staircases weren't—but she could have sworn she'd seen them somewhere before.

Was it a book she'd read, or a lecture series? Gods, she couldn't think with the mirrors and the moving staircases coming at her. She needed to concentrate. No, it was a book. It came to her then, a passage she'd read long ago.

The dominant subject I observed in my last experiment was climbing endless stairs that went to nowhere, a fascinating representation of the futility and horror of the victim's current state . . .

Cazrin's breath caught, and a crawling sensation broke out on her skin. As she felt herself starting to fall again, she thrust out a hand and grabbed the nearest stair rail, pulling herself onto a particularly large, solid-looking stone staircase that hadn't yet moved. With shaking hands, she pulled out her journal and let it hover in the air in front of her.

"Keeper, I need to access the secured entries," she said, her voice tight.

It was one of the many tricks she'd learned from the Ruinous

Child—how to protect and obscure certain entries from prying eyes. She wished she'd had it years ago. It would have come in handy during her childhood.

"Are you certain, Cazrin?" Keeper asked, already flipping through pages until it came to a section dated seven years ago, though the entry below the date appeared to be blank.

Cazrin wasn't at all certain. In fact, the very last thing she wanted to do was revisit this part of her studies. She'd locked it away for a reason. But she needed to find Anson and Uggie and get them out of this.

"Do it," she said.

The page in front of her glowed with silver radiance, and slowly, words materialized on it in loops and flourishes. Cazrin glanced around, but the staircases appeared to have settled for now. That, at least, was a relief. Maybe their movement was linked to her own? If she stayed still, they wouldn't try to kill her.

She turned her attention back to the page. The entry was one she'd copied verbatim from a very old text, one she'd found hidden in a secret compartment in a trunk in her parents' attic. They hadn't known it was there, or they likely would have disposed of the tome long ago. Cazrin had copied what she could before she was discovered and the tome taken away by her mother.

"What's written on these pages isn't fit for decent people to see!" her mother had said, white-faced with what Cazrin had thought was fury.

Looking back with more experienced eyes, she realized that her mother had been afraid.

Cazrin wasn't. How could she be? It was the first time she'd ever seen her ancestress's handwriting in person. Running her fingers over the text had felt like reaching her hand across the centuries to greet her. She'd been giddy with excitement, all too eager to get this glimpse into the life of the most powerful wizard in her family.

But her mother had been right. What she'd deciphered on those pages was shocking, and terrible, and Cazrin couldn't blame her for being afraid.

Trying to separate each individual consciousness amassed and absorbed by the aberration would be a fool's task, but I have observed certain personalities emerge stronger than others, which makes them far more likely to be able to retain a part of themselves. Therefore, the flashes of intelligence, the bits of reality projected by the shattered minds—facilitated by my magic, of course—present a unique glimpse into the remnants of the creature's victims.

For instance, the dominant subject I observed in my last experiment was climbing endless stairs that went to nowhere, a fascinating representation of the futility and horror of the victim's current state. In fact, the path the victim trod often attempted to impede his movements, suggesting perhaps that the remnants of his shattered mind were trying to protect him from whatever lay at the end of the road. Tragic, yet poetic and artful in its own way. I must see if I can peel back further layers of his thoughts and expose them to the light. I will, of course, tread carefully this time. I wish I could record the words of the lost for posterity, but I dare not open myself to it. I had thought a broken mind could endure anything, but even that has proved untrue, judging by the screams.

"Gods, no," Cazrin breathed, as she reviewed the entry.

It confirmed her worst suspicions. As part of their test, the Arcane Brotherhood had chosen to mimic one of her ancestress's most gruesome experiments.

"What's the point of this?" she shouted into the mirrored space, knowing that Vellynne was watching her right now. "This test is about *me*! I'm not my ancestress! I should not be judged by her magic!"

She closed Keeper and slipped the journal back into her satchel. She pushed off the wall, but before she could chant the words of a flying spell, there was a great rumbling beneath her feet. The stone staircase, which had looked and felt so stable, was shattering, breaking apart beneath her feet.

The stone dropped away, and she was falling again.

Cazrin only just managed to hold on to her staff as she plummeted, her body rushing past the mirrors, making her head spin and her stomach heave. Frantically, she chanted another spell to slow her fall. Her staff flared with purple radiance, and as the magic took hold of her body, she once again slowed to a gentle drift. Looking down, she was surprised to see a wide stone platform rising to meet her. As she descended, five more staircases swung out from the walls, connecting to the platform with a loud grating sound.

There were multiple figures on the platform. With a surge of relief, Cazrin recognized Anson and Uggie huddled together, precariously close to the edge. It appeared that they were trying to stay as far away as possible from the third figure on the platform.

Cazrin squinted, trying to see what the creature was—

"Oh no."

Suddenly, her spell was yanked from her, and she was falling again.

She landed hard on the platform, her hip and elbow slamming against the unforgiving stone. A wash of pain swept over her, stealing her breath. For a moment, Cazrin just lay there, gritting her teeth through the pain as she tried to determine if anything was broken.

It was only then that she heard the voices.

Whispers at first. Hissing, sibilant things that had no words in them that she could discern.

Only malice. And fear.

They rose steadily, baritones and tenors, squeaks and yelps and whines, tumbling together, becoming a loud, gibbering murmur that crawled inside Cazrin's mind, vibrating through her body as she lay with her ear against the stone platform.

Get out of my head, she begged, curling into herself to make a shield of her body. She covered her head with her hands and pictured her mind as an impenetrable fortress. Building the walls stone by stone, she pushed away the voices, refusing to let them in. She pictured a sunny village square, a cup of tea on a breezy day, the wind carrying Rane's sweet voice to her.

She couldn't lose herself, not now, when she'd only just found herself.

"No."

That voice she knew. It was Anson. The word came out as an agonized moan, and Uggie whined in response.

The voices were hurting them.

With an effort, Cazrin pushed herself up onto one elbow and made herself look across the platform at the horrific mass of a creature squatting there.

A gibbering mouther.

It was the source of the voices. Cazrin knew it because the pinkish, oozing, liquified form of the creature was covered in mouths. Grins with black gums and broken teeth. Snakelike fangs and grinding molars. The worst of them were the perfect, straight teeth, the pink lips twisted in a euphoric smile even as the voices came out in a tortured wail of unbearable sorrow.

All of it was enough to make her gorge rise, but what snared Cazrin like a hook to the chest, making her unable to look away, were the eyes.

The monster was covered in them. Human eyes, dragonborn eyes, elven eyes, all fixed on Cazrin. Even the eyes of owls and the lambent gaze of wolves speared into her. The mouther was indiscriminate in choosing its victims, absorbing them until only bits and pieces of their bodies and consciousness remained. She'd read about the process in her ancestress's notes, but seeing it like this was unimaginable.

Horror overcame Cazrin, because those eyes, swimming in the liquified matter that had once been living bodies, were *aware*. They knew what they had once been and what they had become. They knew they were damned, for as long as the creature that had consumed them was alive, they could not truly die.

Cazrin lifted a trembling arm, her fingers curling as she prepared to hold the spell and channel it where she needed it to go.

"Burn," she said, her voice a whisper lost in the gibbering cacophony.

But the eyes saw. They saw the burgeoning flame, and as one, they screamed.

Cazrin released the fireball directly into the mass of the abomination.

CHAPTER 30

Of all the wonders Tess thought she might encounter within the Hosttower of the Arcane, one thing she had never expected was to be surrounded by dead, articulated monsters, listening to Vellynne Harpell explain the inner workings of cranium rats and a remorhaz. Mel had warned her that the woman was eccentric, but she also seemed to be an inexhaustible well of knowledge. Under other circumstances, Tess would have wanted to be in the room to see Vellynne and Cazrin discuss magical theory. As it was, they couldn't afford to stand around listening to the woman lecture all day.

Vellynne seemed to sense her impatience. She shrugged one shoulder, and the owl took flight, landing on one of the remorhaz's outstretched legs. "So tell me, Tess, what is so important that Mel sent you to me, and how does it affect the Arcane Brotherhood?"

Finally, Tess thought. "We have reason to believe that the Hosttower has been infiltrated by cultists affiliated with Ashardalon," she said. "Do you know who that is?"

Vellynne's gaze sharpened. "Yes, I'm familiar with that name. It would not surprise me to learn that the greatwyrm had scattered followers within the tower. Members keep their own secrets, and we don't pry into their affiliations unless it threatens the Brotherhood."

"This is more than just a single wizard or two," Baldric put in. "According to our information, the cult has been secretly and aggressively moving into positions of power and influence. Whatever they're planning, it *will* threaten your organization."

"We need your help to root them out," Tess said. "We have names and descriptions, but we don't know who to trust and—"

"Not here," Vellynne said abruptly, cutting her off. She cast a glance around the room, as if someone might be listening, then motioned them toward the door. "If the threat is as grave as you say, we need to continue this conversation in my office downstairs. Follow me."

Tess exchanged a hopeful glance with Baldric and Lark as they fell into step behind Vellynne, leaving the strange specimen room behind. Mel had been right; it seemed that Vellynne was willing to listen and maybe even help them.

"Exactly how big is this place?" Tess couldn't help asking as she tried yet again to track their progress through the tower. Whenever they passed a window, she looked outside to get her bearings, but she was never in the place she expected. It was as if the Hosttower defied all attempts to be understood, at least by outsiders.

Vellynne, never breaking stride, glanced over her shoulder. "Whatever you're thinking, it's likely larger," she said with an enigmatic smile. "How large? I doubt you'll get anyone here to tell."

"Can you tell us how long you've been here? Or how you came to be a member?" Baldric asked. "I've heard of the Harpell family, of course—"

"Oh?" Vellynne said. "Do tell. What have you heard about us?"

"A family of prestigious, eccentric wizards based in Longsaddle," the dwarf continued. "But you don't seem to quite fit with what I've heard of the other Harpells."

"You mean because I'm of the necromantic persuasion," Vellynne said with a raspy chuckle.

"Well, yes," Tess said, exchanging a glance with Baldric. But it wasn't only that. Vellynne struck her as being more pragmatic, more ruthless than the famed Harpells of Longsaddle.

"I found that my ambitions were better understood by the Arcane Brotherhood," Vellynne explained as they turned yet another corner in the twisting, labyrinthine structure. "Their resources are vast, but beyond that, sometimes one needs to step outside the bonds of family to properly find their place in the world."

She and Cazrin had that in common, Tess thought, but she couldn't help also thinking that something didn't add up here. Mel had said Vellynne Harpell was someone they could trust, someone powerful in the Hosttower, but she didn't seem like the type of person Mel would confide in. Powerful, yes, and ambitious, but she didn't seem as concerned about the cult infiltrating the tower as Tess had expected.

She glanced over at Baldric, hoping to catch his eye, but the cleric was staring intently at their surroundings, as if memorizing their passage or trying to work something out in his head.

Vellynne led them to a narrow, winding staircase at the end of a long hallway, and they began to descend. There were no windows along the walls, so Tess couldn't be sure how far down they went, but the air turned colder and colder, and after a while, she noticed thin streams of moisture sliding down the walls.

"Are we underground?" Baldric asked before Tess could. "Didn't know you wizards had chambers this far away from the sun. Aren't you afraid of the books getting moldy?"

Vellynne shot him a raised eyebrow, as if the question were absurd. "We have measures in place to guard against that," she said, "and some conversations and research are better done in peace, away from prying eyes."

"Oh, that doesn't sound ominous at all," Lark said, as they finally reached the bottom of the stairs. Another short hall ended at a pair of double doors, which Vellynne unlocked with a key she wore around her neck. She pushed open the doors and gestured for them to follow her inside.

Tess stepped into a cavernous chamber that soared at least a hundred feet above their heads. Craning her neck, she could just barely make out the stone ceiling, which was interspersed with natural rock and small clusters of toothy stalactites.

"Impressive space," Baldric said, but his gaze was skeptical as he peered around the chamber. There were a few bits of old furniture—tables, chairs, and some desks—covered by dusty sheets, as if the items had been stowed in the room decades ago and forgotten. "Seems like you could do more here than store the things nobody wants anymore," he commented.

"It's used for something," Lark said slowly, squinting at the walls as if he thought they might suddenly grow mouths and bite him. "I can feel that magic fizzing around in my head again."

"This room is a prototype," Vellynne explained. She strode to the center of the chamber and held out a hand, palm downward. There was a low rumbling, and then a triangular column of stone rose from a depression in the floor. It stopped just below Vellynne's fingers. "Many of the testing rooms upstairs were designed after this original. It utilizes a combination of illusion magic and permanent enchantments to assess the abilities of potential candidates for membership in the Arcane Brotherhood."

She made a short, slashing gesture over the stone column, which glowed briefly with purple light in response.

Suddenly, the room began to change.

White patches formed on the walls and floor, creating the illusion of snow and ice. A forest sprang up around them, dense clusters of trees that grew and spread their snow-covered branches. High above their heads, the shadowy ceiling faded to a gray winter sky, with mountains rising in the distance. When it was finished, Tess could almost believe they'd been teleported to the Spine of the World.

She put out her hand, half expecting the snowflakes that drifted around her to feel cold against her skin. So this was what Cazrin was facing right now, she thought, a test of her magical abilities. Tess suddenly felt very far away from the rest of her friends.

And with a sinking feeling, she realized that Vellynne had indeed brought them down here for privacy, but not the sort that would benefit them.

"So," Tess said, turning to face the woman, "when did you take Vellynne's place, Antea?"

Beside her, Baldric and Lark stiffened. Lark cursed, but Tess noticed Baldric didn't look nearly as surprised as the bard. He must have suspected as well.

They'd been so close, Tess thought with a stab of regret. If only they could have gotten to speak to the real Vellynne. She flicked her gaze to Lark and gave the tiefling a subtle nod, the signal that the bard needed to contact Cazrin magically and warn her as soon as he could.

At the same time, Antea made a quick gesture with her fingers. Tess braced herself as several figures in hooded robes walked out of the illusory forest. Their features were obscured by their hoods, but Tess recognized them anyway. They were the cultists who had confronted them on board the ship, along with several additional members. The wizard stepped forward, her features shimmering and shifting before their eyes until Antea stood before them.

"You suspected me before now?" the woman inquired, giving Tess a narrow look. "I suppose I should have expected that." She turned to Lark, who was eyeing the door. "The exits from this room have been sealed," she assured him. "You'll die here, and then we'll find and take care of the rest of your group."

"Before you come for us," Baldric interjected, "I have a deal to propose."

Antea laughed. It echoed unpleasantly in the cavernous room, which still looked like a snowy landscape. "You're in no position to bargain with me," she said.

"Aren't I?" Baldric countered. He touched a hand to his chest, and Tess imagined the red tether they'd seen in Baldric's vision. "You're angry about this connection between me and Ashardalon. I felt your rage when we fought on the ship. You've done a lot for your master, and naturally, you want something in return."

"I want only what was *promised*," Antea hissed. Her eyes flashed, pupils swallowed by black, and Tess took an involuntary step back. "I was to be the leader of the faithful, first among Ashardalon's chosen."

"And you were passed over; Ashardalon came after me instead," Baldric said, holding his ground against the woman's anger. "But we can help each other, Antea. I'm never going to serve the gods, and I'm certainly not going to swear fealty to a dragon that wants to keep me like a pet." He waved a hand. "And look at you. You're Ashardalon's highest-ranking servant, his most loyal follower, and yet he pits us against each other and just sits back and enjoys the show. He doesn't care about you, except for how he can use you. Help me break the connection to him. Show Ashardalon that you won't be his plaything. Make him *earn* your loyalty." He added, "And if he doesn't, you walk away, and you can say you stuck it to the charred old wyrm."

Tess kept an eye on the gathered cultists as Baldric made his case. They were waiting, gathered in a loose circle around their group, eyes locked on their mistress. Baldric could be very persuasive when he wanted to be, and Tess held on to a kernel of hope that his offer would entice her and they could do this without bloodshed.

But when Tess looked into Antea's eyes, the woman's calculating gaze slid inexorably back into hatred. It was strong, too strong for reason or even an appeal to her pride to work.

All she wants is our deaths, Tess thought.

"You may be right," Antea said, staring down Baldric. "Your connection to my master, if severed, may restore me to my rightful place. Or Ashardalon may strike me down for my presumption. Either way, if you believe I will leave you alive in the world, a temptation, a toy for Ashardalon to pursue according to his whims, you're mistaken. Your death guarantees that I never have to see or worry about you again."

Antea made a sweeping gesture with her left hand, similar to what Tess had seen Cazrin do when she ended one of her own spells. The shadow Antea cast on the snow-covered ground seemed to darken and spread, rising up around her like a cape of magic. Tess couldn't tell if it was her own power or a function of the chamber, but as the dark curtain surrounded her, Antea seemed to grow larger before their eyes. Her skin darkened, and her hair lengthened, lashing around her shoulders like snakes with glistening scales.

Scales.

"Oh," Tess managed, as the rest of the cultists raised their arms in deference to Antea. Or, to the thing that Antea was becoming.

This is why we couldn't reason with her, Tess realized. She would never bargain with Baldric because she never considered him an equal.

Antea's body continued to swell, black scales covering her pale flesh as she filled the chamber. Her neck elongated, her eyes turning to slitted amber. Her arms became two great black wings that unfurled above their heads.

When the transformation was complete, a black dragon towered over them and the cultists.

Tess found herself rooted in place. She wanted to run but couldn't. She wanted to raise her daggers in defense, but the weapons felt like sticks in her hands.

A dragon. She should have known. The highest servant of Ashardalon would not be human.

Her face was skull-like, with forward-swept, bone-colored horns that darkened to black at the tips. A flat, forked tongue darted from her mouth, dripping slime that smelled like acid and burned the inside of Tess's nostrils.

"Did you see that coming?" Lark asked in a strained voice as he too stared up at the dragon. "Because that revelation caught me by surprise."

"No," Baldric said hoarsely. "No, I think that one had all of us flat-footed." His expression hardened into a mask of defiance as he addressed the dragon. "We could have had a powerful partnership. We didn't have to be enemies, Antea."

The dragon's booming laugh filled the chamber. "My name is Antezzaravitae, first scion of Chardansearavitriol Ebondeath." She angled her serpentine neck down toward Baldric. "I serve none of the lesser creatures of this world."

"Is it because none of them will take the time to pronounce that name?" Lark chirped. "Because I'd be willing to learn, except putting it into a song might be a challenge."

The dragon reared back, her chest expanding as a sizzling gurgle travelled up her throat.

"Take cover!" Tess cried.

CHAPTER 31

Cazrin watched her fireball streak across the platform toward the gibbering mouther. Crimson flames wreathed a core of deepest black as the spell exploded on the creature, sending a column of fire skyward. The brilliant orange radiance was reflected hundreds of times in the surrounding mirrors, so bright and hot that Cazrin had to duck and cover her head to protect herself.

The whispers momentarily ceased, and Cazrin raised her head in time to see Anson and Uggie jolt, as if they'd been awakened from a nightmare.

Anson looked around in confusion. "What's happening?" he demanded. "Cazrin, what—" And then his gaze fell on the mouther. Its skin was charred black in places, and several of its eyes had melted grotesquely into its flesh, but it was still very much alive.

And angry.

"Anson!" Cazrin cried, as the mouther resumed its terrible gibbering. She waved her arms frantically to drag his attention away from the creature. "You have to block out the voices! Do you hear me? Block them out, or they'll take you over. Uggie! Come here, girl.

That's right." Uggie loped over to her, her mental voice temporarily drowning out the mouther.

Hate this.

Uggie afraid.

Uggie wants to go home.

"So do I, girl," Cazrin said, patting the otyugh with a shaking hand. "Anson!"

"I'm all right—I've got it." Anson clambered to his feet, shaking his head to clear it. The mouther was bearing down on them, slithering across the platform as if the stone beneath it were covered in oil.

Anson drew his sword and charged to meet it, putting his body between the creature and Cazrin and Uggie. He gave a shout of alarm as his boots sank into a soft, gooey substance on the platform, causing him to stumble the last few feet and miss his first swipe at the creature.

"What in the Hells?" He recovered on a backswing that sliced off a protruding lump of flesh. It slapped wetly to the platform. "This thing is terrifying! What kind of a test is this?"

My kind, Cazrin thought grimly, or rather, her family's kind. Would she never escape that woman? She'd been gone so long, but her shadow still loomed large over everything Cazrin tried to accomplish.

She shook those thoughts away. They wouldn't help anyone now. "It's the floor!" she shouted as Anson shifted his stance and plunged the broken end of his sword into one of the creature's bigger eyes. "The mouther transforms the area around itself." Frantically, she tried to remember anything else she'd read in her ancestress's writings. "Don't let it bite you," she warned. "It'll try to absorb you."

"Fantastic." Anson grunted as he wrenched his sword free, flicking some of the monster's liquified flesh off the blade in disgust. "Don't worry about me, just get another fireball ready if you can."

"Not while you're that close!" Cazrin raised her staff and thrust it toward the creature. A stream of blue missiles launched at the mouther, finding more of its eyes and streaking down the fang-filled mouths. The monster roared in pain, and Anson took full advantage, slashing and hacking as hard and as fast as he could.

But the voices were relentless. They rose again in a terrifying chorus of misery and hate. Cazrin imagined she could hear what the mouther's victims were saying.

Make it stop.
Kill me. Kill us.
Die.
You'll join us.
You'll be one with us forever.
DIE.

There was a ringing in Cazrin's ears. She held her staff poised for another spell, but the words wouldn't come to her lips. Vaguely, she felt Uggie grab her wrist and shake her. Anson was yelling something at her, but she couldn't hear him over the voices.

Gods, the voices . . . how had her ancestress been able to bear it for those gruesome experiments?

I wish I could record the words of the lost for posterity, but I dare not open myself to it . . .

Cazrin sucked in a breath as the realization struck her: her ancestress had closed a part of herself off. She hadn't been hearing the voices with her ears. She'd reached out with her thoughts to touch the victims' minds directly. She must have created some sort of mental protection for herself beforehand. Cazrin didn't have those resources to work with, but using that theory, she *could* do something about the voices.

Quickly, she chanted the words of a spell that she'd never tried to use on herself before. Well, no time like the present to push herself. This was a test of her abilities, after all.

As she was finishing the spell, her gaze fell on Anson, but he was too far away to include in the casting, so she turned her attention to Uggie, making one quick change in the wording of the magic to target her.

Sorry, girl, Cazrin thought, *but this will benefit us both in the long run.*

The spell took effect, and suddenly, blessed silence washed over her as Cazrin was deafened by the spell. Uggie shook herself, prancing around in confused fear.

No sound.

Uggie doesn't feel good.

What's happening to Uggie?

Cazrin put her hand on the otyugh in a calming gesture, but she didn't have time to explain her actions.

Across the platform, Anson reared back, his mouth open in a scream that Cazrin could no longer hear, as one of the mouther's teeth-filled maws latched onto his shoulder. The viscous flesh surged up hungrily, as if trying to envelop him.

Over my dead body, Cazrin thought, and Uggie must have felt the same, for she charged across the platform, newly energized and free of the encroaching voices. She waded through the doughy ground created by the monster and sank her teeth into its flesh, catching two more of its eyes. The creature quivered and pulled back, giving Anson an opening to rip his shoulder free of the grasping mouth. Blood flowed down his arm, and his legs trembled, but Cazrin had seen Anson recover from worse. She watched him grasp his broken blade tightly and close his eyes, as if drawing strength from the weapon and his connection to it. Then he opened his eyes and met Cazrin's gaze, his chest expanding on a deep breath, as if using her as a focal point as well, blocking out all other distractions.

When he was in this state, a place of pure concentration and purpose, the pain of his wounds couldn't touch him. His body became an extension of his sword, and he moved with a grace and deadly intent that nothing could impede. He was a wonder to watch.

But the gibbering mouther had its own deadly purpose, and Anson did not have the protection of the magical deafness Cazrin had employed.

As Anson swung his sword, cleaving through another of the creature's eyes, the mouths flexed, and though Cazrin couldn't hear them, she felt the vibration through the stone platform. She saw the moment it hit Anson. The fighter staggered, his eyes going unfocused and his sword slack in his grip.

He turned, as if unsure for an instant where he was or what he should be doing. Then his gaze snapped to Cazrin, and a strange, wild light entered his eyes. He raised his sword and came at her.

"No, Anson, don't!"

But her entreaty couldn't cut through the magical confusion the voices had stirred in Anson's mind.

He swung.

It was a wild, unfocused attack, with nothing like the precision he usually had. Still, it took full advantage of their difference in size.

This is really going to hurt, Cazrin thought as she raised her staff just in time to block.

She caught the blade, and if her staff hadn't been magical, Cazrin had no doubt the strike would have broken it in two. As it was, the blow shuddered painfully through her arms, and she teetered at the edge of the platform, a hair's breadth from plunging off into the abyss. Her staff flared with purple radiance, and she held on, just barely holding back Anson's weight as he tried to shove her over the edge.

"Anson!" Cazrin shouted at him, letting the deafness spell fade. She needed all her senses back so she could snap him out of this. "Wake up! It's me! I told you, you have to fight the voices! Block them out or that thing is going to kill us!"

Glancing over, she saw the mouther rearing back, and a sharp chemical smell filled Cazrin's nostrils. The largest mouth opened wide and launched a sizzling, dripping glob of something foul at them.

"Anson, look out!" Cazrin yelled, and the fighter blinked, coming back to himself just in time to see the projectile.

Before Cazrin could react, he grabbed her staff where it tangled with his blade, using it to turn them, switching their places so that his body acted as a shield, blocking her view of the creature for a second.

The chemical blob hit him square in the back. Anson grunted in pain, and there was a sudden flash of brilliant white light. Cazrin ducked, instinctively pressing her face into Anson's chest to protect her eyes. He curled his arm around her, but his body was trembling, and she could hear the harshness of his breathing.

"Sorry . . . about that," he rasped when Cazrin pulled back to look at him. The chemical smell made her eyes water. Anson smiled weakly. "How . . . do you think . . . we're doing . . . on the test?"

Cazrin saw the pain in Anson's eyes that he was trying to hide. Beyond him, Uggie was furiously tearing into the mouther, but there were bite marks covering her body, and she was limping, her attacks beginning to slow.

And Cazrin had had enough.

"We're getting out of here," she declared. She reached into one of her satchels and pulled out a healing potion, folding Anson's trembling fingers around the vial. It was the strongest potion she carried. "Take this, and when I give you the signal, see if you can feed some lightning into that creature. I'm going to work on our exit."

"Best idea I've heard all day," Anson said, tipping back the vial and draining the contents. Then he spun and charged back into the fray, flanking the creature with Uggie and slashing down with his sword.

Cazrin scanned the walls, firing off a quick spell to reveal the layers of magic, all the enchantments and illusions that had been used to build the testing room. This time, she was braced for the barrage of magic and refused to let it overwhelm her.

Ah, but there were weak spots, she noted. The room wasn't as big as the mirrors and the shifting staircases made it seem. The test subjects wouldn't immediately realize it, because of the warped perspective and the mouther's presence overwhelming their senses. Clever, devious, but shortsighted in the end. Cazrin made a note to herself to give the Arcane Brotherhood a few suggestions of her own for these tests.

She selected a point on the wall, memorized it, then turned her attention to the mouther. "Uggie!" she called. "Get clear! Now, Anson!"

The battered otyugh obediently pulled back, limping to Cazrin's side, just as Anson let out a shout and brought his sword in a diagonal swipe across the creature's body. Lightning whipped along the blade, arcing right into the mouther. It shrieked, its body contorting in hideous poses amid the screams and ululating cries of its chorus of mouths.

"Perfect!" Cazrin cried, seeing the mouther struggling to hold itself together in the wake of the lightning strike. "Now get out of there!"

Cazrin forced herself to focus amid the cacophony, channeling power into her staff. She brought it down against the platform with a thunderous *crack*. A wave of rippling force rolled across the platform just as Anson dove out of the way. It slammed into the mouther, driving it back and off. The screams rose in volume until Cazrin was forced to cover her ears to block out the horrific noise.

She ran to the edge of the platform to look down. The mouther had hit one of the staircases about a hundred feet below. No longer able to hold its form, it splattered into amorphous pools, eyes and mouths dissolving, the screams of its former victims slowly fading as they were finally allowed to die.

"Now that that's done," Cazrin said, glaring at the spot on the wall that she'd chosen. She raised her hand, fingers splayed wide, and began the chant that would summon flame.

"Are the Brotherhood going to be upset if we set the building on fire?" Anson asked, though he didn't seem overly concerned about that outcome. In fact, he looked downright eager.

"I don't think we *could* set this building on fire," Cazrin said when she finished her chant. Flame roiled in her grasp, and she cast her last fireball right at the weak spot on the wall, then skittered back to watch the brilliant conflagration. "But it will probably get their attention."

CHAPTER 32

Baldric had seen a dragon's breath weapon deployed once before, when he'd glimpsed a wizard battling a young red from the safety of a mountain lookout. He'd been very young, and it was long before he'd left home.

His mothers had taken him up to observe the fight in secret, and though they were safely out of range of any potential wild spells or dragon attacks, he'd felt the tension in both of them as they'd watched the deadly duel play out. He'd been captivated by the display, but afterward, when he'd thanked his mothers for letting him watch, they'd both turned to him with that familiar look of annoyance they adopted when he'd missed something they considered to be obvious.

Do you think we wanted to entertain *you by showing you that bit of death?* they'd said. *We did it so you'd learn, so if you ever face something like that, you'll be ready.*

Baldric had nodded soberly, absorbing their admonishment and vowing to remember.

Now, as the black dragon's rain of acid breath enveloped the chamber, burning in his lungs and catching him in the shoulder when he desperately tried to dive for cover in this fake snowy wilderness at the bottom of the Arcane Brotherhood's tower, he had the urge to laugh hysterically.

Nothing, not one bit of what he'd seen as a child, could have prepared him for being in this place, with a burning rain of death bearing down on him and his companions. Oh, if his mothers could see him now . . .

Baldric got to his feet and ran, weaving through an illusory clump of trees, Tess and Lark right behind him. He touched the acid burns now riddling his right shoulder and winced in pain. If his mothers *could* see him, they'd probably call him a fool for thinking he could take cover behind trees that didn't actually exist.

"Kill them!" the dragon commanded. "Kill them all!"

Two of the cultists ran for the trees where they were hiding, and the other three went for the stone column in the middle of the room.

"They're going to deactivate the illusion magic," Tess said, nudging Lark urgently. "That's our only advantage right now. Can you stop them?"

Lark tilted his head, considered for a split second, then pulled his lute off his back and played a few chords, his voice rising in accompaniment with the words of a spell. Just as the cultists reached the column, a cloud of yellow gas billowed up from the floor around them, obscuring them and the column from view. Though Baldric couldn't see them, he heard the sounds of coughing and retching coming from within the noxious cloud. With luck, it might incapacitate the cultists, or at least keep them distracted for a while.

"Nice work." Baldric wiped his eyes, which were streaming from a combination of the acid fumes and the gas from Lark's spell.

"If we stay around the edges of the cloud and use the illusions for cover, we can get into position to attack the dragon," Tess said.

"What about the rest of the cultists?" Lark asked, still playing his lute and focusing on his spell. "They're coming this way."

"I've got them," Baldric said, hoping he could deliver on that promise. "Get in position on the dragon, Tess."

The rogue nodded grimly and disappeared deeper into the illusory forest.

Baldric concentrated, searching his memory for the god with

whom he currently had the most goodwill built up. He couldn't afford a prolonged negotiation, and he needed something strong to take a few of the pieces off this board. They were badly outmatched, and they all knew it.

"Mystra," he murmured under his breath. "Your sanctuary of magic has been overrun. Ashardalon will do nothing but harm here. Help me root his followers out, and I'll protect your followers here in return. And," he added, to sweeten the deal, "the next magical tome we find on a mission, I'll make Cazrin donate it to your followers. I swear it."

He waited, forcing his breath to remain steady, bracing for a sign that Mystra had heard him and was in favor of his plan. He sagged in relief when he felt the familiar tingle of power in his fingers and the weight of the promise, the bargain struck, that settled on his shoulders as he felt Mystra's attention briefly settle on him. Then he had no more time to think; he had only to concentrate as he channeled that magic energy toward the two cultists who were just coming into view around the illusory trees.

Their eyes widened when they saw the spark of magic light flash from Baldric's fingertips. He swept them both up in the spell, and they disappeared.

Baldric let out a relieved breath. Two targets banished, and the other three were caught up in Lark's spell.

That still left one large dragon to deal with.

She was hovering near the ceiling, her massive wings beating the air, shattering the brittle stalactites and sending them crashing to the floor. In order to get a better look at the creature, Baldric took cover behind a large boulder that was, thankfully, not an illusion but a natural part of the cavern. He felt a surge of hope when he realized she was smaller than he'd first thought. Her segmented horns were not as long or aged as a full-grown or ancient wyrm's would be, and her obsidian scales were smooth and shiny with youth.

Maybe they weren't quite as doomed as he'd feared.

Baldric drew his mace and uttered a silent request to Tyr to be with him now. He was going to need all the divine help he could get.

He stepped out from behind the boulder, but his mace refused to flare with its holy fire. Anger surged in Baldric. Was Tyr really going to abandon him *now*? He raised his weapon anyway, waving it to get the dragon's attention.

"You going to linger up there all day, Antea?" he taunted. "Or are you going to come down and get your hands dirty?" Out of the corner of his eye, he saw Tess scrambling up one of the larger stalagmites, keeping out of the dragon's line of sight.

"She'd rather preen and threaten us from afar," Lark said. The tiefling was still playing his lute, tucked up behind a stone outcrop about thirty feet away from Baldric. "Antea the dragon in human's clothing, playing servant to the Arcane Brotherhood while nursing futile hopes of glory." Lark snorted in amusement. "Did you think you'd take over here and turn this tower into a shrine to Ashardalon? I've heard of some prideful, inane schemes in my time, but this is a whole new era of hubris."

The words were laced with magic, and Lark's aim was good.

Too good.

Antea twisted in pain and rage, wings flattening against her body as she went into a dive straight toward Lark.

"All right, I distracted her, now please help, please help, please help!" Lark cried as he ducked more fully behind the boulder.

Baldric watched as the dragon flew past Tess's hiding spot. The rogue threw her dagger, and for a heart-stopping second as the blade spun through the air, Baldric thought she would miss the beast entirely. But it tore through the soft bit of membrane near the base of the dragon's wing and embedded itself in the thick scales.

Almost immediately, Tess vanished, reappearing with her hand on the dagger's hilt, driving it in deeper and holding on to the dragon for all she was worth.

Antea let out a surprised roar, pulling up from her dive so sharply that Tess was nearly flung off by the force of it. She held on by the dagger hilt as Antea barrel-rolled in midair, trying to dislodge the elf and the sting of pain on her back.

Tess stabbed the dragon with her other dagger, and now she had two handholds, Baldric thought, for as long as she could maintain them.

Antea landed on a stretch of illusory snow, and Baldric didn't hesitate. He charged the dragon, his mace leading. He brought it around in a wide arc, using its weight to power the strike. He hit the dragon's leg a solid blow. Antea roared again and whipped toward him, pulling back and bringing her tail around to strike at him.

"Baldric, look out!" Tess shouted.

Baldric saw the solid weight of the tail coming at him and tried to duck, but he wasn't nearly fast enough. The blow caught him right in the chest, sweeping him across the room. He hit the floor hard on his left side and rolled. His chest was on fire, and for a few agonizing seconds he couldn't draw breath.

Distantly, he heard Lark singing, a wild, desperate song that Baldric hated to tell him would never win him any new fans in the local taverns, but then suddenly the fire in his chest cooled and he was able to suck air into his lungs. Looking down at himself, he saw a bit of golden magical radiance sinking into his skin.

Healing magic, he thought. Lark had healed him. The bard usually saved his magical reserves for flashier spells and things that would protect himself. The fact that he was healing Baldric meant he was truly scared.

Baldric didn't blame him.

He rose shakily to his feet in time to see Tess using her daggers as pitons, climbing up the dragon's back toward her head. The cords of the rogue's neck stood out, and she was red-faced, trying to hold on and dodge when Antea whipped her head around to try to bite her leg off.

"Lark!" Baldric shouted to the bard. "Have you contacted the others? We need them!"

"Do you honestly think I don't know that?" Lark shouted back incredulously. "That was the first thing I did after Antea transformed!"

"And?" Baldric said hopefully.

"Cazrin said something about a test and voices, an abomination from her worst nightmares—" Lark broke off with a yelp as the dragon's tail smashed into the rocky outcrop he was hiding behind, sending shards of stone spraying into his face. "She said they'd be here soon!" he shouted as he took off running for better cover. "Which I thought was a staggering bit of overconfidence on her part, but there you go. Help will be here soon!"

They just had to not die in the meantime.

And as if that thought had been a prophecy, the dragon made a sharp turn and flew straight up with such force that Tess was torn off Antea's back, daggers flying in multiple directions. Tess twisted in the air and managed to land in a crouch, but she was right in the dragon's path.

Antea wasted no time. She brought her scaled claw up and raked it across Tess's back as she tried to spring away. Bright blood welled, and Tess fell prone, unmoving on the floor.

"Tess!" Lark shouted in alarm.

Baldric was already moving. His chest still ached from the dragon's tail, but he ignored the pain, skidding to a stop next to Tess. With a surge of relief, he realized she was still conscious. Making a quick decision, he dug out a healing potion and slapped it into her hand, leaning close to whisper, "Get ready to run."

Dazed, she could only nod in response.

Baldric turned, putting his body between Tess and the dragon, holding his mace in both hands. It flared brighter with each step he took closer to the dragon, even though everything inside of him wanted to run away.

Antea regarded him, her horned skull tilted in curiosity. "Are you going to try to bargain with me again, Baldric?" Her voice filled the chamber, and her forked tongue snapped out at him. "Offer me a negotiation like you would one of your gods, when all the while your friends fall around you? You dare to call *me* prideful? How much longer will *you* let your companions bear the consequences for your arrogance and pride?"

"Don't listen to her!" Tess called out weakly from behind him. "We stand with you, Baldric. To the death."

Baldric's chest burned suddenly, a searing bolt of fire that stole any reply he might have made. He didn't want to look down. He was afraid if he did, he would see the tether blooming from his chest like a scarlet flower. And inside his head, the burning gaze loomed large. He felt the greatwyrm's presence hovering over him.

I can give you the power to strike her down, Ashardalon whispered in his mind. *Embrace our bond, and you will have dominance over mightier wyrms than she. You will have the power to protect all that you hold dear. No one will ever touch them.*

Baldric didn't want to be tempted by those promises. He'd sworn that he wouldn't give in. But the greatwyrm knew just how to strike at him when he was the most vulnerable. When his friends were bleeding, pinned down and desperate.

But how could he trust anything Ashardalon promised? The greatwyrm was willing to sacrifice one of his most loyal followers. In fact, he reveled in it. He could feel Ashardalon's enjoyment. The greatwyrm relished seeing two of his toys pitted against each other.

Only the powerful and the ruthless survive, Ashardalon's voice hissed in his mind. *My servants know this. It is the game we all play—to lose is death, but the rewards for those who succeed are vast.*

A game, is it? Baldric thought. A game played to the death.

An idea crept up on him, teasing the back of his mind like an ominous premonition.

He had also made a decision, long ago, to play a game of his own, juggling the favor of the divine and bargaining for power. Hadn't he known then what dangerous powers he toyed with? Tyr had told him as much. He had walked that line and also reveled in playing the gods off one another in his own small way.

Maybe that was why Ashardalon had been drawn to him, in the end. The realization was not a comfortable one, that he and the greatwyrm might have something in common, something that could truly cement the creature's hold over him.

"Am I no better than both of you?" Baldric murmured.

But his friends hadn't seen it that way.

They'd accepted that the path he'd chosen was part of who he was, a way of leaving his own mark upon the world. They'd respected him for it. And he had never used his powers to trample others. He'd been selfish sometimes, and cowardly, but never cruel. Ashardalon was the one playing the cruel game, because there was no winning, not truly. No matter what he did, he would have to sacrifice something, and the price was simply too high.

That didn't mean there wasn't a way out. On his own terms.

Ashardalon had enemies of his own. They'd seen as much in the depths of the Sunless Citadel. They'd been told that powerful entities like Tiamat weren't welcome there.

Baldric gripped his mace tightly in one hand and reached into his pouch with the other, feeling around until his fingers rested on the fruit of the Gulthias Tree. At the same time, he sent out a silent call to Tyr. It was risky. The god of justice had already ignored him once in this fight, but he had a feeling that of all the divine beings he'd ever dealt with, Tyr was the one who would be watching him now. Watching and—Baldric hoped—approving of the choice he was about to make.

He raised his mace, and the fire flared, the heat eclipsing the painful burn in his chest. "Come on, then!" he shouted up at Antea. "Just you and me, and I'll show you the power I can wield! I don't need your master or his gifts! I've plenty of my own!"

In his mind, he shut out Ashardalon, and he charged the dragon.

CHAPTER 33

Cazrin strode purposefully away from the smoking hole her fireball had left in the stone wall. Anson walked on one side of her, Uggie on the other. She'd given them the last of her healing potions, and they were looking much better, but Cazrin's anger at them being hurt in the first place was not likely to fade soon.

"That was the most impressive exit from a battle I think I've ever seen," Anson said, grinning at her. He glanced over his shoulder. "We've got company," he said.

Vellynne caught up with them. "A fine display," she said to Cazrin. "You've done your ancestress proud—"

"We don't have time for this," Cazrin interrupted her with a glare. She turned to Anson. "Lark sent me a magical message. He says they're trapped in an underground chamber, fighting Antea, who is actually a *dragon* in disguise."

"What?" Anson's grin vanished. "Where are they? Did he tell you?"

"What's going on?" Vellynne demanded.

"Our leader, Tess, and the rest of our party are in danger," Cazrin said. "We were told by her mentor, Mel, to seek you out because cultists of Ashardalon have infiltrated the Hosttower."

"And now they have a dragon here too," Anson said.

"Cultists?" Vellynne stiffened. "You said you came here to apply for membership."

Cazrin rounded on her. "It wouldn't have mattered whether I came here for membership or not. You were interested in nothing that *I* had to offer. Your only thought was what you could learn about my ancestress." She shook her head sadly. "We could have learned so much from each other, but you're so mired in the past that you failed to see what was right in front of you."

There was a time when she might have been hurt by that. But she'd grown in the last few months, and she'd learned a lot about herself, so that all she felt now was disappointment at the shortsightedness of a group of wizards she'd admired from afar.

She took a step toward Vellynne, and her expression must have been formidable, because even the seasoned wizard blinked. "If you're really a friend of Mel's, help us find her student."

"They're somewhere underground," Anson said. "It'll be a room big enough for a black dragon. Do you know a place like that?"

Vellynne stared at them intently, but Cazrin refused to back down or be intimidated. She'd put more fireballs through as many walls as she had to if that's what it took to find the others.

Vellynne must have read something of her determination in her expression, because the corner of her mouth quirked in something that was not quite a smile but somewhere in the vicinity. "You remind me a bit of myself in my younger days," she commented. "I regret misjudging you." She nodded to Anson. "I think I know where they went. I'll point the way, then alert the rest of the tower to the potential threat and see that adequate security measures are taken. After that, we'll provide you with aid."

Good enough, Cazrin thought. She just hoped the others could hold out long enough for help to get there. If they were walking into a fight with a black dragon, she was going to be ready.

But she had one thing left to do first.

Quickly, Cazrin cast the spell to send a message of her own. She kept it brief, picturing the golden-haired eladrin in her mind.

"I'll be there," she told Rane firmly, "at Verin's Crossing, in a month." There were no more doubts, not after what she'd just faced and what she was about to do. "I'll look for you."

The answer, when it came, was equally simple, but the words conveyed an affection and warmth that surrounded Cazrin, chasing away the coldness of the Hosttower.

"I'll be waiting," Rane said.

ANSON POUNDED DOWN the stairs after Cazrin, looking back to make sure Uggie was still following them. The otyugh barreled down as fast as her short legs could carry her and showed no signs of tiring. It felt like they'd been descending these steps forever, searching for the hidden chamber where Antea had taken their friends.

"Are you sure we can trust Vellynne's word?" Anson asked. He had his sword out and ready, his palms sweaty with fear that they might be too late.

"We don't have a choice," Cazrin said. "Hopefully she and the rest of the Arcane Brotherhood can find the other cultists—do something helpful for once." She kept her eyes on the stairs in front of her and didn't look back at him. There was a thread of steel in her voice that Anson didn't think he'd ever heard before.

"Glad you're on our side," he said with a chuckle.

Cazrin looked startled. "Sorry, do I sound callous?" she asked.

"After what they did in that test?" Anson shook his head. "I think you sound just right."

"To think, they would use my ancestress's own history against me!" she said, aghast. "That was part of her research, you know—*Studies of the Gibbering Mouther, an Annotated Account*. The Brotherhood was trying to see how closely I'd studied her work."

"But what did they hope to gain?" Anson asked, and then, with a flare of anger, he answered his own question. "They wanted to see if you were following in her footsteps, didn't they? They wanted to use you to learn more about her." He sniffed. "Well, they made a big mistake, and they're missing out on an alliance with a powerful wizard."

Cazrin smiled. "I never intended to join them, remember? This was just a ruse."

"Still," Anson said, "it's their loss."

"Thank you," Cazrin said, flashing him another smile. But the expression faded as they reached the bottom of the steps and a distant roar shook the stone walls around them.

"I think we found the right place." Anson moved ahead down the hallway, which ended in a set of doors. He automatically went head down into a charge, intending to bust right through.

"Wait!" Cazrin grabbed his shoulder, stumbling as she pulled him up short. She raised her staff and cast a spell on the door. A line of red-glowing runes inscribed along the door flared briefly crimson and then were slowly erased as if they'd never been there. "Go ahead," she said when they were gone. "Break it down."

Anson didn't need to be told twice. He opted for a kick that splintered the wood and sent the doors flying back against the walls of a cavernous chamber that was covered in . . .

"Snow?" Anson stepped inside—or outside—to a landscape of mountainous terrain enclosing a snow-covered wood. He wasn't as surprised as he might have been before coming to this place. After the mirrors, the staircases, and the gibbering mouther, he didn't think he had any surprise left in him.

Until he saw Baldric swinging a mace at a black dragon. The creature reared its spiked, horned head back, its chest expanding as it prepared to release its acid breath.

"Baldric!" he shouted at the same time as Cazrin. Then the three of them were running across the chamber. Anson couldn't feel the snow on his boots—ah, an illusion. He wished that all of this could have been an illusion, a nightmare that he was just waiting to wake from. But as the dragon's breath weapon filled the chamber, making his eyes burn, Anson was forced to look away from Baldric.

When he looked back, the dwarf was on the ground, unmoving.

"No!" The cry tore from his chest as he charged the dragon, his sword swinging wildly.

He'd promised to protect them.

Too late. He was always too late, too slow, not good enough.

No, please.

CHAPTER 34

Death was more of a bore than Baldric had anticipated.
 He'd heard it sung about by the bards and described in detail by the poets, as if they'd experienced it firsthand. Perhaps they had. Powerful magic could snatch a person from death's grip, after all. But the poets and the tale-tellers had made it seem so . . . momentous. A culmination of his entire life flashing before him in that instant before he passed from one existence to whatever came next.

Baldric had not felt any of that. He simply floated in a dark void, surrounded by a great deal of nothingness and silence. It was peaceful, but it felt temporary, transitory, and he was impatient to see how this all played out.

Could the dead *be* impatient?

Maybe he wasn't dead.

But the pain he'd experienced, and then the nothingness—it had felt very much like an ending. And in those scant seconds before the end, he'd called out, reaching for someone who could help him, asking for—

"I have come."

The glowing eyes appeared first, lighting up the void with a dull radiance. Baldric felt the heat, the flare of pain in his chest. Then Ashardalon materialized, but not as a creature of smoke and fear and dreams. For the first time, set against the darkness, Baldric saw the greatwyrm in all his terrible glory.

He had seen breathtaking paintings of red dragons poised with their claws above their prey in flight, or releasing a stream of fire hot enough to melt the strongest metal. Ashardalon was nothing like those depictions. Ashardalon was a dragon and a fiend all in one. The balor that had been grafted into his body had changed him in fundamental ways. The horns atop his head were demonic, not draconic, and his chest was large and swollen with a field of glowing red coals, as if the heart of a volcano beat within. The heat was so intense that Baldric could not look directly at the greatwyrm for long.

"What, even in death, I can't escape you?" Baldric said, trying to keep the tremble out of his voice. "Just can't bear to be without me, can you?"

"Your bravado is amusing, but I smell your fear." The greatwyrm's voice, no longer in Baldric's head but all around him, was like the shaking of the earth itself, the grind and collapse of vast caverns in the depths of the Underdark. "You can never escape me. In death, I can claim you where others will not."

"Bit premature of you, isn't it?" Baldric felt the pull of the tether that was still with him, even in the lightless void. "I've made deals with all manner of deities. You may have to fight them for me."

Ashardalon laughed, a malicious roar accompanied by a wave of heat. It shuddered through his body, but Baldric refused to back away.

"You made your bargains, but you swore fealty to no god," the greatwyrm said. "Time and again you told me you serve none."

"I'm holding to that," Baldric said, steeling himself. "There's nothing wrong with a give and take—power for power. You've no place to judge me for who I am."

"On the contrary, you are exactly as I wish you to be," Ashardalon said. "A conduit, proud and defiant. But that defiance means that you stand before me alone. No bargain can save you in death. You're mine now, and with you comes a link to the divine, streams of power flowing from you that will be a banquet for me to consume. Once I've had my fill, I will be as powerful as any god."

"Is that really how you think this will play out?" Baldric demanded. "You believe that my bargains with all the different deities have generated a strong enough link for you to feed on, enough power to make you into a god?" He snorted in disbelief. "If you ask me, hubris has gotten the best of you over the centuries."

"And where has your pride brought you?" Ashardalon snarled. "To me, as I always told you it would. No gods stand ready to help you now."

"Oh, but that's where you're wrong," Baldric said, in the tone of a teacher correcting a smug student. "A deal *can* be made, even here in the void, before I leave this mortal shell behind. You of all creatures, who preyed on my desperation once, should understand—all it takes is the right offer."

Timing was everything at moments like this, Baldric knew; he was standing on the precipice, not knowing if he would fly or fall. In those brief seconds, as a single breath went in and out of his lungs, he thought of the Fallbacks.

He thought of Cazrin and her unquenchable spirit. She'd faced her own demon in the dark and come out stronger than before.

He remembered Anson's resolve. The fighter never gave up, and he'd chosen not to run from his mistakes, instead accepting his flaws and vowing to be better.

And Lark. Baldric and the bard were more alike than he'd known. They were afraid, and they'd rather deny that fear and protect themselves. But Lark had taken a chance and chosen to show himself, chosen to trust, in a world that often didn't reward that kind of vulnerability.

Even Uggie, the creature most unlike them, had made the confounding choice to take them all as her family, without hesitation.

Then there was Tess. Their leader. She'd seen the best qualities among them long before Baldric had, and she never stopped trying to draw them out, to drag them kicking and screaming toward being the best versions of themselves. And she'd done all that while keeping them alive.

If he did fall here, Baldric thought, he would die safe in the knowledge that he'd had a good run with the best people.

He turned his face up to Ashardalon, no longer caring if the fire burned him, and just as he did, there was a rumble of thunder in the distance, deep and vast like a warning.

Timing was everything.

The greatwyrm turned toward the sound, its fiendish head cocked in uncertainty.

"Did I not mention that I called out for aid just before your servant struck me down?" Baldric said. He waited for the greatwyrm to turn that fiery gaze back to him. "I didn't ask for mercy or saving. I just thought to myself, with all your grand schemes for seizing power, what must your fellow dragons think of what you've been up to? Surely, at least one of them would be interested in how you want to siphon the power of the divine in order to make yourself as strong as a god. A challenger, fighting for dominance?"

The distant rumbling grew louder, closer, and a light was suddenly visible in the void.

"Say, for instance . . . Tiamat?"

Ashardalon's head jerked up. "You lie!" he roared, and the greatwyrm's massive claws ate up the distance between them, grasping at the darkness as if it were something the entity could hold. "She rots in her prison in the Nine Hells!"

That was true, and it took all the confidence Baldric could scrape together not to flinch under the greatwyrm's fiery rage and disbelief. But his heart thudded with the thrill of knowing that he had a winning hand. Tiamat was the creator of the chromatic dragons. Ashardalon sought the power of a god, but Tiamat already *was* a god among dragons and expected all to bow before her.

"Are you sure?" Baldric prodded. A smile crept across his lips. "Do you really want to take that risk?"

"You insignificant worm! I will rip you apart!"

Pain flared in Baldric's chest, the tether flaring bright red. But he heard the fear and uncertainty behind the greatwyrm's rage. Maybe Ashardalon really would rip him apart and this was the end. But that light was growing brighter, a storm drawing nearer and nearer.

Ashardalon threw back his head and roared. A geyser of fire

erupted from his mouth, the blistering heat washing over Baldric, finally making him stagger back and curl into himself in the void. The tether seared him, and suddenly, Baldric was roaring too, his body writhing as that connection that had haunted him for so long—that burning pain and those terrible eyes always watching him from the depths of his mind—was torn out of him all at once.

Baldric pulled back, his thoughts scattered as he whirled and twisted in the void, no longer able to see that approaching light. But he felt the cooling of the air around him, and gradually, each breath he took became a little easier.

When he was able to focus again, Ashardalon was gone. The burning that had been inside him—the physical pain and the burden of his fear—was instantly lifted. It was such a change that for a moment Baldric couldn't comprehend it. He gasped, his chest heaving as panic and relief warred inside of him.

But what now? What now?

He was still lost in the void. He didn't know up or down, didn't know the way to escape. And he'd lost sight of that light, the approaching storm that felt as if it were still on the verge of breaking. He had to face it, he knew. Whatever happened, however his actions were judged, he would face it.

CHAPTER 35

The cultists reappeared when Baldric's banishing magic faded, but they didn't have a chance to react before Lark's spell struck them. The thunderous energy slammed them into the back wall, and they slid to the ground and didn't move. Lark ducked behind some stalagmites and moved on.

He never thought he'd find himself wishing he were back in the battle with the lich and the purple worms—he usually tried very hard *not* to think about it, unless he was composing a song.

He wanted to be back there now, with a clear path to saving the day. He wanted someone to tell him what to do. Tess, specifically. He wanted Tess to tell him exactly what he needed to do to save everyone in this gods-forsaken fun house of a death-trap chamber.

Except there was a black dragon standing between him and the rogue, so she couldn't tell him anything. He wasn't even certain she was still alive. He'd lost sight of her after that last round of acid had rained burning death down on them.

On Baldric.

The cleric was facedown on the far side of the room, looking very much like he wasn't going to get up again. Just a few short months ago, these circumstances would have sent Lark fleeing from the room.

Instead he was creeping along the back wall, rage quivering inside him, looking for some cover that wasn't a damned illusion. *Strike hard, strike fast, stay on the move, and keep hidden if you can.* That was Tess's lesson when you were outnumbered or outmatched by a superior foe. He couldn't let himself be pinned down.

What else had she said? He needed to think. Concentrating on the lessons was keeping him from panicking. *Find a weak point and exploit it every chance you get.* Baldric had given him that. He'd attacked the dragon's right front leg, pummeling it with his mace. Lark could work with that. If he could lame the creature, limit her flying, that would give him an advantage.

Gods, all those lessons and strategies really were paying off, Lark thought with a groan. Tess was going to be so smug when he told her.

If she was still alive . . .

Finally, he located a large nest of stalagmites near the back corner of the room. He scrambled up into it and found a Y-shaped nook where he could settle himself and have his hands free. Then he took the Last Resort off his back.

If ever there were a moment for an aptly named weapon, this was it.

Just then, a furious shout echoed from the opposite side of the room, a familiar voice that had Lark fumbling the loading of the crossbow. He looked up, hardly daring to believe that it might be them.

He wasn't hallucinating. Anson, Cazrin, and Uggie charged into view, heading straight for the dragon. They hadn't seen Lark yet, but they must have seen Baldric fall. Anson had such a look of rage on his face that if Lark were on the other end of his broken sword, he would have thrown himself to the ground and begged for mercy.

Unfortunately, the dragon was not nearly so intimidated.

"Finally," Antea growled, swiping at the approaching trio with her tail. Uggie dove to the ground and caught a glancing blow, while Cazrin and Anson stayed just out of reach. "The rest of the rats have come out to play."

Oh, we're going to play, Lark thought grimly. He knew false bravado when he heard it. Antea had weakened them with her acid breath, but her cultists were dead on the ground, and now his group had backup.

He aimed the crossbow and released. Bolt after bolt he put in or near the dragon's hurt leg, hoping that Anson and Cazrin got the message that that was where they needed to aim their arsenal.

From his bird's-eye view, he watched Uggie get her teeth into the left wing when the dragon stumbled on her wounded leg. Uggie ripped and tore at the fleshy membrane while the dragon struggled under the onslaught of Cazrin's glowing missiles. They found her unerringly, no matter how she tried to dodge.

With a frustrated growl of pain, Antea beat her wings, ripping Uggie off of her and trying to take to the air. That was when Anson darted in close, stabbing deep into the bad leg, pumping the wild lightning of the broken sword into the dragon. For an instant, the whole cavern lit up with the blue-white light. The dragon keened as the lightning shuddered through her body.

She was weakening.

Lark put away his crossbow. His arms felt heavy, aching from the number of bolts he'd put into the monster. Now that the dragon's attention was on Anson, maybe he could try to get to Baldric and see how badly the cleric was hurt.

I can use his lantern, Lark thought, adjusting his lute more securely on his back as he started to climb down the stalagmites. Surely, it would work to help bring him back. He couldn't be dead. The dwarf was too stubborn and tenacious to die. He would never stand for—

Lark saw the dragon coming at him almost too late.

While he'd been distracted, Antea had managed to get airborne again, dragging Anson with her. The fighter was clinging to his sword for all he was worth, the blade still embedded in the dragon's leg. Blood flowed liberally from multiple wounds all along her flank.

But she had seen Lark, the songbird that was stinging her from afar. She arrowed straight toward him.

Lark dove from the stalagmite, hitting the ground just as the dragon flew over him and smashed into the stone. Shards flew, and there was a confusion of beating wings and claws all around him. Desperately, Lark rolled, trying to get out of the way, but a heavy weight slammed down on his back, pinning him to the floor.

Pain flooded Lark's body, and he heard an ominous *crack* that made him break out in a cold sweat. Either he'd just had his spine snapped by a dragon's foot and would soon be tasting the sweet darkness of oblivion . . . or . . . something worse . . .

The weight abruptly lifted, and Lark instinctively rolled away, desperate to get out from under the dragon and feeling like the mouse trying to escape the cat. He was bruised but whole, and he reached behind him for what had taken the brunt of the impact.

His lute.

When he clambered to his feet, he could feel the instrument hanging flimsily by its strap, no longer taut and elegant against the muscles of his back. He couldn't bear to look at it now and couldn't have spared the time if he wanted. He was too busy running, dodging the swiping tail, but fortunately, the dragon had turned her attention back to Anson and Cazrin, the latter of whom continued her spell barrage with streaks of flame that tore across the room. Lark seized the opening to half limp, half run across the chamber toward Baldric.

Then he stopped short. Baldric was gone, his body disappeared.

Lark felt a burst of hope. It had been a ploy after all. Something Baldric and Tess had cooked up together when the fight had broken out. He should have known. Tess always had a plan . . .

And then he caught a flash of blond hair weaving in and out of a stand of trees—or illusions; damn this magical fun house anyway. He moved closer, and there she was. Tess was dragging Baldric's body deeper into the illusory wood. Her bruised face was set and stony, and Lark felt dread churning in his stomach again.

Moving as stealthily as he could so as not to draw attention to Tess, Lark made his way over to them. He grasped Baldric's arm just as it slipped out of Tess's grasp. "Let me help," he said.

She glanced over at him and then did a double take. "What happened to your lute? It looks like—"

"Don't," Lark said tersely. "I don't want to know." He helped her tuck Baldric into a corner, as far from the dragon's notice as possible. "Is he alive?" he asked.

"I don't know," Tess said, and for the first time, Lark heard the edge of panic in her voice. "I think he's breathing, but it's so faint and slow, and when I tried to heal him with a potion, nothing happened."

Lark bent closer to examine the dwarf. He was covered in partially healed burns from the acid, but there were still several deep wounds along his left side. He shifted the cleric's arm so he could get a better look, and a small red object fell from Baldric's slack hand.

The fruit of the Gulthias Tree—or what was left of it. Several large bites were missing from the healing fruit.

"What about that?" Lark asked, pointing. "Shouldn't the fruit have saved him?"

"I don't know!" Tess repeated, her voice rising in frustration.

"I thought you and Baldric had this planned!" Lark countered, his own fear and anger getting the better of him. "You always have a plan, Tess!"

"I didn't get consulted on this one!" she snapped. "I was bleeding on the ground, and the next thing I knew, Baldric was kneeling next to me, healing me and whispering that I needed to guard his body. He said to trust him."

His body. Ah, Gods.

Across the room, the dragon threw Anson off at last. Her chest expanded, and another hellscape of acid rained down on the others.

"Damn it!" Tess jumped to her feet. "Stay with Baldric. I have to put her down." The elf's expression hardened. She stepped away from him and raised her teleportation dagger. The light from Cazrin's fire spells glinted off the blade.

She moves like poetry, Lark thought, composing the verse in his head because it kept him from panicking. The blade was her compass, her guide. So small to a dragon—a needle in the dark. But even a needle could bring down the mighty, when it was aimed by a hand like Tess's.

The blade spun through the air, a tiny, flashing bit of metal that streaked unerringly toward its target, allowing for the frenetic movement of a dragon's head, the chemical stench of acid making the air itself into a poison. *End over end goes the needle,* Lark thought, *and the black dragon lifts her head unknowingly, straight into the path of death.*

Well, his own rendering might need some work, but the point was, the dagger buried itself deep in the dragon's right eye, and Tess vanished while she was still in the act of finishing the throw.

She reappeared clutching the dagger's hilt, bracing her feet on the dragon's skull. But the dragon's head jerked, and she slipped.

Lark reacted at once, calling on his magic. "You have her, Tess!" he shouted. "Your name's going in my next song! Tess, the black dragon's bane!"

And then Lark could only watch, slack-jawed, as Tess regained her footing, bore down, and buried her second dagger in the dragon's other eye.

The howl of rage and pain that Antea let loose in the chamber had Lark dropping down beside Baldric and covering his ears, as if the roar itself would blast them all into oblivion. He looked up in time to see the dragon throw her head back, hoping to rip Tess off. But the elf hung on, stubborn and wicked as a thorn embedded deep. The dragon dipped, still howling in pain, and hit the ground hard, fighting to keep herself upright.

And Anson was just waiting for his chance. He charged in below her, found a tender spot where the dragon's injured leg met her body, and drove his sword in. Then he was scrambling back, stumbling to get out of the way as Antea, proud and terrible even in her death throes, slowly sank to the ground.

Tess rode the dragon all the way down, only yanking her daggers free and jumping off Antea's body when she was sure the dragon was truly dead.

There was an eerie silence in the chamber in the wake of Antea's fall, and Lark bent his ear to Baldric's chest to see if Tess was right and the cleric was still breathing. It took an agonizing second, but finally he heard the slow, even breaths. They sounded too much like a body struggling on the verge of death for Lark's comfort.

He was in the middle of casting a healing spell when the rest of the Fallbacks gathered around.

"Is he dead?" Anson asked tightly. He had his arm around Cazrin, though it was unclear who was supporting whom.

Lark had just opened his mouth to answer when a concentrated ball of otyugh shoved past him and collapsed next to Baldric. Uggie whined and nudged the cleric's shoulder gently, her tentacles touching his head, shoulders, and beard, as if trying to wake him up.

"Give him some space, girl," Tess said. She knelt opposite Lark and pulled the otyugh away. "He's going to come back to us." She laid her hand over Baldric's. "Wherever he is, he's coming back."

CHAPTER 36

When the rolling thunder finally reached Baldric, the Aspect of Tyr made its presence known in the void, a familiar dwarven visage manifesting out of the darkness. As ever when he addressed his requests to the god of justice, Baldric felt like a child being scrutinized by a parent he hadn't asked for. He knew he would be found wanting.

"You felt that way because I expected much from you, and in the past, you've refused to attempt to live up to that expectation."

Baldric's head snapped up. "Are you reading my thoughts now?" he asked the Aspect. "That doesn't seem fair of you."

"You speak of 'fair' as if the gods should obey rules that mortals shun at every turn. There is nothing of 'fair' in this path we walk, Baldric Goodhand. But you should be glad that I am here."

"Because you saved me," Baldric said, chastened. "For a moment, I wasn't sure you would, but you imitated Tiamat so well, I thought I actually had summoned her." Wouldn't that have been a fine mess? Probably the last one he ever made in his life. "Thank you for what you did for me." He touched his chest, the cooling spot of skin where the tether was no more. "I'm not sure how I can repay you."

They hadn't gotten to that point of the negotiation.

A thread of amusement spilled out from the Aspect. "I believe you promised me whatever I desired."

Ah, Baldric thought. He'd been half hoping the Aspect would forget that he had, in a moment of despair, used those exact words.

"Is this the part where you reassure me that you won't take advantage of my moment of weakness?" he asked hopefully.

The sense of amusement vanished like the tide ebbing from the sand.

"What you did was not weakness. You faced your tormentor with the ultimate ruse in order to win back your life, but you prepared yourself to die in the attempt, both to protect those you care about and to safeguard the world at large. That ability to look outside yourself and to be willing to give your life to a just cause is what I had always hoped for you."

And for the first time, and much to his shock, Baldric felt an overwhelming sense of something he could only describe as . . . pride coming from the Aspect of the god of justice. It was strange and new, and it stirred a complex stew of emotions inside Baldric, feelings he didn't know if he was ready to deal with.

He swallowed hard, gathering his composure. "This doesn't change anything," he said. "I'll pay my debt to you, whatever it is, but I won't agree to serve you, or any other god."

He waited, the breath caught in his chest, to see if he'd roused the Aspect's anger. There was a long moment of silence in the void. Baldric wondered how long he'd been here. It could have been an age, a century, or only a moment.

But when the Aspect finally responded, Baldric sensed a distance, as if his presence were receding, or Baldric were being pulled away, back to the realm of living mortals.

"You've chosen your path, and you've accepted the risks that come with it. I will not try to change you. As for the debt you owe to me, it is substantial, and I will claim it when the moment is right."

Baldric suppressed a groan as he felt himself fading, being pulled back into his body. The idea of Tyr coming for him "when the moment is right" screamed to Baldric that it would be the worst possible time for him and his friends.

He opened his eyes. He was back in the illusory winter landscape of the Hosttower. Snow drifted from the gray sky above him, and though he couldn't feel the thick white flakes falling on his skin, it still put him in mind of the peaceful softness of a winter's day.

His party members were gathered around him. Baldric's first feeling at seeing them was a soul-deep relief. They were all alive and in one piece.

They hadn't gotten away unscathed, though. All of them were battered, some bleeding, some burned by Antea's acid breath, and he looked with dismay at the broken lute Lark was cradling in his arms.

When they saw he was awake, they gave a shout and leaned toward him at once, with Uggie leading the way, her tentacle wrapped around his left arm.

"Give me . . . a minute," Baldric said, surprised at how hoarse his voice sounded. "Then I'll . . . heal everyone."

Tess gave a watery, incredulous laugh. "You can take more than a minute," she assured him. "We were worried that you weren't coming back. I take it your plan worked?"

He nodded. He started to sit up, and Anson immediately leaned in and supported him. He patted Uggie on the head and gently nudged her back to give him some space to breathe.

"It's all right, girl," he said soothingly. He looked up and caught Lark's gaze, then glanced down at the lute. He searched for the right thing to say, to tell the bard how sorry he was for the loss of the instrument.

Lark spoke first. "Tough crowd tonight," he said, deadpan. "No appreciation for the classics."

Baldric sputtered, and a laugh rose up unexpectedly inside him. He tried to hold it in, but seeing the impish expression in Lark's gaze, it was too much. He laughed, so did Lark, and the others joined in, and a bit of the tension and fear of the battle eased for them all.

After that, Baldric got out his healing lantern and shined its light over the party. As he did so, he looked over at the body of the black dragon sprawled in the center of the chamber. Several members of the Arcane Brotherhood were gathered around the creature, talking in low voices and occasionally shooting glances over at the party.

"They arrived too late to contribute to the battle," Cazrin said, in a tone that said she wasn't in the least surprised.

"We didn't need them," Tess said. "The Fallbacks took care of things."

"But you'd have been pleased to hear how Tess negotiated a substantial reward for us for exposing the cultists' presence in the tower," Anson said, squeezing Tess's shoulder. "That's two rewards now—one from the Harpers and one from the Arcane Brotherhood—not to mention the gratitude of both groups."

Baldric nodded in approval. "Did you use my almost dying as leverage?" he asked.

Tess started to shake her head, but Lark cut in. "I absolutely mentioned it," he assured the cleric.

Baldric nodded. "Good."

Tess sighed in exasperation at both of them. "Thankfully, you're *not* dead, though you gave us all a tremendous scare. But are you all right?" She looked at Baldric in concern. "What happened with Ashardalon and the tether?"

"Both gone," Baldric said, and he smiled at the looks of relief that came over his friends' faces. "I'll give you the details later, but I couldn't have done it without all of you fighting for me." He cleared his throat. "I won't . . . that is . . . I won't ever take this"—he gestured to their group—"for granted. We know what we've got here, all of us. I'm going to work to protect it, and to do what's best for everyone, wherever they want to go." He glanced at Tess. "With you leading us. I'll follow you."

"So will I," Anson said immediately.

The others chorused their agreement, and Baldric felt a sense of peace settle over him. He knew there were loose ends. Remnants of the cult would be out in the world and might come looking for revenge. They would have to be prepared for that, and for Tyr to claim his payment.

But those were worries for the future. Baldric hadn't felt this sense of contentment in a very long time, and he intended to revel in it for as long as he could.

EPILOGUE

Tess was more than happy to leave the Hosttower of the Arcane behind. They spent several more nights in Luskan and arrived back in Baldur's Gate in time to report to Mel and Keevi before the Harper's work took them away from the city.

The Elfsong Tavern was crowded that night. Tess and Cazrin managed to wrangle a table in the back corner that would fit them all, but Mel was running late, and Anson had said he'd meet them there in an hour, so she saved a couple of chairs for them, positioning sheepdog Uggie as a guard so no one would try to swipe them. Then Baldric, Lark, and Keevi went to the bar in search of drinks. Tess noticed the tiefling shooting a few longing glances at the stage, where a trio of performers were singing and juggling knives at the same time.

"Has Lark gotten a new lute yet?" Cazrin asked, glancing after the bard as she settled into a chair next to Tess.

"No, he hasn't," Tess said. She scratched Uggie under the chin to help settle her down. "He told me he's not ready to let go of the old one yet, but with the extent of the damage . . ." She spread her hands.

Cazrin nodded in sympathy. "He just needs time," she said. She glanced toward the door. "Did Anson say where he was going tonight?"

"He just said he had an errand to run, something to check on." She shrugged.

Cazrin folded her arms on the tabletop, eyeing Tess in concern. "You don't think he's looking for Valen again, do you?"

Tess shook her head, idly watching the knife throwers. Their technique was all wrong. If they weren't careful, they would put someone's eye out. "He's long gone from the city by now," she said. "Anson won't be chasing him."

"So you're not . . . worried?"

Tess turned her attention from the knife throwers back to Cazrin, noticing the wizard wore a faint smile. She smiled back. "No, I'm not worried," she said. "Whatever Anson's doing, he'll tell us when he's ready."

Though, by the way Anson had been hanging around Lark's room lately, Tess had a fair idea what he was about. She just didn't want to ruin the surprise.

Tess stood when Baldric, Lark, and Keevi returned to the table laden with drinks and food. The tortle was shaking their head as Baldric finished telling them of his brush with death, greatwyrms, and divinity.

"You filled them in on everything that we did since leaving Baldur's Gate during your trip to the bar?" Tess asked in exasperation. "I thought we were going to wait until everyone was here."

"Tell me about it," Lark said forlornly, taking a bite of buttered bread. "I had a magnificent poem I was composing for the occasion. Since I have no accompaniment," he added.

"I just told them my part of it," Baldric said. "I left plenty of gaps for you to fill in about that heroic dragon fight."

Keevi picked up their tankard and drank deeply. They wiped their mouth and looked at Baldric in amazement. "You know, after we last spoke, I envied you your unique power and position among the gods."

"And now?" Baldric asked, with a quirked brow.

The tortle chuckled and patted Baldric's shoulder with one large hand. "Now I think I'm content to be a servant to Mielikki alone. Anything more is too perilous."

"That's saying something, coming from a Harper," Tess observed.

There were chuckles all around the table. In their wake, Keevi raised their tankard. "Regardless, I offer my thanks and congratulations on behalf of the Harpers, for all that you've accomplished. I hope that we may work together again in the future."

They drank, and Tess exchanged a significant look with Baldric. A partnership with the Harpers could lead to some very lucrative and high-profile work, and they both knew it.

"Did I miss anything?" said a familiar voice at Tess's elbow.

She turned to see Anson standing behind Lark with a cloth-wrapped bundle cradled in his hands. The fabric was green velvet and shimmered in the light.

Tess smiled to herself. He was going a bit overboard with the presentation, she thought, but then again, of all of them, Lark would be the one to truly appreciate a grand gesture.

"We saved you a seat," Cazrin said, waving him over.

"And some food," Baldric added.

"I may have had a bit of your bread," Lark said. He hadn't turned around to greet Anson and so hadn't seen the bundle.

"My thanks," Anson said. He leaned past Lark and laid his present on the table in front of the bard. "I picked up something for you while I was out," he explained. "I hope you like it."

Tess noticed Lark's eyes widen when he saw the size of the gift, but they clouded with dismay when he recognized the telltale shape of it. The bard sighed. "I appreciate what you're trying to do," he said as he gingerly peeled back the cloth, "but I'm not ready to let go of an instrument that's been with me for—"

He stopped when the fabric slid off, revealing his old lute. It had been completely repaired, repainted, and polished, with new strings and a glimmer of what was unmistakably magic shining from the neck.

"How . . ." Lark had to clear his throat several times to get the words out. "I thought it couldn't be fixed. It was in *pieces*."

"I had some of the folks at Sorcerous Sundries take a look at it after you left it in your room," Anson explained. He took the seat Cazrin had saved for him. "They told me it would take a significant amount of magic and coin, but they said it could be repaired and reinforced with enchantments to make it sturdier and pack in a few surprises along the way." He ran his hand over the back of his neck self-consciously. "Do you really like it? I described everything I could remember about how it looked so the maker could get it right. I hope they did a good job."

"It's perfect." Lark ran his hands reverently over the lute, picking it up as if he were cradling a newborn. He looked up and met Anson's gaze. "Thank you," he said, swallowing. "This is . . . well, it's probably the best gift I've ever received."

Anson's face split in a boyish grin. Cazrin clapped her hands in delight. Keevi initiated another toast, and the rest of the Fallbacks leaned in to examine the lute more closely and give their praise. Lark even let Uggie give it a lick of approval.

Amid the talk and laughter, Tess caught Anson's eye and raised her wineglass in her own silent toast. *Well done,* she mouthed.

Cheeks reddening, he nodded back at her, looking happier than she'd seen him in a long time.

Tess's gaze strayed over the fighter's shoulder then, and she caught sight of another familiar face sitting at the bar. Tess shook her head in fond exasperation, picked up her wineglass, and headed to the bar.

She took the empty seat next to Mel. "You could have joined us at the table, you know," she gently chided her mentor. "How long have you been here?"

Mel smiled enigmatically. "Long enough to see you've made all the necessary repairs in your party," she said. "Well done, Tessalynde."

Tess felt herself glowing under the praise. "You were right about everything," she said. "About what I needed to do."

"I usually am," Mel said with a throaty cackle. She motioned for the bartender to refill her glass. "But it's good that you've made your group strong again." She gave Tess a sidelong glance. "You'll need that strength in the days ahead."

"What makes you say that?" Tess asked suspiciously. It was true they still had issues to deal with—like Lark's pursuers. Tess had resolved to find out who they were and what they wanted with the bard as soon as possible. And Cazrin had requested an extended stop in some place called Verin's Crossing, so there was that too. But her mentor usually didn't make ominous-sounding predictions like this.

"You've attracted the attention of powerful forces," Mel said, lifting a shoulder. "The Harpers and the Arcane Brotherhood. *Those* you know, but I may also have mentioned your exploits to certain friends. By thwarting Ashardalon's latest bid for power, you've done them a favorable turn." She waggled her eyebrows at Tess. "They'll be watching to see what you do next."

"And I assume, by your cryptic-ness, that you won't tell me who those friends are," Tess guessed. "It doesn't matter. As long as we don't encounter any more dragons in disguise. I've had enough of that deception."

Mel snorted. "Says the woman who walks around with an otyugh disguised as a sheepdog." She leaned in closer. "And how do you know you haven't *already* encountered another dragon in disguise, eh?"

Tess chuckled and nudged her mentor in the ribs. "By the gods, Mel, if you're about to tell me *you've* been a dragon in disguise this whole time, I swear—" She stopped as Mel just stared at her with the satisfied expression of a cat lording over a dish of cream.

Tess's mouth dropped open, but then she shook her head and grinned. "Nice try," she said. "I may be inexperienced in some things, but there are others I'm certain of, and one of them is that you are a halfling, and you're my mentor. Always have been and always will be."

"True enough." Mel smiled, picked up her glass, and tapped the rim of Tess's. "Child, I could not be prouder of the things you've accomplished, as an adventurer, a leader, and a person of character. However, there are very few things in this world that are exactly as they seem. You would do well to remember that."

ACKNOWLEDGMENTS

Every time I sit down to write out acknowledgments like this, I can't help but marvel that after all these years, I still get to do this thing I love, writing about a game that's helped shape the course of my life. And I continue to get to work with amazing people along the way.

Thanks as always to Alex Davis, Elizabeth Schaefer, Lydia Estrada, and the whole team at Random House Worlds. You all are the best editors and cheerleaders, and you always laugh at the parts I want you to laugh at. To Paul Morrissey, Sarra Scherb, and the team at Wizards of the Coast, it's such a privilege to work with people who have so much passion and love for D&D. It comes through in everything you do. Thank you for having my back on this adventure.

To my amazing agent, Sara Megibow, thank you for being there when the waters are calm and when they're rough, and for everything in between. Onward, always.

To my brother, Jeff, and to my husband, Tim, you've both kept D&D and gaming in our lives. You'll always be my favorite players, and you're my favorite people.

Finally, to Dad, it breaks my heart that I won't get to give you this book like I have all the others, but I know how proud you were of me, and that means everything. And you were wrong about my love of writing and stories—I didn't get it all from Mom. It came from you too. I love you so much.

ABOUT THE AUTHOR

JALEIGH JOHNSON lives and writes in the wilds of the Midwest. Her debut middle grade novel, *The Mark of the Dragonfly*, was a *New York Times* bestseller. Her other books include *The Secrets of Solace*, *The Quest to the Uncharted Lands*, and *The Door to the Lost*. She has also written fiction for Marvel and Dungeons & Dragons: Forgotten Realms, including *The Fallbacks: Bound for Ruin* and *Honor Among Thieves: The Road to Neverwinter*. Johnson is an avid gamer and lifelong geek.

jaleighjohnson.com

ABOUT THE TYPE

This book was set in Caslon, a typeface first designed in 1722 by William Caslon (1692–1766). Its widespread use by most English printers in the early eighteenth century soon supplanted the Dutch typefaces that had formerly prevailed. The roman is considered a "workhorse" typeface due to its pleasant, open appearance, while the italic is exceedingly decorative.